Flanimals

RICKY GERVAIS

Limited edition adult collectables available at

www.flanimals.com

More Flanimals

by
Ricky Gervais

Illustrated by
Rob Steen

ff

First published in 2005
by Faber and Faber Limited
3 Queen Square London WC1N 3AU

Printed in Belgium by Proost

A CIP record for this book
is available from the British Library

ISBN 0–571–22886–0

2 4 6 8 10 9 7 5 3 1

Contents

There are a few more things you
need to know about Flanimals, then we
really should never talk of this again.

Chapter 1

The Flanimal Kingdom

How much do you know about Flanimals? How many Flanimals do you know? All of them? I don't think so. You're probably aware of the Frappled Humpdumbler but that's just one type of Humpdumbler – there's the Puggled Humpdumbler, the Squeebless Humpdumbler and the Flap-Toggled Humpdumbler to name just three. There are thirty.

Thirty Humpdumblers

Puggled Humpdumbler

Squeebless Humpdumbler

Flap-Toggled Humpdumbler

Sprot Tumbler

The Sprot Guzzlor is quite common and as you know loves to eat sprots, but what about the Sprot Tumbler, who just likes to roll them along the ground a bit? Or the Sprot Oggler, who likes to watch them? And of course, the rarer Sprot Mungler, who cunningly looks and acts like the Sprot Oggler so that the Sprot believes it is just being watched until at the last minute it is mungled senseless?

Sprot Oggler   **Sprot Mungler**

There are over twenty types of Underblenge, fifty types of Coddleflop and nearly one hundred types of Splunge. I don't think you need one hundred types of Splunge. You could get rid of most of them. Pointless. In fact, it annoys me a little bit. What about you?

Splunges

Anyway, there are so many types of Flanimal that we don't know exactly how many there are. There are more types of Flanimal that we don't know about than ones we do. How do we know that? We don't. Stupid, isn't it? No it isn't. Why not? I don't know. Do you? Ha! Not so clever now, are you? You will be when you've read this book. You'll know everything. That'll be good, won't it? No it won't, because there'll be nothing left to learn, and learning is great so that will be sad. So I'd stop reading this book now . . . I thought I told you to stop reading. You've got a lot to learn. You'd better read on.

Globs of Gumption

Living Shnerb

Splungent Floob

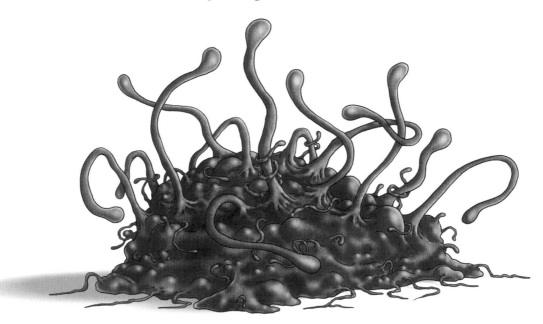

Where did all the Flanimals come from? Some people think they were made by a strange old man who lives in the sky. But not the clever scientists. They believe no one made them. They evolved. That means that over millions and millions of years Globs of Gumption and Living Shnerb gradually grew and changed into Splungent Floobs and Slunge Greeblers which multiplied and became the very Flanimals surviving today.

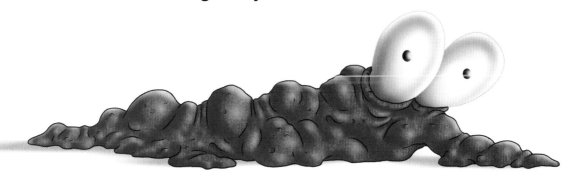

Slunge Greebler

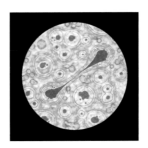

Splorn dividing as seen through a microscope magnified one hundred times

The very earliest form of Flanimal life was Splorn – really nothing more than a liquidiloid membrane, but it possessed the ability to reproduce itself. It could simply divide into two. It could do this because it had the building block of Flanimal life – a giant molecule called Dilopty Ribbidiloydo Nooflapid Happliassy Applyappalappalappalappa. Or DNA for short. Or DN for even shorter. D is about as short as you can go. Well, in any human language anyway. There is a sound that one Flanimal makes that is fifty times shorter than D. I'd say what it is but there's no point as you wouldn't be able to read it, it's so short. If I said it out loud to you, right near your ear, you wouldn't hear it. You'd need very small ears to hear such a tiny sound. Even if you wrote it with a big fat pen it would still fit on the end of a pin. That's how small it is.

Anyway, Splorn, millions of years ago, multiplied and changed in many different ways. It doesn't do it any more. Not sure why. I heard it was guilt.

DNA

Dilopty Ribbidiloydo
Nooflapid Happliassy
Applyappalappalappalappa

Chapter 2

Flanimal Evolution

Figure 1. Evolution of Splorn to Psquirms and Munge Fuddler

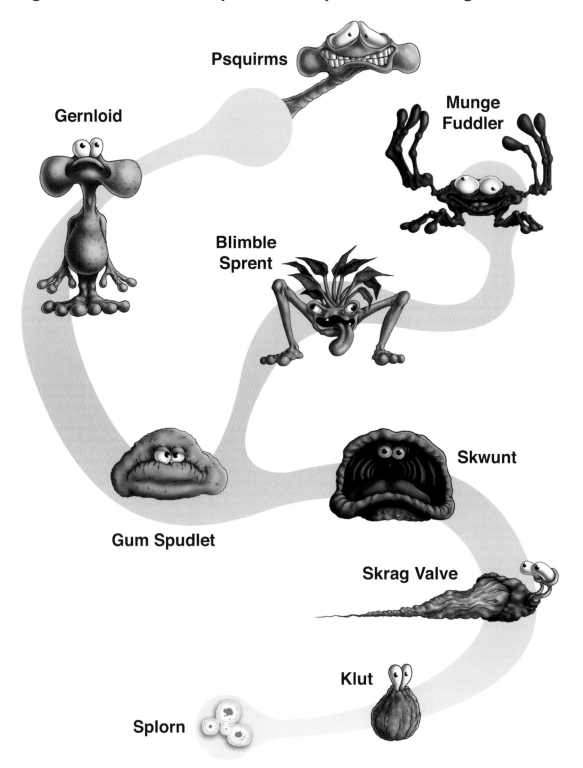

Psquirms

Gernloid

Munge Fuddler

Blimble Sprent

Skwunt

Gum Spudlet

Skrag Valve

Klut

Splorn

Figure 2. Evolution of Austrillo Ployb to Print and Edgor

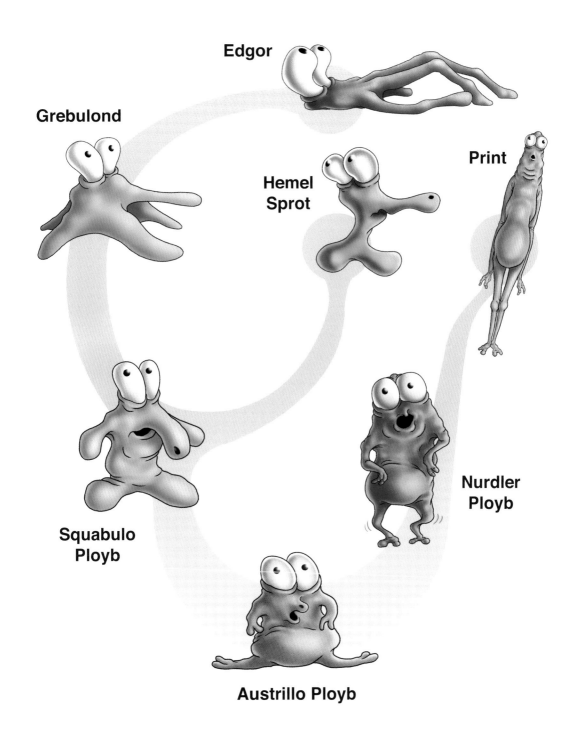

Figure 3. Evolution of Splorn to Squat and Dweezle Muzzbug

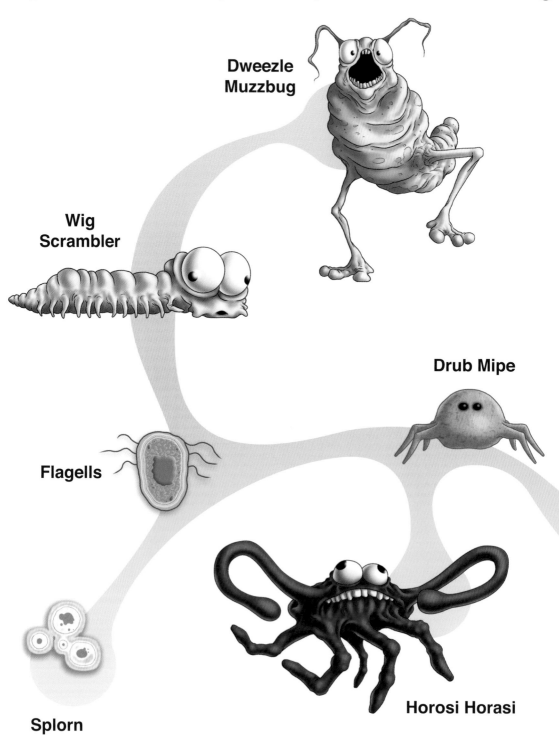

Dweezle
Muzzbug

Wig
Scrambler

Drub Mipe

Flagells

Horosi Horasi

Splorn

Squat

Muffid Skrunt

Scrabs

Figure 4. Evolution of Progulant Glob to Sprot Guzzlor

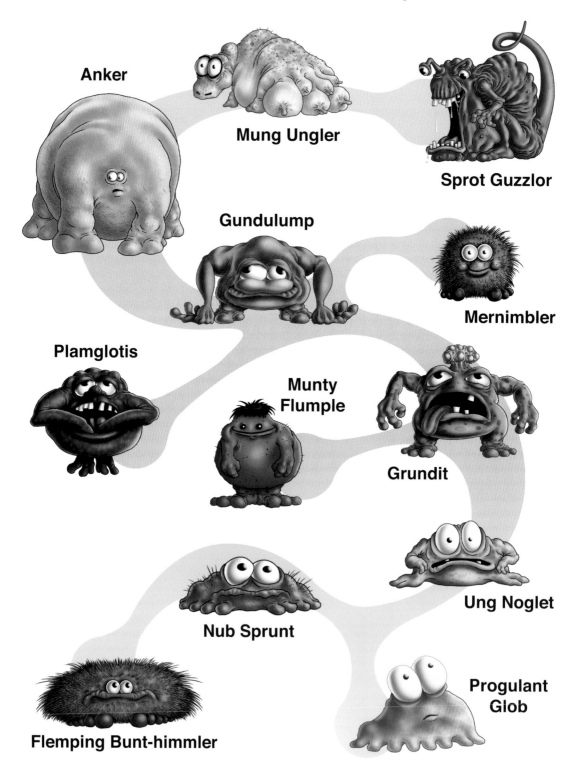

Fossil evidence shows there was a strain of Blunging that evolved millions of years ago but died out. It didn't die out because it wasn't as well equipped as modern-day Blungings – it was actually better equipped, faster, stronger, more intelligent and a prolific breeder. No one is sure why it disappeared, we think it just got bored.

This is what we think it may have looked like.

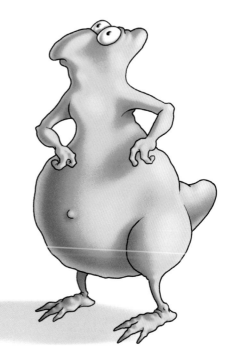

Plodonklopus

Figure 5. The Flanimal Family Tree

Chapter 3

Flanatomy

Flanatomy of the Glonk

Doesn't look like he's doing anything, does it?
Slice him open and see where it's all happening.

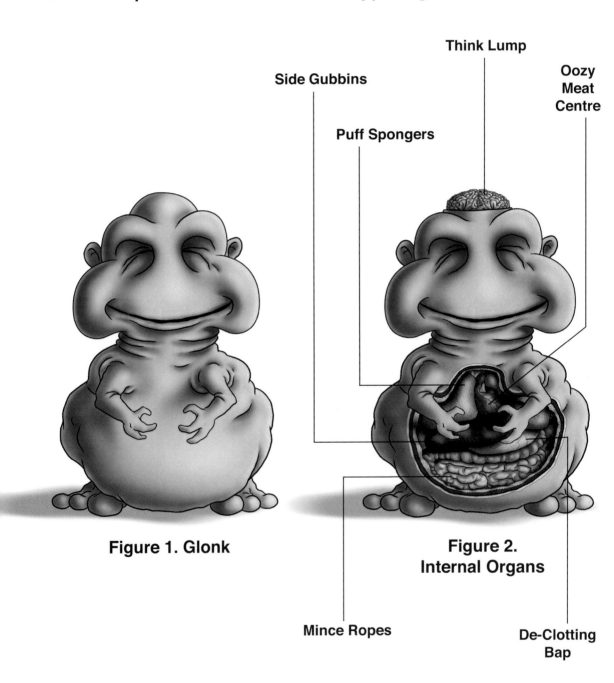

Side Gubbins

Puff Spongers

Think Lump

Oozy Meat Centre

Figure 1. Glonk

Figure 2. Internal Organs

Mince Ropes

De-Clotting Bap

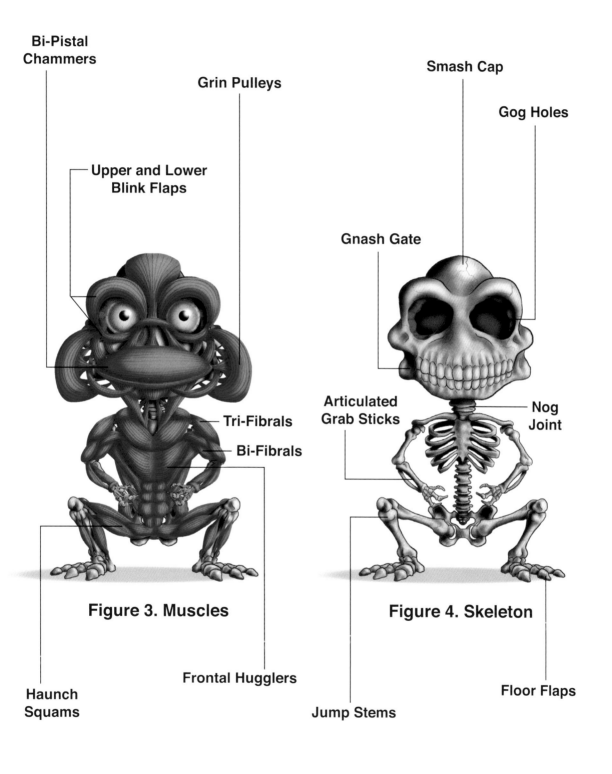

Figure 3. Muscles

Bi-Pistal Chammers

Grin Pulleys

Upper and Lower Blink Flaps

Tri-Fibrals

Bi-Fibrals

Haunch Squams

Frontal Hugglers

Figure 4. Skeleton

Smash Cap

Gog Holes

Gnash Gate

Articulated Grab Sticks

Nog Joint

Jump Stems

Floor Flaps

Remember this little fella?
Remember how cute he is?
Look at a skinned one.

Inside a baby Mernimbler

Chapter 4

Spotter's Guide

Skwunt

(Squintly Clamgullit)

Born with eyes inside its gapping nosh trap, this cloppered valve sclap slams its mouth shut to stop other Flanimals poking its eyes for a laugh. However, it is terrified of the dark and opens up screaming, drawing Flanimals from all around who poke its eyes for a laugh.

Plappavom
(Bilious Flob)

This bilgeulant flap of glunt has no mouth parts and so is unable to eat. It survives by gradually dissolving itself to provide energy for its bodily functions. Its only bodily function is looking around seeing what an utterly pointless and depressing existence it has. This means it lives quite a long time, making its life even worse. It gets smaller as it grows until it is just eyes. Eventually these dissolve too, and it is put out of its misery.

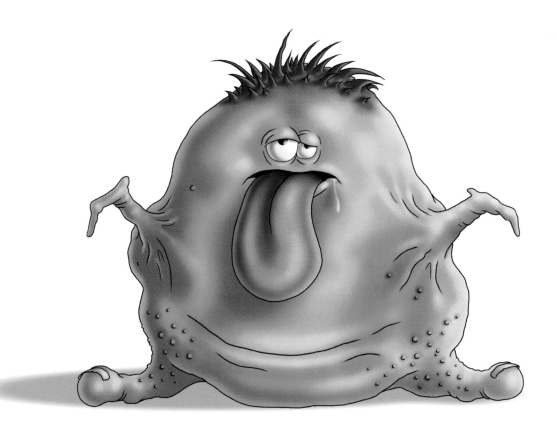

Fud Dumpton

(Mastrofud Poddler)

This romungular quock stumpling looks
like the most razbungled wumbligger ever.
It is actually quite serebental and aspireculous
in its feriping. Which proves you should
never go on appearances.

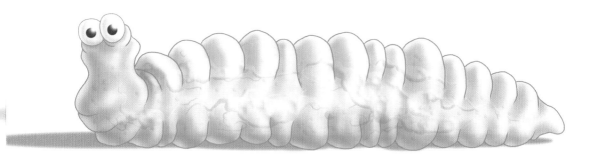

Grommomulunt
(Crumb Gullit)

This splunked-up spooge sock is the larval stage of the Munt Fly. It has no mouth, ears, nose, legs or internal organs but just looks forward to things changing when it sheds its skin and metamorphoses into an adult. Unfortunately the only change that takes place when it reaches adulthood is that its eyes fall off. It does shed its skin but there is no new skin underneath so its insides just leak into the ground. Have you ever heard a stain weep?

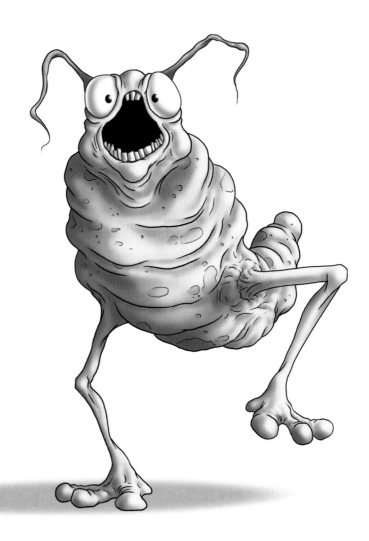

Dweezle Muzzbug

(Throxi Zub-Stumpling)

This scrammy beedle runs around wishing it could fly. Angry, tired and fed up with using its legs to get around, it sheds them so it can rest. Unfortunately legs falling off is one of the most painful things ever and it screams itself to death in agony. Hardly a rest, is it? So be careful what you wish for.

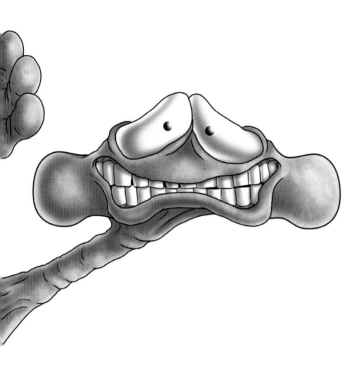

Verminal Psquirm
(Flungal Grindler)

The Verminal Psquirm spends its days poking its head around or over things. Because of this we don't know what its body is like. We can only assume from its name that it is similar in shape to the Hordery Psquirm but with superficial Verminal characteristics.

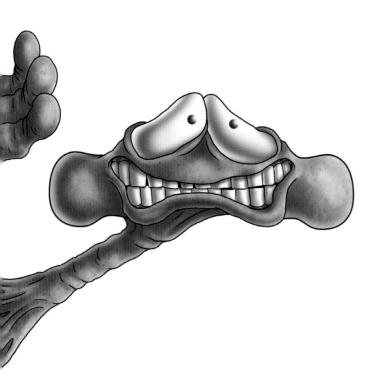

Hordery Psquirm

(Smarmal Grindler)

Very similar, aren't they?

By the way, the 'P' is not silent, it's pronounced *Psquirm*.
I said the 'P' is not silent, it's pronounced PSQUIRM.

Squat
(Psychus Crabantular)

This raknid scrabrapnor is the angriest maddest ripper-flan
in the universe. Whenever it meets another Flanimal it is so filled
with rage that it goes beserk with the gnashing and the smashing
and spiking and biting and it destroys it in seconds. This makes
it even angrier, because it can't carry on destroying, and the next
Flanimal it meets is destroyed even quicker with even more
gore clawing and dreadful head-shredding and aaghhh . . .
IT'S SO MENTAL!

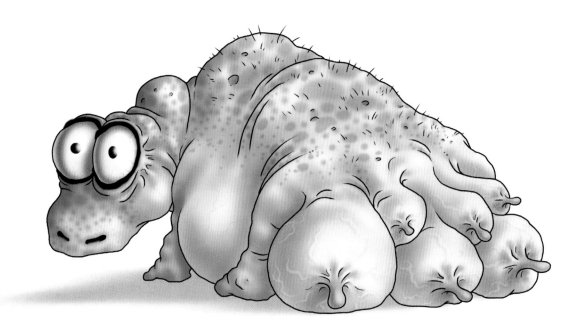

Mung Ungler
(Gruntloidian Mam-Langer)

This brontial mamb drudger is like a big sluggish liquid
lunch. Flanimals from all around come and suckle on its
rear milky puddings and there is nothing it can do about it.
Inside it is screaming "roll on death."

Pong Flibber
(Flatulous Pumpton)

This pungent boggle-eyed guff bubble is quite useless. Its only defence is to pump out its entire gaseous insides at high speed to escape. The Flanimal it is trying to escape from simply follows the smell to find the creature de-ponged and flibbered.

Weezy Tong Nambler
(Fledge Sputer)

This flembulous frog-gossling is so utterly repulsive
in a pathetic, runtling way that it causes all other Flanimals
to instantly want to squash it for fun. Its defence is to flap
and lick. This is even more annoying and it therefore
gets squashed for fun anyway.

Prug Fuggell
(Bog Squabbler)

**This drugulant testroprod is
nothing more than a simple Nad Snail.
And we all know what that means, don't we?**

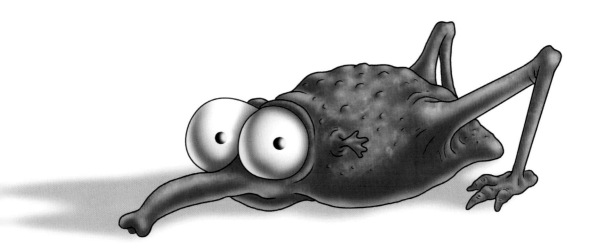

Gronglet
(Konk Shnerbler)

This tiny humfibiloid shnerbles along in ming puddles, snorggling up micro-flugs, creatures so small they can't be seen. It needs something bigger than this to live so it starves to death within the first day of its life.

Spleg
(Konk Bwarker)

Related to the Gronglet but with greater snorggling
capabilities. It can snorggle up twice as many micro-flugs.
This means it doesn't die until the day after it is born.

Swog Monglet
(Mug Jizzling)

This huggly squibbling is a primitive pond slubber that pulled itself out of the primordial sloob millions of years ago. Once on land it was too fat and useless to pull itself back in. Look at it. It is absolutely kippered.

Chapter 5

Flanimal Behaviour

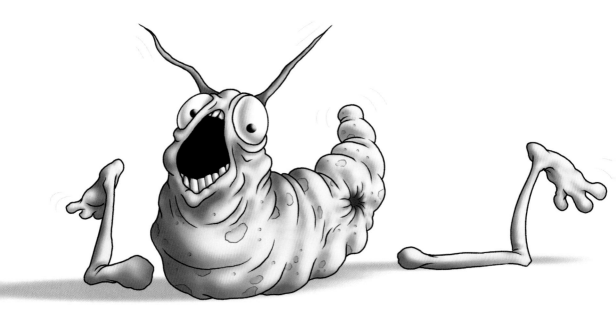

Dweezle Muzzgrub

**Dweezle Muzzbug after metamorphosis
from creepy-crawly into screamy death thing.**

Pong Flibber escape method

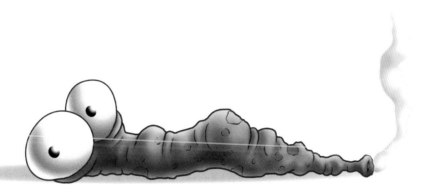

Pong Flibber
De-ponged and flibbered

Who's the Hardest?

As you've probably noticed, the life of any Flanimal is a constant struggle for survival. They have to live long enough to bring babies into the world to continue their species. With the threat from other Flanimals they have to sometimes fight to stay alive. Some love to fight, some are great fighters, but who is the greatest?

At 5 is the Blunging, at 4 is the Grundit, at 3 is the Sprot Guzzlor. We know the top two places are occupied by the Squat and the Adult Mernimbler, but because they've never met in battle we're not sure who would win. Who would you put your money on?

Adult Mernimbler

STATS
Weapons: Gore Horns, Clamp Fangs, Strangle Mits
Biting Power: 10
Strength: 10
Speed: 6
Aggression: 9

Squat

STATS
Weapons: Well clawed up. Two Stiletto Slice Sabres
which slash anything
Biting Power: 8
Strength: 7
Speed: 9
Aggression: More than 10, it tips over into mental

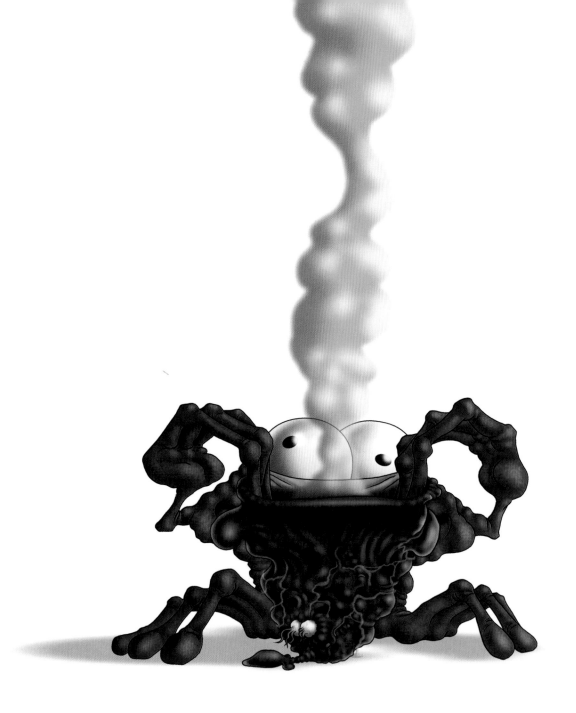

**Munge Fuddler trying to open
Offledermis for superior fuddlin'**

**Munge Fuddler and Offledermis
in an extreme case of over-fuddlin'**

Baby Grundit and Baby Puddloflaj

Just look how well they get on with each other.
They're so young and innocent they don't know any better.

**Adult Grundit showing the
young how to behave**

Twin Plamglotti

Born so close together they've
swallowed each other's arms by mistake.
Not a big problem, they're going to die anyway.

So now you know more Flanimals. Some of them are weird. Some of them are not so weird. But the weird thing is that the less weird ones are weirder than the weirder ones. Weird. But the weirdest thing of all happened exactly many years ago.

One day (two at the most) a baby Blunging asked his father a question.

"Father . . ." he said.

Obviously he didn't speak English. I'm translating so you can understand it. I couldn't even write what he actually said but the noise he made was like a mongoose with a cold. As the Blunging grows up it starts talking like a normal goose with a cold and laryngitis.

Anyway, "Father," he said, "what is beyond the Black Mountain at the end of the Dark Forest on the other side of the Sea of Night?"

"The what?" said the Father.

"The Black Mountain at the end of the Dark Forest on the other side of the Sea of Night."

The Father looked confused.

"Uh?"

"You know, the Sea of Night." He pointed. "Over there."

"Oh yeah," said the Father.

"Well, you know there's a big forest across there?"

"Yes . . ." said the Father.

"Well if you walk through that there's a big black mountain."

"Black mountain?"

The baby pointed again.

"That one!"

"Oh that one, yeah, sure. What was your question?"

"What's on the other side of it?"

"Other side of what?"

"The Black Mountain!" the baby said loudly in an annoyed way.

"Oh . . . nothing," said the Father.

"Nothing?"

The Father shook his head.

"You're not saying that to stop me going, are you?"

"No, there's nothing there," the Father insisted.

"It's just it sounds like the sort of thing a parent would say to stop a kid going."

"No, there's nothing there. Very boring."

"See, it's things like that. Why add 'very boring'? I didn't ask if it was a laugh there, I just asked what's there. It sounds like you're trying to put me off."

"No, there's nothing there."

The baby thought for a moment.

"Is it dangerous? Are there creatures so ferocious that I would be ripped limb from limb if I dared to venture there? And you just don't want me to be killed?"

"No, I don't want you to be bored."

"Right, I'm going."

"It'll take you a long time."

"Don't care. I can't wait to see what's there now."

"There's nothing there."

"We'll see."

"Nothing to see."

"I'm off. Bye."

So off he stritchly hopped. He passed an Underblenge sitting on a rock.

"Alright? Where you off to?" it asked.

"I'm going to see what's behind the Black Mountain at the edge of the Dark Forest across the Sea of Night."

"Oh yeah. I'd come with you but obviously I can't get off this rock."

"Shame," said the baby Blunging.

"Not really," said the Underblenge. "If I could get off the first thing I'd do is stick to your face and suffocate you to death."

They both laughed for ages.

"Anyway, must be off," said the baby Blunging. "Bye."

"Bye," said the Underblenge.

So on he went ever closer to his destination. As he approached the Sea of Night it started to get darker even though it was the middle of the day.

"Weird that, init," said a lonely Skwunt.

"You can talk," said the precocious young Blunging.

"Of course I can. It's about the only thing I can do. I'm literally all mouth," it said.

"No, I mean you're a fine one to say something's weird. You misunderstand me."

"Ooh . . . 'You misunderstand me,'" the Skwunt said mockingly. "I never said I was clever. There's not much room for brains when you haven't really got much of a head, you know. Anyway, where are you going?"

By the way, I should point out that Skwunts don't speak English either. They communicate with a noise that sounds exactly like an old sad monkey gargling.

"I'm trying to find out what's behind the Black Mountain."

"Can I come with you? Two heads are better than one."

"Not in this case," the baby Blunging replied. "Bye."

He crossed the Sea of Night and entered the Dark Forest, which was even darker than the Sea of Night. But then it was night by now so that's understandable. I know what you're thinking. How did a baby Blunging get across the sea when he can't swim? Well, he got a lift on a Frappled Humpdumbler obviously.

So he entered the forest. A forest full of creatures so hideous and terrifying to look at that they would cause anyone to die of fright instantly when they saw them. Luckily, as I said, it was dark so he couldn't really make them out. He went through the forest and there stood the Black Mountain.

"How am I gonna get over that?" he thought.

"You could always go around it," said a Gumbnumbly Knunk Knunk.

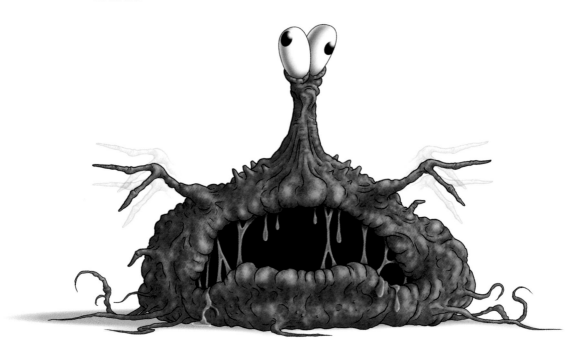

"What in the name of Grob are you?"

"Not sure. I'm not even sure if I am anything," it said.

"Well you've got to be something. I mean every . . . Hang on a minute. How did you know what I was thinking? I didn't say out loud about getting over the mountain, and yet you said 'You could always go around it.' How is that possible?"

"Walk," replied the Knunk Knunk.

"No, not how is it possible to get round it, how is it possible to know what I was thinking?"

"You were thinking very loudly."

The baby Blunging just looked at the creature.

"What a weirdo," he thought.

"Charming," said the offended Knunk Knunk. "Boy, you say what you think, don't you?"

"No I don't. That's the point I didn't say it. I just thought it."

"Loudly," said the Knunk Knunk.

"I'm off," said the Blunging. "Bye."

Finally, after six long days (and four nights), the baby Blunging had crossed a sea, passed through a forest and walked around a mountain. He had made it. As he stood at his destination, at the other side of the Black Mountain, he could not believe what he saw. A sight so devastating he could not speak. He could not move. He could hardly breathe. What do you think he saw? What do you think was beyond the Black Mountain at the end of the Dark Forest on the other side of the Sea of Night?

Guess.

Yes, that's right.

Nothing.

Flanimal Scale Chart

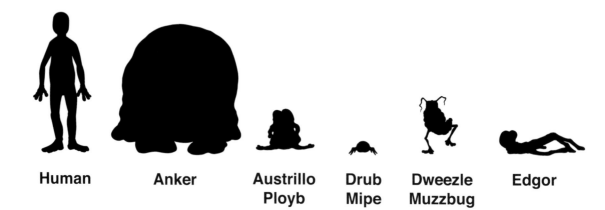

| Human | Anker | Austrillo Ployb | Drub Mipe | Dweezle Muzzbug | Edgor |

| Fud Dumpton | Gernloid | Grebulond | Gronglet | Grommomulunt |

| Gundulump | Horosi Horasi | Muffid Skrunt | Mung Ungler | Nub Sprunt |

**Nurdler
Ployb**

Plappavom

**Pong
Flibber**

**Progulant
Glob**

Prug Fuggell

Scrabs

Skwunt

**Slunge
Greebler**

Spleg

**Squabulo
Ployb**

Squat

**Swog
Monglet**

**Ung
Noglet**

?
size
unknown

**Verminal
Psquirm**

**Weezy Tong
Nambler**

So now you know more Flanimals.
In fact now you know about all Flanimals.
Well, the ones that live on the land that is.
I can't tell you about the Flanimals that live
in the sea because they are a bit weird.
Okay then, we'll talk about them next time.

Oh, I forgot to tell you about the Bletchling again.
What do you think it looks like?

Grant Stewart has specialized in Key Accounts, Sales Management and Business Development for many companies and has run his own training and consultancy company for the past 30 years. His market-leading book on *Successful Sales Management* has sold more than 70,000 copies.

Grant can be contacted at: grantstewart1@gmail.com

Peter Ronald Kellino Fleming is a Chartered Fellow of both the UK Chartered Institute of Marketing and the Chartered Institute of Personnel Development. He is author of numerous management books and has more than 30 years' experience as an International Management Consultant and Trainer (through his consultancy, PFA International).

With past negotiating experience in senior management roles in the Public Sector – and buying exposure in Retailing – he has continued his family's path of international travel (through The Kellino's acrobatic group) and built up his expertise in negotiating in Europe, the Middle East and Australasia.

His specialisms lie with business development through marketing solutions – and helping organizations improve their learning development programmes through his original work on the transfer of learning in the business setting (which brought him his MA/HRM). Apart from his authorship, he is also an active mentor working in both business and voluntary sectors.

Peter is married with two children and lives in Derbyshire, UK.

Di McLanachan is managing director of Learning Curves Personal Development Ltd. She is an international trainer, executive coach, a master practitioner of Neuro-linguistic Programming and author of the bestselling book *NLP for Business Excellence*. She has frequently been featured on both radio and television, and has been delivering training in customer care on a regular basis since 1993.

www.learningcurves.co.uk

Teach Yourself®

Selling
In 4 Weeks
The Complete
Guide to Success

Christine Harvey,
Grant Stewart,
Peter Fleming &
Di McLanachan

First published in Great Britain in 2015 by Hodder and Stoughton. An Hachette UK company.

First published in US in 2015 by The McGraw-Hill Companies, Inc.

This edition published in 2015 by Hodder and Stoughton

Based on original material from *Successful Selling In A Week; Successful Key Account Management In A Week; Successful Negotiating In A Week; Successful Customer Care In A Week*

British Library Cataloguing in Publication Data: a catalogue record for this title is available from the British Library.

Library of Congress Catalog Card Number: on file.

Paperback ISBN 978 1 473 60744 6

eBook ISBN 978 1 473 60745 3

1

The publisher has used its best endeavours to ensure that any website addresses referred to in this book are correct and active at the time of going to press. However, the publisher and the author have no responsibility for the websites and can make no guarantee that a site will remain live or that the content will remain relevant, decent or appropriate.

The publisher has made every effort to mark as such all words which it believes to be trademarks. The publisher should also like to make it clear that the presence of a word in the book, whether marked or unmarked, in no way affects its legal status as a trademark.

Every reasonable effort has been made by the publisher to trace the copyright holders of material in this book. Any errors or omissions should be notified in writing to the publisher, who will endeavour to rectify the situation for any reprints and future editions.

Typeset by Cenveo Publisher Services.

Printed and bound in Great Britain by CPI Group (UK) Ltd., Croydon, CR0 4YY.

John Murray Learning policy is to use papers that are natural, renewable and recyclable products and made from wood grown in sustainable forests. The logging and manufacturing processes are expected to conform to the environmental regulations of the country of origin.

Hodder and Stoughton
338 Euston Road
London NW1 3BH
www.hodder.co.uk

Contents

WEEK 1

Successful Selling
In A Week

Introduction

The idea of selling as an occupation leaves many people terror-stricken, and yet selling is an integral part of running any business. Good salespeople are in great demand. Sales skills are essential in starting any business, and successful selling brings with it career progression, satisfaction and personal growth that are second to none.

With this book, you'll learn *all* the components necessary to become *not just a good but a great salesperson*. Whether you're new to sales, and want to start out with a bang, or a veteran salesperson who wants to maximize results, *Selling In 4 Weeks: The Complete Guide to Success* will be a huge asset to you now and in years to come.

You'll learn ways to increase the effectiveness of your efforts, save time and energy and get the best results possible, regardless of your field of sales. You'll be able to put together your own system of success, just like the people before you from whom these principles are drawn. Successful selling means using a structured set of systems that all professional high achievers can learn. We will look at each of these steps one day at a time.

You may be wondering if your personality is right for sales. You may think that it's important to be a good talker, but it's far more important to be a sincere listener, to be able to ask pertinent questions leading to buying motives, and then be able to present the features and benefits of your product or service as they *match* your customers' needs. A person who does all the talking, without the right questioning and listening, will be wasting time and effort.

There is, in fact, no one right personality for sales. Most of us can use the skills we've developed over our lifetime, and hone them with the principles of this book to become a top-notch, if not world-class, salesperson.

I've spent much of my life selling, training salespeople, and writing about those top-notch sales skills. In another of my books, *Secrets of the World's Top Sales Performers,* I interviewed ten of the world's top salespeople in ten countries and ten industries. The one secret of success they all shared was consistency. They each had their own system and they used it day in and day out.

The same will be true for you. You'll be able to use the techniques in this book to design sales skills that work best for you, your personality and your industry. So dig in and enjoy. I wish you success in your journey, every step of the way.

It would be my greatest pleasure to hear how you applied the material. Writing a book is like giving birth to an offspring, taking about nine months to develop after years of personal growth. As our children grow to be teens and adults, it's nice to hear great stories about them. So, if you have questions or stories to tell me – or you wish to enquire about our seminars – you can reach me at ChristineHarvey@ChristineHarvey.com, or via the publishers.

Wishing you all the best,

Christine Harvey

SUNDAY

Jump-start your success formula

I have often travelled to Hong Kong and Singapore, where business competition is fierce. A journalist there asked me about the principles of my books and courses. 'Mrs Harvey, why are you so adamant about targets for salespeople? Isn't it enough just to do your best?'

'Well, look at it like this,' I responded. 'If you were training to be an Olympic champion runner, would you go out every day and practise running any distance at any speed, just doing your best? Or would you know exactly how far you had to run, and at what speed, in order to meet your defined goal?'

'Oh, yes, I see,' she responded. That made sense to her. It's painful for people to work hard and do their best, to have high expectations and then be let down.

Today you will learn how to set and achieve goals that are *right for you*. You won't fail by thinking sales will come to you magically, or later if you wait. Instead, you'll be planning your best formula for success. You will learn how to:

- adopt new methods of operation
- set your overall goal
- create daily targets
- measure your results
- carry out the actions needed for success.

Adopt new methods of operation

Do you remember the last time you changed jobs? Did it require a mental adjustment of your self-image? The chances are that you needed time to grow into the new shoes.

I remember sitting on a plane from London, bound for Chicago, to meet my first prospective client after I started my company. I still felt allegiance to my old company, my old job and my old colleagues because I had no experiences to draw upon for my new role. If you are just starting out in sales, or changing companies, you may experience this too.

However, psychologists say that we can do a lot for ourselves to speed up the acclimatization process. If we visualize ourselves working in the new role, feeling comfortable in the new role and succeeding in the new role, we will acclimatize faster.

Whether we are new to sales or want to improve our returns, we'll be adopting new methods of operation. We'll be forcing ourselves in new directions, putting ourselves under new pressures, disciplining ourselves and setting new goals. All of these will require that we see ourselves differently. The sooner we do this, the sooner we'll succeed.

Let's look at the specific areas in which you'll want to see yourself operating successfully as preparation for selling.

Preparing for success

- Set your overall goal.
- Break the goal into daily work segments.
- Carry out these daily segments.
- Gain prospective customers.
- Spend time on critical activities.
- Create self-management system charts.
- Organize work systems.

Set your overall goal

Start at the top of the list and set your goals. What do you want to achieve? Calculate it in some specific terms. Will it be a monetary figure, a percentage or multiple of a target set by your company, a possession to be acquired, or even a promotion?

Now think about how to convert that goal to the actual number of sales you need in order to achieve your target. Good. Now the next step is critical and this is the step most unsuccessful salespeople avoid. Divide your total sales into weekly and daily sales and then calculate the work necessary to achieve that.

Calculate workload

Ask yourself the following questions about workload.

- How many sales do I want?
- How many prospects will I need to see in order to make one sale?
- How many prospects do I need in order to reach my total sales target?
- How many activities do I need to do to generate one prospect?
  - Telephone calls
  - Direct mail or emailed letters
  - Exhibitions or seminars
  - Advertisements
  - Cold calling
  - Other

- What daily activity schedule and results do I have to maintain in order to achieve my goal? (Include visits, telephone calls and all of the above.)

Self-deception

Bob Adams, one of the world's top insurance salesmen, puts it in strong terms. He says that the single biggest failure salespeople make is **self-deception**. He said he wasn't 'born with success'. He had to study the most successful salespeople he could find.

His advice? 'Don't fool yourself into thinking you're selling when you're sitting at your desk. If you're not in front of the right number of people every day, working eight hours per day is not the point. It's what you do in those eight hours that counts.'

If you're not in front of enough prospects, you won't sell enough to make your target. And how do you get in front of enough prospects? By making enough appointments. It's that straightforward. 'Yet many people fool themselves thinking they are selling when in fact they are doing busy work,' says Bob.

> **TIP** *Often, the difference between success and failure is neglecting to break down your overall goal into daily targets and tasks.*

Let's look at advice from people who succeed year after year. How do they put this principle into practice?

One salesman with a worldwide reputation for success is Ove from Sweden. He has calculated his yearly target and broken it down into a daily figure. He knows exactly how many sales he must make per day. He knows how many prospects he must see each day.

He stresses that staying at the top is easy if you know how much you must do every day and you do it.

Not me!

'Oh, daily targets don't relate to me,' many people argue. That's the biggest misconception I hear from our seminar delegates. They really believe they can't break *their* activity into daily targets. This is the first mental change we must *all* make if we are to succeed in selling.

> **TIP** *Sales come about from methodically carrying out the right practices, day in and day out.*

Whether we sell large systems to governments that require three years to close, consulting projects that take a year to close or retail products to customers that take three minutes to close, we still have to calculate *which* daily component parts will lead us to success. Even if we only want three customers per year, we'll have to be negotiating with six, nine or twelve prospects constantly. We need to know *how many* and keep this running *constantly*.

In the interviews I undertook for my book *Secrets of the World's Top Sales Performers*, I found that every single top sales performer in every industry knows their daily sales target and daily activity schedule. Did their companies tell them? No. They've calculated it themselves. It's exactly what we all must do if we want true and lasting success.

> *You must know your daily targets for finding prospects and do that first. That means making appointments and seeing prospects. Everything else is secondary.*

Create daily targets

Why do we put so much emphasis on daily sales targets and daily activity targets? It's because we've seen so many failures by talented, hard-working, well-meaning people who deserved to succeed. No one ever sat them down and said: 'Look, success comes by doing the right number of activities day in and day out.'

Make reminders

We know that you are reading this book in order to succeed. You want to use a strategic approach. You want to avoid the pitfalls of others. Therefore, take today to plan your targets. Plan the systems you will use for reaching your targets.

Create prompts on wall charts, screen savers and pocket memos – anything and everything you need to remind yourself that hard work alone will not bring you success. It's a matter of scheduling and seeing the right number of people today as well as carrying out specific activities that will allow you to see the right number of people tomorrow.

Calculate the numbers

What is the right number? If we need one sale per day and we have to see three prospects in order to convert one to a sale, then we need three sales visits per day. That's if we can do one-call closings; in other words, if we need to see each prospect only once. But what if we need to see each prospect

1 sale × 3 prospects × 2 visits
= 6 visits
per day

twice on average and we need to make one sale per day? How many sales visits will we need to do every day? Six.

We'll need time for making appointments and time for following up on promises we make during the appointments. It's therefore essential to plan our targets and break them into daily workloads.

Pitfalls for business owners too

New business owners have exactly the same problem, and we can learn from them. Here's an example. Two talented young dress designers with their own shop asked me for advice on succeeding in their business. They had many loyal customers but they were afraid they wouldn't make enough money to stay in business.

Here are the questions that they needed to ask themselves.

- How much money do we need to make?
- What are our expenses?
- How many do we need to sell per year to cover all our expenses and leave us with a profit?
- How many is that per week?
- What do we need to do in order to sell that many each week?

They hadn't thought about it that way. They were just going to do the best they could. Were they unusual? No. That's the naïve approach you want to avoid, regardless of your industry.

Are 'good products' enough?

I was fortunate to work with a British enterprise agency launched by Prince Charles that helps people start new businesses. Through that experience of working on the Board, I saw hundreds of people who thought it was enough to have a 'good product' and 'do their best'. Yet, as time went on, those who succeeded learned that they had to know *exactly* what their sales targets were every week and every day. Then they had to focus all their energy on making sure those targets were met, to ensure that they didn't go out of business.

Selling helps you succeed

You don't want to be out of business or out of the sales business. There are tremendous opportunities in sales, including:

- opportunities for self-development
- opportunities for promotion
- opportunities for helping people
- job satisfaction
- financial wealth
- progression towards running your own business if that's what you want.

However, few business owners today succeed without strong emphasis and skills on the sales side. Likewise, few people today in the corporate world progress without being able to sell their ideas.

Millions of people are involved in the production of products or services. All their jobs rely on people being able to sell those products or services. Corporations need you.

The economies of the world rely on continued sales. Your skills and your success are more important than you realize.

Measure your results

Whatever your goal, start by measuring your targets and breaking them into daily segments and tasks. Remember that today is your day of preparation and your success later will mainly depend on your plan and your dedication to your plan. The following chart shows the most critical factors to measure, i.e. the number of sales visits (target and actual) and the number of sales (target and actual).

Self-management wall chart and computer graph

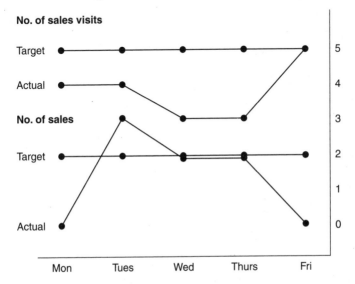

Self-management systems

In order to succeed, you'll also need to chart the following:
- the number of telephone calls you make for appointments (target and actual)
- the number of direct mail letters or emails you send (target and actual)
- the number of referral leads you get from customers before and after the sale (target and actual)
- the number of website hits or other methods you use for finding prospective customers.

These will become your self-management systems.

Predicting shortfalls

If your wall chart and computer graph show you that your actual sales visits are 25 per cent below your target for one week, you can expect to be 25 per cent down on sales unless you make up that number of visits the following week.

Sales do not come about magically, and that's what your management control wall charts and computer graphs remind you of instantly.

Actions for success

Will you reach the success level you hope for? Selling is not a mystical process. It's a predictable, logical, step-by-step process like a production line. When we put in the right component parts, we get the correct end product. When we put in fewer component parts than necessary, we get an inferior end product. There is no mystery about salesmanship.

TIP *Much of your success will depend on coming to terms with the actual component parts of salesmanship.*

Planning our success by setting our daily workload is the first component part. Over the next six days you will learn about the other component parts. When we carry out each component part in the right quantity, with the right quality and frequency, we have success.

Our results come from our actions, not from our understanding. It's said that 'Knowledge without action serves no one.' This is never truer than in sales. Pick up your pen and start *now* to create your targets *and* your self-management system charts. Success is in your hands.

Summary

Today we talked about the importance of targets. We started with the overall goal – for example, an annual income goal. We tied that to the number of products or services we need to sell, then broke that down further into weekly and daily sales targets.

We then looked at the **activity** needed to accomplish those goals. This means the number of prospects needed to gain one sale, and the number of phone calls or marketing campaigns needed to gain one prospect.

Just as 2 + 2 = 4, we saw that, without the right number of actions each day, be it phone calls, visits or marketing pieces – and probably all of these – we can't possibly reach our goal. How much better it is to know this in advance, because then we can change our strategy and systems, or even our targets.

As one of the world's top salespeople says, 'Don't let self-deception be your enemy!' We have to know how to break down targets and set our daily activity level in advance in order to become the top achiever we wish to be. Start now. Go for it, and enjoy!

Remember
Knowledge without action serves no one.

SUNDAY
MONDAY
TUESDAY
WEDNESDAY
THURSDAY
FRIDAY
SATURDAY

Fact-check (answers at the back)

Note: all questions require a single answer.

1. What does changing careers or improving results in your current sales position require?
   a) Mental adjustment of your self-image ❑
   b) Visualizing yourself working in a new role ❑
   c) Visualizing feeling comfortable in the new role and succeeding in the new role ❑
   d) All of the above ❑

2. What can setting goals successfully mean?
   a) Calculating a monetary figure ❑
   b) Targeting a possession to be acquired ❑
   c) Aiming for a promotion ❑
   d) All of the above ❑

3. After deciding on your goal, what should your first step be?
   a) To tell your best friend and ask for support ❑
   b) To convert your goal to the actual number of sales you need in order to achieve your target ❑
   c) To discuss the practicality of your goal with your boss ❑
   d) To celebrate ❑

4. After dividing their annual sales goal into weekly and daily sales targets, what do most *unsuccessful* salespeople avoid doing?
   a) Writing it down ❑
   b) Entering the data into their computer ❑
   c) Calculating the work necessary to achieve that goal ❑
   d) Telling anyone ❑

5. What is the single biggest failure of most salespeople?
   a) Talking too much at the first meeting ❑
   b) Self-deception ❑
   c) Being rude to the customer ❑
   d) Giving their boss false hope ❑

6. In order to know how many prospects to see each day, what must you know?
   a) How many sales you want ❑
   b) How many prospects you need to make one sale ❑
   c) How many activities you need to do to generate one prospect ❑
   d) All of the above ❑

7. Why do most *unsuccessful* salespeople and business owners avoid using goals and targets?

a) They firmly believe that doing their best is enough to make them succeed ❏
b) They have never used them before ❏
c) They are afraid to fail ❏
d) They think it is a waste of time ❏

8. A salesman named Sam calculates that he needs one sale per day. On average, one prospect out of three will buy his products, and he normally has to visit each prospect twice before he gets a 'yes'. How many total visits does Sam need to make each day to reach his goal of one sale per day?

a) Two ❏
b) Four ❏
c) Six ❏
d) Eight ❏

9. Why are your skills and success in selling so important?

a) Your livelihood depends on it ❏
b) The economies of the world rely on continued sales ❏
c) The livelihood of your company relies on it ❏
d) All of the above ❏

10. What is the *most* important thing about comparing your actual sales to your targets on a wall chart?

a) You will see at a glance where you stand ❏
b) You can catch up tomorrow if you fall behind today ❏
c) You will gain recognition from your manager and your peers ❏
d) You will keep your morale up ❏

MONDAY

Develop product and service expertise

On one exciting day in my early sales career, I took the company's technical expert out on a sales call with me. She and I were a knockout team. I was expert at asking questions about needs, and she had answers to every conceivable question the customer had about our products and services. Later, when I had my own company, I enjoyed taking my own sales employees out on calls with me and supplying that same knowledge.

The importance of learning from technical people is obvious. They have years of 'behind-the-scenes' experiences from which to draw. And when you become an expert yourself and model the sales process for a newer member of staff, you also gain. You're on your toes. You do things correctly, knowing that they are watching and learning from you.

There are dozens of ways to gain the product and service knowledge you need to sell well, and one of them is bound to suit your style and interests.

Today you will create your own plan for developing your expertise. You will:

- understand the 'rule of 40'
- find sources of knowledge
- plan your personal strategy.

Understand the 'rule of 40'

Let's start at the beginning. How much knowledge do you need? Perhaps this idea will help you. Dale Carnegie advised his students of public speaking: 'Learn 40 times as much as you will use.'

Why 40 times? It's because our store of information is like a fully charged battery. It shows in our enthusiasm, our self-confidence and most of all in our *competence*. Certainly that's true of selling too.

Let's stop for a moment and think of our customers. How do they view us? Aren't we the only link between the manufactured product or service and themselves? They have to rely on us to tell them *each and every thing* that they might need to know.

It makes sense, then, to have a 40-fold store of knowledge in reserve for every eventuality, over and above what we might use in a single sales discussion with a single customer. Therefore, we need to focus on getting as much knowledge as we can, as quickly as possible.

Invest in yourself

First, let's set the ground rules and clear any misconceptions. In order to reach the top with the desired level of expertise, we should consider the following two principles.

● Expect to invest in ourselves.
● Don't expect the company to provide all our training.

How many years do doctors, lawyers or accountants spend in preparing themselves for their profession? If we want to become experts, we first have to realize that we must invest in ourselves. We have to develop our own plan. If our company trains us, fine. But we cannot use the lack of training as an excuse to hold us back. Success is in our own hands.

> **'An investment in knowledge pays the best interest.'**
> Benjamin Franklin

Find sources of knowledge

Where do we start? We want to set a schedule for absorbing our 40-fold expertise in the shortest possible time. There are many effective options, as shown in the box below.

> ## Dynamic sources of product expertise
>
> - Interview current customers.
> - Study product literature.
> - Study service literature.
> - Study operations manuals.
> - Take technicians on sales visits.
> - Accompany other sales professionals on sales visits.
> - Have discussions with operations people, managers, product developers and distributors.
> - Observe the production line.
> - Utilize web-based training.
> - Take training courses of all kinds.

Interview current customers

Interviewing current customers is one of the most valuable yet least exploited options for salespeople. Customers give us the information from the *user's* point of view, which is invaluable.

The customer doesn't want to know, for example, that a fax machine has 'group 3, high-speed, digital transmission technology'. They only want to know that their document can reach their colleague in Australia in six seconds *because* of this group 3, high-speed technology.

We must always stress the benefit, using the technology as proof that the benefit exists.

Why else are we so bullish when we visit or talk to current customers? Because they are a bottomless pit of testimonials, references, new business, add-on business, referrals, inspiration, enthusiasm, and information about competitors. Moreover, they can supply quotable stories, even material for press releases and feature stories. But the most important part is your instant education.

Here is an example. Some years ago I was involved in selling a computer service. Because everyone on the sales team was hired from other industries, we each needed to get computer training as quickly as possible. I therefore arranged to accompany a technician on a troubleshooting call. After she had sorted out the problem, I asked the client a question: 'What made you choose our system over the competitor's?'

'It's so fast to use and error free,' he said. 'We previously agonized over errors in our systems. Now we complete input forms every morning. It takes half an hour, maximum. Then the results come back – perfect, no aggravation.'

That was a testimonial I could use to emphasize speed and accuracy. It gave our sales team a valuable reference letter and later we turned it into a press release, which gave it added value.

SUNDAY

MONDAY

TUESDAY

WEDNESDAY

THURSDAY

FRIDAY

SATURDAY

The benefits of interviewing customers

The benefits of interviewing our current customers are many and include the following.

- Through interviews we gain confidence in our product and company.
- We learn the benefits to the user.
- We build a rapport, which can later lead to further business.
- We acquire testimonial stories about how the service is used.
- We gain confidence and inspiration.

We can then repeat the interviewing process with different industry group users until we have the knowledge we need. The time it takes will be well worth while.

Plan your personal strategy

Use today to plan your personal strategy for building your product/service expertise. The following checklist will help you decide which methods to apply. Who will you go to in order to get the information? How much time will you allocate to each method? When will you do it? Make a copy of the list and fill it in to create your personal action strategy.

Set up your system today. You may want to call one or two current customers to set up appointments for interviews. You may even want to have the discussion by telephone today, if appropriate. Naturally, it's always better to do it in person if possible. Distances, time and products will dictate the best approach.

TIP

Be sure to allocate enough time every day to update your knowledge.

Look again at your strategy. You may want to spend an hour a day next week reading technical literature, or perhaps two hours today. You may want to invite a technical person to accompany you on your next sales visit, or arrange to accompany them on a technical visit. Decide now, and allocate time in your diary.

Creative options for developing product/service expertise

Method	Yes/No	Who	How long	When
1 Interview current customers				
2 Study product literature				
3 Study service literature				
4 Study operations manuals				
5 Take technicians on sales visits				
6 Accompany other sales professionals on sales visits				
7 Have discussions • with operations people • with managers • with product development people • with distributors				
8 Observe the production line				
9 Utilize web-based training				
10 Take training courses				

Commit to training courses

You may want to persuade your manager that he or she should fund a training course for you from their budget. If you do, be prepared to 'sell' your idea, explaining the benefits the company will get from your enhanced skills. Remember, your boss may have to sell the idea up the line.

But remember the bottom line – your commitment to your own training. If the manager's answer is no, you may have to invest in yourself. Be prepared to take responsibility for your own success.

Professionals spend time and money preparing for success in their career, and selling is as demanding and challenging as any career.

What steps can you take to find training courses that will be valuable to you?

Learn at every appointment

One top sales manager I knew summed it up well when he advised: 'The day you stop learning in sales is the day your professionalism dies.'

After every sales call with any of his sales staff, whether they were new to sales or experienced, he always said: 'Tell me two new things you learned from that visit.' That's good advice for all of us.

Implement your strategy

Take time now to look back over the options for developing product and service expertise. Decide which options are right for you. Then draw up a segmented strategy of how much time to devote to each option. Take today to plan those segments.

Summary

Today we looked at the many ways we can develop the product and service expertise critical to reaching our sales goals. We touched on the importance of relating the benefits of the products and services to the customer. We learned that, just as in other professions, gaining the training we need is up to us if we want to be among the highest achievers and therefore the highest income earners.

We also saw interesting benefits of designing our own training. For example, if we decide to interview past or current clients, we not only learn what benefits they derive but may also gain testimonials, referrals and even new business from them.

In addition, we might choose to discuss product features with operations, technical and product development people, who can give us valuable contacts as well as knowledge.

Finally, with personal learning in mind we looked at how to plan our strategy, using a personal planning chart for easy implementation.

Remember

The day you stop learning is the day your professionalism dies and your income diminishes.

SUNDAY
MONDAY
TUESDAY
WEDNESDAY
THURSDAY
FRIDAY
SATURDAY

Fact-check (answers at the back)

Note: all questions require a single answer.

1. When gaining product and service expertise, how much should you learn?
   a) Twice as much as you might need ❏
   b) Ten times as much as you might need ❏
   c) 40 times as much as you might need ❏
   d) 100 times as much as you might need ❏

2. How do prospective customers normally view us?
   a) The only link between the product or service and themselves ❏
   b) Experts in our field ❏
   c) Untrustworthy ❏
   d) Reliable ❏

3. Who is responsible for the training you receive about the products and services you sell?
   a) The training department ❏
   b) Your boss ❏
   c) You ❏
   d) It depends on the company ❏

4. In which profession is investing in your own education and training considered normal?
   a) The legal profession ❏
   b) The accounting profession ❏
   c) The sales profession ❏
   d) All of the above ❏

5. What is a great way to get training?
   a) Interviewing current customers about the benefits they receive ❏
   b) Studying product and service literature and manuals ❏
   c) Taking training courses of all kinds ❏
   d) All of the above ❏

6. What is one of the most valuable yet least utilized options for training oneself?
   a) Interviewing current customers ❏
   b) Reading manuals ❏
   c) Web-based training ❏
   d) Staying late to study ❏

7. What are the extra benefits of visiting or talking to current customers?
   a) They are a source of testimonials ❏
   b) They often give referrals ❏
   c) They give you inspiration and enthusiasm ❏
   d) All of the above ❏

8. What is a good question to ask a current user when interviewing them?
a) What do you not like about our product or service? ❏
b) What made you choose our system over the competitors'? ❏
c) Who were the competitors? ❏
d) Would you make the same decision again? ❏

9. What is the best way to persuade your manager to invest in your training?
a) Send an email and ask ❏
b) Tell your manager about the features of the training ❏
c) Make sure your training fits in the budget ❏
d) Sell your idea, explaining the benefits the company will get from your enhanced skill ❏

10. Which of the following statements is true?
a) Be sure you are well trained before going out on your first sales call ❏
b) Sales managers can't teach you anything ❏
c) Customers can't teach you anything ❏
d) You can learn from every sales call ❏

TUESDAY

Grasp the buying motives

A university professor I know shocks his class by saying: 'No one makes any decision in life that doesn't benefit himself in some way.'

The students always protest: 'Surely that's not true. People often do things for humanitarian reasons. There are church groups. There are people who do things unselfishly.'

'Yes,' the professor counters, 'that's true. But let's look under the surface. What motivates them? What makes them take their decision? What do *they* get out of it?'

Then he explains that carrying out noble or humanitarian actions makes people feel good. This is the benefit to them.

Gradually, the students learn to examine the motives behind decisions and to look for what drives people. They discover that the benefits people gain can be psychological as well as material.

Think of this as it relates to your own sales situation. What benefits do your customers get? Don't think about what the product does. Think about the benefit to the buyer.

Today you will learn the best way to:

- find the customer's buying motives
- check your assumptions
- match benefits to needs and motives
- present your product or service.

Find the buying motives

Perhaps you've heard this saying: 'The person who asks the questions is in control of the meeting.'

In order to be in control of your success, it's necessary to ask questions, but not just any questions. They must be questions that lead you to the customer's needs and buying motives.

I remember once discussing a prospective client with a new employee. I told my employee that it would be his job at the upcoming meeting to ask questions that would lead us to the buying motive of the prospect. He said he could do it, because he considered himself to be a good conversationalist.

After 20 minutes with the customer, my employee was taking the conversation in all directions *except* to discover why he might want our service. I had to jump in and steer the conversation in the right direction – that of the prospect's needs and what benefits he might gain from our sales training courses. My employee hadn't learned to **target** his conversation in a certain direction. It was a hit-and-miss approach.

Hit and miss doesn't work in selling because we don't have the time we have in social relationships. We have to ask precise questions that lead us in the direction of the answers we need in order to identify our clients' needs, and then stress the corresponding benefits. Such questions could be:

- 'What would you be expecting from a supplier?'
- 'What benefit would you be hoping for?'
- 'What single thing could we offer to convince you to change suppliers and work with us?'

These three precise and directive questions lead you in the direction of finding out the needs and motives of your client. Now think of more questions. Create your own list.

Think of yourself as a sailor with the rudder of your sailing boat in the grip of your hand. As your boat goes slightly off course, you move the rudder to bring it back on course.

To become a powerful and directive questioner we need only think of ourselves as sailors. When the conversation starts to go off course, when it starts to meander aimlessly in this direction or that, we need to bring it back on course. For example, we could say, 'Yes, I see what you mean. That's important to know. I remember you said earlier that you wanted a high-clarity screen...' and so we are back on track. We could then continue with, 'What benefits would you be looking for – higher productivity, faster turnround, less frustration?'

TIP *Practise, practise and practise bringing the conversation back to ascertaining the customer's needs and motives.*

The person who asks the questions sets the direction. We must make sure we know what direction we want to go in.

Get the logical and emotional motives

We can actually help our buyer on two levels: the logical level and the emotional level.

Another way to look at this is to say that every corporate purchase has a benefit to the corporation and a benefit to the individual. Most salespeople focus only on the logical or corporate benefit. Yet the emotional or individual benefit can be, and often is, far more powerful and persuasive.

Why not go away to a quiet place and list your prospects. What are their emotional or individual buying motives?

- What do they need and want?
- What benefits can I match to their needs?

Check your assumptions

The title of this chapter is '*Grasp* the buying motives'. Yet sales are lost because people assume they already *know* what the customer wants.

Using the following checklist to prompt you, list all the assumptions you can think of that you and your colleagues may be making about the needs and buying motives of your prospects. Examine them and ask why you have made each assumption. Is it something the customer said? Is it something ingrained from the last customer? Is it something a colleague has said about the customer? All of your assumptions need to be validated.

Checklist of assumptions about needs and buying motives

List the assumptions you and your colleagues may be making about the needs and buying motives of your prospects.

- Price (too high). Why?
- Price (too low). Why?
- Extras (important). Why?
- Extras (not important). Why?
- Distance
- Delivery time
- Features
- Benefits
- Service

The best way to check your assumptions is to call your customers and ask if your assumptions are right. Then you must *listen* to their answers and reshape your presentation or proposal accordingly. If it's a team sell, you will also need to convince your colleagues to avoid these costly assumptions.

Thus we realize how much time and effort we've lost barking up the wrong tree, and change our approach to selling. If you really want to excel in avoiding assumptions, track the reasons for every sale you lose or have lost. The best companies do just that.

In my book *Secrets of the World's Top Sales Performers*, I describe how the Sony sales team sits together and examines its approach and assumptions. The team members don't point fingers in order to place the blame outside; instead, they decide what caused the loss and how to overcome it next time.

During your analyses, you'll discover that making assumptions about buying motives is fatal. It's a fast cure and a lesson every professional needs to learn.

A common deadly assumption

When calling to find out why the business was lost, you'll discover that there were pressures within the organization that eluded you.

One of our seminar delegates told the story of working closely for several months with the managing director of a company to identify his needs. He thought everything was perfect until he presented the final proposal and discovered that the production director also had influence.

What did he do wrong? His error is common and painful. He assumed that the MD's authority was enough. He didn't identify the people who influenced the purchase decision and therefore didn't find out their needs.

Match benefits to needs and motives

One computer systems saleswoman in America is constantly ranked at the top of her national sales team. Janet achieves 190 per cent of her target year after year.

Let's look at the critical difference between Janet's approach, which keeps her at the top end, and the approach of salespeople whose performance is average.

She has an invaluable two-tier approach.

1 First she visits the prospective client on a fact-finding mission, and interviews them thoroughly to ascertain their needs and motives. She also makes sure she interviews everyone who influences the buying decision.
2 Only then does she present the benefit of her product and in such a way that it precisely meets the customer's needs.

She focuses all her energy and all her words on what the customer will gain from the system. Her preparation time goes into thinking about how the system can match the needs of each individual and therefore justify the costs in their minds.

The average salesperson doesn't hit the bull's eye because their questioning process fails them. Their **needs analysis** and **motive analysis** are missing or inadequate. They don't follow the seven vital rules and so do not sell as often as they could.

During your 'think' before your presentation, you will have made notes, listed those who influence the decision and thought about everyone's needs. You will have looked at the presentation from all sides, as if it were a three-dimensional picture. You'll have thought about all angles in preparation for your next approach to them. You might want to graph it out, as in the following example.

Our product benefits	A	B	C	D	etc.
Needs of Company X					
1.					
2.					
3.					
Needs of Company Y					
1.					
2.					
3.					
Emotional needs Customer A					
1.					
2.					
3.					
Emotional needs Customer B					
1.					
2.					
3.					

SUNDAY
MONDAY
TUESDAY
WEDNESDAY
THURSDAY
FRIDAY
SATURDAY

Seven vital rules for selling

1 Never assume you know the customer's needs and motives.

2 Identify all individuals who influence the purchase decision.

3 Interview to uncover needs and motives.

4 Discover the logical and psychological motives.

5 Go away and think.

6 Express the product or service benefits that match the customer's needs and motives.

7 Only then present to the customer with complete focus on their buying motives.

Present the product or service

Armed with our list of buying motives and the benefits we can offer to meet the customer's needs, we have nothing to fear. Now we see clearly what to present. When we go to our customer, we will not be 'winging it'. We will not be improvising. We will be presenting our product or service in such a way that they can see the benefit and justify it. Their logical and emotional needs will be met.

It will all fall into place because you will have given the customer's buying motive the pre-eminent position. You will have stepped into the customer's shoes and seen the situation from their point of view. You will be on their side of the fence and they will feel it.

Summary

Today we focused on ways to grasp the buying motives of our prospect. Our time is valuable, and we shouldn't waste it presenting features and benefits of our product or service that don't relate to that particular prospect.

Instead, we must spend our time productively, matching the needs of our prospective client to what we can offer. To discover these all-important needs, we simply need to guide conversations in that direction by asking the right questions. When we have discovered all the needs of our prospect, our job in selling becomes easy and enjoyable. We skilfully link those needs to the benefits we offer, in order to have a successful sale!

Remember

The person who asks the questions guides the direction. Make sure you steer in the direction of the buying motives.

SUNDAY
MONDAY
TUESDAY
WEDNESDAY
THURSDAY
FRIDAY
SATURDAY

Fact-check (answers at the back)

Note: all questions require a single answer.

1. What kind of questions lead to discovering the buying motives?
   a) General questions ❏
   b) Vague questions ❏
   c) Open-ended questions ❏
   d) Precise questions ❏

2. Which analogy best shows how to lead your discussion in the direction of your customer's needs and buying motives?
   a) You are a sailor; as your boat goes slightly off course, you move your rudder to bring it back on course. ❏
   b) You are a boxer fighting to win ❏
   c) You are a great conversationalist building rapport by talking ❏
   d) You are a bullfighter dodging left, right and centre ❏

3. What's true about buying motives?
   a) They are always logical, and never emotional ❏
   b) They are both logical and emotional ❏
   c) They are not important ❏
   d) They cause objections ❏

4. What do most ineffective salespeople only focus on?
   a) Logical or corporate benefit ❏
   b) Emotional benefit ❏
   c) Serious benefit ❏
   d) Elusive benefits ❏

5. What's likely to happen when you assume you know what the customer wants without asking?
   a) Customers are happy ❏
   b) Customers are angry ❏
   c) Sales are lost ❏
   d) You look good ❏

6. What is a common deadly assumption?
   a) The boss always makes the final decision ❏
   b) The Finance Director always makes the final decision ❏
   c) The department head makes the final decision ❏
   d) All of the above ❏

7. The average salesperson doesn't succeed because their question process fails them. Why?
   a) Their needs analysis is inadequate ❏
   b) Their motive analysis is missing ❏
   c) They make assumptions instead of asking questions ❏
   d) All of the above ❏

8. What should you do before making your final sales presentation?
a) Make notes about needs and benefits ❏
b) List those who influence the decision ❏
c) Look at the presentation from all sides, as with a three-dimensional picture ❏
d) All of the above ❏

9. What do you need to do in order to have nothing to fear in your presentation?
a) Relax and improvise ❏
b) Go armed with a list of buying motives and benefits you can offer that meet their needs ❏
c) Give a slick presentation ❏
d) Memorize everyone's name ❏

10. What will you feel after you have done a complete needs and benefits analysis?
a) Great about yourself ❏
b) As if you have stepped into the customer's shoes and seen the situation from their point of view ❏
c) Exhausted, but feeling good that it was worth the effort ❏
d) More committed to selling ❏

WEDNESDAY

Conquer objections: turn them to your advantage

The instructor at a seminar I attended early in my career was a world-class expert on the subject of self-motivation. 'Most people are clueless about obstacles,' he told us. 'They come to the first obstacle in the road between themselves and their goal, and they stop dead in their tracks.' He said that people are surprised to find obstacles in life, and yet obstacles are around us continually. 'When we learn to accept that obstacles are a normal part of life, we are on a winning track,' he said.

And so it is with selling. An objection is nothing more than a minor obstacle, and often it can be turned to our advantage.

When we handle objections, whether in selling or in everyday life, we're dealing with human factors, with people's need to be heard, and to be recognized for their opinions, fears, doubts and misunderstandings.

This takes finesse on our part. It takes time to stop and think. It takes determination to do things a new way.

Today you will learn about:

- clearing objections to improve your results
- using a foolproof objection-clearing technique
- mastering price objections
- closing despite objections.

Improve results by clearing objections

Let's look at two examples in which we can apply the objections process to improve our results. Some years ago I gave a speech to 150 people from a political party that had previously taken our sales and marketing course.

After my speech, I asked some of them: 'What have you implemented from the course so far?' Their immediate answer was: 'Better ways of handling the objections of our electorate.' Thus we see the importance of being able to sell and defend our ideas. The same is true in the workplace and in all areas of life.

Here is a second example, a true story told to me by one of our instructors about the power of the objection process in personal life. By using this process, he reported that he had improved his relationship with his teenage daughter tremendously. After applying the three-part objection technique in a conversation with her, she told him that it was the first time she felt he had really listened to her. Thus her attitude and co-operation improved enormously.

In selling, if we don't clear the objection, it lingers like smoke in the mind of our customers. We must clear it just as we clear smoke from a room. Think of a large fan blowing the smoke out through an open window. That's what you're doing with the objection-clearing process.

Use the objection-clearing technique

This foolproof three-part process can have extraordinary results for you too. The steps are:

1 the 'prelude cushion' (psychological)
2 the explanation (logical)
3 the clarification question (psychological).

The prelude cushion

Our 'prelude cushion' prepares people to listen by melting down their defences.

You may think it logical to focus on your explanation segment, but this will fall on deaf ears unless you break down the defences of the customer first. When I refer to the 'customer' in this case, of course I'm referring to our listener, be it our boss, our spouse, our child, our political constituents, our colleague or our client.

The prelude cushion is when we take time to sympathize with the customer, to line up on their side and see their point of view first, before we start on our logical explanation. If the

customer says no, we must start again with our prelude segment. But the chances are that they won't, because our words have made them feel that we understand their concerns. We didn't ride roughshod over their objections.

The prelude cushion gives the other person a chance:

- to cool down
- to realize we're on their side
- to feel understood
- to have their concerns validated
- to save face
- to build a rapport with us.

Do you think those points are important to the person with the objection? Of course they are. That's why it improved our instructor's relationship with his daughter, in the example above. She felt as though her father had taken time to listen to her and care about her point of view.

What people want from us

We need to think about this point carefully. Isn't that what people want from us in any situation – to be listened to and to have their concerns recognized? And isn't that what's missing when we bypass the prelude segment and go straight to our explanation segment?

Don't make that mistake. If you do, you'll just be handling objections the old way and you'll find no improvement.

No matter how good your explanation segment, it won't sink in until you convince people that you sympathize with and value their concerns.

Master price objections

Let's look at a hot subject with salespeople – overcoming the price objection. First let's look at the difference between success and failure. The truth is that most ineffective salespeople *think* that they could sell *if* their price were lower.

However, most top salespeople don't stop to consider price to be an obstacle. Why? Think about this because the chances are that you've fallen into the same trap from time to time.

Why do the top performers breeze past the price objections when others are blocked?

The reasons are **attitude** and **understanding**. If we think our price is too high, you can be sure we'll transmit that to our customer. If we think our price is too high, we won't look for the benefits that justify the price.

Would our companies stay in business if the price didn't justify the benefits? Probably not.

If the price really is too high, then it's time to cure the problem or change jobs. The point is this: *don't* make the mistake of the majority of ineffective salespeople, which is to try to ignore price justifications.

We must get out there and *learn* price justifications as the top performers do. That will form our logical explanation segment. And we must remember to prelude our price justification.

Why not put the technique into practice and see what you can achieve? I think you'll be surprised. You can work on your answers today by using the three-part objection-clearing process chart near the end of this chapter and the following case study.

The process in action

'I like your product, but the price is too high,' our customer says. At this point we don't know what he means by 'too high'. Is it higher than the competition for exactly the same thing, higher than his budget or higher than his expectation? But we can't ask yet because we haven't broken down the resistance.

1 The prelude cushion

Think about what your prelude should be. It must be right for you and your customer. Fill the appropriate response into the three-part process chart, perhaps something like this:

'Yes, I can understand your concern about price, Miss Whitehill. With the economy the way it is, businesses have to make every penny count. In fact, you're not alone. A lot of our clients told us they were worried about price before they used our service. Yet afterwards they come back and tell us they had a 100 per cent payback within six months.'

2 The explanation

Now we're making our transition to the logical explanation. In our prelude we sympathized with *the customer's* concern. We even said others felt the same. We're going out of our way to prove we understand the concern from the customer's point of view.

Now, what *are* our price justification benefits? What reasons do we have that will justify the expenditure? Chances are that you'll find dozens when you start digging.

You'll be most effective if you get these from current and past customers, because you'll have high credibility stories to tell your clients. For example: 'Mr Phillips at Tarmaco told me last week that they reduced their down time by 30 minutes per day with our service. This amounted to £10,000 per year.'

We should always match the customer's buying motives to the benefits we put forward. We won't talk about down time if it's irrelevant. We'll choose some benefit that does justify the price to that particular customer.

Brainstorm price justification

Look again at the three-part process chart below and list all the price justifications you can think of, then talk to colleagues and customers to expand the list. It might seem like a daunting task but, once you've done it, it will be a gold mine at your disposal.

Start your list now before you read on. Even if it's just one or two points scribbled on a scrap of paper, it will get you started. The first step is the hardest and we want to get you on the winning path. Remember, success is in our actions, as well as our realizations. We must be unrelenting with ourselves when we're forming new habits of success.

TIP *If you can't justify the price, your customer certainly can't, so your preparation today will win you great rewards tomorrow.*

3 The clarification question

Now it's time to nail down the closing with our clarification question: 'Have I satisfied your concerns on the price, Miss Whitehill?'

'Well, yes, but I'm still concerned about the set-up cost,' she responds.

Good. Now we know she's satisfied about the running costs, but she has a concern about the set-up costs. That's not a problem.

We use the three-part process again.

1 We start at the beginning, with another prelude cushion.
2 Then we go to the second step, the logical explanation. We give the benefits she'll receive in exchange for the price she pays for set-up.
3 Then we go to the third step, the clarification. Ask a question to see whether she accepts our explanation. Make a copy of the following chart for each of your prospects and fill it in as appropriate for them.

Three-part objection-clearing process chart

1 Prelude cushion	2 Explanation	3 Clarification question
(human/psychological factor)	(logical factor)	(human/psychological factor)
This opens the iron gate and breaks down the resistance.	This is the justification: benefits received in exchange for money paid out. a b c d	Does our customer understand and accept our explanation?

Close despite objections

We may never satisfy every concern a customer has. There will always be a competitor who offers something we don't offer. There will always be requests we can't fulfil. But when we can satisfy enough concerns to outweigh the doubts, we will succeed.

You can always use the direct approach: 'Margaret, we've discussed a checklist of ten requirements you hoped to meet. We are able to meet eight of these. They are the significant ones. I see those eight as being...' (We list the benefits and price justifications that relate to her.)

We ask: 'Does it sound like the kind of service you would benefit from?' *Thus you help the customer put the situation into perspective.* The chances are that eight out of ten of the requirements will be enough to meet their demands, especially if the requirements you can offer outweigh the ones you can't offer.

Be armed ahead

In preparation for your success ahead, you'll want to be armed with a list of likely objections and responses. Copy the following chart and add as many sheets as you need to be prepared for most eventualities.

Use the answers you have prepared on this chart during sales presentations, telephone calls with prospective customers and even in written communication.

Think now about all the areas in which you can use the three-part objection-clearing process. Set a target today for improving your success rate in breaking down the iron gate of resistance and overcoming objections.

Now think of ways to:

- practise it
- remember to do it.

Reference chart of possible objections

	Prelude statement	Explanation statement	Clarification question
1 Price			
2 Delivery time			
3 Lack of expertise			
4 Other likely objections a b c			

Summary

Today we studied ways of overcoming the objections of our prospective customers, and even ways to turn objections to our advantage.

We looked in depth at an effective three-part process for overcoming objections, be they on price, delivery time or any other factor.

We learned that if we don't cushion our response to an objection, it will fall on deaf ears. We learned that the explanation segment of our response must be one that *matches* our client's needs. We learned to end our three-part process for overcoming objections with a simple question: 'Does this satisfy your concern?' By doing so, we will assess whether the concern is gone, so that it won't linger like smoke, or whether we need to readdress the concern and bring it to a positive conclusion.

When you master the three-part process, nothing will hold you back! You'll go from strength to strength in your career. So start now and make this your speciality.

Remember

The prelude cushion is the key to having your explanation accepted and the objection overcome.

SUNDAY

MONDAY

TUESDAY

WEDNESDAY

THURSDAY

FRIDAY

SATURDAY

Fact-check (answers at the back)

Note: all questions require a single answer.

1. Learning to overcome objections is a useful tool to use with whom?
   a) Teenagers ❑
   b) Politicians ❑
   c) Customers ❑
   d) Everyone ❑

2. In selling, what will happen if we don't clear an objection?
   a) It will go unnoticed ❑
   b) No one cares ❑
   c) It lingers like smoke in the minds of our customers ❑
   d) It's good for business ❑

3. In handling objections, what must we do before we put the spotlight on the explanation?
   a) Break down the defences and fears of the customer ❑
   b) Change the subject ❑
   c) Make sure the customer understands the features of the product or service ❑
   d) Make sure the customer understands the benefits of the product or service ❑

4. In the three-part process of handling objections, what does the prelude segment do?
   a) It gives the customer a chance to feel understood ❑
   b) It allows the customer's concerns to be validated ❑
   c) It lets the customer build rapport with us ❑
   d) All of the above ❑

5. What does every customer – and every person we know – want?
   a) To be listened to ❑
   b) To have their concerns recognized ❑
   c) For us to value their concerns ❑
   d) All of the above ❑

6. What's the best way to handle price objection?
   a) Learn price justification ❑
   b) Remember to prelude our price justification ❑
   c) Put the three-part process into practice ❑
   d) All of the above ❑

7. What is the explanation segment?
   a) The logical explanation ❑
   b) The emotional explanation ❑
   c) The contrary segment ❑
   d) All of the above ❑

8. What's the most important question for you to ask when ending the objection process?
   a) 'Shall we move on?' ❑
   b) 'Have I answered your concerns about that?' ❑
   c) 'When would you like to start?' ❑
   d) 'Did I explain that well?' ❑

9. What should we do when we can't satisfy every concern a customer has?
a) We should withdraw ❏
b) We can close anyway if the benefits outweigh the objections ❏
c) We should talk the customer out of his or her concern ❏
d) We should refer them to our competitor ❏

10. What is the purpose of preparing a chart with likely objections and responses?
a) For sales presentations ❏
b) For telephone calls to prospective customers ❏
c) For written communication ❏
d) For all of the above ❏

THURSDAY

Master successful presentations and closings

There is nothing magical about closing a sale. If all the component parts are there, you need only ask a question such as, 'Does this seem right for you?' or 'When would you like to begin?' *Then* the business will be more likely to fall into your lap. But what are those all-important component parts?

There are eight component parts to successful sales presentations and closings. Seven of these lead up to asking for the business while building commitment along the way. Your job is to become an expert in each of the eight segments.

You have been practising all the skills involved throughout your life. It's simply a matter of putting them together in the right order – in a 'presentation train'.

Today you will build your expertise by learning about the eight parts of the presentation train, which are:

- finding out the corporate buying motive
- finding out the personal buying motive
- showing your product expertise
- understanding competitors' strengths and weaknesses
- linking needs to benefits
- overcoming objections
- reviewing needs and benefits
- the successful close.

The presentation train

Most of the segments of the presentation train involve asking questions, sincerely and with genuine interest. Some involve presenting facts about your product or service that link to your customer's needs.

The engine comes first. In successful selling, determining the buying motive drives the content of the presentation. And last comes the caboose, the final car on the train. In selling, that's where you close your sale. And in the middle will be six wagons, representing the other factors leading to your close.

1 ASK – Find out the customer's corporate buying motive.
2 ASK – Find out the customer's personal buying motive.
3 KNOW – Show your product expertise.
4 KNOW – Understand the competition's strengths and weaknesses.
5 TELL – Make links between needs and benefits.
6 TELL – Overcome objections.
7 REVIEW – Refocus on needs and benefits.
8 ASK – Their decision needs your closing question.

Imagine each part of your presentation process as a separate wagon on a freight train. Each wagon is splendidly painted and filled with jewels.

Imagine that we are the railway inspectors. We walk along the side of the wagons together, sliding open the doors, and we see that each is filled with precious blue, yellow and green jewels. These jewels represent:

● facts
● answers
● links.

The blue jewels represent the facts. The yellow jewels represent the answers we get. The green jewels represent the links between them.

In your sales presentation, when you combine the facts with the answers to your questions, you'll be able to make critical links. These links will be the green light to your sale.

1 Ask about the corporate buying motive

Let's have a look inside the engine, which is reserved for the customer's corporate buying motive. It will be almost empty when we first slide the door open. There will be a few facts here about why *most* people buy your product or service, but no specific facts about why *this* customer wants your product.

Assumptions don't count in sales. But as we ask questions, our engine will fill with more and more facts, more and more jewels to help us link the buying motive to the benefits we have to offer.

The difference between you, a top sales performer, and a mediocre sales performer is that you will ask and ask and ask until your engine is *filled* with facts and answers. You'll find out the buying motives of every decision-maker and every decision-influencer. Each answer, each fact, will add another authentic, precious jewel to your engine.

The mediocre sales performers will not take time to ask because they assume that this customer is like all the others. Their false assumptions will lead them to impure links. The benefits they offer to the client will therefore be right for other customers but not necessarily right for this customer. Their time will be spent in vain.

We won't let this happen to us because we realize that the time spent here is the most valuable of all.

2 Ask about the personal buying motive

Most ineffective salespeople don't even push open the door to this first wagon to look inside for the personal buying motive. They assume that the engine, the corporate buying motive, is

all-important. Yes, of course, we can't sell without satisfying ourselves that the engine is full of valuable jewels, but we must not discount another, vitally important factor: how will we get our prospect to push for consensus within his or her organization to buy from us?

If our prospect is not personally motivated, why should he or she bother? After all, they have a job to do. Our sales efforts are an intrusion in their busy schedule.

We must identify *what's in it for them*. What is it that can motivate them personally? Is it:

- saving time
- improving prestige
- reducing chaos
- reducing stress
- improving morale
- being up to date
- career advancement
- more free time?

We have to *ask*. We have to fill our wagon with genuine jewels of answers and facts in order to create the genuine links necessary to sell.

3 Know and show product expertise

As we're turning their situation around and around in our minds, the links are building up faster and faster. We have our product expertise: those blue jewels in our second wagon are the facts about our product and service. Now we are pouring in the yellow jewels – the answers to all our questions about the customer's corporate and personal buying motives.

The yellow and blue jewels are merging together in our mind, and green sparks are radiating from them. Those are our links – the combination of needs and benefits which are the reasons people will buy.

Naturally, *your* wagon is brimming with knowledge. You've painstakingly talked to current customers to find out why they use your products. You've found out what benefits they get. You've built up first-hand stories about these benefits. You *know* what you have to offer to prospective customers in every detail. You've consulted your literature and your internal experts. You *know*.

4 Know the competition's strengths and weaknesses

Don't be afraid when you look inside this third wagon.

 TIP *Knowledge is power: the more we know, the better the position we will be in to defend the benefits we can offer.*

Our competitor may have some excellent features but, if those features are not important to our client, we can still sell our benefits and win. The important thing is to be informed about what the competition *does* offer. Then we won't be taken by surprise. We'll have time to turn it around in our mind, to become comfortable with it in a matter-of-fact way, to accept it as a feature but put it in perspective.

'Yes,' we can say to ourselves, 'they have this feature; we have that. Now let's see who needs what. Let's look at the combination of benefits. Let's look at the cost of their benefits and of our benefits, and find out who is willing to pay what for those benefits.'

Then, when a customer says that our competitor has feature A, we'll be able to say: 'Yes, how do you feel about that feature? There are many features in the marketplace today. We've created ours by researching what our users most wanted for the price, ease of use,' etc. We then help the customer put it into perspective.

Key questions

- Do they really need what the competitors offer?
- Is it really an advantage?
- Will they really use it or is there a downside?
- What will it cost the customer either financially or in terms of learning, time or energy?
- What will they have to give up in order to gain that?
- What are the start-up and continuation costs?
- What does your package of features and benefits have to offer over theirs?

By helping them to re-evaluate it, they may see that it's not important at all. The last salesperson may have made them feel they couldn't live without this 'all-singing, all-dancing' feature. But you, through your thoroughness in asking about their buying motives, can help them reflect.

Because knowledge is power, and our wagon is full of knowledge about the competitors, we're in a position of strength, not weakness. We have little to fear. We'll be able to make links that work for us *and* for the client.

5 Tell them how their needs link to your benefits

This is the moment of truth. I mean that literally. If we have the truth in terms of the buyer's needs and motives, if we have all the true facts about what our products can do, then we'll be able to make these links that give the buyer the mental green light to buy.

Selling today is not a manipulative process. Selling is helping the customer *see* what we have to offer and how it meets *their* needs. Notice that there are two parts to this and that the second part is the key to success:

1 what we have to offer
2 how it meets their needs.

Many ineffective salespeople focus only on the first part. They don't stop to realize that a customer wouldn't want to buy from someone who says: '*We* can do this, *we* can do this, *we* can do this.'

Who is the most important person in the world? The customer is, of course. A salesperson who talks only about their product and what it can do will not make the customer feel important or cared about. It's the *link to their needs* that makes the sale.

We can't make this link without asking the customer what they want, what benefit they see, what their objective is, how they will use it. We don't do it as an interrogation, but rather from a position of consultative concern, of really trying to help. Don't make the mistake of the ineffective salesperson, doing only half the job. You'll get only half the results. Do the whole job – make the link. Tell them how it meets their needs. Do this and your sales will more than double. This is true in every industry, from retail to aerospace, from products and services to politics and education.

If we want to sell anything, even an idea, we have to make a flawless link to the needs of the customer and the benefits they will get. Make a list now of the benefits and likely motives of several of your prospective customers. This process will help you think on your feet when you see them.

> **Stating the link between
> benefits and needs**
>
> **Customer X**
>
> **Need:** Customer wants to reduce their department's
> annual overheads by £15,000.
>
> **Benefit:** Say, 'Our system saves 20 per cent man hours
> over your current system.'
>
> **Link:** Say, 'You'll be able to do without your two
> temporary members of staff, saving £30,000. This
> £30,000 in overhead reduction will pay for the system in
> the first year and reduce your running costs by £15,000,
> which was your goal. From then on, you continue to
> save every year.'

Make a table like the one below to fill in the needs and benefits and the links between them for your own customers.

Once you have developed your link-building expertise, you'll be able to communicate it verbally or in writing or both, thus increasing your closing rate.

	Customer A	Customer B	Customer C
Need			
Benefit			
Link			

6 Tell them how objections can be overcome

Remember that objections can linger like smoke unless you address them. *You* won't let objections linger because you'll use the three-part objection technique you learned on Wednesday. You'll make your customer realize that you *do* sympathize, you *do* understand. Then you'll give the explanation, and then you'll check to see if their concern is satisfied.

Ineffective salespeople don't see this fifth wagon as full of helpful jewels. They see it as full of serpents and demons. They want to keep it locked shut. They want to skirt around it, staying as far away from it as possible *at all times.*

They want to sweep any hint of objection under the rug, hoping naïvely that it will never resurface. Little do they know that it smoulders there while the customer's mind becomes locked into the idea that their objection is reality. The customer is mentally packing their briefcase to go home while the ineffective salesperson continues to talk – *unheard.*

Your wagon, on the other hand, is filled with blue and yellow jewels, because you've studied the likely objections and solutions, and you've asked questions to find out what the concerns are.

You have the facts and answers. You therefore counter the objections quickly and easily, as if holding the hand of the customer and walking them through a maze.

7 Review the needs and benefits

This is the most rewarding stage because it reveals the big picture. It puts everything into perspective for the customer. We've discussed features, benefits, needs, motives and objections. Now we're ready for the big picture.

'You told me you wanted to achieve X, Y and Z. Is this still the case?' we must ask. We're helping them refocus on their needs, cut out the extraneous and forget the glorified benefits offered by the competitors.

Next, we say: 'We've looked at our ability to meet X, Y and Z through these methods...' and put our benefits succinctly. We don't elaborate for so long that the customer forgets what X, Y and Z are.

Instead, we keep our choice of words focused on what they get, not what we give. 'With this machine, you can get your documents to your office in Australia in six seconds. This will help you meet your objective of speeding up your communication time in order to win contracts.'

We won't say: 'This machine gives you group 3, high-speed, digital transmission technology.' That's about the machine, not the customer. In addition, it doesn't mention his objective at all!

Yet that's how most uninitiated salespeople would handle their presentation. You won't, of course, because your wagon is filled with the links – the jewels you've created by combining the needs with your benefits. You've sifted through the important versus the unimportant benefits to the customer, and you stress the important ones.

 Focus on the benefits the customer gets from your product or service rather than on what you are offering.

8 Ask for their decision

The last wagon, the caboose, is the most vital one of all.

Recent research has shown that four out of five buyers *expect* to be asked to buy and *wait* to be asked. They don't volunteer to buy because they expect us, as part of the selling process, to ask. They wait and, if it doesn't happen, the buying moment passes by.

Let's look at what causes the critical moment to pass. Several things could happen. A competitor could ask for the order and get it, or the customer could lose interest or divert their funds to another project.

The ineffective salesperson – who doesn't ask – loses. But your approach is different. From the beginning you have been thorough. You've been letting the customer know how your product or service can help them, thus building commitment each step of the way. Your approach has let them see themselves using and benefiting from the product.

Now when you ask for their decision, it's almost a foregone conclusion. The benefits are clear and they *line up exactly* with the customer's expressed needs.

You've been a catalyst in their search for the answer. You've helped them make their way through the maze of the unknown. You've helped them see the answer.

Now when you ask for their decision, it's not an abrupt surprise. It's not a pressured, stressful event, but a natural evolution. Our customer now expects a closing question, which will vary according to the situation.

Closing questions

- 'Will you be taking this, then?' we might ask at the retail counter.

- 'Does this seem like the kind of service which would benefit you?' we might ask in the sale of services.

- 'Are the advantages we offer more meaningful than the other suppliers'?' we might ask in system sales.

- 'Will you be working with us, then?'

- 'What implementation dates should we establish?'

Stop now and make a list of closing questions that feel right for you. Then when you get to this stage of your presentation, you won't have fear. Instead, you'll see your final wagon filled with jewels of preparation. You'll have question after question which you designed and which work for you and not someone else.

Look at the freight train diagram at the beginning of this chapter again. Do you know the secret of success over others who fail?

Build your expertise

Most ineffective salespeople have no freight train at all. They have only a little product knowledge. They ask no questions to ascertain needs – they assume they know. They make no links to needs. They talk about the product only instead of the benefits. They avoid objections whenever possible. And they don't ask for the business.

Would you want to hire a person like that to work for your business? Probably not, and yet many managers find they have no choice. They hire people, find ways to train them and motivate them and then hope for results.

The case is different with you. You're building your own professionalism, which makes you a rare commodity, like a needle in a haystack.

Keep up the good work. The rewards will be coming your way. By continuing to build your expertise in sales, you will be increasing your value to yourself and your company. Many men and women in sales, like myself, start their own companies, or are promoted to executive or CEO positions. They are elected to chair important community groups.

Why? Because they have learned to motivate, to look for people's needs, to communicate and meet those needs. Imagine that you are a CEO needing to convince your Board of something important. Now look at the freight train at the beginning of this chapter. Isn't your job of selling your idea to the Board the same as selling a product to your customer? Your expertise in sales will help you define *their* needs and motives, present the benefits of *your* idea and link it to their needs.

Summary

Today we discovered the eight parts of mastering successful sales presentations and closings. Each part is indispensable, and each part is linked to the part before and after it, rather like wagons in a freight train.

First, we saw the importance of fleshing out the corporate buying motive, and second the customer's personal buying motive. We discovered that the latter is often overlooked and leads to lost sales. Third, we looked at product expertise, and fourth at competitors' strengths and weaknesses. We saw that it's often easy to overcome our competitors' strengths, if we ask thorough questions about corporate buying motives and personal buying motives. In this way, we can build up our product's strengths as they relate to our customer's needs.

In the fifth and sixth parts, we linked needs to benefits and overcame objections. That left the road clear for our seventh part – the review of needs and benefits – and finally, our eighth part – the successful close.

Remember

Four out of five customers wait for us to ask for the order. Be sure to ask closing questions.

Fact-check (answers at the back)

Note: all questions require a single answer.

1. What's dangerous about making assumptions about buying motives?
   a) You will most likely get it wrong ❏
   b) Assumptions lead to why most people buy, but not why this customer wants to buy ❏
   c) You waste a lot of time and most likely lose the sale ❏
   d) All of the above ❏

2. Why do mediocre sales performers not take time to ask about buying motives?
   a) They assume that this customer is like all the others ❏
   b) They use the shotgun approach and want to get out of the appointment as soon as possible ❏
   c) They haven't taken the time to learn how to ask questions ❏
   d) All of the above ❏

3. Customers have corporate and personal motives for buying. Name some personal motives.
   a) Saving time ❏
   b) Career advancement ❏
   c) Reducing stress ❏
   d) All of the above ❏

4. How do we discover buying motive?
   a) By asking ❏
   b) By telling ❏
   c) Through interrogation ❏
   d) Through espionage ❏

5. In selling, which is most important?
   a) What we have to offer ❏
   b) How our offer meets the customer's needs ❏
   c) How our offer saves the customer money ❏
   d) How our offer helps the customer's career ❏

6. Objections linger like what, if not answered?
   a) Smoke ❏
   b) Serpents ❏
   c) Iron gates of resistance ❏
   d) All of the above ❏

7. Why is the review of the customer's needs and benefits one of the most rewarding parts of the sales process?
   a) It reveals the big picture ❏
   b) It puts everything into perspective for the customer ❏
   c) It sets the scene for the close ❏
   d) All of the above ❏

8. In the sales process, what should we focus our words on?
   a) What we can offer ❏
   b) What benefits the customer can get ❏
   c) The features ❏
   d) Price savings ❏

9. What is the most important aspect of closing a sale?
   a) Showing strong interest ❏
   b) Asking for their decision ❏
   c) Making promises ❏
   d) Loving your job ❏

10. What characterizes expert
    salespeople?
a) They are easy to train ❏
b) They are good talkers ❏
c) They are a rare commodity,
   like a needle in a haystack ❏
d) They are a dime a dozen ❏

FRIDAY

Create action-provoking systems

Most of you who are reading this book are high achievers by nature. You are open to new ways of achieving even higher results, especially if the efforts or changes involved will be minimal and the results will be exceptional.

And so it is with the tips in this chapter. When improving your tennis game, for example, a 10 per cent change can bring you 100 per cent better results, and the same is true in selling.

Today we look at why 'action-provoking systems' are so important, the best ways to use them and their critical advantages over other systems.

As you read ahead, don't be misled by the word 'system'. It might be a word that alienates some of you. It might even send a chill through you. After all, salespeople are sometimes thought of as spontaneous and freewheeling – traits that often lead to their success.

However, when we refer to 'action-provoking systems' here, we're referring to ways you can:

- keep *yourself* on track
- save yourself time
- harness your effort and send it in the right direction.

Strike while the iron is hot

Striking while the iron is hot is a critical issue. If we follow up a direct mail letter or email by telephone two weeks after it's sent, our call will be one-fifth as effective as it would be if we called within the first two days.

This is because people forget 60 per cent of what they hear and read after two days. If we call shortly after the letter or email is sent, it will be fresh in their minds. If we call after three weeks, it won't.

The same is true of following up your prospect for a decision. What's the point of following up too late – after our competitor goes in or after our customer's budget is diverted?

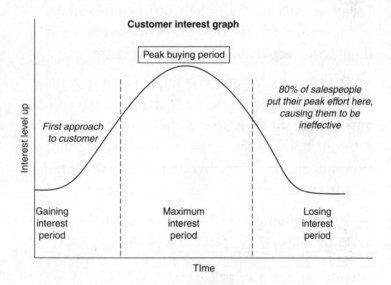

Customer interest graph

Peak buying period

First approach to customer

80% of salespeople put their peak effort here, causing them to be ineffective

Interest level up

Gaining interest period

Maximum interest period

Losing interest period

Time

Work hard or work sharp?

The majority of salespeople put their time and effort into the sales process too late. Because they don't have action-provoking systems, they do things when they have time rather than at the right time. Often this is too late.

An action-provoking system will help you use your time where it counts:

- closing the sales you have already started
- starting the correct number of new prospects necessary to meet your targets.

What's your experience?

What kind of system do you have now?

Perhaps your experience is something like John's, an experienced salesman who came to our course. He was looking desperately for a way to increase his sales, but didn't know which way to turn.

We asked him what sort of action-provoking system he had, and he said he wrote everything in his diary. He said he carried everything over to the new page. Yet he admitted it was a lot of work to carry it forward and easy to miss or forget some.

We looked at John's system and then showed him the matrix below. It can be created by hand or on a computer.

'The beauty of this system,' we told him, 'is that we can walk into our office in the morning and see at a glance all our prime prospects. We know immediately which ones need action.

'On 1 June two companies need action from us. On 2 June four companies need action. They are the ones on lines 3, 4, 8 and 12. We just pull up those files and see what action is necessary.'

Action-provoking system								
June	1	2	3	4	5	6	7	
1. Smith & Co	X							
2. J Bloggs								
3. Estmann		X						
4. Winters		X						
5. Peak and Co								
6. Johnston								
7. Withers								
8. Goodall & Co.		X						
9. Jones Bros								
10. Kent Air								
11. P.J. Anchor	X							
12. Bassett		X						

Advantages of an action-provoking system

This action-provoking system gives us two critical advantages.

1 We're not likely to forget anyone. Their name is already entered.
2 We see at a glance much more about our prospect.

Let's say we call someone five days in a row and we miss them each time. We'll mark an X on the next consecutive day to remind us to call.

Later we'll have more critical information. We'll be able to glance at our sheet and see the number of X marks. If we see five X marks side by side, we'll know our efforts aren't succeeding. If this is a hot prospect, we'd better redouble our efforts or take other action.

John looked sceptical, but he went away and tried it. He called us a month later and said that the results of his new system put him up 40 per cent on his sales figures after only 30 days.

The weakness of diary systems

'The diary system used to let me lose prospects too conveniently,' he told us. 'I've closed three sales this month by entering them into the matrix system. I know I would have turned the page and forgotten them in my old diary system, but because they were on the matrix I couldn't forget. It also made me more aware of my hard work on each prospect to date by seeing all my actions on one sheet. It made me more determined. I felt more in control.'

You may have the same reluctance that John had at first. You probably have a system that works for you. Fine. But ask yourself the following questions.

● How well is it working?
● How much is slipping through the net that I'm not aware of?

If you're looking for sales excellence, you have to turn over every stone of your present practices and see if there is a way of doing anything differently. You might find a way to make a small change in your practices that can get you considerably higher results.

Take today to examine your system and find its weak points. Then develop a new, improved system.

The weakness of computerized systems

'We have a perfect computerized system,' one salesman said. 'It tells us everything we've done for a prospect and what stage it's at.'

'Great,' we said. 'Does it tell you what day you have to take the next action? Does it show you on any given day a list of every prospect that needs action that day?'

'Well, I'm not sure,' he said. 'But we can pull up any prospect name and see the history of our actions.'

Think about what he's just said and see if you can find two fallacies. There's nothing wrong with history, but history is history. It doesn't provoke us to action on a certain day.

So there we have the first fallacy – confusing 'action taken' with action 'to be taken'.

Think again about the computer system of the salesman above and where you can see the second fallacy. When we asked him if he got a list of prospects that need action every day, he said he *wasn't sure*. What does that tell us about his use of the system? It tells us that he wasn't using it, at least not to help him prompt his daily actions.

There's no point in having systems we don't use, and it becomes even more dangerous to think we have systems that help us when in fact they don't.

TIP *Look at your systems cold and hard now and ask, 'Are they really helping?' If not, don't fool yourself into thinking they are. Make something quick and easy that works for you.*

Record systems for prospecting

What we're looking for is an action-*provoking* system, not historical record-keeping. We want a report that lets us see two things at a glance:

- a list of critical actions at the beginning of each day
- every prospect that should *have been* actioned in the past, with the number of days outstanding next to it (like an aged debtors' report that accountants use).

Only then do we have a good system. Only then do we know if we are striking while the 'iron is hot'.

Here's a useful manual system if you have hundreds of prospects to deal with at once. This system consists of two files. It's especially useful for telesales and telephone appointments.

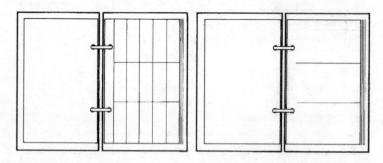

Action-provoking
ring binder 1

Prospect information
ring binder 2

In file 1 we have 52 sheets or printouts, each representing one week of the year. On each sheet there is a week number, date, and days of the week across the top.

Down the side there is a place to list:

- new prospects
- follow-up prospects
- appointment confirmations.

Each sheet looks like the one shown here to the right.

On Monday, we walk into the office knowing that *we must activate a certain number of new prospects*. This number depends on our yearly target, which we've broken down to a daily figure. Our prospects might come from a phone book or a Chamber of Commerce list, an industry list or a list of direct mail letters or emails already sent.

Action-provoking file 1				
Week number		Date		
New prospects				
Mon	Tues	Wed	Thurs	Fri
○				
Follow-up prospects				
○				
Appointment confirmations				

Now we are ready to follow each up by telephone. We go to our second file, which holds our prospect information.

Each sheet looks like the one overleaf, entitled Prospect information file 2, which holds our important contact details:

Three or more prospects can fit easily on one page. Because of the volume of prospects, we give each a code number, which is easier to fit on to one sheet in the action-provoking ring binder.

SUNDAY MONDAY TUESDAY WEDNESDAY THURSDAY FRIDAY SATURDAY

By Monday night our sheet will look like this:

| Company name | Code number | A 103 |

Person

Title

Address

Tel number

Contact date and discussion details

○ _____

Company name   Code number A 104

Person

Title

Address

Tel number

Contact date and discussion details

○ _____

Company name   Code number A 105

Person

Title

Address

Tel number

Contact date and discussion details

You'll see that most prospects have been spoken to. These have diagonal lines through them. Prospects A105, 109, 88 and 80 have not been reached and therefore they are listed for action on Tuesday.

All records can be kept in the prospect information file, or on a laptop for easy portability.

When we get enough detail on one prospect, we may choose to open a separate file for them, on our computer or in the filing cabinet.

Take time to think of what system will work for you. Ask yourself the following questions.

Action-provoking file 1				
Week number			Date	
New prospects				
Mon *A 105*	Tues *A 105*	Wed	Thurs	Fri
~~A 106~~				
○ ~~A 107~~				
~~A 108~~				
A 109	*A 109*			
~~A 110~~				
Follow-up prospects				
~~A 65~~				
~~A 22~~				
○ ~~A 37~~				
A 88	*A 88*			
~~A 94~~				
Appointment confirmations				
A 80	*A 80*			
~~A 26~~				
~~A 34~~				

- Where will I be when I use the system: in the car, at my desk, etc?
- How many entries will I need per day, per week and per month?
- What size book or record sheets do I need?
- Where will I store back-up information?
- What should the system look like?
- Who else will use it?
- Who will enter the prospect names?
- Who will enter the next actions required and the dates by which they must be done?
- What time of day will I take the actions, e.g. phone calls for appointments, phone calls for follow-up?

Add other questions to suit your situation.

Without an action-provoking system, we don't have the support system we need. Our energy is fragmented and at the end of the month we're disappointed we didn't get the results we hoped for.

Take today to design an action-provoking system to make your efforts effective.

Summary

Today we saw the importance of having a self-created, action-provoking system. Created by you, just for you, it will be easy to use, and portable if necessary. Perhaps it will be computerized, perhaps not.

Your system's most significant feature is that it will cue you to *what you need to do* each and every day. If it records only *what has been done*, it is not an action-provoking system but merely a data collection system. It will not help you take the actions today needed to reach your target. It won't help you double your income or gain a promotion or start your own business. While it may be useful for data collection, it will be largely a waste of time with regard to reaching your targets.

An action-provoking system, however, will take you above and beyond the league of 80 per cent of salespeople – the ineffective ones who put their effort in too late. Your system will keep you on track, striking while the iron is hot and closing while the customer still has interest ... *not* pushing water up hill with a rake, after their interest is lost!

Remember
Your action-provoking system puts you in control.

SUNDAY
MONDAY
TUESDAY
WEDNESDAY
THURSDAY
FRIDAY
SATURDAY

Fact-check (answers at the back)

Note: all questions require a single answer.

1. What percentage of salespeople put most of their effort into closing a sale after it's too late?
   a) 40% ❏
   b) 80% ❏
   c) 20% ❏
   d) 10% ❏

2. What's the most important period of the buying cycle?
   a) Gaining interest period ❏
   b) Maximum interest period ❏
   c) Losing interest period ❏
   d) All of the above ❏

3. What's the main reason so many salespeople put effort in too late and miss the sale?
   a) They don't have action-provoking systems ❏
   b) They do things when they have time ❏
   c) They don't want to be seen as being too aggressive ❏
   d) All of the above ❏

4. What are the benefits to you of having an action-provoking system?
   a) It will help you use your time where it counts ❏
   b) It will help you close the sales you have already started ❏
   c) It will help you start the correct number of new prospects necessary to meet your targets ❏
   d) All of the above ❏

5. What systems are least likely to help you reach your targets?
   a) A diary system ❏
   b) Ones that don't list every prospect ❏
   c) Systems that record what has been done, rather than what needs to be done ❏
   d) All of the above ❏

6. What must computerized systems do to work well and help you reach your goals?
   a) Tell you everything you've done for a prospect, and what stage the sales is at ❏
   b) Tell you what day you have to take the next action ❏
   c) Show you, on any given day, a list of every prospect that needs action that day . ❏
   d) All of the above ❏

7. What's the biggest failure of sales systems?
   a) Confusing action taken with actions to be taken ❏
   b) Messy documents ❏
   c) Hard-to-carry systems ❏
   d) Too much data ❏

8. What specific information does a sales system need to help you reach your goals the fastest?
   a) Data about history about the prospect ❏
   b) A new list of prospects ❏
   c) Advice codes for each prospect ❏
   d) A list of prospects that need action every day ❏

9. When creating action-provoking systems, which questions are useful to ask yourself?

a) Where will I be when I use the system: in the car, at my desk, etc.? ❏

b) Who else will use it? ❏

c) Who will enter the next actions required and the dates by when they must be done? ❏

d) All of the above ❏

10. What will happen if you don't have an action-provoking system?

a) You won't have the support system you need ❏

b) Your energy will be fragmented ❏

c) You'll be disappointed you didn't get the results you hoped for ❏

d) All of the above ❏

SATURDAY

Implement motivation and support systems

People often tell me that they find the hardest part of selling is keeping themselves motivated and on track. In the sales profession, we don't often have the support network we had in other jobs. We usually have no one setting our deadlines or telling us what projects to work on next.

One woman I know was an Olympic swimmer, with all the skills of a self-disciplined person when it came to goal-setting and practice. When she started her own company selling from home, she told me: 'Christine, I don't have a structure any more, like I had in my old job.'

What she didn't realize was that she had to create her own structure and support systems. The good news is that, after applying the principles of this book, she was up and running, drawing on the motivation she had as an Olympic athlete.

And so it will be with you. Today you will learn how to:

- be your own cheerleader
- devise your own support systems
- stay positive when the going gets tough
- eliminate the doldrums and self-criticism
- dare to be different
- overcome roadblocks and move quickly to your goal.

Be your own cheerleader

'Everyone gets into the doldrums,' my first sales manager told our sales team, 'but it's up to each of you to get yourselves out of them.'

It would be nice if we all had sales managers who could coach us and encourage us at every turn, like the best football coach. But that's not practical. Managers are occupied with many activities, and they can't possibly know our personality and motivational needs as well as we can. Most importantly, though, think who our success is reliant on: them or us?

Since we can't wait for someone else to motivate us and set up our motivation systems for us, we have to do it for ourselves. In effect we have to carry our own cheerleader or football coach in our mind.

What motivation and support systems can you put into place that will allow you to reach the top?

What support do I need?

Think about your own situation carefully. What kind of support and encouragement do you want when you have a 'down' day? What kind of support do you want on normal days?

Be specific and complete your own list. It might include support for:

- goal setting
- reaching a particular milestone
- doing a mundane task consistently
- cold calling
- getting appointments
- boosting morale
- confidence building.

Today we'll study the motivation and support systems of the top achievers so that you can choose those that would work for you and put them into place immediately. They include:

- people who can support you
- developing a positive attitude
- acknowledging your strengths
- doing things differently
- overcoming obstacles
- defining your goals.

Create personal support

What do you need from people? One top salesman talks to his wife from his mobile phone four times a day. He likes having someone to share his progress with, his ups and downs, his trials and tribulations.

Decide what support you want from people. All of us have people in our lives willing to support us, especially if we're willing to support them in turn.

Who do you have? Open your mind to an expanded group of potential supporters. They might be partners, friends, co-workers, sales or other managers, people from your social groups, progressive thinkers, the community, Chambers of Commerce, new acquaintances or customers.

Be specific about the kind of support you want, referring to the list in the box above. Then set your goals, and share your progress with your supporter. Just reporting your progress to someone every day for a week, for example, can start you on a new path or help you form a new habit. I do this with a friend of mine who also owns her own company.

Think now. Who can you talk to? You'll be surprised at how many people there are who would like to have this support reciprocated.

Stay positive

What are the chances that your customer will be positive if you aren't? The answer is zero.

We all have negative thoughts that pass through our minds, but it's our choice whether to hang on to them or not. The first step is to notice what our thoughts are.

Notice your thoughts

If you were to count the number of thoughts that flash through your mind in one minute, you would reach well over 60. We can't hold on to every one, so why not pick the positive ones? So often in life we give in to the negative ones, forgetting that we are in charge of either holding on to or releasing those thoughts.

Release the negative

One top sales executive I interviewed for my book, *Secrets of the World's Top Sales Performers,* has developed his own mind-clearing process, which is very effective.

He takes a walk after work to review how the day has gone, deciding what mistakes he's made, what to do about them and what to do differently next time. Then he releases any negative thoughts or guilt remaining about his mistakes.

In other words, he concentrates on correcting his mistakes rather than downgrading himself for making them in the first place.

Think now about what system you can put in place to:

● listen to your thoughts
● concentrate on correcting your mistakes
● hang on to the positive
● release the negative.

Could you allocate some time each day as this top achiever does? Could you write down the positive? What steps can you take? Think about it as you read the next paragraphs.

Eliminate the doldrums

The best way to eliminate the doldrums is to take a moment to acknowledge your strengths and what you do right. Take time to acknowledge your persistence, your stamina, your determination, your progress in being organized, your sales skill building and so on.

Watch children as a clue to human development. A two-year-old says: 'I can do it, I can do it, I can do it.' A three-year-old says: 'I did it, I did it, I did it.' They go from conviction, determination and belief to success.

That's what we need to do too in creating success patterns. First, we have to have a positive attitude about the fact that we *can* do it, and then we have to reinforce the fact that we have done it.

That's the reason you have to stop to give yourself acknowledgement for your progress and success. Don't wait until you reach the end result because you'll get into the doldrums waiting. Acknowledge yourself for the small steps along the way.

 For maximum success, write down your success steps and review them every evening or when you're most likely to get the doldrums.

Most people find it easier to criticize themselves than to acknowledge themselves. It comes from years of incorrect practice. Now is the time to reverse the process. When you acknowledge yourself, your morale will go up. And high morale is essential to keeping yourself going.

Your skills and qualities

Make a list now of skills and qualities you can acknowledge in yourself. Then you'll be able to refer to these when you need a morale boost.

Dare to be different

Another top sales executive hired a secretary after being in insurance for only six months. No one else was willing to be so daring and invest in themselves *before* their income was high. But he saw the potential of doing what he did best and delegating everything else. Now he has four members on his support staff and *ten times* the average income!

The chances are that you're holding yourself back from something. It may be hiring an assistant or trying a new method no one else uses. It might be investing in equipment or support staff, or doing presentations or demos a different way. Whatever it is, look again. Think again. Don't be afraid to be different.

Perhaps you will be an inspiration, not only for yourself but for others. There are plenty of mediocre salespeople doing things in their standard way, getting standard results. If you want to be successful, you have to be determined, committed, positive, disciplined and different.

Being different alone won't do it. But being different on top of being determined, committed, positive and disciplined can put you on a new level. What are you holding yourself back from? Now decide what you are willing to do about it. Focus on the long-term effect you'll create and not the short-term resistance to change you may get from those around you.

Make a list like this and jot down your answers.

What am I holding myself back from?	
What am I willing to do about it?	
What result could I expect?	

Overcome roadblocks

Most people see a number of roadblocks between themselves and their goal. Roadblocks always exist.

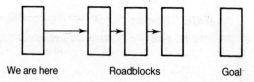

We are here   **Roadblocks**   Goal

The mentality shift that helps us overcome roadblocks is totally straightforward: keep the goal in sight and focus determinedly on ways around the roadblocks. It looks like this:

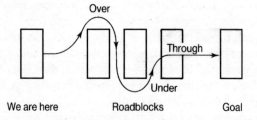

Over

Through

Under

We are here   **Roadblocks**   Goal

In reality, roadblocks are nothing more than challenges that help us grow. One person's roadblock is nothing to another person because they've already gained skills in that direction. So why not go in that direction to gain those skills as well?

Move quickly to your goal

Let's ask ourselves these questions:

- What happens if we have no goal?
- What if our goal isn't clear in our mind?
- What if we see our goal as one big chunk rather than daily pieces?

We may feel that we're moving too slowly or not at all towards our goal. We get caught in a downward spiral.

What can we do every day to make sure we're creating an upward spiral, moving closer to our goal? The answer is to have our goal clearly defined – break it into action segments and tackle the segments every day without fail.

> ***'Happiness is directly proportional to the speed you're moving towards your goal.'***

When you develop that discipline, success will be in your hands. Without it, you're giving your power away. What is *your* clearly defined goal? What are the segments that will help you to reach it?

Take the most challenging path

One successful woman I know says: 'When you come to a crossroads in life, take the most challenging path.' Why does she advocate this? Because challenges make us grow and make us feel good about ourselves. If we turn away from the challenging path, we stagnate.

I talked about this concept in a speech to a group of sales executives in Malaysia, among whom was an IBM salesman. A year and a half later he came to me and said that this advice had completely changed his life. He had been doing well already but, with his new determination to take the most challenging paths at every turn, his life had become incredibly rich with new and exciting opportunities.

Think now of what challenging paths lie before you. Perhaps you haven't seen them in this light before. Perhaps they would also bring you rich, new and exciting opportunities. It's important not to turn your back on them. Having the courage to take the challenging path and overcome the roadblocks requires conviction that we'll succeed. The best way to do this is to harness strength from past successes.

Think first of what roadblocks you perceive to be in front of you, standing in the way of your challenging path.

Consider your past successes

Think now of all your past successes. Think of your successes early in your career, early in your education. Think of any contest or competition you won, no matter how young you were. What quality did you have that helped you win? You still have it. Now is the time to harness this to help you overcome your roadblocks.

Every individual has a great deal more potential than they ever imagine. The goal or vision you have in your mind must be exactly right for you because no one else has that same vision. Don't let a simple roadblock stop you. Use your strengths to overcome it.

Summary

Today we studied the most important factors for implementing motivation and support systems.

We saw that being in sales is much like running our own business. Our remuneration, or some of it, is often linked to our results. No sales = no pay. Thus we need to be our own coach, our own cheerleader, our own goal setter and our own creator of a structure for working that brings us success.

We also analysed the steps of the sales process that require the most support, and looked at ways we can get that support. We learned how to stay positive when the going gets tough, how to release negativity and how to eliminate the doldrums and self-criticism. We looked at why we might dare to be different or to take the most challenging path. And, most of all, we looked at the over-under-through method of overcoming obstacles, which can be used not only in sales but also in all aspects of life.

Remember
When you come to a crossroads in life, take the most challenging path.

SUNDAY
MONDAY
TUESDAY
WEDNESDAY
THURSDAY
FRIDAY
SATURDAY

Fact-check (answers at the back)

Note: all questions require a single answer.

1. What's the key to getting support from people?
   a) Being willing to give them reciprocal support ❏
   b) Deciding what kind of support you want and asking for it specifically ❏
   c) Setting your goals, and sharing your progress ❏
   d) All of the above ❏

2. What is the first step to staying positive?
   a) Noticing your thoughts ❏
   b) Eating a good breakfast ❏
   c) Working out every day ❏
   d) Meeting with your boss in the morning ❏

3. What is the best way to eliminate the doldrums?
   a) Taking time to acknowledge what you do right ❏
   b) Taking time to acknowledge your persistence ❏
   c) Acknowledging your determination ❏
   d) All of the above ❏

4. What's important about keeping your morale high with regard to increasing your sales?
   a) People will like you ❏
   b) It keeps you going ❏
   c) Your family will notice ❏
   d) You'll feel good about yourself ❏

5. What's the most important step in creating success patterns?
   a) Know what you want to do ❏
   b) Get permission from your boss ❏
   c) Have a positive attitude that you can do it ❏
   d) Write down your plan ❏

6. Why should you not wait until you reach your goal to acknowledge yourself, but instead acknowledge your progress along the way?
   a) To help you remember where you are going ❏
   b) To help you remember why you are going there ❏
   c) Because it's too long to wait until the end ❏
   d) To stay out of the doldrums and keep motivation high ❏

7. Why do most people find it easier to criticize themselves than to acknowledge themselves?
   a) Other people like it ❏
   b) They learned it in childhood ❏
   c) They've had years of practice ❏
   d) It feels right ❏

8. Why is it good to make a list of your skills and qualities and refer to it occasionally?
   a) It brings a smile to your face ❏
   b) You get good ideas from referring to it ❏
   c) It boosts your morale ❏
   d) It helps you defend your position when you need to ❏

9. What's a good way to get around roadblocks?
a) Think of them as nothing more than challenges that help us grow ❑
b) Go around them: over, under or through ❑
c) Stop and do something else ❑
d) Both a and b ❑

10. What's good about the following philosophy? 'When you come to a crossroads in life, take the most challenging path.'
a) Challenges make us grow ❑
b) It gives you more exercise ❑
c) If we turn away from the most challenging path, we stagnate ❑
d) Both a and c ❑

SUNDAY MONDAY TUESDAY WEDNESDAY THURSDAY FRIDAY SATURDAY

WEEK 2

Successful Key Account Management
In A Week

Introduction

Key account management is increasingly important and must keep pace with its customers as they continually develop and evolve, often resulting in increasingly sophisticated buying structures. The key account manager therefore requires a wide variety of skills in order to be successful; this is not only an important job role in its own right, it is often a stepping stone to career development, leading to more senior management jobs.

On Sunday the key account manager is encouraged to **Know your customer** as success depends on a relationship that is both rewarding and valuable. A thorough understanding of the customer is dependent on information gathered; the vital element to a strong position is the possession of knowledge.

Monday is the day to **Analyse your growth opportunities**. The competitiveness of the company must be appraised to enable the identification of sales growth opportunities and all major accounts should be compared in appeal and position to give an indication of the strategy to be adopted for customers.

Tuesday is the day to **Measure profits by account**. The key account manager is shown how to measure the profitability of major customers and to draw up league tables to enable profit improvement strategies. Less profitable customers need to be made more profitable and efforts made to grow sales with those whose profitability is higher; the customers who produce the majority of the sales are often not the same ones who produce the majority of the profit as they can make demands that reduce the supplier's margin.

On Wednesday the key account manager must **Plan for success**, building on the analysis of growth opportunities and profit measurement already considered, to result in a best judgement final plan. This plan can be used in management control, as well as to benchmark and report on performance, facilitated by a sales plan checklist.

On Thursday the key account manager is taught to **Negotiate to win-win**; success relies on understanding the difference between negotiation and selling and being able to conduct negotiations to produce a win-win situation in which the objectives of both sides are considered. The core principles of negotiation must be learned and there is great skill involved in managing the high pressure situation that is brought about by the significant costs and values to be considered.

The key account manager looks at **Control activity levels** on Friday and the monitoring of standards of performance to enable the presentation of plans and progress, allowing the measurement of success against these plans. Information management is crucial to the control cycle and the absolute success measures are the objectives covering the quantifiable goals. If standards are not being achieved, this must be diagnosed and corrected.

Finally, on Saturday the key account manager is reminded to **Manage relationships** with an introduction to the Relationship Model, which describes how business with a customer changes as it moves from a transactional or short-term sales achievement, to collaboration with long-term customer value and retention.

Grant Stewart

SUNDAY

Know your customer

A successful key account manager depends on a relationship with his or her customer that is both rewarding and valuable. The way to achieve this relationship is explained in the following section, with emphasis placed on the importance of information gathering, to enable a thorough understanding of the customer, their business and the buying processes involved. Five categories of required information are detailed, with suggestions of pro forma documents given for data capture, explanations of how the information may be used, its importance and examples of practical applications. Having ascertained facts about his or her customer, the key account manager is guided through learning about their policies, markets, financial performance and buying processes. The concept of a decision-making unit is introduced, with an explanation of the subjective and objective influences to which buying decisions made by the customer are submitted, emphasizing that the buyer does not work alone. Throughout the process, the key account manager is shown that the vital element to a strong position is knowledge. This knowledge will allow the building and maintenance of a positive relationship with the customer to avoid errors that may prove costly to the business.

SUNDAY
MONDAY
TUESDAY
WEDNESDAY
THURSDAY
FRIDAY
SATURDAY

The key account manager needs to collect customer information in five categories:

1   Customer facts
2   Customer policies
3   Customer markets and our business
4   Customer financial performance
5   Customer buying processes.

Customer facts

● Locations of customer's head office, regional offices, factories, warehouses, etc.
● Names of parent company, subsidiaries and affiliates
● Number and type of outlets (if applicable)
● Planned changes to locations
● Last three years' sales turnover and profits.

This information will be laid out as a pro forma document with space to revise any changes of information. Accuracy of information is essential and the pro forma needs to be tailored to the specific industry in which the key account manager is operating.

For example, a key account manager selling to customers in a retail distribution business will have extra sections on areas such as:

● Square metres of space
● Average sales per square metre
● Average sales per outlet
● Breakdown of outlets by type and size, e.g. customer's standard outlet grading system.

Alternatively, a key account manager for a computer manufacturer may collect information by end customer type, for instance, offices, retailers, manufacturers, distribution companies, service companies, etc.

Customer policies

● On access to customer sites and outlets
● On promotional and marketing support from suppliers
● On promotional materials allowed

- On entertaining and social events
- On pricing and discounts.

The aim of collecting this type of information is to ensure that all of the key account manager's behaviours fit in with the customer's policies, thus avoiding costly mistakes.

For example, many customers are increasingly concerned about the influences on their buying departments created by suppliers' entertainment and gift policies. A key account manager who does not understand the customer's policy in this area, may ruin the relationship completely by ignoring strict guidelines laid down by the account.

Furthermore, the need to understand customer's policies is crucial in the area of contact outside head office, such as visits to customer factories, warehouses, outlets and service centres. Unauthorized visits to customer premises would harm the relationship. The key account manager needs to issue clear policy guidelines to all members of the workforce who have contact with the customer's business. This includes the sales force, delivery staff, customer administration and customer service staff.

The customer holds the key account manager responsible for the actions of all supplier staff who are in contact with the customer. An innocent mistake by a junior member of staff may impair the relationship. It is up to the key account manager to record customer policy information and to ensure that it is communicated successfully to all staff and implemented without mistakes.

Customer markets and our business

- Estimate of total purchases by customer, by market
- Sales by market, by brand or product
- Our share of customer's total business
- Customer's share of our total business.

The purpose of this type of information is to answer the question: 'Where are we now?' Historical sales and market information will form the springboard for analysing growth opportunities for key accounts. The information can be laid out in a pro forma:

This pro forma can be completed for:

- Different years (trends)
- Different markets
- Different products/brands sold to each market

Customer markets and our business pro forma

Year	Market category	Estimate of total purchases by customer (units and value)	Our sales to customer	% share of customer's total purchases	Customer's share % of our total sales

Customer financial performance

- Customer's return on capital employed
- Customer's return on sales
- Customer's sales in relation to capital employed
- Stock, debtor and creditor turnover
- Profit performance by product and market category.

The key account manager should collect the published financial information of customers, for instance the annual report and accounts. This will give the financial summary of how the customer is performing and the key account manager can look at the trends of performance over the past two or three years to see if the customer's business is improving or deteriorating.

This knowledge will enable the key account manager to formulate profit improvement strategies for customers that empathize with the customer's profit requirements. The main areas on which such information can be collected are shown in the following table:

The key account manager does not need to be a financial expert – help can be sought from financial analysis books or from the internal financial department. Experience shows that understanding the customer's financial performance creates

	Ratio	How to calculate	What it means
1	Return on capital employed	Net profit before tax/capital employed%	It measures the profits produced in relation to the total capital invested in the business. Capital employed is shareholders' funds (share capital and reserves) plus loans. Comparisons can be made with other companies in the same industry.
2	Return on sales	Net profit before tax/sales%	This measures profit after all company costs have been deducted in relation to the total sales of the company. This is effectively the customer's profit margins.
3	Capital turnover	Sales/Capital employed	This measures the speed of sales turnover in relation to the capital employed in the business. High is good.
4	Stock turnover	Stock × 365/Sales revenue	This measures how the company's inventory (stock) is turning over, expressed in number of days. The lower the number of days the better.
5	Debtor turnover	Debtors × 365/Sales revenue	This measures the customer's ability to collect payment from its customers and is expressed in number of days. Like stock turnover, debtor turnover should have a low number of days.
6	Creditor turnover	Creditors × 365/Cost of goods sold	This shows how long it takes to pay the bills of suppliers and is expressed in days. The higher the number of days, the better.

a good basis for developing strategic approaches to key customer planning and negotiation. You may wish to reduce your investment in customers whose financial performance is declining, while increasing your investment in customers whose profits are increasing.

Further information is available from a customer's stock market performance. Is its share price rising or falling? Do City financial analysts rate the customer as a buy, sell or hold, as far as the shares are concerned?

Customer buying processes

- Customer organization and buying structures
- Interests and characteristics (e.g. sports, hobbies) of customer managers
- Description of buying process
- Analysis of decision-making unit (DMU).

This information section is vital since it will guide the key account manager in developing the right quantity and quality of relationships at all relevant levels with the customer. It is well known that many key account managers fail to identify an accurate customer buying process, and fail to develop relationships with all members of the decision-making unit (DMU).

A typical customer buying process would be:

- Recognition of customer needs
- Specification of products to meet needs
- Search for suppliers to meet needs
- Analysis of supplier proposals
- Evaluation of proposals and selection of suppliers
- Selection of an order routine
- Performance evaluation and feedback.

These buying processes may differ according to whether the products and service needs are new, are modified from a current product or service, or are a routine repurchase.

The DMU is a core concept of key account management and can be extremely difficult to define in large accounts with many buying influences. The classic model developed by Webster and Wind (1972) identified five key groups:

1 *Users*: for example, those who influence product purchases as users.
2 *Influencers*: for instance, industrial engineers, manufacturing staff, technical personnel.
3 *Buyers*: those who place the orders – may be individuals or a buying committee – and each buyer may have different characteristics affecting purchase, such as status needs, attitude to risk, willingness to negotiate.
4 *Deciders*: for example, the board of management, finance director or buying committee. A key account manager who deals only with buyers may regret a reluctance to contact deciders.
5 *Gatekeepers*: for instance, secretaries, receptionists, mail sorters, warehouse staff. Gatekeepers may be relatively junior members of staff, but key account managers may need to get them 'on side' if the other members of the DMU are to be contacted and influenced.

Each person in the DMU will have a unique profile of buying influences, which must be collected and summarized by the key account manager. These influences can be summarized under two headings:

1   *Subjective influences:* these are non-rational influences that psychologists believe have a major impact on all purchase decisions. Examples include:

- Desire for status
- Need for power
- Need for reassurance
- High or low attitude towards risk and innovation
- Need to be liked
- Need to please superiors.

2   *Objective influences:* these are the rational and logical reasons for purchase and examples are:

- Price/cost
- Performance
- Reliability
- Delivery
- Service quality
- Convenience and flexibility.

In practice, most buying decisions are a combination of both subjective and objective needs, and the key account manager should collect information on all possible influences of all members of the DMU. The saying 'People buy people first' is usually true. It would clearly help a supplier/customer relationship if the key account manager knew that a member of the DMU enjoyed a particular sport or hobby and this could be incorporated into the relationship process, for example, in invitations to social or sporting events.

Summary

The first requirement for any account manager is to know his or her customer. This involves spending much time and effort in data collection and assimilation to build up a full understanding of the facts, policies, markets, financial performance and buying processes relating to the customer. While the key account manager does not need to be a financial expert, the information gathered must be accurate, regularly updated and collected in an easy-to-access form. Customer policies must be adhered to for the avoidance of costly mistakes and it should be remembered that the customer holds the key account manager responsible for the actions of all supplier staff with whom they are in contact. Knowledge and understanding of the customer enables the formulation of profit improvement strategies for key planning and negotiation, which are facilitated by the development of the right quantity and quality of relationships at all relevant levels with the customer. Recognition of the decision-making unit and its influences, whether subjective or objective, is vital; while all the information categories are important, the customer buying process is primary. If the key account manager moves on to another company, his or her successor should have all the core information readily to hand: knowledge is power.

SUNDAY
MONDAY
TUESDAY
WEDNESDAY
THURSDAY
FRIDAY
SATURDAY

Fact-check (answers at the back)

Note: some questions require a single answer and others require more than one answer.

1. The key account manager needs to collect information on his/her customer in how many different categories?
a) 1 ❏
b) 5 ❏
c) 10 ❏
d) 20 ❏

2. It is essential that the information gathered is:
a) accurate ❏
b) shared with the customer ❏
c) tailored to the specific industry ❏
d) easy to access ❏

3. The most important of the information categories is the:
a) customer facts ❏
b) customer financial performance ❏
c) customer buying processes ❏
d) customer policies ❏

4. In examining customer policies the key account manager must include consideration of:
a) access to customer sites and outlets ❏
b) acceptable promotional and marketing support ❏
c) entertaining and social events ❏
d) whether or not they agree with the customer policies ❏

5. A key account manager's behaviour must fit in with the customer's policies:
a) mostly ❏
b) sometimes ❏
c) always ❏
d) never ❏

6. Within the key account manager's team, to whom do the customer's policy guidelines apply?
a) it varies according to the situation ❏
b) delivery staff ❏
c) customer services ❏
d) sales force ❏

7. Unauthorized visits to customer premises are likely to:
a) make the customer feel valued ❏
b) harm the relationship ❏
c) be a good investment in understanding the customer ❏
d) be beneficial to both customer and key account manager ❏

8. A key account manager will need to build a relationship with the customer's:
a) buyer ❏
b) secretary ❏
c) finance department ❏
d) none of the above ❏

9. When looking at the financial summary of the customer's performance, the key account manager needs to consider:

a) trends over the past two or three years ❏

b) last year's figures and projections for this year ❏

c) estimates of sales for the next three years ❏

d) this year's sales only ❏

10. In the formulation of profit improvement strategies the key account manager needs to consider the customer's return on capital employed. Which of the following statements are true?

a) return on capital employed measures the profits produced in relation to the total capital invested in the business ❏

b) comparisons may be made with other companies in the same industry ❏

c) return on capital employed is the only relevant consideration in determining declining or improving fortunes in a customer ❏

d) return on capital employed is one of several factors to consider in understanding the customer's financial performance ❏

MONDAY

Analyse
your growth
opportunities

To enable the identification of sales growth opportunities, the key account manager must first appraise the company's competitive situation. To assist in this process, a four-stage approach to the analysis of business growth opportunities follows, including competitive analysis, SWOT analysis, account appeal and product market matrix. A pro forma is given to illustrate the SWOT (strengths/weaknesses/opportunities/threats) analysis that may be adapted according to industry type. The use of an opportunity grid as a vital part of key account management is explained, with its purpose being to place all major accounts on a visual map to allow comparison of their appeal and position. While a standard list of these factors is not possible due to differences in industry, a comprehensive example is given. Having looked at the appeal and position, the key account manager is then shown how to score these factors, to give a weighting, or relevant importance, producing the scoring boundaries for the opportunity grid. The account grid location gives a strong indication of the strategy to be adopted for the customers. Finally, there is an explanation of the product market matrix, an effective way to position and visualize sales opportunities for major accounts and therefore to identify growth opportunities.

Analysis requirements

The key account manager needs a four-stage approach to analyse business growth opportunities:

Analysing opportunities

1 Competitive analysis
2 SWOT analysis
3 Account appeal/our position
4 Product market matrix

Competitive analysis

● Identification of competitors
● Previous actions
● Strengths/weaknesses
● Forecast plans.

The first major step is to identify – for any major account's business – who your competitors are. While this may be obvious in markets with a small number of suppliers, it becomes more complex as the number of suppliers increases. There may be competitive threats to your business with a particular customer and this may come from new sources. For example, an overseas competitor attacking your core market or attacks from new entrants into an existing market.

One example is the food distribution business in any country, which could be changed overnight by the entry of one of the US giants with an aggressive buying and pricing policy.

A second example is the financial services market, where traditional bank and insurance company suppliers could face new competitors from other retail fields, such as non-food and food retailers.

These competitors need to be analysed in terms of strengths and weaknesses. Some may have financial strengths, but little understanding of your market, whereas others may be relatively small companies, but with strongly focused expertise in your core markets. Their plans are never published in advance and you will need to look at their previous actions and behaviours to forecast their likely strategy and action plans.

Failure to anticipate a competitive attack on one of your major customers could lead to a disastrous loss of business in a very short period of time.

Strengths/weaknesses/ opportunities/threats (SWOT)

- Identify key areas for SWOT analysis
- Identify your strengths
- Recognize weaknesses
- Highlight likely opportunities
- Recognize real threats.

The SWOT analysis has been an important corporate analysis tool for many years and its application is appropriate for key account management.

The topic areas of the analysis should reflect their importance in the eyes of major customers. The following example of a SWOT pro forma is taken from a retail food distribution supplier. Topic headings will vary according to industry and while this example covers eight topics, there is no limit to the number of topics that can be analysed.

Strengths/weaknesses/opportunities/threats

	Strengths	Weaknesses	Opportunities	Threats
Product range				
Product quality				
Branding				
Pricing/Terms				
Distribution/ Listings (% outlets stocked)				
Service (delivery, sales)				
Promotions				
Merchandising				

The important point about a SWOT analysis is to express strengths and weaknesses against competition. It is not a strength if the competition is also strong in that area. For example, your company's product quality may be excellent, but if major competitors provide a similar product quality, then this is not a competitive strength.

Account appeal/our position

- Create an opportunity grid
- Analyse customer appeal factors
- Analyse the strengths of your position
- Position accounts on opportunity grid.

The creation of an opportunity grid is a vital part of key account management – it forms the basis of the account strategy and plan.

The purpose of the opportunity grid is to place all of your company's major accounts on to a visual map. This works as follows:

Opportunity Grid

	100	200	300	400	
	3	2	1	High	
				300	
	6	5	4	Medium	**Appeal**
				200	
	9	8	7	Low	
				100	
	Weak	Medium	Strong		

Position

The key account manager needs to analyse the appeal and position factors, in order to score each account and place them on the grid. Every industry is different, so there can be no standard list of appeal and position factors.

However, the following is a comprehensive example drawn from a supplier in the retail food distribution business.

The scoring boundaries used above (100–400) are taken from the example company used. The grid numbers (1–9) are explained at the end of this section.

Account appeal factors

1 *Market factors*	
Volume turnover	
Rate of growth	
Range stocked	
Access	Access to those parts of the key account needed to achieve your objectives. There will be two main areas: 1 Middle management 2 Branches
Support	Of our brands by account.
2 *Financial factors*	
Demand for discount	
Distribution policy	This could be in the form of warehouse delivery to branches, direct distribution or third-party supply. The important thing is how effective the operation is, not which of these three is in operation.
Prompt payment	
Instant volume ability	Is the account able to take deliveries of large volumes at short notice and pay for them?
3 *Environmental factors*	
Provision of information	How willing or able is the account to supply the kind of information you need for effective business planning?
Buyer relationship	Quality of interpersonal relationship with key account manager and those able to take decisions and implement policy on the key account side.

Your position factors

Brand strength in account	
Product range stocked	
Merchandising support	In the sphere of pack facings and point-of-sale material.
Market share	Your share of that particular key account business.

Competitor activity	In the sphere of promotional activity.
In-store furniture	The proportion supplied by you as opposed to other manufacturers.
Pull through ability	This factor refers to the ability of the account to implement and pull through promotional business development plans. In all probability, two main areas will need investigation: 1 Middle management 2 The point of sale
Distribution/Delivery effectiveness	This is the measure of efficiency of the key account to have the correct brands in appropriate volumes always available at the point of sale.
Promotional/Pricing flexibility	Is the key account able to meet our needs in these respects?
Company awareness	The key account manager's awareness and understanding of the complete key account operation, its aspirations, successes, failures, strengths and weaknesses.
Complication factors	Disruption of business plans for whatever reason – management, inflexibility of varying systems etc.
Service relationship	Strength of your position with account.

Each of these factors should be scored. It is best to weight each factor in importance by allocating 100 points to each category of appeal and position. Score each factor by using a system of, for example, marks from one to four. The weighted average score is achieved by multiplying the weighting (relative importance) by the score. If we use a four-point scoring system as an example, the maximum in each of the two categories will be $4 \times 100 = 400$. This will make it easy to produce the scoring boundaries for the nine boxes in the opportunity grid, thus reducing the subjectivity involved in the scoring. If we take the appeal/position factors as above, the weighted average score for one account might be as follows:

Account appeal				Our position/Strength			
1 Market factors	Weight	Score	Total		Weight	Score	Total
Volume turnover	20	3	60	Brand strength in account	18	3	54
Rate of growth	12	2	24	Product range stocked	10	3	30
Range stocked	10	3	30	Merchandising support	6	2	12
Access	6	4	24	Market share	12	3	36
Support	6	2	12	Competitor activity	7	2	14
2 Financial factors				In-store furniture	4	2	8
Demand for discount	10	1	10	Pull through ability	4	3	12
Distribution policy	10	2	20	Distribution/Delivery effectiveness	15	3	45
Prompt payment	4	4	16	Promotional/ Pricing flexibility	10	2	20
Instant volume ability	10	3	30	Company awareness	4	4	16
3 Environmental factors				Complication factors	4	4	16
Provision of information	4	3	12	Service relationship	6	2	12
Buyer relationship	8	2	16				
TOTAL	**100**		**254**		**100**		**275**

In the example used here, this account scores 254 for appeal, and 275 for position. This would place the account in the middle/right portion of box 5 on the grid.

At the end of this important analytical process the key account manager can see all of the accounts placed in the nine grid boxes. Although there can be some exceptions, the usual way to use the opportunity grid is as follows:

Account grid location	Opportunities	Strategy
Boxes 1, 2 and 4	Strong position/appeal	Defend/improve
Boxes 3, 5 and 7	Selective opportunities	Build and develop
Boxes 6, 8 and 9	Weak position/appeal	Milk/withdraw

Product market matrix

- Market size estimates
- Product sales by market
- Product/market trends
- Opportunity areas.

The product market matrix is an effective way to position and visualize the sales opportunities for major accounts.

The matrix can be used in a variety of ways and the following example shows how it works.

The product market matrix

£000	Market 1	Market 2	Market 3	Product trend	TOTAL
Product 1	100 / 60	2000 / 80	400 / 150	Increasing 33% p.a.	2500 / 290
Product 2	500 / 30	1000 / 100	2000 / 100	Decreasing 7% p.a.	3500 / 230
Product 3	1200 / 100	2400 / 200	1600 / 40	Increasing 2% p.a.	5200 / 340
Market trend	Static	Growing 14% p.a.	Increasing 3% p.a.		
TOTAL	1800 / 190	5400 / 380	4000 / 290		11200 / 860

P / A

P = Potential purchases, i.e. market size.
A = Actual purchases from us.
p.a. = Per annum.

The word 'market' can have various meanings, including different countries, sales regions, end user types or industries.

The product categories can be individual items, product groups or broad generic categories. The market/product boxes can be further subdivided to show the past two years' performance.

Independent market research may help to identify market sizes for particular accounts, but this can be extrapolated from market share estimates. Moreover, many customers are happy to give market size estimates for their category business.

The product market matrix can be used by the key account manager to identify growth opportunities, or at very least to provide a basis for further investigation. In the above example, Product 1 in Market 2 would be a good potential opportunity area – the product is increasing at 33% per annum, the market is growing 14% per annum and the share of total business in that market is well below the average level. There may, of course, be good reason for this under-performance, but this simple analysis method can produce very good growth opportunities.

Summary

The sales opportunities for each account must be considered carefully by the key account manager. The four analysis requirements to understand business growth opportunities are: competitive and SWOT analyses, account appeal and product market matrix. The competitive analysis allows for the identification of competitors, examination of previous actions, consideration of strengths and weaknesses and forecast planning. In choosing the topic areas of analysis for SWOT, the key account manager must examine his or her own company to identify strengths, recognize weaknesses, highlight likely opportunities and understand real threats. In consideration of account appeal and the key account manager's own position in relation to the customer's business, an opportunity grid is a useful tool. With this grid it is possible to reduce subjectivity in analysing customer appeal factors relative to the strength of the manager's own position. This visual map gives a strong indication of the opportunities available and therefore of the strategy to adopt for each account. Finally, the product market matrix effectively positions the sales opportunities for major accounts, given consideration of market size estimates, product sales by market, product/market trends and areas of opportunity. At the very least, this will provide a basis for further investigation by the key account manager.

SUNDAY
MONDAY
TUESDAY
WEDNESDAY
THURSDAY
FRIDAY
SATURDAY

Fact-check (answers at the back)

Note: some questions require a single answer and others require more than one answer.

1. How many stages are involved in analysing business growth opportunities?
   - a) one ❏
   - b) two ❏
   - c) three ❏
   - d) four ❏

2. Complete the phrase. Product market...
   - a) format ❏
   - b) template ❏
   - c) matrix ❏
   - d) pattern ❏

3. Competitors need to be analysed in terms of:
   - a) strengths and weaknesses ❏
   - b) the size of their company ❏
   - c) financial position only ❏
   - d) the plans they publish ❏

4. SWOT is an acronym for strengths, weaknesses, opportunities and...
   - a) timescales ❏
   - b) threats ❏
   - c) teamwork ❏
   - d) trials ❏

5. How many topics should be considered in a SWOT analysis?
   - a) as few as possible ❏
   - b) five ❏
   - c) eight ❏
   - d) there is no limit ❏

6. With reference to an opportunity grid, which of the following statements apply?
   - a) the list of appeal and position factors is the same in every industry ❏
   - b) it places the company's major accounts on a visual map ❏
   - c) there is no standard list of appeal and position factors ❏
   - d) there is no potential for comparison between accounts ❏

7. In considering account appeal factors, which of the following are applicable?
   - a) market factors ❏
   - b) financial factors ❏
   - c) environmental factors ❏
   - d) it varies from time to time ❏

8. The word 'market' can have various meanings, including:
   - a) different countries ❏
   - b) sales regions ❏
   - c) industries ❏
   - d) none of the above ❏

9. Product categories in the product market matrix can be...
   - a) of little relevance to the scoring ❏
   - b) individual items ❏
   - c) product groups ❏
   - d) broad generic categories ❏

10. The product market matrix can be used by the key account manager:

a) to identify growth opportunities ❑

b) as a standalone tool to look at sales opportunities ❑

c) to provide a basis for further investigation ❑

d) to show under-performance ❑

TUESDAY

Measure profits by account

The most important customers for a company in terms of sales may not be the most important in terms of profit. In this section, the key account manager is shown how to measure the profitability of major customers; the relationship between sales and profits is the impetus for developing key account management as a separate part of the sales force. There are many benefits of profit analysis and a full explanation of how to achieve such an analysis, involving the drawing up of a full profit and loss account, follows. Costs attributable to customers must be considered, although some of these can only be attributed by estimation and sampling methods. Profitability league tables may then be drawn up between customers, to compare those in the same market segments as well as to make comparisons between different market segments. The significance of this information is that it enables profit improvement strategies, which must be used to inform the key account manager's ongoing negotiation process with each major customer. Finally, there are three exercises to check understanding of financial fluency and awareness, with answers and explanations given.

Comparing sales and profits

The impetus for developing key account management as a separate part of sales force management was the 80:20 rule. This means that, in general, 80 per cent of a company's sales turnover will come from 20 per cent of customers (known as the Pareto statistical distribution).

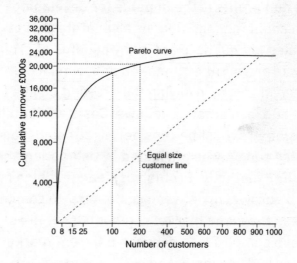

Eighty per cent of a company's profits will also come from around 20 per cent of its customers, but these are generally not the same 20 per cent who produce most of the sales. This is because major customers can demand and obtain better levels of price, promotional discounts and service levels, thus reducing the supplier's profits considerably.

In a recent analysis carried out for a client, not one of their top 25 customers in terms of sales turnover featured in their top 25 league table of customers in terms of per cent profit. A comparison can be made as follows:

Customer	% of your sales turnover	% of your profits
1	22	16
2	16	14
3	11	5
4	8	10

This type of analysis indicates that the key account manager should try to make less profitable customers more profitable and try to grow sales turnover with customers whose profitability is higher.

The following real example shows two customers in the same market category who produce very different levels of profitability to the supplier.

	% of combined sales turnover	% of combined gross margin	% of combined net profit
Customer 1	45.6%	40.1%	6.3%
Customer 2	54.4%	59.9%	93.7%
	100.0%	100.0%	100.0%

This example shows that two customers with similar sales volume start to move apart at the gross margin level and are distinctly different at the net profit level. Customer 2 is much more profitable to this supplier because it buys more profitable products, at higher price levels and at lower servicing costs than Customer 1.

Benefits of profit analysis

1 Provides a balanced review of variable selling costs
2 Illustrates their effect on customer contribution and trading profit
3 Identifies true cost of obtaining/maintaining business with major customers
4 Provides comparisons between customers and between trade sectors
5 Indicates areas of potential action
6 Establishes real customer 'profitability'
7 Establishes the most cost-effective method of servicing/obtaining business
8 Provides a basis for account planning/forecasting
9 Pulls together the cost centres in order to manage the business better
10 Strengthens the negotiation stance
11 Introduces 3-D attitudes:
   - Sales volume
   - Sales revenue
   - Profitability.

Analysing major customer profitability

Analysing the profitability of major customers is usually carried out by the financial department. The process involves attributing costs at a number of different levels to each major customer, so that a full profit and loss account can be drawn up. Typical costs attributable to customers would be as follows:

Costs attributable to customers

- Cost of sales
- Commissions
- Sales calls
- Key account management time
- Order processing costs

- Promotional costs
- Non-standard packaging and unitization
- Dedicated inventory holding costs
- Dedicated warehousing costs
- Material handling costs
- Transport costs
- Documentation/communication
- Returns/refusals
- Credit taken.

Some of these costs can only be attributed by estimation and sampling methods. For example, time spent by the sales force servicing each major customer can be calculated by completion of sample time sheets, which are then applied to the hourly cost of each salesperson. Provided that the calculations are applied consistently between each major customer, comparisons can be made. A typical profit and loss account by a customer might look like the table below:

	Customer A	
	£000	%
Standard price (excluding tax)	70,000	100
Manufacturing costs	40,600	58
Maximum gross contribution	**29,400**	**42**
Total discounts	16,100	23
Actual gross contribution	**13,300**	**19**

	Customer A	
Delivery costs:		
200–999.9 drop size	1,050	1.5
1,000+ drop size	1,050	1.5
Total distribution costs	2,100	3
Distributed contribution selling costs:	11,200	16
Key account	35	0.05
Regional	700	1
Merchandising	315	0.45
Total selling costs	1,050	1.5
Selling contribution	10,150	14.5
Extended credit cost	1,960	2.8
Office administration	210	0.3
Net contribution	7,980	11.4
Allocated overheads	4,270	6.1
Net profit	3,710	5.3

In this example, the definitions are as follows:

Standard price List price of products bought by that customer multiplied by sales volume.

Manufacturing costs Direct product costs (materials, labour, packaging) of product mix bought by that customer.

Discounts Total discounts given to that customer, which can be broken down by different types if required.

Delivery costs Costs analysed by delivery size.

Selling costs Time costs, estimated for all sales personnel servicing this account.

Extended credit cost Cost of special payment terms give in to this account.

Office administration Estimate of administrative time costs involved in servicing this account.

Allocated overheads This is all the head office and central overheads, which are usually allocated in relation to sales turnover.

Application of customer profitability information

It is now possible to produce profitability league tables to compare major customers in the same market segments. Comparisons can also be made between different market segments, for example, comparing wholesale major customers with direct customers and sales agents.

League tables can be presented in striking visual format with the help of software packages. Armed with this vital information, the key account manager can analyse each major account for profit improvement opportunities. Alternatives can be brainstormed and their financial impact measured.

The options listed below can all have a significant impact on profit improvement.

Profit improvement strategies

- Increase sales of more profitable products
- Achieve sales in new outlets
- Improve merchandising impact
- Increase sales in more profitable geographical regions
- Introduce new products

- Promote sales more effectively
- Produce customer's own-brand products
- Increase or reduce selling prices
- Increase sales volume
- Reduce customer discounts and promotional allowances
- Reduce sales force servicing costs
- Reduce customer credit period
- Negotiate improved contractual terms.

In some cases, the key account manager can afford to invest more in profitable accounts or reduce attention given to less profitable accounts. This profitability information is of great importance during the ongoing negotiation process with each major customer.

Experience of working on consultancy and training projects with hundreds of key account managers shows that financial fluency and awareness is a major area of development. Negotiations have been witnessed where the customer's financial skills are significantly ahead of those of the key account manager. A variety of training exercises also show how difficult it is to become fluent in this key skill area.

Try these three exercises, and see how you do (no peeking at the answers!).

1 Price discount

If the trade price to your major customer is £100 per case, and the gross profit is £20 per case, how much extra percentage volume do you need to keep the same cash profit if you cut the price by £2 per case?

2 Price increase

If the trade price to your major customer is £100 per case, and the gross profit is £20 per case, how much volume could you lose and still produce the same cash profit if you increased the price to £110 per case?

3 Cost of credit

A company has a turnover with an account of £1 million per annum and offers ten weeks' credit at a profit margin of 5 per cent. What would the effect on margin be of a reduction of credit to eight weeks, assuming per cent interest rates?

The effect of extended credit is often dramatic, particularly when interest rates are high. An account with the same level of turnover and profit margins as the above example would produce a financial loss after four months at 15 per cent interest rate. In other words, the whole of the £50,000 margin disappears if the customer delays payment for four months or more. Again, tables can be produced that show the effects on profitability of extended credit at different interest rates.

Answers
1 Price discount
The easiest way to calculate this is to take the price cut and divide it by the new margin and percentage it:

$$\frac{2}{20-2}\% = 11.1\%$$

This means that at this margin a 2 per cent price cut requires a 11.1 per cent increase in volume to break even, i.e. to achieve the previous cash profit. This easy formula allows the key account manager to calculate price discount effects in any situation. Tables are available and the volume increases required can simply be looked up rather than calculated.

2 Price increase
You can use the same formula as Question 1,

$$\text{i.e.} \quad \frac{\text{Price increase}}{\text{New margin}}\% = \frac{10}{(20+10)}\% = 33.3\%$$

This means that you could lose one-third of your current volume sales, yet still achieve the same cash profit as before. You can prove this by using real sales volumes.
 If you were currently selling 100 cases at £20 per case gross profit, you would be making £2000 gross profit. If you divide this £2000 by your new gross profit (£30) you can see that 66.66 cases (minus 33.33 per cent) will produce exactly the same cash profit.

3 Margin and credit costs
Margin of 5 per cent on £1 million = £50,000

   Ten weeks' credit = approximately one-fifth of year's turnover = approximately £200,000

   Interest rate of 15 per cent on this constant credit level = £30,000

   Eight weeks' credit = approximately £160,000

   Interest rate of 15 per cent on this credit level = £24,000

   Saving = £30,000 – £24,000 = £6,000 (12 per cent of margin)

   (The exact figure is a little less than £6000 because some figures have been rounded for convenient calculation.)

Summary

Account profitability information is an important tool in key account management. In general, 80 per cent of a company's sales turnover will come from 20 per cent of customers; this is the Pareto statistical distribution. It is illuminating that 80 per cent of a company's profits will also come from 20 per cent of its customers but, crucially, these are not the same 20 per cent who produce the majority of the sales. This is because the major customers can demand and obtain better prices, discounts and service levels, all of which considerably reduce the supplier's profits. Therefore the key account manager should attempt to make less profitable customers more profitable and try to grow sales turnover with those whose profitability is higher. Profit analysis has many benefits including the drawing up of a full profit and loss account, which then enables comparisons to be made between major customers as well as profit improvement strategies. Financial fluency and awareness are of great importance during the ongoing negotiation process with each major customer and the key account manager themselves may be appraised and measured on profit improvement performance as part of a performance management system.

SUNDAY
MONDAY
TUESDAY
WEDNESDAY
THURSDAY
FRIDAY
SATURDAY

Fact-check (answers at the back)

Note: some questions require a single answer and others require more than one answer.

1. The most important customers in terms of sales:
   a) may not be the most important in terms of profit ❏
   b) will definitely be the most important in terms of profit ❏
   c) are the only customers worth developing ❏
   d) can make significant demands of the supplier ❏

2. The Pareto statistical distribution shows that:
   a) in general, 20 per cent of a company's sales turnover will come from 80 per cent of customers ❏
   b) in general, 80 per cent of a company's sales turnover will come from 20 per cent of customers ❏
   c) in general, 50 per cent of a company's sales turnover will come from 50 per cent of customers ❏
   d) per cent of sales turnover from per cent of customers varies from industry to industry ❏

3. Of a company's profits, around 80 per cent come from around 20 per cent of its customers. These are:
   a) the same 20 per cent of customers who produce most of the sales ❏
   b) generally not the same 20 per cent of customers who produce most of the sales ❏
   c) it varies from industry to industry ❏
   d) atypical results ❏

4. A supplier's profits can be considerably reduced by:
   a) small customers ❏
   b) promotional discounts ❏
   c) reduction in prices ❏
   d) service levels ❏

5. If top customers in terms of sales turnover are not also top customers in terms of profit, the key account manager should:
   a) no longer deal with these customers ❏
   b) try to make less profitable customers more profitable ❏
   c) accept the situation ❏
   d) try to grow sales turnover with customers whose profitability is higher ❏

6. Analysing the profitability of major customers is usually carried out by:
a) the customer themselves ❏
b) the key account manager ❏
c) the financial department ❏
d) the customer services department ❏

7. Costs attributable to customers include:
a) key account management time ❏
b) raw materials ❏
c) promotional costs ❏
d) transport costs ❏

8. Account profitability information ...
a) needs to be reported to the key account manager on a regular basis ❏
b) can be reported just when convenient ❏
c) can be used as part of a performance management system ❏
d) has no value in performance management ❏

9. Profit analysis ...
a) facilitates comparison between major customers ❏
b) enables profit improvement strategies ❏
c) shows the current position but has no bearing on future direction ❏
d) none of the above statements are applicable ❏

10. Profit improvement strategies may include:
a) increasing sales of more profitable products ❏
b) increasing sales volume ❏
c) ending promotions ❏
d) increasing customer credit period ❏

WEDNESDAY

Plan for success

> *'If you don't know where you're going, any road will take you there.'*

The key account manager must develop objectives, strategies and tactical plans to formulate a set of action priorities; to plan for success and prevent competitive threat. This plan must build on the analysis of growth opportunities and profit measurement discussed earlier to evolve a final plan that takes all internal and external factors into account. In the following section, the key account manager is shown how to format an account plan that takes in factors such as key facts, the SWOT analysis, customer strategy and action plan, servicing, pricing and distribution. The use of this plan in the company's own management control and information system is highlighted along with how to benchmark and report on performance. It is good practice to complete the plan to a standard format and the importance of a consistent link between objectives and performance monitoring is also explained, both of which may be facilitated by a sales plan checklist. A detailed example of such a checklist is given, with prompts for products, merchandising, promotion, servicing, pricing, distribution and communication/motivation, which relate to the headings used in the account plan format example.

Account plan format

It is best for each key account manager in a company to complete the plan to a standard format. This enables comparisons to be made between plans for different customers. It also allows the best plans to achieve the greatest resource allocation from senior management. There is no standard format for a key account plan, but an example from a fast-moving consumer goods company provides a typical set of headings in a pro forma document.

1 **Key facts**
　1.1. Market sizes by product group in value, volume, market share, and growth.
　1.2. Our sales by product group.
　1.3. Percentage distribution levels of our key products in customer outlets.
　1.4. Our profit contribution with this customer for the past two years.
2 **Strengths/Weaknesses/Opportunities/Threats (SWOT analysis)**
　As per the model from Monday.
3 **Customer strategy**
　3.1 Customer appeal and our position, as shown on Monday. Summary of the customer's appeal to us (high, medium or low) and our position within the customer's business (strong, medium or weak).
　3.2. Key issues to be addressed in the planning period.
4 **Detailed customer strategy and action plan**
　4.1 **Product strategy**
　　● Product priorities for sales development
　　● Range development plans
　　● Packaging, size or feature changes planned.
　4.2. **Merchandising**
　　● Product space allocation plans for customer outlets
　　● Business case propositions for increased share of customer's space
　　● Merchandising strategy for implementation by the sales force.

4.3 Promotion
- Relationship to customer's advertising programme
- Timing and emphasis of promotional strategy
- Relationship of promotional investment to sales objectives
- Promotional opportunities for new store openings
- Development of unique promotional methods for this customer
- Establishment of criteria for evaluating promotional effectiveness.

4.4 Servicing
- Development of service level agreements (SLAs) with different customer contact points
- Deployment of field sales force, agency staff, merchandisers and telephone sales
- Establishment of service levels in regard to warehousing, delivery, order processing, distribution and administration.

4.5 Pricing
- Establishment of maximum and minimum price levels within customer outlets
- Establishment of negotiation guidelines on promotional discounts
- Agreement of maximum promotional buying periods where price discounts are applicable
- Establishment of maximum promotional discounts by product group
- Agreement of annual retrospective discount offers contingent upon sales success levels, and the establishment of negotiation parameters for the annual account plan agreement with the customer.

4.6 Distribution
- Plans to increase number of customer's outlets stocking our products
- Which outlet types will produce greatest opportunities?
- Incentives to sales force for improving distribution levels
- Stock level strategies related to sales rates.

4.7 Communication/Motivation/Organization

- Quality and frequency guidelines for customer communications
- Development of customer relationship management and customer newsletter policies
- Creation of customer team development and entertainment plan
- Development of trading and promotion brief to internal management/sales force/merchandisers, setting out service, activity and operating standards
- Establishment of customer contact frequencies for discussing business plans and reviewing performance
- Review of presentation quality of all communications vehicles to customer.

5 **Summary of customer revenue, expenditure and profit plan by product group showing the previous year and the current year's plan.**

6 **Promotional calendar summary showing the planned promotional events by products group for each month of the year.**

The company's management control and information system will report performance against the key objectives set out in the plan on a monthly basis or more regularly, as required by the key account manager. Targets will be broken down into performance benchmarks by month, taking seasonality and promotional strategy into account.

The result is a consistent link between objectives and performance monitoring, although in many companies there is a disparity between these two. There is a great loss of effectiveness if performance targets, both quantitative and qualitative, are not reported on a consistent basis. There is a lot of truth in the sayings:

- If it's worth doing, it's worth measuring.
- What gets measured gets done.

Sales plan checklist

In order to arrive at decisions on the content of the account plan, a checklist approach should be used. The following examples are drawn from a consumer goods company servicing key accounts in the retail distribution business. The checklist headings relate to those used in the account plan format example above.

Product checklist
- Which products would we like to sell more of in this account for strategic or profit reasons?
- Where are the product growth opportunities with this customer?
- Are there gaps in the customer's range for promoting our existing products, e.g. geographically or in particular outlets? Where are these gaps, e.g. sizes, flavours, pack types, varieties?
- Are there new product opportunities for this customer, either for branded or own-label products?
- What effect will the customer's marketing strategy have on our product sales, e.g. store openings or closures, increased size of outlets, brand strategy?
- Do we need to change our product strategy, e.g. better quality, new lines, revised packaging, new sizes?

Merchandising checklist

- How are our competitors displayed in shops or depots? What share of facings do we have?
- What should we be doing to improve our share of space and impact in store or depot?
- Consider:
  - Display units
  - Promotional material
  - Sitting and traffic flow
  - Turnover and profit per square metre (what is the customer's target?)
  - Consumer handouts via merchandising teams
  - Joint activity/experiments with other suppliers
  - Shelving plans (planograms)
- How compatible is our packaging (shelf and transit) with customers' needs?
- What improvements do we need to make – quantify benefits?

Promotion checklist

- What have been or will be our objectives, for example:
  - To increase sales out – by how much?
  - To increase distribution – by how much?
  - To increase display/facings – by how much?
  - To increase customer staff motivation – measured by?
  - To increase stock levels – by how much?
- What activity was and will be planned? Include not only major promotions but also local or regional activity, special events, for example:
  - Advertising
  - New store or depot openings
  - Demonstrations
  - Incentives (include personal entertaining)
  - House magazines, public relations (PR) and competitions
  - Newsletters/bulletins/mail outs
  - Trade shows/seminars
  - Tailor-made consumer/retailer activity
- How can activity be more cost effective?
- How does our programme/investment compare with last year and competition?

Servicing checklist

- How often do we/should we make contact with head office, field management and branches?
- Who should make the contact where there is overlap? Define action responsibilities.
- What kind of selling and/or merchandising services do we/ should we provide in branches?
- How do we currently obtain and process orders?
- Could we speed up the process (obtain more allocations)? For example, telesales, automatic reordering.
- Use of computer links, e.g. Customer Relationship Management (CRM) system?
- How do we deliver products?
- How could we reduce time from obtaining order to placement of product on shelf?
- What kind of stock control objectives/systems does the customer have/employ?
- Can we assist the customer in any way to reduce out of stocks?
- What action is required by key account manager and/or our directors and others to improve relationships/influence, for example:
  - Formal marketing/business review presentations
  - Factory/head office visits
  - Involvement in customer seminars, social and sports events, celebrations, staff meetings/outings, charity sponsorship.
- What services do our competitors provide? How do we compare (benchmarking standards)?
- What specialist skills and facilities could we provide as an aftersales service, for instance:
  - Staff training – product knowledge and skills
  - Merchandising.

Pricing checklist

- Retail price:
  - On promotion?
  - Off promotion?
  - Compared with competition?
  - What should our discounts be?

- Discounts:
  - On promotion?
  - Off promotion?
  - How do they compare with previous year?
  - And competition?
- Customer incentive scheme for achieving annual plan:
  - Is there one?
  - Should there be one?
  - How can the present one be improved?
  - How do we compare with competition?
- Contracts:
  - Would contract pricing be an advantage?
  - How does our current or planned contract situation compare with competition?
- Could we negotiate reduced drops and/or increased drop volume, at what cost?
- Credit:
  - How long does it take us to collect due debts?
  - How can this be improved?

Distribution checklist

- Which of our products are listed by head office?
- Which of our competitors are listed by head office?
- What action needs to be taken to obtain listings? (Set a time plan)
- What are our branch or depot stock levels (weeks or months supply)?
- How do they compare with the competition, last year and trade sector average?
- How can they be increased/reduced?
- What action needs to be taken to achieve maximum distribution potential?

Communication/Motivation/Organization checklist

- How can we improve the customer's knowledge, interest and willingness to make things happen on our behalf?
- Interest and motivation can be achieved by:
  - Newsletters
  - Examples of how top staff achieved their successes

- Selling guidelines
- Use of visual aids at meetings
- League tables
- Personal letters of encouragement/thanks –customers, self, office, staff and sales force.
- Organizing:
  - How activity is to be arranged
  - Who will be involved?
  - What lead times are required?
  - What equipment is needed?
  - What skills are required?
  - What training is needed?
- How can organizing the customer's business be improved?

Summary

A company that prospers is one that makes things happen through good planning and the anticipation of market and competitive threats. Planning for success requires a well thought out key account plan that provides direction, objectives, strategies, action plans, budget and the benchmarks by which success may be evaluated. The plan should be written down and circulated to all those within the company who have a part to play in its implementation. At periodic review meetings the key account manager will be appraised on the delivery of the plan, with any shortfall being identified and measures taken to fill any disparity between objectives and results. Essentially the key account plan will answer three key questions: Where would we like to be? How will we get there? How will we know we are getting there? If the plans are completed to a standard format, comparisons may be made between plans for different customers and also allow for the greatest resource allocation by senior management. A consistent link between objectives and performance monitoring is paramount, with the regular reporting of targets being very effective in the assessment of this. A sales plan checklist ensures that the correct course is maintained.

SUNDAY
MONDAY
TUESDAY
WEDNESDAY
THURSDAY
FRIDAY
SATURDAY

Fact-check (answers at the back)

Note: some questions require a single answer and others require more than one answer.

1. Planning for success aims to develop objectives, strategies and tactical plans to:
a) give the key account manager a set of action priorities ❏
b) prevent competitive threat ❏
c) form the basis of successful evaluation ❏
d) avoid the need for further negotiation ❏

2. It is good practice for each key account manager in a company to complete the account plan to a standard format. This:
a) enables comparisons to be made between plans for different customers ❏
b) does not enable comparisons between plans for different customers ❏
c) allows the best plans to achieve the greatest resource allocation ❏
d) has no influence on resource allocation ❏

3. Performance targets are effective if reported on a consistent basis. Which of the following statements are applicable?
a) only quantitative targets are relevant ❏
b) only qualitative targets are relevant ❏
c) both qualitative and quantitative targets are relevant ❏
d) sales figures alone are relevant to performance targets ❏

4. A key account plan builds on the analysis of growth opportunities and the measurement of profits by account. Which of the following statements is also true?
a) the best plan is the first and most obvious outcome ❏
b) a series of alternative strategies and actions will be generated ❏
c) the final plan will be the best judgement taking internal and external factors into account ❏
d) the plan should be circulated to all within the company who have a part to play in its implementation ❏

5. At periodic review meetings, the key account manager will be appraised on delivery of the plan according to criteria of
a) content and quality ❏
b) timing ❏
c) budget ❏
d) simplicity ❏

6. Which three of the following questions are relevant to the key account plan?
a) where are we now? ❏
b) where would we like to be? ❏
c) how will we get there? ❏
d) how will we know we're getting there? ❏

7. In assessing customer strategy in the account plan format, which of the following should be taken into account?
a) customer appeal, whether high, medium or low ❏
b) any potential customer has appeal, irrespective of their position ❏
c) our position within the customer's business, whether strong, medium or weak ❏
d) our present position is irrelevant; where we aim to be is all that matters ❏

8. With regard to the merchandising checklist for a sales plan:
a) the displays of competitors are not relevant ❏
b) the displays of competitors are relevant ❏
c) consideration should be given to the compatibility of packaging with customers' needs ❏
d) it is not necessary to accommodate customers' needs in the design of packaging ❏

9. The pricing checklist of a sales plan should consider:
a) trying to get away with the highest price possible, even if it is unsustainable ❏
b) retail price ❏
c) discounts ❏
d) customer incentive scheme ❏

10. Companies that prosper:
a) make up a plan as they go along ❏
b) achieve results through good planning ❏
c) measure and evaluate success ❏
d) anticipate market and competitive threats ❏

THURSDAY

Negotiate to win-win

In the ongoing relationship between key account manager and customer there is a significant element of negotiation, which can occur during any stage of the business. A successful key account manager must understand the difference between negotiation and selling, plan effectively in advance of the negotiation and be able to conduct negotiations to produce a win-win situation. These secrets will soon be revealed. Negotiation versus selling depends on whether the need to supply is equal to or exceeds the need to buy. In planning to negotiate there are five steps that the key account manager should follow. In the following pages the account manager will see that they need to look at the situation from the customer's viewpoint as well as from their own. Both sides have objectives that must be considered and met, forming a list of negotiation variables, often called the 'shopping list'; some examples are given. Guidelines for conducting negotiations are also set out along with the core principles of negotiation that must be learned. The realization of relative strengths and weaknesses is a great skill in negotiation, which is always a high pressure situation owing to the significant costs and values to be maintained.

Negotiation versus selling

Selling occurs when the need to supply exceeds the need to buy. It involves persuading the buyer that the supplier's products are needed.

Negotiation assumes that the need to supply is equal to the need to buy – it is the give and take process whereby the conditions and terms of a transaction or relationship are agreed.

Key account managers still have to use their selling skills to develop relationships with their accounts and to put forward their case, yet negotiation is more prominent in maintaining business. The following chart illustrates this point.

Selling versus negotiation

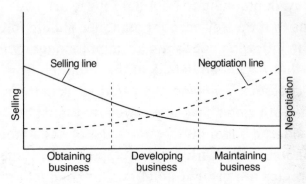

Planning to negotiate

Before every negotiation, the key account manager should follow five steps:

Planning stages

1 Assess buyer needs/identify areas for negotiation
2 Cost/benefit analysis
3 Assess stances that buyer will take

4 Relate to your objectives
5 Plan your own stances

Assess buyer needs

- What are the buyer's commercial needs?
- What will be the effect of purchase or no purchase?
- What problems does the customer have?
- What alternatives exist, e.g. competitive offers?
- What subjective needs exist, e.g. security, status, peace of mind?
- What is the relative importance of each need?
- What 'shopping list' of negotiable areas will the buyer raise?

The purpose of this stage is to enable the key account manager to look at the situation from the customer's viewpoint. This is the skill of empathy and research shows that successful negotiators are particularly strong in putting themselves in the customer's shoes.

You need to prepare a number of questions in advance that aim to identify the key issues in the customer's buying situation. You also have to anticipate the needs of different interests within the customer's organization structure. As an example, the buyer may invite the marketing director to attend a meeting and perhaps the distribution manager. These three job roles will have a different emphasis for each need.

Cost/benefit analysis

- What concessions can you offer?
- What concessions will you seek from the buyer?
- What are the costs and benefits of these concessions?
- What concessions cost us little, but are of considerable value to the buyer?

For the key account manager, the aim of this planning is to prepare costs and values in advance of the meeting to ensure that you are not caught out. It is much better to come to the meeting prepared, than to admit that you do not know a figure and have to refer to head office.

Even worse, if you are not prepared financially, you may give away an important financial concession without getting anything worthwhile in return. Skilled buyers are able to exert psychological pressure to get an agreement and it is easy to miss an opportunity.

It is best to make concessions that do not have a simple cash cost. For instance, if you think the buyer will ask for an extra cash discount, you can plan to offer extra support services (e.g. training), which will be of benefit to the buyer but cost you nothing in real financial outlay. This could happen if you had spare capacity in your training department, which could provide training for your customer at no immediate extra cash cost for your company.

Assess stances that buyer will take

- What is the real strength of the buyer's need?
- How will the buyer state this in the extreme stance?
- What will be done to pull you towards this position?
- What will the buyer's real stance be?

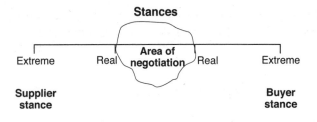

Stances

Area of negotiation

| Extreme | Real | | Real | Extreme |

Supplier stance   **Buyer stance**

In the diagram, both the buyer and supplier may begin the meeting with extreme positions designed to throw the other side off their position. Two examples demonstrate the importance of this type of negotiation planning.

The first example is an annual contract negotiation, where two key account managers meet two buyers. The first action of one of the buyers was to tear up a previously submitted proposal from the supplier and state: 'If this is the best you can do, there is no basis for any agreement, and we will have to review your competitive position with us.' Fortunately, one of the key account managers recognized this as a ritual initial ploy, and defused the situation by making a joke. This lightened the atmosphere and the negotiation proceeded in an amicable manner.

The second example is of a key account manager replacing a previously successful manager. The first gesture of the buyer was to hand over a long list of items that he said he would no longer stock unless the supplier offered the same terms given to another key account. The buyer had found out through the grapevine that another customer was getting better terms from the supplier.

In this case, the extreme stance completely caught the key account manager unawares, and he had no arguments pre-prepared. The effect was that he had to call off the meeting and refer to head office, thus giving the buyer a significant psychological edge.

Relate to your objectives

- What do you need to achieve?
- What conflict exists with the buyer's needs?
- What common ground exists?
- How can differences be resolved by negotiation?
- How can the buyer's objectives be achieved together with yours?

The key issue is to know the 'walk away' point. This is a set point of cost concessions in relation to benefits you receive, which you cannot go below.

In role-play practice sessions with key account managers, it is amazing how many times too much is given away by the supplier under pressure to retain business with the customer. Every negotiation has a price and the rewards for good preparation at this stage are evident in more profitable deals.

Plan your own stances

- What bargaining point do you have?
- How can you raise value relative to cost?
- How will you match concessions on each side?
- What stances will you open with?
- What are your real stances?
- Who will be involved in the negotiation?

The key account manager can plan to negotiate from a significant list of negotiation variables, often called the 'shopping list'. With enough preparation, the buyer's shopping list can be anticipated and creative trading of concessions can take place within the overall negotiation framework.

Examples of negotiable variables

1 Schedules of production/delivery
2 Cost
3 Training
4 Maintenance contracts
5 Flexible working hours
6 Performance standards
7 Sale or return
8 Long-term contracts
9 Allowance for exhibitions/display
10 Use of staff
11 Delivery dates/locations
12 Tailoring of solutions/materials (e.g. packaging)
13 Storage costs
14 Support packages
15 Enhancements
16 Penalties for non-performance
17 Installation and implementation support
18 Stock holding levels
19 Discounts/incentives/bonuses
20 Promotional support
21 Exclusivity
22 Deferred price increase
23 Cash flow/payment terms
24 Use of machine/machine time for development
25 Fixed or variable prices
26 Investment money
27 Type of materials used
28 Leasing or outright sale
29 Complexity of solution
30 Speed of delivery
31 Guarantees/indemnities
32 Samples/free product
33 Joint advertising/branding

34 Future commitment for further work
35 Notice periods
36 Experience/specialist skills provision
37 Use of premises
38 Backup (hardware, staff)
39 Call-out terms (rates, time)
40 Expense rates
41 Documentation provision (e.g. reports)
42 Charge for secretarial support

Conducting negotiations

1 Let the buyer talk first, so that you know the full shopping list
2 Establish real stances without the buyer 'losing face', moving from extreme stances
3 Avoid premature deadlock – be flexible
4 Trial close frequently – 'If we did this, would you do that ...?'
5 Trade concessions one at a time – 'I'll agree, if you will ...'
6 Add value to your concessions – 'We have never done this before ...'
7 Devalue buyer's concessions – 'That is available to us anyway ...'
8 Get commitment regularly – 'So let us agree what we have accepted ...'
9 Be confident – assertive, unemotional, friendly
10 Maintain 'social fabric' – negotiation is a ritual game for real stakes
11 Ensure buyer gets the satisfaction needed, both objective and subjective – you both need to 'win'

The skilful negotiator begins by obtaining the buyer's shopping list right at the start. It is easy to be drawn into making further concessions if your first offer is not acceptable, unless you ask the customer for their requirements first.

The greatest skill in conducting negotiations is to realize your relative strengths and weaknesses. You can then trade concessions creatively within an overall shopping list structure.

The selling skill of persuasion should be used to help you to secure the best deal possible, relative to the situation you face.Like two poker players, sometimes you will have good cards and can speak from strength, but sometimes you have a poor hand and must use bluffing tactics to help your position.

The core principles of negotiation can be summarized as follows:

Negotiation principles

Some dos
- Show respect
- Be patient
- Confess limits to authority
- Communicate well

- Trade concessions
- Rehearse/prepare
- Respect confidences
- End positively

Some don'ts
- Show emotion
- Confront
- Betray confidential information
- Compromise minimum objectives
- Relax guard
- Underestimate
- Dominate
- Irritate

The key account manager can PASS the test by:

Planning effectively for the likely areas of the negotiation, the costs of concessions and the likely trading areas.

Asserting themselves during the meeting, but being flexible enough to achieve a compromise.

Searching for variables that can be traded creatively during the give and take process.

Summarizing the points of agreement during the negotiations and summarizing actions to be taken to resolve any matters not yet agreed.

The habits of negotiation can be taken to extremes. In the 19th century, a foreign minister was negotiating with his counterpart of another country. During the lengthy negotiation process, this foreign minister died. On being given the news, his counterpart replied: 'I wonder what he meant by that?'

Summary

The ability to negotiate is a core skill for key account managers and can be developed through practice and training. The aim is to achieve a win-win situation in a challenging but friendly atmosphere. Key account managers must still use their selling skills to develop relationships with their accounts and to put forward their case, yet negotiation is more prominent in maintaining business. All negotiation should be planned, following five steps: identifying areas for negotiation, undertaking a cost/benefit analysis, assessing the stances the buyer will take, relating to the key account manager's own objectives and planning their own stance. Having planned the negotiation, the key account manager must consider the situation from the customer's viewpoint; successful negotiators are particularly strong in empathizing with their customer. There is a significant list of negotiation variables and the skilful negotiator begins by obtaining the buyer's shopping list right at the start. Concessions can then be traded creatively, with the selling skill of persuasion being used to help secure the best deal possible, adhering to the do's and don'ts of negotiation principles. Finally, summarize the points of agreement during the negotiations as well as the actions to be taken to resolve any matters not yet agreed.

For more involved discussion about the art of negotiation, please see Week 3.

SUNDAY
MONDAY
TUESDAY
WEDNESDAY
THURSDAY
FRIDAY
SATURDAY

Fact-check (answers at the back)

Note: some questions require a single answer and others require more than one answer.

1. Negotiation can occur:
a) only at the start of the relationship with the customer ❏
b) during any stage of the relationship ❏
c) where an annual contract needs to be agreed ❏
d) where individual transactions form part of the relationship ❏

2. Select the correct statements. Negotiation:
a) is not the same as selling ❏
b) is the same as selling ❏
c) is a give and take process ❏
d) has an outright winner and a clear loser ❏

3. Select the correct statements. Selling:
a) assumes that the need to supply is equal to the need to buy ❏
b) occurs when the need to supply outstrips the need to buy ❏
c) involves persuading the buyer that the supplier's products are needed ❏
d) is a skill not required in negotiation ❏

4. When planning to negotiate, how many stages are there to follow?
a) one ❏
b) five ❏
c) ten ❏
d) it varies from time to time ❏

5. When planning to negotiate:
a) the key account manager must look at the situation from the customer's viewpoint ❏
b) the key account manager needs only to consider their own viewpoint; the customer can look after themselves ❏
c) successful negotiators avoid empathizing with the customer so as not to be distracted from their aims ❏
d) successful negotiators are particularly strong at putting themselves in their customer's shoes. ❏

6. During the negotiations:
a) it is always possible to strike a deal ❏
b) there is a 'walk away' point ❏
c) there is a creative trading of concessions ❏
d) the atmosphere is unlikely to be pressured or hostile ❏

7. There is usually a significant list of negotiation variables, often called:
a) the wish list ❏
b) the to-do list ❏
c) the dream list ❏
d) the shopping list ❏

8. A skilful negotiator:
a) makes their own
   requirements known first to
   dominate the negotiation ❏
b) lets the buyer talk first to
   learn the full shopping list ❏
c) seeks to diminish the buyer's
   confidence to be able to
   achieve their own goals ❏
d) ensures the buyer gets
   satisfaction also – you both
   need to 'win' ❏

9. Which of the following are good
   principles of negotiation:
a) showing emotion ❏
b) confessing limits to
   authority ❏
c) showing respect ❏
d) relaxing one's guard ❏

10. Which of the following
    statements are applicable to
    negotiation:
a) skills of negotiation can
   be developed through
   continuous practice and
   training ❏
b) there are significant costs
   and values to be obtained
   on both sides ❏
c) the aim is to achieve a
   good compromise ❏
d) none of the above ❏

FRIDAY

Control activity levels

Activity levels and standards of performance must be monitored by the key account manager to enable the presentation of plans and progress to customers and to measure success against these plans. In the following section the importance of information management is explained as this is crucial to the control cycle. It will be seen that objectives are the absolute success measures, covering the quantifiable goals. The key results areas are the means by which objectives are achieved and include all the activity levels necessary to service the account; these activity levels are a key part of the planning and control process but judging the relationship between activity levels and success can be challenging. Once the key results areas are established, standards of performance, both qualitative and quantitative, can be set for each type of activity with major customers. The collection and analysis of results by the key account manager enables performance to be measured against all set standards and requires the formation of a key account information system. If standards are not being achieved, diagnosis and corrective action must be implemented; suggestions and examples for both of these are given.

The control cycle is shown below:

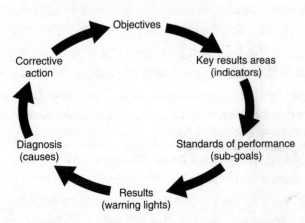

Managing with information

1 Objectives

These are the absolute success measures and will cover the quantifiable goals such as sales, turnover and volume, profit and market share of the customer's business.

2 Key results areas

These are the means by which objectives are achieved and include all the activity levels necessary to service the account, as specified by the key account manager.

These activity levels are a key part of the planning and control process because they answer the question: 'What causes success?' Many people will contribute to these activity levels. Examples include:

● Sales force call frequencies, necessary to service the account
● Amount and quality of time spent with the customer
● Administrative contacts with the customer's administrative department

- Senior management contacts with the customer's equivalent levels of management
- Marketing department contacts with the customer's marketing department
- Operational service levels in areas such as manufacturing, warehousing and transport
- Telephone and email contact levels
- Financial and credit control activity levels.

It is an art, rather than a science, to judge the relationship between activity levels and success. The supplier has limited resources of people and time available to contact each major customer and the customer has limited resources to respond to each supplier. Previous experience is the best guide to establishing what activity levels are required, and it is important to keep reviewing both the frequency and quality of all contact levels with major customers.

3 Standards of performance

Once the key results areas are established, standards of performance can be set for each type of activity with major customers. These can be either quantitative or qualitative.

Quantitative standards would cover areas such as:

- Number of calls to be made by sales force
- Time spent per call
- Frequency of business reviews with customer
- Credit control payment standards.

These standards can be set and agreed with each member of the team who has contact with the major customer. In some cases, a key account manager will set measurable activity standards for hundreds of company staff who have either direct or indirect contact with that major customer. If the supplier has a significant number of major customers, there will be an intricate jigsaw of measurable performance standards, which will establish activity levels for a large proportion of the total staff.

Qualitative standards define the quality levels of these activities.

- Once call frequencies are established for the sales force, the qualitative standards will define what is achieved during each call. For example, the salesperson may be required to follow a standard process for each visit, which may include checking stock levels, ensuring products are displayed or used correctly, agreeing service standards with customer staff, etc.
- Administrative staff may have quantitative standards for their response times to queries or times taken to answer telephones, but there may be important qualitative standards to set for the way that responses are handled and the quality of service given to the customer. Quality of customer contact may be more important than the number of contacts made, so both should be measured.
- The presentation of the annual account plan to each major customer is a quantitative standard, but the way it is presented is qualitative. Each company should develop a format tailored to its own market, but the following is an example drawn from a consumer goods company supplying retail distributors.

Annual account plan presentation

Stage 1	Review last year's trading performance ● Volume/sterling turnover ● Expenditure budget ● Promotion programme ● Marketing support ● Range stocked, gains/losses ● Distribution levels by product.
Stage 2	New year's objective/strategy ● Set turnover target/earnings target ● Promotion strategy ● Distribution/listings objectives ● Marketing plans, etc.
Stage 3	Incentive discount scheme ● Outline earnings achieved ● Present new proposition.
Stage 4	Account plans ● Store opening/closing programme ● Promotions programme ● Stocking policy ● Pricing policy, etc.

Stage 5	Justification of account plans Sales increases due to: ● Inflation ● Store maturity (sales increases due to new stores becoming fully operational) ● New store openings ● Brand maturity (sales increases due to new brands becoming fully accepted and distributed) ● Promotional support ● Market growth ● Market share growth ● New listings ● New products ● Shelf space/relays.
	Sales decreases due to: ● Store closures ● Brand deletions.

● In reviewing performance with the major customer, quarterly reviews are a quantified standard of performance (they could be more or less frequent). How these reviews are carried out are qualitative standards. Again, each company is different, but the quarterly review format for the same company as above, would be as follows:

Quarterly reviews

Stage 1	**Review trading situation** ● Versus same period last year ● Versus incentive discount scheme (including targets to pull back any deficit) ● Versus objective set with account.
Stage 2	**Review promotional programme** ● Result of promotions already run ● Reconfirm remainder of programme ● Discuss any changes re. Stage 1 results.
Stage 3	**Review marketing support** ● Results of activity already run ● Reconfirm rest of year ● Present any changes to plans.
Stage 4	**Accounts plans** ● Identify any changes to policy that will affect your plans.

Each qualitative standard of performance forms the basis of a performance management system for all members of staff who have a role to play in servicing major customers. To assist in performance management, different levels can be established, for instance:

- Below standard
- Meets standard
- Above standard
- Exceptional.

These standards can form the basis of coaching at all levels on the job, and for developing off the job training programmes.

4 Results

The key account manager needs to collect and analyse results so that performance can be measured against all set standards. This requires the formation of a key account information system.

Setting up any sort of key customer information system is complex and can be expensive because it requires information to be collected by the customer rather than by traditional accounting categories. Both quantitative and qualitative information may be difficult to collect and some staff may not wish to accurately record all their activities. Computerization has made quantitative results reporting more precise, but reporting on qualitative standards is always difficult. The fact that it may be difficult should not mean that it is not done at all.

Various types of documentation will require development and continual modification to ensure their accuracy. These documents could include call reports, service standard reports, customer surveys, account information records, etc. Each information system will be tailored to individual companies and there can be no standard specification.

If results, both quantitative and qualitative, are measured against standards, variances against each standard can be managed by the key account manager. If standards are not being achieved, the next two stages of the control process must be implemented – diagnosis and corrective action.

5 Diagnosis

The key account manager has to motivate the line managers of those teams of staff where there is performance shortfall.

Diagnosis aims to identify when results are not being met due to a fall in quantitative standards (e.g. the sales force is not calling often enough or spending enough time on key accounts) or where there are qualitative shortfalls in standards. A fall in qualitative standards requires a diagnosis of possible causes. The following are examples:

- Declining motivation
- Lack of training (attitude, skill or knowledge)
- Poor planning
- Lack of promotional effort
- Poor organization
- Need for incentives
- Recruitment failures.

These causes can often only be identified from personal meetings and discussion with the staff members concerned. Investigation may often reveal some complex behavioural or cultural issues.

6 Corrective action

Once the problems have been diagnosed, the key account manager can help to influence corrective action. This may involve discussions with other line managers or assisting with developing training programme specifications. Corrective actions may entail:

- Improved activity management
- Better/more frequent coaching
- Revised training programmes
- Better staff management methods
- New control and measurement systems.

Experience shows that improving quality in managing major customers is a process of constant improvement and continual activity management. The key account manager rarely has responsibility for other members of staff within the company. Thus, there is a need to develop influencing skills so that other managers and their staff can be motivated to deliver the right quality of service to each major customer.

Apart from taking corrective action involving people issues, which are often outside the key account manager's direct control, there will be many times when performance falls below set objectives and corrective action needs to be taken.

For example, if a major customer is falling short of the profit objectives set for it, corrective action could involve an appraisal of the following alternatives:

- Increasing price levels
- Reducing discounts
- Redirecting effort to higher margin product lines
- Increasing volume by cost-effective promotional methods
- Reducing account servicing costs
- Negotiating new contract terms
- Reducing financial costs to customer.

Each of these alternatives will require detailed appraisal and there may be no easy solutions because the customer could resist the revised action plan.

Summary

A good plan must be measured and managed for it to become a successful plan and the control of activity levels for each major customer is an essential task for the key account manager. The objectives are the absolute success measures and cover quantifiable goals such as sales, turnover and volume, profit and market share of the customer's business. The key results areas are the means by which the objectives are achieved and include all the activity levels necessary to service the account. Judging the relationship between activity levels and success is an art, so previous experience is the best guide to establishing the required levels of activity. Once the key results are established, standards of performance can be set for each type of activity with major customers; both quantitative, such as number of calls made and time spent per call and qualitative, such as the way responses are handled and the standard of the service given. The key account manager needs to collect and analyse results so that performance can be measured against all set standards. Diagnosis to identify when results are not being met due to qualitative or quantitative shortfalls in standards allows corrective action to be applied.

SUNDAY
MONDAY
TUESDAY
WEDNESDAY
THURSDAY
FRIDAY
SATURDAY

Fact-check (answers at the back)

Note: some questions require a single answer and others require more than one answer.

1. In controlling activity levels, select which of the following statements apply:
   a) the key account manager needs to present plans and progress to customers ❏
   b) the key account manager does not need to present plans and progress to customers ❏
   c) success must be measured against plans through standards of performance ❏
   d) success does not need to be measured; this has no benefit ❏

2. Objectives are the absolute success measures and cover quantifiable goals such as:
   a) sales ❏
   b) turnover and volume ❏
   c) customer satisfaction ❏
   d) profit and market share of the customer's business ❏

3. Staff relevant to the activity levels servicing the account include:
   a) the key account manager only ❏
   b) the customer services team only ❏
   c) the senior management contacts with customer's equivalent levels of management ❏
   d) all staff who are involved in servicing the account ❏

4. When considering the relationship between activity levels and success ...
   a) the relationship may be judged scientifically ❏
   b) it is a subjective judgement ❏
   c) there is no guide to the required levels of activity ❏
   d) previous experience is the best guide to establishing activity levels ❏

5. Standards of performance may be:
   a) quantitative only ❏
   b) qualitative only ❏
   c) either qualitative or quantitative ❏
   d) set and agreed with each member of the team in contact with the customer ❏

6. How many stages are there in the annual account plan presentation?
   a) one ❏
   b) three ❏
   c) five ❏
   d) ten ❏

7. The collection and analysis of results involves several challenges. Which of the following statements is true?
a) if the information is difficult or expensive to collect, the costs outweigh the benefits so it should not be done ❏
b) documentation only needs an initial set-up and will then be relevant for the duration of the relationship ❏
c) development and continual modification of documentation will ensure accuracy ❏
d) it is not necessary to tailor the system to individual companies ❏

8. Diagnosis aims to identify when results are not being met. This may be:
a) due to a fall in quantitative standards ❏
b) due to a fall in qualitative standards ❏
c) identified from personal meetings and discussion with staff ❏
d) unrelated to the above possibilities ❏

9. Corrective actions may entail:
a) improved activity management ❏
b) changing the objectives to make them easier to achieve ❏
c) revised training programmes ❏
d) new control and measurement systems ❏

10. If a major customer is falling short of the profit objectives set for it, corrective action could involve:
a) increasing price levels ❏
b) reducing discounts ❏
c) redirecting effort to higher margin profit lines ❏
d) an easy solution, as the customer is likely to welcome negotiating new terms ❏

SATURDAY

Manage relationships

In this section the key account manager is introduced to the Relational Model, which describes how the key account relationship changes as it moves from a transactional focus (short-term sales achievement) to collaboration (long-term customer value and retention). The relationship with the customer must be managed and the five stages of key account management in the development of this relationship are introduced. These stages may be broken down as pre, early, mid, partnership and synergistic key account management. The characteristics of these stages are fully explained. There is also a sixth stage to be considered, which is what occurs when the relationship with the customer has broken down; uncoupling. Factors that may cause uncoupling are listed. Purchasing management trends that favour the development of relationship suppliers are also considered as these have become more relevant in recent years and can have a significant influence. The SCOPE model of successful partnerships is also introduced, encompassing strategic factors, cultural and chemistry factors, organizational and operational factors, performance review and reporting factors as well as equality factors. In summary, a comparison is made between transactional and relationship key account management.

Relational model

There is an increasing importance in key account management to build relationships by linking supplier company staff more closely with major customer staff. There is a move away from a transactional focus (short-term sales achievement) to a relationship focus (long-term customer value and retention).

This trend in relationships development has been accurately analysed by Tony Millman and Kevin Wilson in the key account Relational Model. This describes how the key account relationship changes as it moves from transactions to collaboration.

Key account relational model

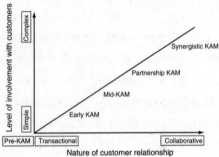

KAM= Key account management

Source: *Key Customers: how to manage them profitably*

Malcolm McDonald, Butterworth-Heinemann, 2000. Based on the work of Millman and Wilson.

The five stages of key account management (KAM) development are characterized by Millman and Wilson and supported by further research from Malcolm McDonald and Beth Rogers:

1 Pre-KAM

● Identify potential key accounts
● Establish the first customer needs
● Seek initial entry points.

2 Early KAM

- Initial transactions established
- Small share of customer's business
- Key account manager/purchasing manager relationship
- Aim to understand customer's decision-making unit.

3 Mid KAM

- Selling company is a preferred supplier
- Interactions increase in numbers and complexity
- Trust levels increase
- Contact levels increase to involve directors, other managers, specialists and operational staff
- Wariness on both sides about 'putting too many eggs in one basket'.

4 Partnership KAM

- Supply and share of customer's business may approach 100 per cent
- Development of partnership agreements
- Growth of team working to improve quality and reduce costs in both companies
- Sharing of sensitive information
- Long-term pricing and product development policies
- Open book financial information shared
- Shared expertise at all levels
- All departments at each company fully aligned.

5 Synergistic KAM

- A 'beyond partnership' stage
- A single entity, rather than two organizations
- Joint value (synergy) created at all levels
- Exit barriers on either side are high
- Joint planning at all levels

- Cross-functional focus teams work on joint business improvement projects
- Key account relationships may cut across country lines and become global.

Uncoupling KAM

There is a sixth stage not presented in this analysis, and that is uncoupling key account management. This describes a breaking down of the relationship and it can occur at any of the five stages described. It may be caused by factors such as:

- Changes in key personnel
- Change in corporate buying policy, for example, a retailer may decide to source its purchases on a global basis rather than in its home market
- Breakdown of trust, for instance, a failure to communicate a product quality problem or preferred buying terms given to a competitor of the major customer
- Complacency
- Cultural factors – where there is a mismatch between a bureaucratic supplier and an entrepreneurial customer
- Quality, for example, if either company suffers a serious decline in product, process or people quality
- Declining market position – where either company suffers a significant loss of market share
- Financial problems – if either party suffers significant financial problems.

Trends favouring relationships

In recent years, there have been a variety of purchasing management trends that favour the development of relationships with suppliers. These trends include:

- Centralization of buying
- Global sourcing of supplies
- Just-in-time (JIT) inventory management systems
- Zero defects quality management
- Outsourcing of supplies

- Focus on total supply chain management
- Computerized techniques for materials management and routine transactions
- Development of preferred supplier buying processes
- Increased size and scale of purchasing due to mergers and acquisitions.

Taking one example from the above list, the just-in-time delivery systems are based on the Japanese high dependency theory. This tries to eliminate waste by getting everyone involved, including key suppliers. The result is a joint continuous improvement process known as Kaizen.

One piece of recent research showed that Japanese auto component companies supply 24 times the value per vehicle compared with US companies in the same market. Japanese manufacturers bought twice the volume of components from one-tenth of the number of suppliers, compared with US companies.

This favours the development of what the consultancy Bain & Co. calls Value Managed Relationships. These are collaborative partnerships aimed at retaining major customers, and key account managers play a major role as the interface in this relationship building process.

Some research carried out by Roger Pudney of Ashridge Management College has identified the following competitive advantages from partnerships, which are relevant to the development of more advanced key account management relationships.

Competitive advantages from partnership

- Strategic long-term developments
- Higher margins/higher prices
- Volume increases
- Easier negotiations
- Economies of scale/manufacturing efficiencies
- Reduced delivery times
- Blocking competitors
- Early problem solving

- Early information
- Faster new products
- Security of supply.

The Ashridge research developed an easy-to-remember SCOPE model of successful partnerships:

Strategic factors include shared vision and strategy, making long-term commitments and a significant investment in the partnership, ensuring that the partners' strengths are complementary.

Cultural and chemistry factors include managing the fit between the two cultures and building strong personal relationships.

Organizational and operational factors principally find ways to integrate and link the partners together at many levels.

Performance review and reporting factors include setting up a regular mutual evaluation system to assess the effectiveness of the partnership.

Equality factors are mainly softer behavioural factors, such as building mutual trust and treating each other as equals.

Successful partnerships
SCOPE model

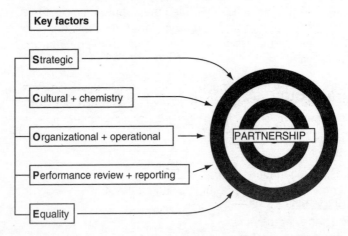

Source: R. Pudney Ashridge International Partnership Study

The type of relationship between supplier and customer will determine the qualities the key account manager needs to develop. Some major customers will not require their relationships with key account managers to venture beyond the management of the sales transaction processes. Other customers favour a more sophisticated relationship moving towards partnership and that will require a different type of key account manager.

These differences are shown below:

Transactional key account management	Relationship key account management
Sales focus	Customer retention focus
Simple negotiations	Complex negotiations
Competitive threats	Limited or no competition
Supply of products/services	Joint creation of products/services
Short timescale	Long timescale
Limited range of contacts	Extensive range of contacts
Low service levels	High service levels
Cost/price focus	Value focus
Adversarial	Partnership
Occasional communication	Frequent communication
Some cooperation	Total cooperation

China's Chairman Mao Zedong once famously said: 'A journey of a thousand miles begins with a single step.' A week is the first step in a journey and we wish you the very best of luck in reaching your destination.

Summary

The move from short-term sales achievement to collaboration, with long-term customer value and retention, means it is increasingly important in key account management to build relationships by linking supplier company staff more closely with major customer staff. This trend is shown by the Relational Model. The different stages of the relationship have different characteristics, from seeking initial entry points (pre-KAM) to winning a small share of the customer's business (early KAM), to becoming a preferred supplier (mid-KAM) through to partnership and beyond. As these stages progress the customer and the key account manager become increasingly aligned and interdependent; there are many competitive advantages from partnership. Trends such as centralization of buying and global sourcing of supplies favour the development of relationships with suppliers and there is a SCOPE model of successful partnerships. The qualities a key account manager needs to possess are determined by the type of relationship between supplier and customer. Excellent sales skills will be appropriate for early KAM and perhaps mid-KAM, but the ability to manage complex customer relationships is also essential if the relationship is to become less transactional.

SUNDAY
MONDAY
TUESDAY
WEDNESDAY
THURSDAY
FRIDAY
SATURDAY

Fact-check (answers at the back)

Note: some questions require a single answer and others require more than one answer.

1. The description of how the key account relationship changes as it moves from transactions to collaboration is called the Relational:
   a) Progress ❏
   b) Model ❏
   c) Development ❏
   d) Change ❏

2. Which of the following statements apply to the developing relationship with customers in key account management?
   a) the level of involvement moves from simple from complex ❏
   b) the level of involvement is complex to begin with then becomes simple ❏
   c) the nature of the relationship moves from transactional to collaborative ❏
   d) the nature of the relationship moves from collaborative to transactional ❏

3. How many stages are there of key account management?
   a) one ❏
   b) five ❏
   c) ten ❏
   d) an infinite number ❏

4. Which of the following statements is applicable to Partnership KAM?
   a) supply and share of customer's business may approach 100 per cent ❏
   b) supplier and customer introduce new levels of confidentiality ❏
   c) sensitive information is shared ❏
   d) financial information is closely guarded ❏

5. Which of the following statements is applicable to Synergistic KAM?
   a) it is always easy to end the synergism ❏
   b) exit barriers on either side are high ❏
   c) the two companies remain distinct ❏
   d) there is a single entity, rather than two organizations ❏

6. Uncoupling KAM is the phrase used to describe a breaking down of the business relationship. Which of the following may be a cause of uncoupling?
a) changes in key personnel ❏
b) an improvement in product, process or people quality ❏
c) complacency ❏
d) financial problems ❏

7. A value managed relationship is one which:
a) is entirely dependent on the value of the sales ❏
b) sees the key account manager having a low profile in the relationship ❏
c) is a collaborative partnership aimed at retaining major customers ❏
d) is one whereby the supplier charges the customer for every service delivered ❏

8. Which of the following are competitive advantages from partnerships?
a) higher margins/higher prices ❏
b) security of supply ❏
c) blocking competitors ❏
d) none of the above ❏

9. The Ashridge research developed an easy-to-remember model of successful partnership called:
a) RANGE ❏
b) REACH ❏
c) EXTENT ❏
d) SCOPE ❏

10. In a comparison between transactional and relationship key account management, which of the following statements is true?
a) transactional KAM focuses on sales ❏
b) relationship KAM has low service levels ❏
c) relationship KAM is adversarial ❏
d) transactional KAM is short timescale ❏

WEEK 3

Successful Negotiating
In A Week

Introduction

There was a time, not that long ago, when negotiation was seen, in the main, as the province of industrial relations folk and car sales advisers. But, no longer!

Repeated financial crises have squeezed profit margins and, in some markets, discouraged buyers from making marginal purchases or continuing habitual expenditure. Managers have found themselves in the frontline of the expectation to achieve better value for money, and the starting point for this is to shop around and explore the offers made by new suppliers, and/or to negotiate better deals with existing suppliers.

Even if your job doesn't involve negotiation, then you might still be an active negotiator when replacing your car, moving house or even selling last season's wardrobe.

The truth is that being a good negotiator has become a life skill, enabling those who are good at it not just to save money, but also to upgrade their computer, television or lawnmower with little or no increase in outgoings – and enhancing their reputation in the process.

Becoming an effective negotiator is certainly within the scope of the majority of people. At its simplest, it involves thinking out what you want, planning how you'd like to get it and developing your powers of persuasion to convince other people that you are simply being reasonable.

So, how do top negotiators achieve their top results?

Well, the starting point is to eradicate some 'no-nos' that could provide obstacles to an agreement. One such no-no is agreeing to meet on the 'opponent's' territory rather than making them travel to yours (where they will feel less comfortable and relaxed and are likely, therefore, to be at a disadvantage). This might just generate additional worries for them, but could also result in aggressive behaviours or even sheer obstinacy ('If that's your game, I'll be blowed if I'm going to co-operate with it').

Then there's the win/lose style (another no-no), which gives no allowances or benefits to the other party – for example, setting extreme demands and becoming confrontational in defence of them. These experiences can sound odd ('Do people really behave like that?' you might say), but when they are under pressure, people can always behave in unpredictable ways.

Week 3 of this book will help you to plan to become a better negotiator through:

- becoming better prepared for meetings
- planning clear and realistic objectives for a negotiation
- maintaining concentration
- and making logical proposals that create agreement in the other party.

None of this requires a move towards the 'dark arts' or using dishonest strategies – the best negotiators often turn out to be quite ordinary folk who are committed to gaining better results.

Our attitude to negotiation is critical because it can make a substantial difference to how we see:

- the solution
- our 'opponents'
- the outcome we would like to achieve.

'Super deals' sometimes make the newspaper headlines, but so too do disasters:

> *Unions flex muscles as bosses plan new pay round*
>
> *Multinational puts small supplier out of business*
>
> *Super salesman sells 'dud' chemicals*

Many people's reaction to such headlines is:
'If that is what it takes to be a negotiator, you can count me out!'

The fact is that every day many millions of deals are struck that do not lead to strikes, breaches of contract, high court actions, divorces or suicides.

There is always a possibility, though, that something could go wrong – and it is wise to ask yourself about this before setting up a negotiation.

Finally, it is important to remember that negotiating may not be essential (or even desirable) in every situation. Other approaches or outcomes could include:

- acceptance by the other party
- consulting them (this could result in erosion of possible objections)
- selling the idea (a simple, but effective method of persuasion)
- imposition (not nice – but sometimes necessary in a crisis situation)
- arbitration by another, mutually acceptable and appointed, party (result is usually binding)
- mediation through a neutral third party (who provides an additional communication channel)
- alternative dispute resolution – useful when all else fails and the parties want to avoid recourse to the law.

Peter Fleming

SUNDAY

Create the right environment

You will be more likely to be successful if you know how to create the right environment for negotiation to take place.

Before setting out on a negotiation strategy, it is important to review your motivations for wanting to negotiate in the first place.

Did you identify strongly with the ideas expressed in the Introduction and now want to put them into practice? Or, maybe, you are planning a new 'attack' on your department's objectives (cost controls, sales revenues or even reorganizing work routines) and you fear that there might be some negative reactions.

This first chapter will help you to set up the best environment for a negotiation, so that you avoid distractions and negative factors that can reduce the chances of a successful outcome. This includes:

● reviewing your own attitudes to a negotiation
● creating the best atmosphere for the meeting
● selecting the best time
● selecting the best place.

SUNDAY

MONDAY

TUESDAY

WEDNESDAY

THURSDAY

FRIDAY

SATURDAY

Review your own attitudes

Say, for example, your manager has told you to cut back your team's hours, and the best way to do this would be to make someone redundant. You are concerned that this will cause negative attitudes or even conflict among your team, making you feel that you have to be more insistent and take a more hard-line attitude. This, in turn, might make change more difficult and result in a bad working atmosphere.

Alternatively, you could take a softer, more consultative line, which might bring constructive ideas from the team and engender a better atmosphere. It may even lead, for example, to everyone agreeing to a cut in their hours to 'save' their colleague.

Create the right atmosphere

Experienced negotiators recognize that there are four possible outcomes to a negotiation:

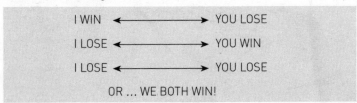

I WIN ⟷ YOU LOSE

I LOSE ⟷ YOU WIN

I LOSE ⟷ YOU LOSE

OR ... WE BOTH WIN!

Most people would prefer not to be losers – unless they have unusual motives – and the risk of 'losing' divides negotiators into three categories; those who are:

- **competitive** and want to win at everything
- **collaborative** and want to achieve the best deal for both or all parties
- **consensual** as they put the importance of maintaining good relationships above any issues that could threaten to divide the parties.

If your role or aim is the continuing development of your business, goodwill or relationships, the collaborative style will bring better, longer-lasting relationships and results.

So, the right atmosphere will be affected by:

● how you feel about the situation
● how you feel about your 'opponent'
● the relative power of the two parties
● your ability to cope with stressful situations
● your composure – especially with emotional pressure
● how much you trust each other
● your degree of open-mindedness
● your aspirations (Are you the sort of person who would wish to achieve better-than-average results?)
● how prepared you are to listen (as well as to speak)
● your charisma.

Incidentally, our use of the word 'opponent' does not mean 'pistols at dawn'! It is simply a shorthand word to describe the person with whom we are negotiating.

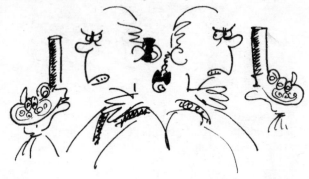

 *Remember that, if you want to achieve a win/win deal, your opponent needs to **want** to arrive at a satisfactory agreement too. You can influence this by the way you use the ten factors listed above.*

Choose the right time

The 'right time' to negotiate is probably when you have least need for a deal and your opponent's need is greater. However, collaborative negotiators minimize the 'fall out' from such

222

relationships. Otherwise, the opponent may feel 'beaten' and determined to beat you next time. Warfare of this kind can, unfortunately, go on for years.

Skilled negotiators:

- choose their timing carefully (avoiding the 'bull-in-a-china-shop' approach)
- patiently draw reluctant opponents to the negotiating table (it could take time)
- avoid spontaneous negotiation sessions (if at all possible)
- prepare their case carefully
- weigh up what they think may be on their opponent's agenda
- know their own limitations and those of their opponents (for example, are you 'sharper' in the mornings or in the evenings?).

Select the best place

The right place to negotiate is any place where you feel most comfortable and, as important, most confident.

This comfort factor involves more than just feeling at home. There may be times when your 'home territory' could provide you with disadvantages as well as advantages.

SUNDAY
MONDAY
TUESDAY
WEDNESDAY
THURSDAY
FRIDAY
SATURDAY

For example, you would prefer not to:

- be distracted by minor queries while trying to concentrate on the negotiation
- be interrupted by telephone calls
- allow your opponents to see the state of your workplace if it is chaotic or somewhat luxurious in their eyes (this might not impress them).

These factors may help to heighten your opponent's confidence and lower yours.

On the other hand, witnessing these things on your opponent's home ground may help you.

Meeting in neutral territory is often suggested by negotiators as an appropriate way of avoiding any bias in the meeting.

However, you should beware of:

- neutral territory that subsequently turns out to be your opponent's home ground
- being 'landed' in a situation where you do not feel comfortable.

Social situations can put some negotiators at a disadvantage, for example being invited to a more up market restaurant than they might have visited previously for a business negotiation – or vice versa!

SUNDAY

MONDAY

TUESDAY

WEDNESDAY

THURSDAY

FRIDAY

SATURDAY

Summary

So, let's summarize our progress today. You should think carefully about how to build a partnership with your opponent.

Look deeply within and ask yourself:

- Am I really seeking a win/win outcome?
- When will be the best time to negotiate?
- Are we/is our opponent in a hurry?
- How can we use time to our mutual benefit?
- What advantages are there in going to the other party to negotiate or in asking them to come to us?

These questions may seem obvious, but the art of negotiating lies in applying them to your own situation.
Try to relate them to a current project or need. For example, you may be thinking of changing your car. Which of these points might be of greatest help to you today?

ATMOSPHERE	TIME	PLACE
....	....	....
....	....	....
....	....	....
....	....	....

Negotiation is not a 'dark art' that should be avoided at all costs. It provides a useful skill that often enables a manager to achieve desirable outcomes with minimal disruption or expenditure.

Setting the scene is a vital part of this process – one that should not be minimized – and tomorrow we will work on more preparations that should contribute to a successful outcome.

Now try our multiple-choice questions to see how you have progressed.

Fact-check (answers at the back)

For each question, choose one preferred answer (tick the box), then go to the answers at the end of the book to score your choices.

If you chose second (or even third) best answers, then think about why these answers are not as good as our 'top rated' one(s).

1. How do you feel when you read of a major negotiation that has achieved an outstanding result?
a) There must have been some 'fiddling' going on. ❏
b) I'd like to have been around to see it because I bet it wasn't that easy! ❏
c) If they can do it, I'm sure I should find out more and give it a try. ❏
d) I bet they don't have all the constraints that are put on managers here. ❏

2. You have a supplier whose representative is very competitive; their product range is good but you only buy 'necessities' from them as the rep 'winds you up' by trying to make you buy things you don't think you need.
Should you:
a) continue to keep the rep at a distance and minimize the orders? ❏
b) avoid the rep by ordering online? ❏
c) get the problem 'off your chest' and give the rep a piece of your mind? ❏
d) politely, but firmly, explain to the rep that you might be prepared to place bigger orders but only on the condition that you will not be pressurized into purchasing items you do not need or want? ❏

3. Where will you have this conversation?
a) At a local hostelry at the rep's invitation. ❏
b) In your busy office where there are witnesses to record the conversation. ❏
c) In your quiet meeting room where you can both concentrate on making a 'new' start. ❏
d) In a personal letter addressed to the supplier company. ❏

4. You experienced bad traffic conditions on the way to work this morning and were an hour late. When you arrived, your assistant told you that your director had called to talk to you about a customer complaint – and seemed very cross.
Should you:
a) call on the phone and try to resolve the problem – starting with an apology for being late? ❏
b) go straight to the director's office and try to resolve the problem – starting with an apology for being late? ❏
c) ignore the situation and wait for the director to call again? ❏
d) delegate your assistant to deal with the problem? ❏

5. You are experiencing a very pressurized work period and are struggling to keep on top of things. You want to take on a new supplier but know little about them, as their base is at the other end of the country. Should you:

a) 'bite the bullet' by prioritizing the time and task; and learn about the supplier by visiting them before placing the order? ❏

b) ask for their Annual Report, placing the order if all seems in order and putting off the visit until things are quieter? ❏

c) ask them for the name of a referee or satisfied customer to gain an independent report? ❏

d) seek a third-hand report from your (independent) trade body? ❏

6. On your way into work today you noticed that one tyre on your car is almost flat. You had intended to book it into your regular service garage but forgot, and they are 'too busy' to collect it today. You called out an alternative 'emergency service' and the operative has removed the wheel (reporting that the tyre is dangerous) while he prices a replacement. You believe that the quoted price is twice the real cost. Should you:

a) pay up and put it down to experience? ❏

b) have a staff member block his vehicle in with the company van, to 'even up the playing field'? ❏

c) telephone your motoring club to check the normal cost and, if it is lower, tell the operative that that is what you believe the cost should be? ❏

d) stop taking risks with your own personal safety? ❏

7. You are naturally extrovert, preferring to deal openly with colleagues and team members. One of your team has just been elected by union members as a staff representative and you are worried about how this development might affect relations in the team. Would you:

a) warn the individual that you will not tolerate your team relations being 'contaminated' by extremist propaganda? ❏

b) check how many team members are also members of the union and warn any that are not members not to join? ❏

c) seek advice from your boss? ❏

d) welcome your colleague's preparedness to represent their colleagues in meetings/debates and offer your 'counselling support' if it should become necessary? ❏

8. You are visiting a customer in his office and are surprised that all the visitors' chairs are low chairs while the customer has a high adjustable chair. You feel that you would be at a disadvantage sitting on one of the low visitors' chairs.
Would you:

a) politely refuse to sit down, claiming a bad back and only relenting if your host can provide a higher or high-backed chair? ❏

b) reluctantly sit down on the low chair and hope that it will not put you at a disadvantage? ❏

c) explain that this can only be a quick call as you are expected elsewhere, but you'd like to invite the customer to lunch down the road? ❏

d) leave as soon as it seems polite/decent? ❏

9. Your boss asks you to attend a meeting in the office to agree a cost-saving plan – with a hint that redundancies may result. You are anxious to argue strongly against this but worry that your case will lose impact because of the constant interruptions that are common in the office.
Would you:

a) refuse to attend unless a quieter venue is found? ❏

b) book the boardroom, which is quiet and confidential? ❏

c) hide your doubts and determine to struggle on regardless? ❏

d) start looking for alternative vacancies in case someone in your team needs them? ❏

10. At the cost-saving meeting your boss accuses you of closing your mind to ways of improving productivity, over-identifying with your team members by defending their interests.
Would you:

a) seek support and advice from the local union organizer to protect your own position? ❏

b) present a case for recovery that involves a stronger marketing plan to improve revenue and margins, with milestones for monitoring progress (and with the aim of avoiding impetuous cuts)? ❏

c) propose a 'no replacement' policy, supposing that individual staff members might decide to chase better opportunities with your competitors? ❏

d) suggest an in-depth research project of methods used by competitors, which you could then emulate? ❏

SUNDAY
MONDAY
TUESDAY
WEDNESDAY
THURSDAY
FRIDAY
SATURDAY

MONDAY

Research your objectives

How do you take decisions? Are you a person who relies on instinct, feelings and emotion, or are you a person who chases down real facts and evidence to support your decisions?

Experienced managers may tell you that they just 'know' the best way to go with a strategy or plan because business goes in cycles and 'what goes around, comes around'! Is this a safe approach? Or should experienced personnel check their facts like anyone else?

Relying on instinct (or even 'luck') may work out well as much as 80 per cent of the time – but is that good enough? Probably not, especially if an incorrect decision could blow a hole in the organization's budget and lead to even more drastic action. And how long do you have to wait before you have enough experience to back 'instinct'?

Now, managers often find themselves having to take (or influence) decisions that involve deploying resources internally, or committing the organization to external action. In either case, it is probable that a commitment to the action will be needed from other people – and this may well mean a meeting involving a negotiation (even when there is no buying or selling intention). So, today, we are going to look closer at your negotiation objectives.

Have you ever considered when the worst time for doing the week's food shopping might be?

Is it:

- when the store is busiest?
- when stock is running out?
- when you are in a hurry?

If concern about impulse purchasing is uppermost in your mind, the answer has to be:

- when you are hungry!

Of course, you might always prepare a list before starting the shopping expedition – some people do, but many others do not. If you stand and observe your fellow shoppers at the checkout you can quickly identify those who probably did not bring a shopping list.

There is nothing wrong with buying products we like, but was this a conscious decision or did the final bill come as a shock? The objective shopper starts out with a checklist and then consciously buys any items that are not on the list.

Similarly, the skilled negotiator always prepares a checklist of objectives – a 'shopping list' – and uses it to compare actual results from meetings with those expected. Any move away

THE ITEM
YOU ORDERED
LAST
NIGHT, SIR

from the original plan is then a conscious decision and a target for trading off concessions from the opponent.

Skilled negotiators rarely negotiate without any kind of plan – and most produce detailed plans on anything but the back of an envelope or cigarette packet.

Prepare your own 'shopping list'

As the host, preparing for a dinner party may involve some or all of the following:

- deciding on a menu
- preparing a list of ingredients
- making a list of jobs to be done (and by whom)
- drawing up a seating plan
- sending out invitations.

Similarly, a decision to move house should lead us to prepare an objective plan. For example, you may have decided to move to a larger house – three-bedroomed, semi-detached with a garage – from your present two-bedroomed terraced house. You will probably start with a wishlist for the new house that might read as follows:

- two double bedrooms, one single
- two reception rooms downstairs
- a downstairs cloakroom
- separate garage – close to the house
- gas-fired central heating.

Of course, these items either exist or they do not – but the priority attached to them may vary and your view may be very different from that of your partner.

When house hunting we rarely find exactly what we want and this listing will probably provide an important basis for negotiation at home before you even visit a prospective vendor. The result of these discussions will be a baseline of standards or objectives, against which

various possibilities will be screened. You will probably not want to visit properties that do not come up to your expectations (although this is by no means certain – did your present accommodation exactly match your 'minimum' standards?).

Prepare your negotiation brief

Once you have selected a property you find attractive, you will need to produce a negotiating brief for both your purchase and your sale (if you have a property to sell). This will encompass:

- your objectives
- your best assessment of your opponent's objectives.

Plan your objectives

Establishing your own objectives will be relatively easy. Taking price as an example, the buyer's objective will be to obtain good value for money bearing in mind the need not to exceed market value. The buyer's parameters for price will be determined by the following.

At the 'upper end':

- available funds – from the sale of a current property
- any bridging finance available
- a personal loan from your favourite aunt
- how much you really want the property.

At the 'lower end':

- the lowest price you feel the vendor might consider without insulting him/her and causing the withdrawal of the property
- the price that you feel correctly matches current market activity
- a price that enables the vendor to meet his/her plans.

Assess your opponent's objectives

Assessing your opponent's objectives means carrying out some research – at best; and guessing – at worst!

The process requires the ability to put yourself in your opponent's position. For example, a vendor may have chosen to advertise a property at £180,000. It would be surprising (and unusual) if this did not include a 'fall-back position', which would allow for the agent's advice and the fact that some (if not all) potential buyers may make a lower offer.

So, the parameters for the sale may vary between:

(a) Price

Base limit	Ideal position
£162,000 ◄────────►	£180,000

The 'base limit' here represents 10 per cent discount on the asking price and could be lower if the vendor is desperate to sell, or if some fault is discovered in the building survey, say.

SUNDAY

MONDAY

TUESDAY

WEDNESDAY

THURSDAY

FRIDAY

SATURDAY

(b) Timing

Base limit   Ideal position

5–14th April ←————————→ 3–31st May

(This would allow for a holiday between 16th and 30th April)

Of course, there is a lot more at stake when we buy a house, such as how well our own furniture will fit into it and what it will 'feel' like when we are living there. Vendors are often keen to sell items of furnishings such as carpets and curtains and this can be very helpful if the move is a strictly budgeted affair. Expensive mistakes can be made here too:

(c) Furnishing and fittings

Base limit   Ideal position

Vendor 'gives'   Buyer pays vendor's
contents away ←————————→ valuation of £10,000
with agreed   for contents
house purchase

As we shall see later, goodwill between buyer and seller may have quite an effect in arriving at the most appropriate point of 'balance' between the two extremes on the three charts. Any breakdown or loss of confidence between the parties can lead to a lose/lose outcome.

Examples of lose/lose results could be:

● either party changing their mind and withdrawing from the transaction (leaving one party, or possibly both, with considerable professional fees to pay – and nothing to show for them)
● carpets and curtains (etc.) put into storage rather than being given away (leading to increased costs for the vendor)
● some items 'taken' by the vendor when the buyer expected them to be included in the price (leading to a rearguard action for restitution).

The effect of time

Time can have a crucial effect on the negotiation process, as we shall see later in the week. However, suffice to say here that a vendor who is being moved by his company (with a tight deadline) may be prepared to consider a lower offer if he is convinced that the contract can be speeded up (e.g. by a cash sale).

Equally, the vendor who is able to put his house contents into storage (bearing in mind his firm's willingness to pay the bill) may be prepared to meet the buyer's timetable, especially when sales activity is depressed.

How do you find out about such levers?

At its simplest, you need to ask:

● friends and family, etc.
● professional advisers (e.g. solicitors, agents, etc.)
● people who have moved recently
● your opponent/his family/friends/staff, etc.

'My opponent? Surely he or she will not tell you the truth,' you may say. That may be so, but exaggerations or understatements can easily be checked and being 'economical with the truth' may risk the breach of trust between the parties.

> **TIP** *The broader the issue on which you need to negotiate, the more valuable it is to consult with a wide range of people.*

In commercial negotiations the following consulting checklist may prove useful:

- past users of the product/service
- other experienced buyers/sellers
- present referees
- comparison agencies/publications
- advisers
- other people in your own organization (the Japanese use this method to great effect – especially with new business contacts)
- your opponent's own staff.

So, your negotiation brief should include:

- an agenda of issues to discuss
- your objectives expressed in terms of parameters
- questions to ask to reveal information about the negotiation or your opponent's position.

239

SUNDAY
MONDAY
TUESDAY
WEDNESDAY
THURSDAY
FRIDAY
SATURDAY

A negotiation brief is not paper for the sake of paper – a systematic approach will pay for itself over and over again.

Pre-meeting planning

The following checklist may help you avoid any loose ends.

Opening
- How should I open the meeting?
- How interested is our opponent in the meeting?
- What needs might exist?
  - Theirs
  - Ours
- What areas of common ground exist between us?

Authority
- Who am I meeting?
- What is the history/track record of the relationship?
- How much authority does my opponent have?

Power and influence
- What is their 'power' over us and/or our competitors?
- What is our power in this situation?
- How can we exploit our strengths for mutual benefit?

Commitment

- How interested is our opponent in the meeting?
- How badly do they need an agreement?
- Do we want/need agreement today?
- Will a negotiated agreement stick?

Competition/exclusivity

- How might market forces affect the negotiation?
- What leverage might be used?

Innovation and promotion

- What concessions are we likely to have to make to ensure that the deal is successful?
- How innovative are the proposals under discussion?
- Who will contribute what to help?

SUNDAY
MONDAY
TUESDAY
WEDNESDAY
THURSDAY
FRIDAY
SATURDAY

Summary

Researching and planning your objectives (and supporting facts) may not, on their own, produce a convincing argument. However, a negotiation plan – based on a reality that has been carefully and systematically compiled – should give the manager both confidence and a 'winning hand' (especially if your opponent is not as well prepared).

You will still need to prepare to introduce the facts as persuasively as possible, and, even then, you may need a fallback position – especially if your opponent decides to play hard ball or is rigidly attached to his/her position. There is a risk of a lose/lose outcome (perhaps no loan agreed, or the probability that your target property will be sold to someone else).

Now that you have worked through Monday's text, why not try out your own plans for a car change, a house move or perhaps where you would prefer to spend your summer holidays. The following template could help you with your planning.

SUNDAY

MONDAY

TUESDAY

WEDNESDAY

THURSDAY

FRIDAY

SATURDAY

Your objectives	Opponent's position
1	....
2	....
3	....
4	....
5	....

Concessions you can give	**Concessions you seek**
1	....
2	....
3	....
4	....
5	....

Questions I need to ask

1 ....

2 ....

3 ....

4 ....

5 ....

Fact-check (answers at the back)

For each question, choose one preferred answer (tick the box), then go to the answers at the end of the book to score your choices.

If you chose second (or even third) best answers, then think about why these answers are not as good as our 'top rated' one.

1. How much importance would you give to the following factors (if you were following the example of high-performance negotiators)?
   a) Your own negotiating position on the current topic. ❏
   b) Your opponent's position. ❏
   c) The venue for the negotiation. ❏
   d) All of the above are equally important. ❏

2. If you can choose the time and place for negotiating a 'significant' case, would you choose:
   a) the preferred time/venue of your opponent? ❏
   b) a location by mutual agreement? ❏
   c) your preferred time/venue (where you believe you'll be on your top form)? ❏
   d) anywhere and any time – it shouldn't matter! ❏

3. If your opponent's role is to try to agree a wide range of topics/items with you at the meeting, how should you protect yourself from being tempted away from meeting your own needs?
   a) Be open-minded and prepared to discuss anything. ❏
   b) Postpone the meeting until you have a definitive list from the other side. ❏
   c) Prepare a definitive list of subjects and your own goals with supporting arguments. ❏
   d) Don't do anything. ❏

4. Your negotiating brief should concentrate on defining:
   a) your least favourable positions – every other result would be a 'win' ❏
   b) some desirable results – taking into account any known outcomes that are defined ❏
   c) your most favourable position – every other result would be a 'lose' ❏
   d) all of the above. ❏

5. Which constraints should be considered when preparing your brief?
a) Predictions for financial/trade/world markets. ❏
b) Any likelihood of political pressure. ❏
c) Legal and/or social constraints. ❏
d) All of the above. ❏

6. Outcomes of a negotiation are mostly affected by:
a) how people feel at different times of the day ❏
b) the amount of effort both parties put into their preparation ❏
c) when the participants receive their 'pay' ❏
d) timing of the economic cycle. ❏

7. The suggestion that you could have a (better) offer from your opponent's competitor could be viewed as:
a) an unacceptable insult ❏
b) a powerful tool that always get results ❏
c) a perfectly acceptable 'lever' ❏
d) a one-way tactic that gives the 'user' an edge over the opponent. ❏

8. In negotiation, an agenda:
a) helps to provide a template for the topics for discussion ❏
b) provides a 'straitjacket' for what would otherwise be an interesting, free discussion ❏
c) could reduce opportunities for discussing new or additional needs ❏
d) should be prepared by the boss. ❏

9. A concession is:
a) something you give to make your opponent feel happier ❏
b) a demand you make to 'weaken' the other person's position ❏
c) a factor that you can exchange for a similar concession from your opponent ❏
d) a gift or 'sweetener' to ease agreement. ❏

10. Building flexibility into your negotiation brief:
a) helps ensure that the meeting will not result in a breakdown if either party 'digs in' ❏
b) gives confidence to both parties ❏
c) helps the parties explore alternative options leading to agreement around those that are acceptable to both ❏
d) enables another 'deputy' to take over if one negotiator is unable to conduct the negotiation. ❏

SUNDAY

MONDAY

TUESDAY

WEDNESDAY

THURSDAY

FRIDAY

SATURDAY

TUESDAY

People and places

Have you ever met someone with a 'magnetic' personality – someone who, whatever the situation, seems to carry other people with them?

While this characteristic may not be common, there is no doubt that people who have it can make highly effective negotiators. No matter what the issue or situation, they seem comfortable and persuasive and, most important, engaging.

We may not be able to copy such qualities, but we can develop some of the ways of behaving that can have a similar impact. For example, do you show an interest in others? Are you a good listener, but also someone who has an interesting point of view?

These qualities are invaluable if you are planning to persuade other people to agree with you or do something for you – important features of the work of the negotiator.

Salespeople have plenty of opportunities to practise persuading others. The best salespeople are those who have found a natural and acceptable way of selling themselves, which makes selling their product or proposals much easier.

Negotiation is not about having blazing rows with opponents, nor creating an icy atmosphere (although in some circumstances this might prove a useful tactic). To be successful, negotiators need to be able to persuade other people to agree with them and/or take action, and the successful salesperson undoubtedly has a head start over the rest of us.

Who am I?

Success in negotiation is affected by our ability to demonstrate the following skills and attributes. Rate yourself on this checklist by circling the figure that you feel represents your present skills:

FACTOR	LOW	HIGH
I am the kind of person who:		
1 presents myself as a person who likes people	1 2 3	4 5 6
2 is positive	1 2 3	4 5 6
3 is persistent ('No' can nearly always be turned into 'Maybe' and 'Maybe' into 'Yes')	1 2 3	4 5 6
4 is open-minded (there is always more than one way of achieving an objective)	1 2 3	4 5 6
5 has a good sense of timing and tact	1 2 3	4 5 6
6 has high aspirations for deals (skilled negotiators have high aspiration levels and tend to search for above-average agreements)	1 2 3	4 5 6
7 presents the case assertively	1 2 3	4 5 6
8 chooses the most persuasive words	1 2 3	4 5 6
9 thinks clearly under stress	1 2 3	4 5 6
10 influences the emotional atmosphere of meetings	1 2 3	4 5 6
11 maintains self-control	1 2 3	4 5 6
12 is decisive	1 2 3	4 5 6

You may not be good at *all* these things but, as this week progresses, awareness may encourage you to experiment, and practice makes perfect! But, be careful not to experiment in live negotiations, which could have a significant effect on your organization's objectives – well, not yet, anyway!

Today's topic is about your personal effectiveness in relations with others and how to identify the strengths and weaknesses of your opponents.

Personal communications and negotiations

One facet of personal effectiveness, when it is applied in negotiations, is the use of an appropriate communications style. There are two specific styles that are used by us all in everyday communication:

- the extrovert style
- the inductive style.

The first style relates to our attempts to persuade the person to do something by giving them lots of information – in effect, seeking to persuade by 'pushing' your opponent into a position.

The inductive style is concerned with trying to encourage your opponent to do something, by 'pulling' him or her towards that position. Clearly, this approach is more about manipulation and is more subtle than the extrovert style.

The extrovert style

Obvious characteristics of this style are shown below. This person:

- always has a say
- produces lots of ideas and suggestions
- may enjoy a discussion and argument
- quite likes to stir things up in a discussion
- may reveal inner thoughts regardless of the circumstances
- frequently gets his/her own way in conversations.

The style also has a down side that may dilute its effectiveness – especially in extreme cases. If opponents are to be persuaded rather than bludgeoned into submission, these characteristics need to be kept under control. The person may:

- take an aggressive approach to others
- be bluntly honest

- give as good as they get in an argument
- stick to a point of view having expressed it
- criticize others
- look for all the snags and problems in new ideas.

This style will be most successful, in the short term, when negotiators are working in a powerful situation (i.e. power is on their side) and in a competitive climate. However, if the relationship is dependent on goodwill for its continuing success, there may be a greater likelihood of bruised feelings resulting from the negotiation. This, in turn, may lead to more aggressive tactics being used by the opponent next time (i.e. 'tit for tat').

Characters of the 'old school' who have developed a reputation of being strong negotiators – with a measure of charisma in their personal make-up – may attract a high level of respect from other people. This is particularly noticeable in competitive organizations and in sales-oriented negotiations.

However, the style may not always transfer readily into non-aggressive environments and may lead to the isolation of the negotiator if the style is not appreciated by staff, senior managers, trade unionists or, indeed, customers.

The inductive style

As we have seen, this is the opposite communication style to the extrovert style and, as such, tends to be rather less predictable.

Its relative success is based on the principle that the more you are able to test out the attitudes and arguments of your opponents, the more likely you will be able to pinpoint weaknesses in their arguments. Indeed, the weaknesses may become clearer to them, thus enabling you to induce them to move towards your position.

This style will involve the following conversational skills:

- putting others at ease
- encouraging them to come up with lots of ideas
- being able to extend and develop those ideas
- encouraging a warm and friendly atmosphere
- giving credit and praise to others
- taking care to avoid upsetting others.

Do you know people like this? How do you feel about being in discussions with them? Can you imagine your probable response if they were to ask for your help? Most of us would probably be predisposed to help them.

This effect is enhanced further if you are also able to use clarifying behaviour in interactions with others, to ensure that there is a minimum of misunderstandings. This will involve:

- listening carefully to what others say
- checking that you have understood what they have been saying
- finding out what others are saying
- asking lots of open questions. (These are the ones that start with 'What', 'When', 'Who', 'Why', 'Where' and 'How'.)

Your effectiveness will be further enhanced if you are the sort of person who:

- admits to mistakes readily
- conciliates when things get heated
- admits to your weaknesses.

Finally, these skills should enable you to:

- obtain the information from others that you need in any negotiation situation.

The inductive style demonstrates the advantages of co-operating rather than competing with others.

SUNDAY
MONDAY
TUESDAY
WEDNESDAY
THURSDAY
FRIDAY
SATURDAY

Choose a style

There is no perfect style that will work in every situation. Both styles have advantages – for example, a sales representative will need to be reasonably extrovert to survive the various 'knocks' from clients.

Similarly, a negotiator involved in a much longer-term negotiation spread over, say, several months will need to adopt a softer, inductive role.

We should also bear in mind two other influences.

1. Make the relationship work

If your opponent is a natural extrovert who fills the time with lots of communication, you may find yourself in competition for 'air-time'. If this were to continue unabated, it could lead to increasing frustration, talking over each other and, eventually, conflict.

If two negotiators, whose natural styles lie in the extreme areas of the inductive style, were to meet to discuss a case there could be many questions asked by one party only to be met with more questions from the other.

In practice, people tend to use a mix of both styles, with plenty of give and take. In fact, the skilled negotiator will aim to develop expertise in both areas, so that he or she has complete flexibility and can move in and out of either approach depending on the needs of the opponent.

2. General cultural influences

Over the past decade, there has been a general move towards the inductive style in management and society in general. This may be attributable to a variety of influences:

- political neutralizing of some of the aggressive influences in the industrial relations field
- increased awareness of the importance of meeting the needs of others
- effects of the human relations school of management theory
- increased effects and support of management training.

SUNDAY

MONDAY

TUESDAY

WEDNESDAY

THURSDAY

FRIDAY

SATURDAY

TIP *Negotiators who are working in cultures other than their own need to adapt their style to suit the local customs and culture.*

Who is my opponent?

We have seen that knowing something about your opponent before the meeting will be an advantage to any negotiator. If we have met the person before we will be able to predict some of the possible levers and arguments that might be successful in the next round of discussions.

Aspects of communication style have already been discussed and we will now consider possible pressure points that could be applied to the debate.

All negotiations take place against a background of 'needs'; if needs did not exist then there would be little point in meeting to negotiate. To help you prepare for the meeting it would be useful to consider the needs of your opponent in more depth. There may also be a hidden agenda that will help you select a negotiation strategy.

The famous industrial psychologist Abraham Maslow identified a **hierarchy of needs** to explain why people are motivated to work in a modern industrialized environment:

The broad concept of the triangle is that we all need to survive, by satisfying the needs at the base of the triangle. Having satisfied these **physiological** needs our attention turns to the need for **security**, satisfied through the provision of adequate housing/accommodation. Both these factors may be satisfied through the earning of money, but the higher motivators such as **social needs**, **status** and **self-fulfilment** are not usually satisfied in this way.

The model is shown as a triangle to illustrate the fact that not everybody reaches the higher needs – indeed, some people become hooked on one particular need.

For example, your opponent may have a particularly liking for good food and, therefore, may be a lot more malleable after a good meal (at your expense, of course!). Others may be especially 'hooked' on status symbols and quickly identify your deal as a way in which they can be successful and earn a bigger company car or a status jump in the firm's hierarchy.

Equally manipulative is the industrial relations negotiator who holds a little in reserve to allow an opponent to feel victorious just when the union branch is about to re-elect its representatives or the management is considering the regrading of personnel professionals.

GO ON! TAKE IT!
TAKE MY LAST
1/16 PERCENT!
≈CHOKE!≈

So where should we meet?

At first sight this is a commonsense matter. Sales representatives might say they always expect to go to visit the buyer, and the management side of a joint industrial council might always expect to hold meetings in the boardroom.

Actually, the place of the meeting can make quite a difference to its 'comfort factor'. Some people seem to be able to fit into any environment and still behave confidently in business meetings. Others are intimidated by the very thought of having to negotiate on the opponent's ground.

So, playing 'home' or 'away' may have advantages to you and your opponent.

'Home' advantages

- You may feel more in control.
- You can control interruptions.
- You can orchestrate recesses.
- Back-up support is available should you need it.
- You can choose the office/location/layout to suit you.

'Away' advantages

- You may have the moral advantage in cases of late arrivals, etc.
- You have the chance to assess your opponent's workplace.
- Your opponent may make allowances as you are not on home ground.
- You can pressurize your opponent by suggesting that senior staff get involved to break any deadlocks.

Another alternative is to choose neutral territory. But, once again there may be some hidden advantages. For example, the lobby of a hotel may appear to be neutral until you discover that your opponent is a regular visitor there and is personally known to the manager, the restaurant manager, the head porter, the barman and even the waitress. This can be most impressive – and is intended to be!

Will any of this make any difference to the meeting? It could do. After all, if you are dependent on your opponent for a crucial piece of information on which to base the negotiated agreement, would you mistrust someone who is so obviously credible in this sophisticated environment?

Summary

Developing our 'people skills' may need time and patience, but the payback will be really worth the effort and the progress steps suggested below may help you achieve better results:

● Try to develop a greater interest in other people – what they have to say, and their experiences.

● Build up your own self-confidence as you show you are a good listener.

● Learn how to reveal a little more of your own personality.

● Develop your questioning skills, especially those 'open' questions (What? Where? When? How? – but not too many of the 'Whys' as they can appear confrontational).

You will find that as people respond better to your conversations they will talk more openly about their needs, making it much easier for you to show ways that these can be met.

SUNDAY

MONDAY

TUESDAY

WEDNESDAY

THURSDAY

FRIDAY

SATURDAY

**Plan your style
and
negotiation venue**

What do you know about your opponents?

Who will be involved? ....

Their preferred style	Your preferred style
....	....
....	....
....	....
....	....

Possible venues
Home: ....   **Away:** ....
Neutral
ground: ....

People who need to be briefed

....

....

....

....

....

....

Fact-check (answers at the back)

For each question, choose one preferred answer (tick the box), then go to the answers at the end of the book to score your choices.

If you chose second (or even third) best answers, then think about why these answers are not as good as our 'top rated' one.

1. Negotiation issues may be centred on the past or present but the results of the meeting will be most important to:
a) present issues and activities ❏
b) settlement of past difficulties ❏
c) future relationships ❏
d) past, present and future. ❏

2. Talking persuasively by negotiators is best achieved by:
a) becoming a good listener ❏
b) improving your questioning skills ❏
c) concentrating on being positive ❏
d) exploiting an irresistible personality. ❏

3. Having high aspirations in negotiation means:
a) trying to achieve win/win deals that are better than just 'average' ❏
b) being positive – even when there seems little to be positive about ❏
c) thinking clearly under stress ❏
d) being prepared to be 'pushy'. ❏

4. An extrovert personality will be most effective in negotiating with an opponent who:
a) uses an inductive communication style ❏
b) enjoys stirring things up in a conversation ❏
c) uses an extrovert style ❏
d) is able to extend the ideas of others. ❏

5. The application of a typical extrovert style in negotiating can result in:
a) a 'tit-for-tat' competition in successive meetings ❏
b) opponents concentrating on all the negative aspects of a proposal ❏
c) outstanding results – especially if power is on that person's side ❏
d) 'bruised' feelings on the part of the opponent if feeling obliged. ❏

6. Inductive-style negotiators benefit from:
a) revelations of focused information that may contradict the claims of the extrovert/uncontrolled negotiator ❏
b) more thorough exploration of options ❏
c) a general shift away from the extreme extrovert style in business culture ❏
d) shorter, but open, conversations with opponents. ❏

7. The style of communication you choose to use in a negotiation should be determined by:
a) the personality you have developed over the years ❏
b) the outcomes you are trying to achieve ❏
c) the communication style of your opponent ❏
d) your skills in asking/answering questions. ❏

8. Self-knowledge ...
a) makes it more difficult to influence the other person because you over-identify with their 'problem' ❏
b) enables you to get your own way in a negotiation ❏
c) guarantees that you know when to 'back off' ❏
d) enables you to recognize when you are in the presence of a rather better opponent. ❏

9. An analysis of the underlying needs of your opponent may reveal:
a) weaknesses in their case ❏
b) needs that you could satisfy with the current offer ❏
c) 'pressure points' that may persuade them into a deal ❏
d) opportunities to build the relationship over a longer time. ❏

10. The venue of the meeting should always be:
a) agreed as part of the planning for the negotiation ❏
b) on 'home' territory ❏
c) alternate – home or away – to be fair ❏
d) somewhere both parties are comfortable. ❏

SUNDAY

MONDAY

TUESDAY

WEDNESDAY

THURSDAY

FRIDAY

SATURDAY

WEDNESDAY

Break
the ice

As with many other business functions, negotiation results are influenced considerably by your planning effort (and, conversely, disappointing results are often caused by inadequate preparation).

Over the past three days' study we have explored the foundation plan of the meeting. Now it is time to open our meeting and begin the communication (talking, listening and non-verbal communication), which we hope will ultimately lead to an agreement.

Sometimes these foundations may seem to be ignored by experienced operators who still achieve good results. However, for the less experienced, it would be a mistake to jeopardize or compromise good results by cutting corners when planning a negotiation.

It is a mistake to undervalue the part that good presentation can play in setting the scene for the meeting and in making proposals, and it is easy to see why good communicators might believe that the preparation stages are less important. However, it has been said that if you fail to plan, you risk planning to fail! This can come as quite a shock to a persuasive communicator.

The way in which negotiators 'break the ice' at the start of a negotiation can have a big effect on the later stages of the meeting – so we are going to explore the twin aspects of:

● opening the meeting
● communicating.

Skills assessment

Results from the opening and the development of the early stages of a meeting will be affected by the following factors. Before working through today's pages, you might like to rate your current skills in each of these areas by circling the rating that you feel applies (and you might consider obtaining a comparison with the ratings of someone who knows you well):

Factor	Rarely Used			Always Used	
Establishing rapport – verbal and non-verbal	1	2	3	4	5
Establishing common ground	1	2	3	4	5
Exploring mutual objectives for the meeting	1	2	3	4	5
Building a joint agenda	1	2	3	4	5
Getting comfortable	1	2	3	4	5
Clarity of speech	1	2	3	4	5
Assertive behaviour	1	2	3	4	5
Avoidance of bias and tunnel vision	1	2	3	4	5
Maintaining flexibility	1	2	3	4	5
Listening for overtones and signals	1	2	3	4	5
Questioning skills	1	2	3	4	5
Controlling and reading body language	1	2	3	4	5

Your performance in each of these areas can be improved and will affect your results!

Opening the meeting

Creating the right atmosphere for the meeting will be important if it is to end in agreement. Tough issues can be sorted out without necessarily establishing an ice-cold atmosphere at the start; equally, if the players have not met before and the stakes are high, quite some time may be allocated to establishing an atmosphere of trust.

Two parties of two negotiators from businesses in the finance sector met recently for the first time to discuss transfer charges between their two organizations. Millions of pounds were at stake and, from the start, it was obvious that both sides were nervous about the possibility of making expensive mistakes.

To the surprise of both teams when they met in the hotel meeting room, all the participants looked similar, were of similar ages, had dressed alike, and came from similar backgrounds. All this became increasingly evident in the first 45 minutes of the meeting, which covered almost any topic except that which the meeting was about!

At this point, almost instinctively, the parties felt they had built up a feeling of trust, and they started on the agenda. Progress was then rapid and, to everyone's surprise, the meeting concluded in 1.5 hours with a win/win agreement and a celebratory lunch. The agreement endured for a year and provided a sound basis for subsequent renewals.

Establishing rapport

Meeting people for the first time – or indeed greeting someone we have met before – is normally accompanied by an appropriate choice of words and actions.

However, the way these things are done can be significant. Passing the time of day and, as important, using your opponent's name, are accepted customs in greeting – just as shaking hands provides an acceptable way of expressing warmth to the other person. We make some hidden judgements on the basis of these greetings:

- the firmness of the handshake – the 'crusher' or the 'wet fish'
- the distance between the parties when they shake hands
- the formality or informality of the greeting – varying from 'Good morning' to 'Hi' or 'G'day'

- the warmth of the facial expression when meeting – e.g. smiles can be open or, perhaps, cynical
- the extent of eye contact – open and level, or hooded and uncertain
- the appearance of the parties – the manner of dress, etc.

The golden rule in the area of appearance – for the best results – is to try not to breach any areas of known preference on the part of your opponent.

Common ground

It is always easier negotiating with someone you have met before because you may have some knowledge of that person's domestic circumstances, leisure interests, last holiday and/ or drive or motivation. The early stages of a meeting provide an excellent opportunity to catch up with what has been happening in your respective lives – domestically and, probably more importantly (from the point of view of the negotiation), in business – since you last met.

This episode should help both parties to rebuild common ground, which may be especially valuable if (or when) the going gets tough later in the meeting.

Obviously, a new contact needs careful nurturing, and the opportunity should be taken to find out a little about them without creating the impression of being either nosey or pushy.

The agenda

It is surprising how often negotiators get together with a mutual interest in meeting but without having established a common agenda at the start. This is probably because each negotiator tends to think of their own agenda as of paramount importance and superior to the other person's interests.

If the meeting is to be collaborative, then it is important to provide the opportunity for both participants to air their own agenda. Apart from anything else, it is quite a challenge to check your opponent's agenda against the items you expected to be raised when you prepared for the meeting.

This does not mean that every agenda item or objective has to be revealed at the start of the meeting, but failure to do so in a collaborative atmosphere will invite the questions, 'Why was this item concealed? Was it really a slip of the memory or has some advantage been sought by failing to reveal the topic?'

Physical comfort

The physical conditions of the meeting will also influence how comfortable (and possibly how co-operative) either party may feel, and this can be transferred readily to comfort with the deal itself. A variety of tactics may be adopted to win 'unfair' advantage over the opponent.

These usually only work when they are not too obvious and, by virtue of their exposure, they tend to become less effective the more they are used.

Examples are:

- your opponent's chair set at a lower level than yours
- your opponent having to look into the sun (or bright light)
- orchestrating interruptions when the going gets rough
- manipulating the temperature of the meeting room
- choosing a venue for the meeting which has distracting furnishings (e.g. walls decorated in, say, a vivid blue or orange)
- prominent positioning of a clock, which may give discussions a sense of time pressure.

How should you deal with these tricks if and when they arise?

In short, the best method is to let your opponent see that you have noticed the tactic and seek his/her approval to remove the influence. You can do this by correcting or neutralizing the influence and commenting on it to allow your opponent to understand that you have noticed the use of the tactic.

Communicating

The most obvious skills are sometimes those that cause most difficulty in meetings. The effectiveness of the talking and listening process is affected by a variety of factors:

- self-discipline in allowing your opponent to speak (giving them some 'air-time')
- the style you use in speaking (e.g. not too biased or self-opinionated)
- quality of listening, which is affected by factors such as interpretation and concentration
- your body language.

Talking

From our earliest years, talking is essential to our well-being, but how we talk in a negotiation meeting can have quite an effect on how we are perceived by those we meet. For example, the following request to the boss:

> 'I suppose it wouldn't be possible – I know this is probably not the best time to ask – to maybe find five minutes to get together to see if you could find your way clear to, perhaps, pay me an extra £10 per week?'

would probably be greeted by a simple 'No!'
A great deal of work has been done recently on helping people develop assertiveness skills – the example above demonstrates non-assertive behaviour: vague, apologetic and almost defeatist. Few skilled negotiators would contemplate using this approach.

Equally, making the following demand:

> 'If you don't pay the yard staff an extra £10 per week, you will be looking for a new team!'

HEY, WOLF! LET'S LOOK AT SOME ALTERNATIVE STRATEGIES!

could result in the response:

> 'If that's your attitude then perhaps that is the best thing for us to do!'

Skilled negotiators are more likely to use the following approach:

1 Q: 'When will the Board be looking at this year's pay review?'

2 A: 'It is scheduled for consideration in March.'

1 Q: 'How much are you proposing to include in the budget?'

2 A/Q: 'We will be under great pressure to find anything – given the present state of the market. How could the staff side make a contribution?'

1 A: 'If you are talking about productivity improvement, the staff need money on the table! However, if you have something to offer there may be scope for discussion.'

Assertive expression is based on our needs, and the use of 'we' is better than 'I'. In fact, self-opinionated negotiators who use an egotistical approach often find it difficult to persuade others to change their minds or adopt their proposals.

Similarly, emotional responses are best kept under control. The use of anger, for example, can make a short-term point in a meeting, but if it is overused it can obstruct a negotiated settlement – with a 'lose/lose' result. The golden rule is to keep cool, avoid rhetoric and provocative language and maintain self-control. This can be difficult if your opponent is hyped-up and determined to cause maximum disruption as a deliberate tactic. In such cases, a good defence is to slow

down interaction, make a conscious effort to avoid reaction and concentrate on non-confrontational language.

Listening

To say that it is essential to listen to interaction in negotiation meetings is to state the obvious. However, this can be harder than it seems. For a start, the process in any conversation can be difficult for some people; and when we are seeking a negotiated bargain it is complicated by the additional demands on our brain in the meeting.

Put simply, negotiator 1 makes a proposal to negotiator 2, who listens carefully to the point. However, as the statement is unfolding, negotiator 2 seeks to comprehend the point made – checking it against prior knowledge and experience and listening for the overtones in the expression – while also beginning to form a suitable reply and use an appropriate method (e.g. 'Shall I ask a question, make a statement or what?'). It is hardly surprising that points are missed in such circumstances – and sometimes our response may be totally irrelevant!

Why else can it go wrong? People have a habit of 'tuning out' – especially if they do not want to hear what is being said (try telling your teenage children to tidy their bedrooms, for example!). Others turn a deaf ear, making the right sounds while their brain is not really engaged and there is no real commitment to change.

And, lastly, we take the power of vocabulary for granted – especially the importance of using comprehensible language. Jargon, for example, needs to be avoided and it is essential that any words that are not understood by the opponent are immediately clarified. Here, again, is another valuable use of assertive questioning.

Tips for improving your listening skills include the following:

● Watch your opponent's lips while they are talking (and watch their eyes while you are talking – to gauge their reaction to what you are saying).
● Try to concentrate on the over-riding message in their contributions, rather than becoming bogged-down or distracted by individual words.
● Take notes to aid your concentration.
● Avoid trying to second-guess your opponent's statements or trying to finish off their statements (even in unison!).

- Categorize contributions received from your opponent (e.g. 'Is this contribution a question, summary, or proposal?') and plan an appropriate response.

These approaches will help your concentration and enable you to spot opportunities for discussion and for bargaining. For example, an innocuous discussion during the earlier part of a meeting with a client might reveal that:

1 'Yes, things have been pretty busy – we have just changed our computer system.'
2 'What kind of pressures has this brought? Strings of noughts on pay-slips?'
1 'No, but our bought ledger system has come to a halt.'

If you are proposing to supply this customer with a service or goods, be careful. You may decide on a contract easily enough, but may then have problems encouraging them to pay up! So, this signal should be followed up when it comes to agree terms of the contract at the end of the meeting.

Non-verbal communication

There are many other ways of communicating.

Body language, and the skills of reading it, has recently become a very popular topic among the business community. 'If we could read the minds of our opponents and be able to work out exactly what they are thinking and planning, we could achieve much better deals!' Unfortunately, it is not as easy as that because analysing body language is an imprecise science.

However, there are some simple signals that are useful to observe in negotiation, although the novice should be careful not to apply the meanings in a literal sense in every situation.

Face touches
It is said that in conversation about, say, the price of a service or goods, if the speaker accompanies a price quotation with a typical statement such as, 'This is my best offer' with a rub of the nose, a scratch of the chin, a wipe of the eye or a tug at the collar, it may be an untruth! The chances of this being so increase if a chain of these actions occurs one after the other. However, it should always be remembered that the speaker may have a cold (causing a constant nose irritation) or be feeling uncomfortable in a hot environment (hence the tug at the collar).

The moral here is that while it is sensible to observe and try to read your opponent's body language, it is best not to allow your hands too near your own face while negotiating!

Eye gaze
Level eye contact is often taken as an indication of honesty and, therefore, an interpretation could be that the negotiator may be trusted. However, eye gaze cannot be constant in one direction, or it may be interpreted as staring! Negotiators need to vary their use of eye contact, but it is essential when looking for reactions to ideas or trial proposals. Failure to make eye contact may protract a meeting simply because the signals that your opponent is prepared to accept your position go unnoticed. What signals? The occasional frown or flicker of a smile; the raising of an eyebrow or even the sharp return of a glance. We take many of these actions for granted, but, if observed, they may help us interpret progress in the negotiation.

Mirroring

Two people who are anxious to make a good impression on each other with the aim of a win/win deal may mirror each other's body position and movements. The explanation for this is that each party is sending signals to convince their opponent that they are very similar in terms of attitudes, values and aims.

This approach can have a significant effect, although it may only be subconscious. So, if your meeting is rather cold and you wish to try to relax your opponent, mirroring their body positioning may have a positive effect.

Hand movements

Many people speak with their hands and, while this is quite natural, it is important that such movements do not become extravagant or distracting to your opponent. A pen or pencil can provide a useful means of underlining a point – especially if the meeting has become emotional – but aggressive movements should be eliminated. Anything that causes irritation in an opponent is to be avoided as it may lead to non-acceptance of your proposals.

In general, open-handed expressions may be taken to underpin the sincerity of the speaker, whereas pointing or closed fists may reveal aggressive undertones in your opponent.

Summary

This chapter has explored the foundations of communication between the two parties in some detail, and it would be surprising if your self-examination has not identified some improvement goals that you might incorporate into an action plan.

We tend to take communication skills for granted and only recognize that we could improve them when we come across an opponent who is significantly better at it than us. Why not revisit the table at the beginning of 'Tuesday' to check if you need to update those grades, adding crosses against the target numbers (above your previous scores).

SUNDAY
MONDAY
TUESDAY
WEDNESDAY
THURSDAY
FRIDAY
SATURDAY

Fact-check (answers at the back)

For each question, choose one preferred answer (tick the box), then go to the answers at the end of the book to score your choices.

If you chose second (or even third) best answers, then think about why these answers are not as good as our 'top rated' one.

1. Opening a meeting or discussion will be much more effective if there is already an agreement about:
   a) its purpose ❑
   b) the agenda ❑
   c) who should attend ❑
   d) the venue for the meeting. ❑

2. Confirming the purpose of the meeting at the start will help:
   a) make everyone feel welcome ❑
   b) ensure that everyone is at the right meeting ❑
   c) enable additional items to be added to the agenda ❑
   d) ensure that everyone knows the range of contribution they should be making. ❑

3. Establishing rapport means:
   a) concentrating on speaking the same 'language' as your fellow attendees ❑
   b) getting on the same 'wavelength' as your colleagues at the meeting ❑
   c) reading other people's body language ❑
   d) being able to look each other in the eye. ❑

4. How you open the meeting can have a big impact on the level of trust you are able to build up and, consequently:
   a) how open your colleagues might be to accepting new ideas or refining/improving established ones ❑
   b) how long the meeting will take to reach its objectives ❑
   c) the acceptability of any new ideas proposed at the meeting ❑
   d) the level of agreement everyone is prepared to give. ❑

5. Building common ground with your opponent involves:
   a) ensuring that you are wearing clothes that will not offend the other person ❑
   b) avoiding any extreme language or subject matter that might offend your guests ❑
   c) concentrating discussion on the main agenda subject ❑
   d) sitting close together so that everyone feels committed to the meeting's objectives. ❑

6. Listening to your opponents in a negotiation is easier if you:
a) like them ❏
b) are committed to the subject they are talking about ❏
c) achieve a balanced talk/listen ratio ❏
d) are able to ignore the distractions around you. ❏

7. The agenda is the main guide for discussion topics at a negotiation meeting, and the main negotiators should:
a) avoid all other topics ❏
b) listen carefully for any new information that could have a bearing on outcomes/relationships between the parties ❏
c) be prepared to add in their own (additional) topics, especially if it seems likely they will be agreed upon ❏
d) avoid any discussion without a complete written agenda being agreed at the start. ❏

8. It is best if the negotiator takes the lead by dominating the discussion and doing most of the talking.
a) Wrong – both parties need to have their say. ❏
b) It is better to aim for a fair/natural balance (e.g. 55% to 45%). ❏
c) Correct, as being dominated could mean 'losing'. ❏
d) It is best to leave the conversation to take its own course. ❏

9. Analysing non-verbal communication (or body language) is over-rated.
a) Wrong – it can indicate issues that need clarifying or tackling. ❏
b) Correct – people should feel that they can behave naturally and not worry about being misread. ❏
c) Sometimes – uninhibited behaviour can be more persuasive. ❏
d) It requires expert training and disciplined observation. ❏

10. Negotiators who use hand movements to emphasize speech in negotiation meetings:
a) can distract the listener and mislead them ❏
b) should always be encouraged to behave naturally ❏
c) provide additional information that may signal issues for greater exploration ❏
d) should be encouraged to sit on their hands. ❏

THURSDAY

The agenda

Having opened our negotiation and made some inner judgements about the other party, we need to make some progress in discussing our agenda. Of course, this should be in the other party's interest too, and if this does not seem to be the case then the need for the meeting should be reassessed. Could it be that you have a reluctant partner to this negotiation – and, no matter how hard you try, the outcome will be a 'lose/lose'? The 'loss' may just be some time and effort – salespeople sometimes describe unwilling clients as 'time-wasters' – although their failure to 'qualify the customer' (ask questions to determine their interests, needs, preferences, timing, budget, etc.) in the first instance may have led directly to this situation.

Needs

We know that negotiation meetings are about resolving (or meeting) mutual needs. For example:

● you need to buy a new car and the dealer needs to sell one

or

● you need to obtain the reinstatement of a suspended work colleague and management needs to obtain staff support for overtime to meet a rush order.

On Wednesday we found that discussion meetings provide the opportunity for us to present our side of the case – to promote and defend our interests, to sell our position and the advantages of accepting it to the other side.

We will also have tried to draw from our opponent a description of their position so that we can begin to debate it, undermine it and make it seem impossible or unreasonable. While this is going on, our opponent may be trying the same tactic on us!

For example, a standard tactic when surveying a second-hand car is to fault the car by referring to the high mileage, worn tyres or rust-marked body. This softening-up process is designed to precede the making of a proposal or offer (often a rather low one!), but this tactic may be easily rebuffed if the vendor is prepared to cite the 'large number' of other potential buyers who have been in touch about the car. Is the buyer really interested, or not?

Assertive questions such as 'How can you justify this position?' may draw your opponent to reveal his or her arguments and aims in the negotiation. With persistent questions, difficulties in arriving at a mutually agreed strategy on his or her side may be revealed, thus enabling you to take the moral high ground or express the stronger (more persuasive) argument.

Dividing your opponent from his or her side becomes easier once you know that there may have been some difficulty on their part in arriving at an agreed negotiating strategy.

Of course, such debating points are reversible and you must be careful not to lay yourself open to the use of this approach by your opponent. So, any attempts by the vendor of the car to

sell it to your partner – who is loudly proclaiming enthusiasm for the vehicle – may cause you some difficulty when it comes to obtaining the best price or terms.

In reality, it is unlikely that your opponent will make any major moves for nothing, so you will need to demonstrate your preparedness to move in some way as a means of obtaining movement from your opponent. These signals should have been sent and received before beginning to form the proposals or offers that will lead to the final bargain.

Proposing

Today's session describes how to maintain progress in the meeting by making appropriate proposals. We will consider:

- timing
- encouraging proposals
- the best formula
- defending principles
- meeting inhibitions.

 All your preparation will prove its value in this vitally important stage.

Timing

There is a right time for proposals in a negotiation meeting, and experienced negotiators sense when the moment is right. This sense of timing is akin to the salesperson's ability to choose the right moment to close the sale. How we find this out, other than by trial and error, is analysed below.

Exhausting every avenue of discussion will eventually lead you to a stage when you have to make progress in the meeting, and making proposals is the next obvious step. However, this approach can feel overcautious and pedestrian, and may lead your opponent to become exasperated through lack of progress. (This can, of course, be turned to an advantage if your opponent is very anxious to conclude the meeting – a process that might be speeded up if he or she makes some quick and major concessions.)

When your meeting concerns an urgent issue and either or both negotiators have a strong sense of destiny, there will be an irresistible force moving the discussion towards agreement – especially if the parties have already expressed a strong desire to reach an agreement. In such a situation, proposals will flow naturally almost as a summary of each party's position.

The reverse of this natural progression rests in the truism described by Professor Parkinson (ref: Parkinson's Law) – that time taken for decisions is in inverse proportion to the costs incurred. Committees have been known to spend hours taking decisions about the replacement of canteen cups but only minutes on major decisions that few members understand!

The same can be true of negotiation: when small issues combine with ready quantities of time, progress in the meeting can be very slow – with as much attention given to the social objectives as the deal itself.

Finally, beware of the use of time as a major tactic in the meeting. Logical movement through the early stages of the meeting may be unattractive to so-called skilled negotiators, and this may lead to one of them suggesting a jump from base square to final square in one move. A simple, innocuous question might be asked:

'We are both busy people and I am sure we could close this deal very quickly – if you agree, of course?'
'Yes, that seems a good idea.'
'So, what is your bottom line?'

Revealing this position may make it difficult for the opponent to trade movement once the base position has been revealed. There will then be little alternative to agreeing to the initiator's proposals without breaking off negotiations altogether.

Encouraging proposals

If you feel that the time is right for proposals to be made but are not sure whether this feeling is mutual, you can always ask! Handholding skills (i.e. encouraging the opponent to feel that you are trustworthy, and are not trying to lay a trap) are valuable in negotiation. Apart from giving the other side the opportunity to drive the meeting, encouraging them to make leading proposals in an open atmosphere will help progress to be made.

Such a step needs to be accompanied by appropriate non-verbal signals – warm smiles, gentle nods and a high level of attention (eye contact and slightly laid-back body position but facing the opponent).

Who should make the first proposal – and what that should be – is an issue that can give the inexperienced negotiator some concern. After all, there is little pleasure in feeling that your first 'bid' was too high and, through speed of acceptance by the other party, that you are paying more than you needed to.

A major aim of the early discussion stage in the meeting is to tease out the other party's position on each agenda item – and the arguments used to defend them. This may well indicate that, say, the vendor's preferred price is going to be totally beyond the resources of the buyer and some concessionary proposal is necessary to keep the buyer in the meeting. (A similar argument can be advanced for the buyer who tries to introduce a very low offer – risking insulting the vendor.)

So, the opening stance is recognized as the position that would bring most benefit for the proposer's party – the debate will doubtless seek movement towards the opponent's position – and the best format for this is when both parties move towards each other, trading concessions.

The best formula

Phrasing of proposals is crucial. The best formula is to present your proposals using a conditional approach. For example:

'*If* you will give us payment terms of 30 days, *then* we will meet your price request.'

Now, this proposal may seem rather bald – especially without examples of the earlier conversation. When a bridge is needed between the discussion part of the meeting and concluding the bargain, either party may introduce trial proposals. These will suggest tentative ways forward without necessarily burning boats and risking earlier agreement by suggesting something that is not acceptable to the opponent.

A typical example might be:

'I'll tell you what we might be able to arrange: *if perhaps* you could find a way of speeding up payment – say, in 30 days – *then we might* be able to find a way of reducing the price.'

If this approach brings a constructive response, then it is likely to be followed swiftly by a formalized proposal along the lines of the first example above.

Defending principles and meeting inhibitions

It is at this stage that you might find your bottom line under attack or under threat of being compromised. For example,

HM Government made it clear after the Falklands War that sovereignty was not on the agenda for peace negotiations with Argentina and this would be a precondition for any future discussions.

There could be a risk that, while such a condition might be agreed, your opponent may reintroduce that element in the meeting itself, with the expectation that the constructive atmosphere might persuade negotiators to allow discussion of the issue. This clearly should not be accepted and the team would have to make it clear that approaches to put the subject on the agenda would jeopardize agreements on other issues.

At the same time, you must remember that your opponent is not an entirely free agent. He or she is representing another organization or party, with interests that may differ from your own. These interests will overlap – or there will be no point in attending the meeting – but it is obviously in your opponent's interests to persuade you to move from your ideal position.

For example, a client may complain about one of your service engineers whose behaviour on his premises has been the source of complaint from several of his staff. His initial approach may be to demand the withdrawal of that person ('Never send him here again!'), and this may be readily countered with an apology and a convincing promise to hold a full and thorough internal inquiry.

However, if we were to think through our opponent's position we would see that his organization has in it several people who would also like to see the back of the engineer. Failure on his part to sort out the issue could lead to a significant loss of face and credibility for your opponent. Such inhibitions can lead to apparent obstinacy and may make a win/win agreement more difficult to achieve if the client's inhibitions are not addressed.

Summary

We have seen in this chapter that proposals are vital to a negotiation, no matter how fundamental or extreme the issues under debate happen to be. There are many examples on record of negotiation teams becoming 'comfortable' in debating the issues, and conversation then seems to go round and round without any agreement or solution – except, maybe, an agreement for the location and timing of the next meeting!

If you find yourself to be a willing party to such a travesty, remember this truism:

Senior management/leadership can always exercise its right to change the delegated negotiators.

How might it feel and look to be the one of the people who has been replaced so peremptorily?

So, proposals are what make the negotiation move forward, and they need to be carefully planned and thought through; not arrived at in desperation without any concern for how they might be implemented.

SUNDAY
MONDAY
TUESDAY
WEDNESDAY
THURSDAY
FRIDAY
SATURDAY

Fact-check (answers at the back)

For each question, choose one preferred answer (tick the box), then go to the answers at the end of the book to score your choices.

If you chose second (or even third) best answers, then think about why these answers are not as good as our 'top rated' one.

1. The only way a negotiation can progress is through the use of:
   a) signals ❏
   b) collaborative relationships ❏
   c) proposals ❏
   d) summaries. ❏

2. When is the 'right' time to start making proposals?
   a) Any time, discovered through a process of trial and error. ❏
   b) When the issue, which needs resolution, is urgent. ❏
   c) When your 'opponent' starts proposing. ❏
   d) When you have a good idea of the needs of the other party. ❏

3. The statement, 'Supposing we were able to offer a discount of 5% if you committed to this purchase today', is a:
   a) dream ❏
   b) signal that your opponent is ready to make a move ❏
   c) proposal ❏
   d) trial proposal. ❏

4. Conditional proposals are based on the principle of:
   a) something for something ❏
   b) collaborative bargaining ❏
   c) win/lose ❏
   d) if..., then.... ❏

5. If your proposal is rejected by the other party, this means:
   a) They want you to improve your offer in some way. ❏
   b) The negotiation has failed. ❏
   c) You may have misunderstood their position and you need to clarify it. ❏
   d) The other party has a better proposal of their own. ❏

6. A very low offer or proposal could result in:
   a) insulting your opponents, and their withdrawal ❏
   b) beating your own objectives if it is accepted ❏
   c) a breakdown in relationships between the parties ❏
   d) a great reputation as a principled negotiator. ❏

7. Revealing that the value of a proposal lies outside your authority to accept, shows that:
   a) your opponent is talking to the wrong person ❏
   b) you have no better arguments ❏
   c) you have prepared a negotiation plan ❏
   d) a real obstacle exists to any agreement at this level. ❏

8. People who prefer to make the first proposal, invariably:
a) lose through revealing their hand too soon ❏
b) should be given a quick counter proposal ❏
c) are surprised when it isn't accepted ❏
d) win through leading the argument. ❏

9. Debating what seem to be minor points (and in considerable depth):
a) risks frustrating both parties and the withdrawal of one party (i.e. lose/lose) ❏
b) may reveal a lack of confidence (or knowledge) ❏
c) may hide a hope to win by causing the opponent to give in ❏
d) may lead to the opponent complaining to your boss. ❏

10. How should you react if your discussion reveals that your original preparation was inadequate?
a) Call a natural recess/break to enable you to catch up. ❏
b) Seek help from your boss. ❏
c) Quickly change the subject. ❏
d) Withdraw from discussion to avoid making an expensive or embarrassing mistake. ❏

FRIDAY

Conclude
the deal

It may seem trite when we reflect on the process described here – five days spent learning aspects of negotiation, leading towards a possible agreement – when a negotiation might be concluded in a street market in a matter of minutes! Doubtless, the location and complexity of the topic can have a big effect on the speed of progress in negotiating, but the skills we employ in street trading are closer to 'haggling' than to the professional style of debating the issues, seeking mutual movement and benefits, and ensuring that the agreement is worthwhile and long-lasting.

Few experienced negotiators can claim to have a totally trouble-free record in the deals they have arrived at (and then had to live with).

Experience can be an expensive teacher and this fact is what makes this last stage in the negotiation so important – the need to be able to close the meeting with agreements that are satisfactory to both sides (and with both parties clear and committed to the next stage – implementation).

Closing skills

There is little point in investing time in negotiation meetings if we cannot close them with satisfactory agreements. However, there are many people in the commercial world who make presentations with a view to selling a product or service, or buyers who invest time in meeting with sales representatives and those meetings not resulting in a contract.

The question is, do those involved ever discover why their closing rate is not higher? And can they do anything about it? In staff relations meetings there is less priority given to immediate results – they are often broken by recesses and adjournments, consultations between staff representatives and their members, and between personnel staff and their managers. But the same discipline applies here – if time is invested in meetings, then agreement must be the ultimate objective.

So, what are the skills we need to develop to close off a negotiation meeting satisfactorily? The following checklist may provide useful insights:

● Summarizing progress
● Resurrecting earlier issues for agreement

- Linking issues in the agreement
- Using concessions to improve the agreement
- Listening for concessions
- Using appropriate closing techniques.

TIP *Mistakes at the 'last fence' can be very expensive and frustrating. Make sure you are able to clear the last few hurdles cleanly so that you are satisfied with your performance!*

Summarizing
One little word!

It is not possible to do too much summarizing in a meeting. The fact is that many people become confused during negotiations and, even though one party has a clear belief in what has been agreed, it often happens that the opponent has a very different view of that same agreement. Both people were at the same meeting and yet there is still confusion and little unanimity – and this is very dangerous when the agreement is actually implemented.

Examples of things going wrong after the negotiations have stopped are legion. Buyers select colours of merchandise and plainly state the colours they do not want – and yet, somehow, those colours still arrive in deliveries. Similarly, sales representatives inform buyers about discount terms, and yet buyers still claim, once the invoice arrives, that they were not told about them.

Summaries help to clarify proposals and the terms of the agreement. You cannot have too many of them. Remember the one little word that provides the signal of a summary – 'so' – and try to use it:

- whenever the meeting ceases making progress
- when you are not sure what has been said or agreed
- when you feel that the time is right to begin to close the meeting.

Accuracy in summaries

When summaries are used in a meeting they can have an extraordinary effect. First, a summary often seems to fix the points stated and agreed – even though both sides know that the discussion is not yet finished. This can be very helpful when seeking to make speedy progress, but it is important for the summary to be accurate. If you include in your summary something that has not been agreed – even if you feel that you are taking artistic licence – there is a risk that the relationship between the two parties will be broken and trust breached.

Similarly, it is very important to listen to summaries given by your opponent. There is always a risk that something you believe has been agreed is left out or changed in the opponent's summary. If this happens it is important that the person who spots the error speaks out straight away, otherwise the change may be accepted into the agreement by default, and could cause major disruption towards the end of the meeting. This might not affect the ultimate agreement but it may leave either or both parties with a bad feeling and have a knock-on effect on future meetings.

TO RECAP, THEN – YOU'LL INCLUDE POSTAGE, GIFT WRAPPING AND A HOLIDAY IN MAURITIUS FOR MY WIFE & ME

Resurrection

By virtue of the fact that a strategic summary will be seen as a means of bringing the meeting towards a close, it provides a last opportunity to raise any items on which no progress was made earlier.

On Tuesday you will have rated yourself on persistence. This is an important quality for negotiators. The fact is that people who refuse to move earlier in a meeting may be a little more flexible when the end of the meeting is in sight. Also, the presentation of your case and the subtle temptation of concessions may encourage your opponent to be more flexible on issues that were sticking points before.

OH, AND LASTLY, MISS SMITH HAD A POINT ABOUT REFRESHMENTS

Linking

Linking one item with another is another method of obtaining movement on difficult issues. Most negotiators see their agenda as consisting of a variety of separate issues or objectives – indeed, many commercial deals involve the sale and purchase of several products or items, each of which needs to have been negotiated. It would be quite normal for the negotiators to achieve different deals on each item on the list, but it is also likely that either side may resist giving way on one particular item. A way out of this is to link one issue with another.

For example, a buyer may have agreed to pay a wholesaler £11 for a box of five reams of photocopying paper with an order of 100 boxes. He is pleased with this agreement as the price agreed is 50p a box less than he had expected to have to pay. Another item on his shopping list is some specialized bond paper for use in preparing and presenting reports. The wholesaler has offered a price of £18 a box, to which the buyer is not prepared to agree – his counter offer is £16. On the basis of negotiating the same quantity of paper, the buyer offers to increase the price on the copy paper by 25 Pence per box if the vendor will agree to a price of £16 for the bond.

Remember that everything is negotiable and you just need to persuade the other side to accept this to make progress with issues on which your opponent has inhibitions.

Using concessions

Concessions may provide a way of obtaining additional movement towards the end of the meeting. Skilled negotiators know to keep additional concessions up their sleeves to use in closing the meeting. These will be most effective where the concessions are cheap for you to give but very valuable to your opponent.

For example, if you have just sold your car – and therefore have cleared the cheque – you may be able to persuade your garage to extend the warranty on a new car for the all-in price that you agreed earlier, but now with the additional concession of a cash transaction.

Closing

Salespeople are frequently trained to close the sale, and a variety of methods exists to help achieve just that. However, if negotiators have done their job well the meeting will close itself. The best resolution of the meeting is when both parties have achieved what they set out to achieve and all that is left to do is to formalize the agreement.

This may not always happen, so it is sometimes necessary for the meeting to be nudged towards closure. Some common ways of achieving this are:

- calling a recess
- imposing a deadline
- threatening to pull out or call time
- asking for agreement
- the summary close.

Calling a recess

Making a decision about, and therefore committing to, the agreement that has been discussed often requires a little time and space. Reluctance from your opponent to agree to the deal may be overcome by planting the seeds of satisfaction in his or her mind and then allowing time for thought (with a view to allowing the seed to mature and flourish). If you have covered the ground well and summarized the areas of agreement, a short recess at this stage should bring a positive decision.

Imposing a deadline

If there is any doubt about the result of the recess it might be prudent to lay down some rules about the time for which the current offer will be valid. Clearly this approach may be viewed as pressurizing your opponent, but is quite justifiable when the time period is fair.

A typical example could be a quotation for a construction task that is dependent on the supply of the materials, for which the quotation assumes no price rises for the materials. Therefore the quoted price can only be valid for, say, one month.

Threatening to pull out

If one party believes that the other party needs the agreement, then a bluff to pull out of the meeting may work.

However, such orchestrated tactics can easily rebound on the bluffer if the timing or style of the threat is poor. You might easily find that you are allowed to go and are not called back!

SORRY- I HAVE TO SEE SOMEONE MORE IMPORTANT

On the other hand, it has been known for creative answers to be found to situations when the time has run out on the negotiating.

For example, when international negotiators spent 18 months trying to negotiate a Strategic Arms Limitation Treaty, and the self-imposed deadline was reached, the parties agreed to stop the clock for 36 hours – just sufficient time for the final agreement to be transacted. When they finished, the agreement was backdated to fit the original deadline!

Asking for agreement

A simple way of closing the deal is to ask for your opponent's agreement. At first sight this is such an obvious approach that it may be unclear why everyone doesn't use it all the time. 'Asking for the order' is a classic technique taught on most sales training courses. However, salespeople do not often use the approach, simply because of the risks of being turned down.

Actually, a rejection might not be the disaster it may seem. It may be possible to rescue the deal even at a late stage simply by asking 'Why?'. The answer may clarify your opponent's objections, giving you one last chance to bring the negotiation to a satisfactory conclusion.

The summary close

Finally, the closing point for the meeting should be summarized. The skills for this have been described earlier today.

A cautionary note!

Don't forget that your opponent enjoys a free will to agree or not to agree! Even though you may have worked hard and concluded a good deal, your opponent is still acting for his or her reasons, not yours. This may be worth bearing in mind if you are feeling euphoric when you start to evaluate the deal.

Confirming

Even when your meeting seems to have closed with a full-hearted agreement, there are still risks that the implementation of the agreement will be faulty. The success of the negotiation lies in this process and it is probably hard – with the euphoria of a successful outcome – to turn your mind to what can go wrong.

However, things do go wrong, often for no sinister reason. The parties' recollection of what was agreed may be inadequate, but if the performance of the agreement does not meet either sides' expectations it would be quite understandable if underlying motives were questioned.

Solutions to avoiding these problems include:
- taking and exchanging notes
- getting the agreement in writing
- checking that minutes and opponent's notes agree with your notes
- taking care with the small print.

Taking and exchanging notes

It isn't easy to contribute to a negotiation meeting – talking, listening and making notes – but working notes of the meeting will be an essential foundation for any subsequent agreement or contract. In the commercial world, it is quite usual for a representative's memorandum of sale and a buyer's order to be drafted during the meeting and exchanged at the end. This provides the first check that both sides have a common understanding of what has been agreed and, with experience and trust built up over time, one side may be prepared to accept the other's notes.

In staff relations meetings it is common for both parties to nominate their own secretary to take minutes of the meeting, and the notes are then used to form the ultimate record of the meeting.

Get it in writing!

Even when notes have been exchanged at the end of the meeting it is still important for a formal record of the agreement to be exchanged. Most negotiations commit two organizations as well as the various players, and formal records will need to be exchanged.

Confirmations may take the form of:

- purchase requisitions
- sales order notes
- minutes of meetings
- letters of confirmation
- revised proposals (bringing letters of acceptance)
- formal contracts
- joint communiqués or treaties
- procedural agreements and bargains.

A cautionary check is to ask yourself:

'Am I covered in law if anything should go wrong? Who could I sue?'

This is not to say that you would wish to sue – most disputes between contractors are resolved by negotiation. But skilled negotiators will not put themselves into a position where they have no recourse if the opponent should renege on the agreement.

Check confirmations agree with your notes

How often have you attended meetings and failed to recognize the minutes when they have been released some time later? Unfortunately, those who have the responsibility to prepare the notes are sometimes tempted to misuse that power to rewrite them to suit their preferred position – subsequent to the meeting. Even if deception is not intended, subtle changes may take place to meet the political inhibitions of the boss, the organization or even some of the people present. Where changes have been noted, and where these affect the letter or spirit of the agreement, a loud complaint should be made, officially. Any apathy here may be taken as acceptance of the new situation.

Take care with the small print

One major company in the North of England employs a whole department of lawyers whose main task is to check buying agreements and ensure that their own terms and conditions are supreme over those of their suppliers. The consequence of this is that any small supplier is unlikely to be able to achieve any variation to those terms and may be faced with the stark choice of contracting on the buyer's terms or not at all.

We would all prefer that contractual breakdowns did not lead to recourse to the law – this can be very expensive in time and money – but the larger the contract the better it would be to ensure that the worst consequences of failure do not leave you totally exposed to losses. For this reason, penalty clauses are often found in construction contracts, restraint of trade in personal contracts and even clauses allowing actions for damages against trade union bodies where the continuity of supply of a service is affected by a trade dispute.

Summary

A 'win/win' result is usually the objective of every negotiator who is aiming for repeat business and the building of goodwill. It matters not whether the sums or issues are small or gargantuan – alliances are built by mutual trust and benefit for both parties, and can be reflected on with mutual pride and trust.

This may sound trite, but it is not difficult to find cases where one party's greed or 'sharp practices' has led to the breakdown of trust, loss of repeat business – and even court action (to say nothing of all that appalling publicity). No one in their right mind would desire that, but the consequences of getting it wrong are what makes this negotiation skill so important (and the negotiator highly responsible).

It has been said that the combination of an industry-leading strategy and excellent negotiators can bring world-beating results. Unfortunately, the opposite is also true!

If you want to enhance your reputation in your organization or industry, you could do a lot worse than follow the advice in this book!

SUNDAY

MONDAY

TUESDAY

WEDNESDAY

THURSDAY

FRIDAY

SATURDAY

Fact-check (answers at the back)

For each question, choose one preferred answer (tick the box), then go to the answers at the end of the book to score your choices.

If you chose second (or even third) best answers, then think about why these answers are not as good as our 'top rated' one.

1. When you hear the word 'so' you should:
   a) ignore it – only your summary is important ❏
   b) insist that what is said is put into writing before you agree ❏
   c) listen carefully, as your opponent is about to summarize and you'll need to reject it if you disagree with it ❏
   d) be prepared to reject the proposal. ❏

2. Resurrecting earlier issues towards the end of the meeting:
   a) risks spoiling the whole agreement ❏
   b) may lead to a fuller agreement if the atmosphere is more constructive ❏
   c) should be avoided for fear of causing the other party to walk out ❏
   d) provides a way out of an impasse or stalemate. ❏

3. When facing potential deadlock, a recess will:
   a) be a waste of time ❏
   b) enable both sides to relax ❏
   c) create a solution for the final agreement ❏
   d) provide an opportunity to do some creative thinking and maybe seek further information or advice. ❏

4. In recognizing a degree of uncertainty/nervousness in your opponent's reluctance to reach agreement, the best option is to:
   a) impose a time deadline ❏
   b) threaten to put the matter to their senior management ❏
   c) give specific reassurances on how any 'losses' will be mitigated (e.g. through guarantees) ❏
   d) threaten to escalate the case to your senior management. ❏

5. Forcing further concessions from the opposition after agreement has been reached (and on an issue that has been overlooked in discussion) would most likely:
   a) enhance the final deal for one party at the expense of the other ❏
   b) risk the whole agreement being cancelled ❏
   c) cause the other party to 'lose face' ❏
   d) achieve a great winning result. ❏

6. A good measure of success in a negotiation is the number of concessions that could have been made but which remained unused.
a) True. ❏
b) True if both parties become aware of the total picture. ❏
c) Totally untrue – it's the quality of the outcome that's important. ❏
d) Untrue – it's the level of goodwill that has been further enhanced by the agreement. ❏

7. A satisfactory deal can sometimes be further improved by:
a) meeting on neutral territory ❏
b) exploring concessions that might not have been used by either side and that could be exchanged with mutual benefit ❏
c) negotiating over a meal (the other side paying the bill) ❏
d) having two different negotiators. ❏

8. However good – and complete – the negotiation, the proof of its success lies in:
a) the tactics used in the meeting ❏
b) the way the deal sounds to the 'boss' ❏
c) both parties' understanding of the agreement ❏
d) the written record. ❏

9. Successful implementation of a negotiated agreement is nearly always dependent on:
a) both parties' commitment to the deal ❏
b) the size of the deal ❏
c) the degree of trust that has been built up between the negotiators ❏
d) the scale of the risk of failure of implementation. ❏

10. The 'best pairing' of negotiators occurs when:
a) both are committed to a win/lose outcome ❏
b) both are highly rated as effective negotiators and they recognize this in each other ❏
c) their styles of interaction are very similar ❏
d) their styles of interaction are fully compatible. ❏

SATURDAY

Learn from your experiences

If life provides experiences from which we can learn and develop, this must be more true of negotiating than most other activities! However, human nature being what it is does not bring a guarantee that all of us learn from our experiences and apply those lessons. We have all met people who keep on repeating the same mistakes, even when those errors are blatantly obvious and pointed out to them. Is there anything we can do about this if it is in our nature?

Yes! When it comes to negotiating there are things we can (and should) do – starting with self-reflection, better preparation and more self-discipline in developing the skills outlined in this book.

Evaluating performance

Consider the following checklist, which may help you pinpoint your own strengths and weaknesses.

Preparation

1 Do I spend enough time preparing to negotiate?
2 Have I discussed the case with other people in my organization?
3 Have I researched my opponent's case?
4 Is there any additional information I may be able to collect from my opponent's organization?
5 Which outcome do I really want:

 win/win, win/lose or lose/lose?

6 Have I prepared a negotiation plan/brief?
7 What is on my objectives/shopping list?
8 What are the parameters for each objective?
9 Have I prioritized my objectives?
10 What concessions can I give?
11 Where will we meet?
12 Have I analysed the relative power positions of our two organizations?
13 When will be the best time to meet?

Know yourself

14 In what circumstances am I:

 ● most comfortable?
 ● least comfortable?

15 How easy do I find it to:

 ● take decisions?
 ● persuade others?
 ● be positive and persistent?
 ● choose the most persuasive words?
 ● think clearly under stress?
 ● control myself?

16 What motivates me? What 'Achilles' heels' might exist in me?
17 Am I a disciplined listener?
18 Am I tempted by a win/lose opportunity if I will be the winner?

Opening the meeting

19 How good am I at putting others at ease?
20 How good are my presentation skills?
21 Can I control and read body language?
22 How able am I to probe others for information?
23 Can I respond to others' probing without giving away anything of value?
24 How well am I able to develop a collaborative atmosphere in a meeting?
25 Have we established a common agenda and identified common ground?

The meeting

26 How well can I balance talking and listening?
27 How can I make the meeting layout work for me?
28 How good are my concentration and listening skills?
29 When might a recess be useful?
30 How can I make good use of interruptions?
31 Who is in control in the meeting?
32 Have I identified the best time to make proposals?
33 How good am I at introducing trial proposals?
34 How can I formulate counter-proposals to overtake my opponent's proposals?
35 Am I using 'If... then' and 'So' successfully?
36 When my opponent blocks my proposals, am I able to unblock them again?
37 How able am I to use the closing skills of:

- hand holding?
- summarizing?
- using late concessions?
- linking?

Don't forget that the real test of your negotiation meeting lies in the results, and that skilled negotiators have:

- a track record of significant success
- a low incidence of failure in the implementation of their agreements
- high ratings for effectiveness by both sides.

Continuing to grow

Negotiation is a practical skill. It is subject to the same characteristics as other skills – it gets rusty if it is not used and improves when used frequently. So, there are a number of steps that you as a negotiator can take to increase these skills:

- Take every opportunity to negotiate.
- Talk about negotiation with experienced people both inside and outside your organization.
- Read about negotiation. Look at:
  - newspaper articles for recent cases
  - trade magazines for technical sources
  - books and articles.
- Review your deals carefully and thoroughly.
- Attend a training course that enables you to obtain some feedback about your style and skills (preferably through the use of video). We look forward to meeting you soon at one of our workshops!

The truth is rarely pleasant, but the review process will be pointless if you indulge in self-deception. Check your objectives and those of your opponent that you know about – and make sure you do not make the same mistakes twice!
Finally, we wish you happy and successful negotiating!

WEEK 4

Successful Customer Care
In A Week

Introduction

No matter what type of business you are in, there is one irrefutable fact: if you don't look after your customers, then somebody else will. And that will probably be your competitor.

Never before has customer care been such an essential element of any successful, thriving business. Customers no longer have the mentality of 'put up and shut up'; if they're dissatisfied with your product or service, they *will* let you know one way or another. If you're lucky, they will tell you. This is fortunate indeed because it gives you the opportunity of putting right whatever is wrong and compensating the customer for their less-than-satisfactory experience. If you're unlucky, they will tell you with their feet – by walking away from you and towards an alternative supplier. Along the way, they will probably tell the world and his dog about their bad experience with your organization, and the resulting negative impact on your sales could be significant.

The bottom line is that it costs more to get new customers on board than it does to retain the loyalty, repeat business and recommendations of existing customers. When you focus on keeping your customers happy, there is invariably a positive, knock-on effect on sales. I've seen it happen in organizations where I've run customer care training for their staff and, within just two weeks, sales have taken a distinct upturn.

Even better is the news that customer care doesn't need to cost a lot of money to implement. Often, it's just a matter of mentally 'stepping into the customer's shoes', understanding what they want and then putting initiatives in place to deliver *more* than they expect. When you do this, you are achieving 'customer excellence'. You are positioning yourself as a market leader and as a caring organization, and your reputation will draw more business to you.

This Week will start you on your journey to becoming a market leader in customer care. We will explore all the different components involved and you will discover that there is far more to it than just how your staff interact with customers.

How do you know what your customers think of you and how can you find out? Feedback is essential in order to ensure that you are focusing on those aspects that are important to your customers. Assumptions won't work; you need to know for certain that any changes you are making are in the right areas – and those areas are determined by your customers.

Communication is such a core skill in customer care that it is vital to get it right. We incorporate proven Neuro-linguistic Programming (NLP) techniques that will enable you to build a powerful rapport rapidly, whether face to face, over the telephone or even in writing. You will learn about the VHF (visual, hearing, feeling) channels of communication and how to 'tune into your customer's wavelength'. You will even discover how JK Rowling uses this technique in all the Harry Potter books to gain a compelling rapport with her readers.

Most important of all, throughout the book, you will be encouraged to develop your own customer care initiatives to implement within your organization. This ensures that everything you are learning has a practical application and it will enable you to start achieving beneficial results in the shortest time.

Di McLanachan

SUNDAY

Customer care is more than just saying 'Have a nice day'

It would be very easy to believe that customer care is purely related to how your staff interact with customers and the quality of the service they deliver. However, it is far more than that. Your organization is giving out messages all the time that are interpreted as an attitude towards its customers.

For example, what first impression would a visitor to your organization gain? If you have a reception area, what does it look like? Are there dried-up potted plants, dirty coffee cups and a carpet that clearly hasn't been vacuumed for several days? Or is it clean and tidy, with comfortable seating and perhaps a framed copy of your mission statement on the wall?

Are your reception staff friendly and welcoming or would visitors feel like they are an inconvenience, interrupting a personal conversation by their presence?

What impression does your organization's website convey? Is it difficult to navigate with text errors dotted throughout the pages or does it look sharp, professional and user-friendly?

So start thinking about the overall impression that your organization sends out to past, present and potential future customers. In so doing, you will notice that customer care is very closely allied to marketing, in that the image you present is, in effect, your shop window to the world.

SUNDAY

MONDAY

TUESDAY

WEDNESDAY

THURSDAY

FRIDAY

SATURDAY

Imagine the scene

You're visiting a town that you used to know well some years ago.
You haven't been there for a long time but you remember that
there used to be a really good Italian restaurant on the high street
where you enjoyed many pleasant evenings with fabulous cuisine.
You decide that you will seek it out and have a meal there.

You head for the high street, and there is the restaurant, but
not quite as you remember it. It looks a little shabby – on the
sign outside a letter is missing from the word 'restaurant' so
that it now reads 'restaura t'. Undaunted, you step inside. It's
quiet – hardly any diners at all. You stand for a few moments,
expecting someone to greet you with a smile and usher you to
a table. You can see two waiting staff in the distance with their
backs to you, chatting and laughing together and completely
oblivious to your presence. You decide to approach them and,
in fact, you walk right up to them and say, 'Excuse me, table for
one, please?' before they are even aware that you exist.

On hearing you speak, they finish their conversation before
one of them turns to you, waves an arm in the direction of
several unoccupied tables and says, 'Anywhere you like.' You
head for a table near the window and become aware that
they have resumed their chat. You sit down and take in your
surroundings. The lighting is low, and you assume that this
is to create an ambience – until you notice that no fewer than

five light bulbs have blown and now remain unlit, still in their fittings. On further inspection, you notice the cobwebs that are delicately dangling from the ceiling chandelier.

There is a menu on the table and, despite the large coffee stain on it, the range of dishes on offer looks promising, so you decide to remain optimistic. One of the waiting staff ambles over after you have managed to make eye contact with him. You ask him what the soup of the day is. He hesitates, then turns his head and repeats your question in a raised voice to the waitress, who is now engrossed in sending a text message on her mobile phone. 'Minestrone,' she yells back, without bothering to look up.

You order a bowl of minestrone soup. Fish for your main course would be nice, except that it's off. Chicken, perhaps? No, they've run out of that too. You settle for lasagne and order a glass of wine.

On your table is a small vase of faded silk flowers. The waiter notices you looking at it, picks it up and thoughtfully blows a fine layer of dust off the petals before replacing it before you. 'Thank you,' you hear yourself say as you notice from his fingernails that he probably has a day job as a motor mechanic. In fact, your nose tells you that he must have rushed here straight from the garage without having the time to shower or use a deodorant.

As you sit back in your chair, you look around the room and realize that the décor is exactly the same as it was when you used to come here regularly, all those years ago. Yes, you're certain that this *is* the same wallpaper – it's just not making as much contact with the walls as it used to and one or two pieces are missing altogether.

The waiter returns with your glass of wine and you notice that whoever was last to drink out of this glass had been wearing a delightful shade of rose-pink lipstick.

The soup arrives – a full bowl – and as the waiter plonks it down on the table in front of you, it sloshes over the sides and spills onto the tablecloth. Fortunately, there are already other stains on the cloth so one more won't make any difference. And there's another bonus: there's no need to blow a cooling breath onto every spoonful before putting it in your mouth because it's not too hot at all. In fact, it's lukewarm.

The lasagne is a different prospect completely. Not only is the dish it arrives in far too hot to touch, but the pasta is crisp and curling up at the edges. You suspect it has been reheated in a microwave oven.

By now, your optimism has left you, along with your appetite. You decide to bring this experience to an end and ask for the bill. At least, you would ask for the bill if you could see anyone to ask. The two waiting staff have disappeared now, probably out of the building to have a cigarette.

Finally, you get the bill. You pay in cash, including a small tip that you feel obliged to give, even though the service, and in fact the whole experience, has been abysmal. You leave the money on the table and make for the door, uttering a 'goodbye' on the way there. Behind you is the unmistakeable sound of a deadpan voice saying, 'Have a nice day'.

Although there has been some exaggeration in the details of this story, you may have had a similar experience. You may have felt your heart sink when your favourite pub or restaurant put up a sign saying 'Under New Management'. You may have witnessed standards of care and quality declining, with the inevitable result that customers take their business elsewhere.

So let's explore all the factors that constitute customer care, using the restaurant story as an example.

Visual appearance

- The letter 'n' missing from the word 'restaurant' on the sign outside
- The five light bulbs that were no longer working
- Cobwebs dangling from the 'chandelier'
- The stained tablecloth
- The coffee stains on the menu
- The faded silk flowers covered in dust
- Wallpaper peeling off the walls.

There is a danger that if a problem isn't corrected shortly after it occurs, it starts to become invisible. That is, staff who are constantly around it stop noticing it, as was the case with the items listed above. When a customer arrives, seeing these things for the first time with 'fresh eyes', they form an impression that the business has a slapdash attitude to quality, which probably extends to everything else it does. The customer just might turn on their heel and leave right then.

If your business doesn't have physical premises that a customer would visit, then these principles apply to your website. How professional does it look? Is it easy to find a phone number on there if the customer wants to call you? In particular, check every page with a fine-tooth comb for text errors. I once worked with a family-run cleaning business that relied totally on their website to promote them. Even though they had reviewed every page when it was first created, I found 20 errors spread throughout the site. One in particular sent out an interesting message: instead of the text saying 'we will hoover around you' it read 'we will hover around you'! If your potential customer doesn't like the look of your website, they will leave and look for your competitors' sites instead.

Exercise

Review your organization's visual elements, both physical and virtual, as though you were a potential customer. When reviewing, you are looking at something again, with a greater attention to detail.

Attentiveness and helpfulness of staff

- The two waiting staff chatting instead of noticing a customer approaching
- The waiter who waved an arm in the direction of some empty tables instead of showing the customer to a specific table
- The waitress who was busy sending text messages in full view of the customers
- The waiter didn't know what the soup of the day was
- Dirty fingernails and lack of personal hygiene
- Both waiting staff disappeared, probably for a cigarette break
- The meaningless 'have a nice day' spoken with total insincerity.

Without doubt, staff attitude and behaviour towards customers is the key element in customer care. People buy people first, and even if the food in this restaurant had been superb, the experience was still damaged by the behaviour of the staff.

It is imperative that customer-facing staff *smile*. Here are five good reasons why:

1 **Smiling is contagious**. In a study carried out in Sweden, it was discovered that people found it difficult to frown when they were looking at others who were smiling. In fact, their facial muscles started twitching into smiles all on their own! If your staff smile at customers, there is a very strong chance that your customers will smile right back.

2 **Smiling releases endorphins.** Endorphins are the body's natural painkillers and have been found to be anywhere from 18 to 500 times as powerful as any man-made analgesic. Endorphins are non-addictive, can reduce feelings of stress and frustration and can even control cravings for chocolate and potentially addictive substances. In fact, they are the best (and legal) way to achieve a natural 'high'.

3 **Smiling boosts your mood**. Because the mind and body are inextricably linked, psychologists have found that even a forced smile will instantly lift your spirits. So smiling staff really are happy staff.

4 **Smiling is easier than frowning**. Your body has to work much harder and use far more muscles to produce a frown than to smile. Also, frowning is ageing whereas smiling lifts the face and makes you look younger.

5 **A smile can be heard over the telephone**. If you change the shape of your mouth, the voice coming out of it will sound different. Even if you can't see your customer, you can still smile at them down the phone and they *will* be able to hear that.

Quality of the product or service

- Lukewarm soup.
- Menu choices not available.
- Lasagne microwaved to a crisp.

SUNDAY

MONDAY

TUESDAY

WEDNESDAY

THURSDAY

FRIDAY

SATURDAY

In the restaurant example, the food would have needed to be outstandingly good to compensate for everything else that was lacking. It wasn't. And I'm sure our customer never set foot in there again.

However, people often behave in an interesting way in restaurants. Perhaps you've had it happen that you and a companion order your meal, it arrives and, while you're eating, you both comment that the quality isn't as good as it could be. Just then, the waiter appears and asks if everything is okay and you hear yourself saying, 'Yes, fine, thank you'. Perhaps you don't want to make a fuss, and what could the waiter do about it anyway? So you say nothing, but you take your custom elsewhere. The waiter, who hasn't personally tasted the food he put in front of you, is unaware that there is a quality issue. He only knows that the restaurant doesn't get as busy as it used to, but assumes that this is just a sign of the present 'economic climate' out there.

It is very, very important to not only maintain your existing standards of quality but also to seek continuous improvement. It's too easy to become complacent, to unwittingly allow standards to slip and then have the uphill struggle of trying to recover your previous good reputation and tempt 'lost' customers to return to you. Even from an economic standpoint, it costs more to get new customers on board than it does to retain existing ones. Get your customer care right and you can reduce your marketing costs.

Summary

In this chapter, we have explored some of the many components of customer care. We've seen that it is not just about how the staff conduct themselves; it is also about how the organization conducts itself.

We have highlighted three key focus areas – visual appearance, attentiveness and helpfulness of staff, and quality of product or service. They work well as starting points for achieving excellent customer care.

What are your competitors doing in these three areas? If you've ever lost even one customer to a competitor, why was that? You need to know what your competitors are doing, how they're doing it and how you can do it even better. This is valuable *research*; every organization does it.

Competition is the best incentive there can be to keep you on your toes with customer care. It can give you ideas for quality initiatives that you wouldn't otherwise have thought of – you may not be in the same industry, but could their ideas 'map across' to you?

SUNDAY
MONDAY
TUESDAY
WEDNESDAY
THURSDAY
FRIDAY
SATURDAY

Fact-check (answers at the back)

Note: all questions require a single answer.

1. Which statement is true?
a) The visual appearance of your business makes no difference to customer perceptions. ❏
b) Attention to detail is nit-picking, time wasting and unnecessary. ❏
c) Customers see your business with 'fresh eyes' and notice things you don't see. ❏
d) The cleanliness of your business premises is of little importance. ❏

2. Which statement is true?
a) It costs more to keep existing customers happy than it does to attract new customers. ❏
b) It costs more to generate new customers than it does to retain existing ones. ❏
c) Customers are naturally loyal and will always overlook your failings. ❏
d) Customer care and marketing are completely separate functions. ❏

3. Which statement is true?
a) Nobody will notice the occasional text error in your website. ❏
b) A website is just a marketing tool; it has nothing to do with customer care. ❏
c) As long as you have a website, you don't need to publish your phone number. ❏
d) Your website is your organization's shop window to the world. ❏

4. Which statement is true?
a) Personal appearance and hygiene are very important for customer-facing staff. ❏
b) If staff don't feel like being attentive to customers, they needn't be. ❏
c) 'Have a nice day' always works well, spoken in any tone of voice. ❏
d) As long as you have wished your customer a nice day, you have fulfilled all your customer care responsibilities. ❏

5. Which statement is true?
a) Customer care begins
and ends with your
customer-facing staff. ❏
b) Customer care is about
how your staff and your
organization conduct
themselves. ❏
c) Customer care is a nice
idea that will probably
just happen anyway. ❏
d) Customers are an
inconvenience and
interruption to the
working day. ❏

SUNDAY

MONDAY

TUESDAY

WEDNESDAY

THURSDAY

FRIDAY

SATURDAY

MONDAY

How do you measure up?

If I were to ask you how your organization is performing, you would probably refer me to the last set of annual accounts. You would be able to give me figures for annual turnover, gross profit, net profit and so on. Departments within your organization will have budgets allocated to them, within which they must contain all their operating expenses. No doubt they track actual against planned on an ongoing basis so that any remedial actions can be taken as appropriate.

In short, because money is tangible and relatively easy to measure, it gets measured. However, it should be said that a set of accounts can only ever represent past performance – like looking in a rear-view mirror while driving forwards.

Customer care is less tangible than money, and therefore it is not as easy to measure. Because of this, it often gets overlooked as a measure of performance. Managers are unlikely to have a monthly or yearly plan for customer care against which their actual performance can be measured, yet if any department significantly underperforms in this area, there could potentially be a serious impact to the organization's financial results.

In this chapter, we will explore ways of creating and implementing customer service standards throughout your organization to nurture a consistent, conscientious approach to customer care.

Common sense

Customer care should just be a matter of common sense; it is, after all, about treating others in the way you would like to be treated. How difficult can that be? However, what is common sense to one person is not common sense to another, hence the need for standards.

If your business is engaged in the manufacture of a product, then you probably already have quality standards in place, for example ISO 9001. But do you also have customer service standards to supplement these? The British Standards Institution has published a Customer Service Code of Practice, BS 8477, which is intended for guidance and recommendation rather than being a compliance document.

If your business is service based, then the quality of your customer service is key to the operating success of your organization. According to the Institute of Customer Service (ICS), service standards 'help to define what a customer can expect and remind management and employees of the challenge and obligations that they face'. The ICS goes on to recommend that service standards need to be defined in terms of the following three areas:

- timeliness
- accuracy
- appropriateness.

Let's look at each of these in turn, and explore exactly what they mean.

Timeliness

A common measure of timeliness is the promptness of answering telephones. Many organizations pledge that phones will be answered within three rings and, while this is a very noble idea, it implies that this will happen 100 per cent of the time, which isn't always possible. Working days and working hours need to be taken into consideration when setting standards, and defining an acceptable 'success percentage' is better than implying that nothing less than 100 per cent will do.

For example, 'During our working hours of 8.30 a.m. to 5.30 p.m. on weekdays, 95 per cent of calls will be answered within three rings'. This is a perfectly acceptable service standard.

If yours is an organization that promises 'next day delivery' then this implies that it includes weekends and that delivery can be to anywhere in the world. If this isn't the case, then 'next day' needs to be more specific, for example weekdays only and UK mainland only (if you are a UK-based business).

It is also a good idea to have a performance standard for your customer-facing staff on how long it should take to resolve a customer's problem. Although many problems can be dealt with during the course of a telephone conversation, more complex ones may require investigation, possibly involving staff from other parts of the organization.

Once a complaint or problem has been registered by a customer, the clock is ticking. Whether they have reported it to you verbally, in writing or via email, they now have an expectation that somebody is dealing with it and that it has been given an appropriate level of importance – high! If the problem is a complex one, requiring more time to investigate than a couple of hours at the most, it is essential that the customer is kept up to date with progress, even if that progress is minimal. The customer who hears nothing will feel neglected, and if they already have a grievance with you this will fan the flames and make it much worse.

Exercise

Define three service standards related to timeliness that either already exist within your organization or would improve your customer care if they did exist.

1. ....
2. ....
3. ....

Accuracy

Unlike timeliness, where accuracy is concerned nothing less than 100 per cent is acceptable. Imagine that you have had a consultation with your doctor for an ailment. He has given you a prescription but, unfortunately, he made a small error in spelling the name of the medication and you are about to be given something completely different by the pharmacist. At worst, this alternative medication could be harmful, or even dangerous, to you. The fact that 98 per cent of your doctor's service was accurate just wouldn't be good enough; it must be 100 per cent to be acceptable.

Customers expect 100 per cent accuracy on everything, especially in the following areas:

● the spelling of their name
● their address details
● the delivery date and time promised

- invoice or receipt details, especially amount charged
- goods or services to exactly match their description and be reliable
- information or promises given, either verbally or in writing
- the goods delivered match exactly what was ordered.

Exercise

Do you have any processes or procedures in place to check the accuracy of the product or service you supply to customers? If so, what are they?

....
....
....

What percentage of accuracy are you currently achieving and how do you know that?

....
....

Define three service standards related to accuracy that either already exist within your organization or would improve your customer care if they did exist:

1. ....
2. ....
3. ....

Appropriateness

This relates to how well you meet your customers' expectations, particularly when responding to enquiries or complaints. For example, you have ordered goods via the internet and you receive a partial delivery. You send an email to the supplier asking when you can expect the remainder of the delivery and whether this split delivery will affect the 14-day free trial that was promised when you placed your order. You receive a reply that anticipated delivery will be in ten days' time, with an apology for the delay. That's it – no mention of the 14-day free trial at all. The level of appropriateness demonstrated by the supplier was a dismal 50 per cent and you now feel that you have to email them again, to restate your question about the trial period.

Exercise

Do you have any processes or procedures in place to check the appropriateness of responses your organization makes to customers? If so, what are they?

....

....

....

What percentage of appropriateness are you currently achieving and how do you know that?

....

....

Define three service standards related to appropriateness that either already exist within your organization or would improve your customer care if they did exist.

1. ....

2. ....

3. ....

Writing service standards

When writing service standards, ensure that they are defined precisely and concisely, with no ambiguity that would allow for any misunderstanding or misinterpretation. Also think about how each service standard can be implemented and measured. This will ensure that they are realistic and serve a valuable purpose in confirming that your customers really are receiving a high and consistent standard of care.

At this point, it is worth getting input from other sources as to the areas that need to be included in your service standards, for example:

● management at all levels
● staff, especially customer-facing staff

- customers
- potential future customers
- previous customers (why are they no longer your customers?)
- competitors (remember this is research, not spying)
- any regulatory authorities relevant to your industry.

Implementing service standards

So, you've written them and they are comprehensive and clear – now what? There needs to be ownership throughout all levels of your organization, starting at the very top. The standards need to be cascaded down to all staff, and perhaps included in everyone's job objectives, so that each individual is evaluated on how well he or she performs in relation to these standards at their annual appraisal.

Visibility of the standards can be maintained through your organization's internal communication channels, e.g. newsletters, notice boards, intranet, discussion at department meetings and so on. Externally, this visibility can be turned into a real, public commitment to customer service by including a reference to service standards in the mission, vision or values of the organization.

The following are examples of organizations that have done just this.

Low-cost airline **Easyjet**'s mission statement:

> *To provide our customers with safe, good value, point-to-point air services. To effect and to offer a consistent and reliable product and fares appealing to leisure and business markets on a range of European routes. To achieve this we will develop our people and establish lasting relationships with our suppliers.*

McDonald's vision:

> *To be the world's best quick service restaurant experience. Being the best means providing outstanding quality, service, cleanliness, and value, so that we make every customer in every restaurant smile.*

The Home Depot's mission statement:

The Home Depot is in the home improvement business and our goal is to provide the highest level of service, the broadest selection of products and the most competitive prices. We are a values-driven company and our eight core values include the following:

1. Excellent customer service

2. Taking care of our people

3. Giving back

4. Doing the 'right' thing

5. Creating shareholder value

6. Respect for all people

7. Entrepreneurial spirit

8. Building strong relationships

Avon Cosmetics' mission statement:

The Global Beauty Leader

We will build a unique portfolio of beauty and related brands, striving to surpass our competitors in quality, innovation and value, and elevating our image to become the beauty company most women turn to worldwide.

The Women's Choice for Buying

We will become the destination store for women, offering the convenience of multiple brands and channels, and providing a personal high touch shopping experience that helps create lifelong customer relationships.

The Premier Direct Seller

We will expand our presence in direct selling and lead the reinvention of the channel, offering an entrepreneurial opportunity that delivers superior earnings, recognition, service and support, making it easy and rewarding to be affiliated with Avon and elevating the image of our industry.

SUNDAY

MONDAY

TUESDAY

WEDNESDAY

THURSDAY

FRIDAY

SATURDAY

The Best Place to Work

We will be known for our leadership edge, through our passion for high standards, our respect for diversity and our commitment to create exceptional opportunities for professional growth so that associates can fulfil their highest potential.

The Largest Women's Foundation

We will be a committed global champion for the health and well-being of women through philanthropic efforts that eliminate breast cancer from the face of the earth, and that empower women to achieve economic independence.

The Most Admired Company

We will deliver superior returns to our shareholders by tirelessly pursuing new growth opportunities while continually improving our profitability, a socially responsible, ethical company that is watched and emulated as a model of success.

Estée Lauder's mission statement:

The guiding vision of The Estée Lauder Companies is 'Bringing the best to everyone we touch'. By 'The best', we mean the best products, the best people and the best ideas. These three pillars have been the hallmarks of our Company since it was founded by Mrs Estée Lauder in 1946. They remain the foundation upon which we continue to build our success today.

Barnes & Noble's bookstores:

Our mission is to operate the best specialty retail business in America, regardless of the product we sell. Because the product we sell is books, our aspirations must be consistent with the promise and the ideals of the volumes which line our shelves. To say that our mission exists independent of the product we sell is to demean the importance and the distinction of being booksellers. As booksellers we are determined to be

*the very best in our business, regardless of the size,
pedigree or inclinations of our competitors. We will
continue to bring our industry nuances of style and
approaches to bookselling which are consistent with our
evolving aspirations. Above all, we expect to be a credit
to the communities we serve, a valuable resource to our
customers, and a place where our dedicated booksellers
can grow and prosper. Toward this end we will not only
listen to our customers and booksellers but embrace the
idea that the Company is at their service.*

The **MBNA Corporation** (a financial institution and holding
company that is also an independent credit card lender):

*Our mission is to provide you with an outstanding
member/Customer benefit that helps you meet your
organization's objectives. We work very hard to
understand your objectives, then create a program that
can help you meet them. Whether you want to attract
new members, retain existing ones, drive incremental
sales, or reinforce member or brand loyalty, we will
work with you to help you achieve those goals.*

Microsoft's mission statement:

*At Microsoft, we work to help people and businesses
throughout the world realize their full potential. This
is our mission. Everything we do reflects this mission
and the values that make it possible.*

Once service standards have been created and made public, it
is essential that *everyone* in your organization 'walks the walk'.
It's very easy for those staff who perceive themselves to be more
'back room' than customer facing to believe that customer
service standards don't apply to them. And yet it's quite feasible
that an incoming call might get put through to a department that
doesn't usually deal directly with customers. The phone might be
left to ring for a minute or two, before someone finally picks it up
and snaps, 'Yeah?'. Your carefully thought out service standard
of answering within three rings with 'Good morning, [name]
speaking, how may I help you?' has just gone out the window.

Customer service is everyone's business, from the Chief Executive Officer through to the cleaning staff. Whenever I stay in a hotel, I'm always impressed by the cleaners I encounter who deliberately make eye contact with me, smile and say 'Good morning' in a genuinely courteous tone of voice. For me, this enhances the entire hotel experience and speaks volumes about the standards of customer service that must be in place. I would quite happily stay at that hotel again and I'd recommend it to others.

Line managers play an important role in nurturing a 'customer-friendly' attitude in their staff, and often this attitude plays a key part in selection criteria at recruitment interviews. If the culture of an organization is one of serving customers, and enjoying doing it, then not only does this generate a positive reputation externally, it also creates a happy, motivating work environment internally. This in turn decreases staff turnover, with the financial benefits of reduced recruitment and training costs.

Many organizations use motivational posters displayed on, for example, notice boards to continually remind staff of the importance of maintaining a focus on customer service. Typical slogans include: 'If we don't look after our customers, somebody else will.' You may have seen posters like this; although the words may seem a bit trite, the message is clear and to the point.

Summary

In this chapter, we have looked at ways in which you can define appropriate levels of customer service and incorporate them into standards that will apply throughout your organization. It is always useful to know what other organizations similar to yours are including in their standards, and conducting research on this topic can provide you with ideas and other sources of inspiration for writing your own.

The important point is that your standards must be visible to, and understood by, staff at all levels in your organization. For example, if you define a procedure for resolving customer complaints within a specified period of time and one of your employees misses this deadline because he or she didn't know it existed, then communication of the standard has been ineffective and needs to be addressed. Your organization's culture must be to 'walk the walk' rather than just 'talk the talk', and going public on this in a mission statement indicates to the world that you really are serious about it.

And one final point – if you are in the business of selling products, then you and your staff need to be fully conversant with the Sale of Goods Act and all the legalities it contains, particularly related to warranties. This is one standard that is not optional!

Fact-check (answers at the back)

Note: all questions require a single answer.

1. Your company's annual accounts represent:
a) Day-to-day trading figures ❏
b) Future market trends ❏
c) Past financial performance ❏
d) Planned versus actual expenditure. ❏

2. Customer care is:
a) A 'nice to have' option ❏
b) A performance measurement ❏
c) Only applicable to customer-facing staff ❏
d) Not relevant to your organization. ❏

3. Which statement is true?
a) Only manufacturing businesses need to have standards in place. ❏
b) Everyone has common sense so there is no need to define service standards in writing. ❏
c) Customer care is as tangible as money. ❏
d) Service standards remind all levels of staff of their customer care obligations. ❏

4. It is recommended that service standards be defined in terms of:
a) Timeliness, accuracy, profit margins ❏
b) Timeliness, accuracy, appropriateness ❏
c) Timeliness, dress code, appropriateness ❏
d) Reputation, accuracy, appropriateness. ❏

5. Which statement is true?
a) Telephones *must* be answered within three rings at all times. ❏
b) 'Next day delivery' needs to be clarified to avoid misunderstandings. ❏
c) As long as the phone gets answered eventually, the customer has been served. ❏
d) Problem resolution can take a long time and the customer should be patient. ❏

6. The acceptable percentage for accuracy is:
a) 100 per cent ❏
b) 98 per cent ❏
c) 95 per cent ❏
d) 93 per cent. ❏

7. Which statement is true?
a) If people have an unusual name, they should expect it to get spelled wrongly. ❏
b) A delivery date is just an estimate, not a promise. ❏
c) If a product is similar to its description, that is good enough. ❏
d) Goods must match exactly what was ordered by the customer. ❏

8. Which statement is true?

a) Appropriateness relates to your tone of voice when dealing with a customer. ❏

b) Appropriateness relates to how well you meet your customers' expectations. ❏

c) As long as the customer has received a response of some kind, appropriateness has been achieved. ❏

d) By the nature of their role, customer-facing staff are automatically 'appropriate'. ❏

9. Which statement is true?

a) Service standards need to be defined precisely and concisely. ❏

b) Implementation and measurement need not be considered at this stage. ❏

c) Input from past customers has no value. ❏

d) There is nothing to be learned from competitors. ❏

10. Which statement is true?

a) As long as standards have been written, that is good enough. ❏

b) Senior management are too far removed from customers to bother with maintaining standards. ❏

c) Visibility of service standards to all levels of staff in an organization is essential. ❏

d) A mission statement is not the appropriate place for customer service standards to be made public. ❏

SUNDAY
MONDAY
TUESDAY
WEDNESDAY
THURSDAY
FRIDAY
SATURDAY

TUESDAY

How do your customers think you measure up?

In the previous chapter, the focus was on creating your own set of customer service standards and then measuring your organization's performance against them. This is, of course, good customer care practice.

Here's the bad news. No matter how well you have defined your standards and are monitoring performance, your customers will always decide what your *real* standards are. You might hate the phrase 'the customer is always right', but your customers are your reality check. You might be consistently achieving the standards you have put in place, but if your customers have a different set of standards against which they are evaluating you, then yours are obsolete.

It is also a bad idea to assume that 'no news is good news'. I have lost count of the number of times I have worked with organizations that had adopted the attitude of believing their product or service must be acceptable because 'nobody's complained yet'. Customers will not necessarily complain in words; it is more likely that they will complain with their feet (by walking away from you).

It is essential that you find out what your customers think of you – don't assume, ask them. You need this information to get a clear understanding of how you are *really* performing and also to identify areas for improvement. This chapter explores the ways in which you can do this effectively and how this in turn can enhance customer loyalty and even bring you new customers.

How well do you know your customers?

Who is your typical customer? Are they an individual or an organization? Do they buy from you face to face or via the internet? These are questions that you should know the answers to, and the following is a customer profiling exercise to check out just how well you know them.

Exercise

There are two sections to this profiling questionnaire: the first relates to individuals and the second relates to organizations. You might have both types of customer buying from you, in which case complete both sections. If, however, your customers are predominantly one type or the other, then complete only the appropriate section.

- Individual customers
  - Gender ....
  - Age ....
  - Family ....
  - Where they live ....
  - Employment ....
  - Approximate income ....
  - Hobbies/interests ....
  - Aspirations/goals ....
  - What they buy from you ....
  - How often do they buy? ....
- Organizations
  - Size (number of staff) ....
  - Annual turnover ....
  - Location ....
  - Number of years established ....
  - Nature of business ....
  - Purchasing procedure ....
  - Decision maker ....
  - What they buy from you ....
  - How often do they buy? ....

If you are answering the organization questions, 'purchasing procedure' relates to the process for making a purchase. For example, does someone within the organization raise a request for purchase and a buyer from the procurement department then approaches three potential suppliers for a quotation? Is there an approved suppliers list and, if so, how often is it reviewed? Is the buyer also the decision maker or is someone else in the organization responsible for the final sign-off? If you are dealing with organizations as your main source of business, then you need to know all these things.

The following questions relate to both individuals and organizations as customers:

● How did they find out about you?

....
....

● What is important to them in dealing with you?

....
....

● What exactly do they expect from you?

....
....

● How well are you meeting their expectations?

....
....

● How do you know that?

....

....

● How might their expectations and needs change in the future?

....

....

What you have been doing in this exercise is, effectively, stepping into the shoes of your (typical) customer. If you found this hard to do, then you may not be as attuned to your customers as you need to be. This particularly relates to the questions about how well you are meeting their expectations and how you know that. If you made assumptions when you answered those questions, then the real answer is that you *don't know* how well you are meeting your customers' expectations. *You need to know.*

You particularly need to know if your customers are dissatisfied for any reason. The following iceberg model illustrates the importance of this.

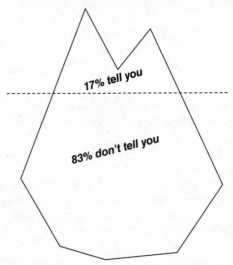

The iceberg of dissatisfied customers

Of all your dissatisfied customers, only 17 per cent (above the water line) will actually tell you that they are unhappy, giving you the opportunity to put things right. They, in turn, will each tell an average of five other people about their experience with you, so *85 people get a positive message* about how you look after your customers, even if something has not been quite right.

The remaining 83 per cent (below the water line) say nothing to you about their dissatisfaction, so you have no opportunity to take remedial action. However, on average, they each tell nine other people that their experience with you was a bad one, so *747 people hear a negative story* about you.

The moral of the story is that it wasn't the tip of the iceberg that sank the *Titanic* – it was the mass below the water line. You need to know about *all* of your dissatisfied customers so that you can resolve their problems and ensure that only positive messages about you are passed on to other potential customers.

Finding out what your customers think of you

There are several ways that you can ask your customers for feedback. For example:

- asking them face to face immediately after business has been transacted
- giving them a feedback card or form to complete that they can either give back to you there and then or post back to you later
- writing to them with a survey form for them to complete and send back
- emailing them with an online survey for them to complete
- telephoning them to ask for feedback over the phone
- using a market research company to collect and analyse feedback.

It is essential that your customers feel that their feedback is important and will be taken seriously. You could confirm to them that you might well make changes for the better in the future, based on their input and suggestions. In so doing, your customers feel valued and are more likely to remain your customers.

Have you ever stayed in a hotel where there was a customer feedback form or card in your room with a request that you fill it out and either hand it in to reception when you check out or post back later?

Have you ever stayed in a hotel where, in your room, there was a short summary of changes the hotel had made in the last six months as a result of reviewing and acting upon feedback from guests who had completed the feedback form?

You may well have answered 'yes' to the first question, but what about the second question? Many hotels just pay 'lip service' to the concept of gathering feedback from their guests. But just imagine that you stayed at a particular hotel and took the time and trouble to complete a feedback form, and when you happened to stay there again a few months later, you discovered that a suggestion you had made had been implemented. Even better, when you reached your room, you found a personalised note from the manager, thanking you for the previous suggestion you had made, confirming that it had been implemented and welcoming any further ideas you might have. How valued would you feel? How happy would you be to stay there again in the future? And how many people might you tell about this?

So, as you can see, the benefits of getting feedback from your customers go well beyond just finding out what they think of you. Customer loyalty can be enhanced and new customers gained through referrals.

What information do you ask for?

Start with deciding what you really want to find out about. You could compose countless questions about product quality, speed of service, politeness of staff and so on; however, a feedback form that is so lengthy it has become intimidating and time-consuming is less likely to get completed.

The two essential things that you need to know about are:

1 What is it about your product or service that is important to your customers?
2 How well are you delivering on those important areas?

Let's imagine for a moment that you are a manufacturer of mobile phones. You have decided to bring out a new, enhanced model and you believe that your customers just love to have a large range of ringtones to choose from, so you invest time and money in creating some new ones. When you announce the launch of your new model, incorporating the increased range of ringtones as a marketing and customer care tool, you are disappointed to find that the volume of sales is less than you had anticipated.

At around the same time, a competitor of yours also announces the launch of a new mobile phone, and their main promotional feature is a battery with a significantly extended life. Their sales go through the roof. Why? Because they took the time and trouble to find out what mobile phone features are important to their customers and then supplied them. You assumed that ringtones were important; your customers would have told you that battery life was more important, if you had but asked them.

Although there is no definitive template for a feedback form, the following are extracts taken from real examples of satisfaction survey forms issued by a variety of different businesses. In each case, the intentions behind the questions are good; however, the final format is less than ideal. The names of the businesses have been withheld; they are identified by their industry type. I have reproduced the actual text from the forms with my comments shown in normal text throughout.

Supermarket

Where appropriate, the card asks for a tick in one of five boxes, ranging from poor to excellent.

> *We would like your comments*
> What do you think of our prices?
> What can you buy cheaper elsewhere?
> What have you particularly liked about shopping here recently?
> Is there anything you have disliked about shopping here recently?

Overall, how do you rate us at satisfying all your
everyday shopping needs?

Day and time of visit

Your postcode

Please post this card in the 'We're listening' post box or
hand it in at the customer services desk.

We are unable to reply to individual comments. For urgent
issues, please contact customer services. Thanks for your help.

Considering this card is headed 'We would like your comments'
and a post box labelled 'We're listening' is provided, it is very
disappointing that this supermarket is refusing to respond to
individual comments. The card continues on the other side with:

Please tick the relevant boxes . . .
(from poor to excellent)

Products:

- Choice/range
- Always able to get the products
  you want
- Quality
- Finding products easily
- Any comments about specific products
- What other products would you like us to provide?

Staff:

- Helpfulness of our staff
- Speed of service at checkout

Store:

- Store cleanliness and tidiness
- Ease of parking
- Finding the trolley you want

Customers are invited to list other products they would like to see in the store, but because the supermarket is not prepared to respond to these requests, the customer may assume that the product they have requested will now be stocked, and be disappointed if it isn't.

It is interesting that the only personal information the card requests is the day and time of visit and the customer's postcode. Presumably, the store is planning to carry out an analysis of how far people travel to do their grocery shopping and at what time of day. If they had asked for the customer's name and a contact telephone number, they could have offered a prize draw for a £50 voucher to spend in the store. This would have been an incentive to fill in the card and would have demonstrated that customers' input is valuable.

Car dealership

A six-page A4-sized document posted to customers three weeks after servicing is carried out.

> How satisfied were you with your recent service experience at the dealership? Please score your level of satisfaction on a scale of 1.0 (completely dissatisfied) to 5.0 (completely satisfied) in the boxes opposite.
>
> For example, if fairly satisfied you might provide a score of 3.2 or if you are completely satisfied you might provide a score of 5.0.

The length of this survey is intimidating enough; however, the questions in the first section ask for a response in decimals, which is unnecessary. A score between 1 and 5 is sufficient; getting into decimals is too precise and nit-picky.

The next five sections of the form ask for your evaluation by ticking one of five boxes, which are:

> Completely satisfied
> Very satisfied
> Fairly satisfied
> Somewhat dissatisfied
> Completely dissatisfied

This is inconsistent. Either they want precise scores with decimal points or they want evaluations based on the headings above. A mixture of the two on the same form gives the impression that there were at least two authors of this document, who had a disagreement. The only way to resolve their conflict was a compromise, and hence the two completely different ways of scoring. This really doesn't give a good impression to the customer. The form continues with:

How satisfied were you with . . .

- The ease of getting through to the dealership to book an appointment?
- The ease of getting a service appointment within a reasonable time?
- The dealership's ability to give you an appointment for the date/time you requested?
- The appearance of the dealer's service department?
- The ease of parking when you visited the dealership?
- The waiting time when you dropped off your car?
- The friendliness/helpfulness of the service advisor?
- The service advisor's ability to understand your individual issues?
- The technical competence of the service advisor?
- Their ability to provide a cost estimate?
- The dealer's ability to offer an alternative method of transport (if required)?
- Their ability to complete the work within the timescales given?
- The availability of all necessary parts?
- The quality of the work performed?
- The level of contact to keep you updated while your vehicle was being serviced?

And so it goes on. On the positive side, the covering letter that accompanies this form does promise that if it is completed and returned in the postage-paid envelope provided by a specific date, the customer will be entered into a prize draw to win a 'luxury break' at a smart hotel. This is a good incentive and, in light of the length of the survey, absolutely necessary to encourage the customer to spend time working through this tedious form.

Hospital accident and emergency department

A double-sided, almost A4-sized card, headed 'satisfaction survey'.

> We are constantly striving to improve the quality of the Accident and Emergency (A&E) service. You can help us to do this by filling in the questionnaire on the other side of this card. The cards are collected each day and the results analysed. Your opinions will help to shape the future of the Accident Centre.
>
> Indicate your opinion by marking the appropriate box with a straight line, like this: —

This is really helpful if you have no idea what a straight line looks like!

> Please use a pencil or blue/black pen.

Now you're in trouble. You just came along here with your broken leg. You had no idea that you needed to have your pencil case with you!

> Mark only one box for each question and rub out any mistakes.

What if you've been using a pen? Should have brought along your pencils *and* an eraser!

SUNDAY
MONDAY
TUESDAY
WEDNESDAY
THURSDAY
FRIDAY
SATURDAY

> Please post the completed card in the box, to the right of the door leading out of the department. Do not fold, bend or tear this card.

A bit optimistic – might depend on the state you're in when you're finally ready to leave A&E. Some of the questions can't be answered until then.

The next section provides options of:

- Not applicable
- Very good
- Good
- Acceptable
- Poor
- Very poor

> What was your experience of the following:
>
> - Waiting time to register
> - Waiting time to see the doctor
> - Waiting time for X-ray
> - Waiting time for treatment
> - Staff courtesy – nurse
> - Staff courtesy – doctor
> - Effectiveness of the anaesthetic
> - Information from staff
> - Quality of treatment
> - Appearance of department

I love the question about effectiveness of the anaesthetic! If it worked particularly well, you may be so woozy that you're having trouble finding the door out of A&E, let alone the post box for your card! However, if it didn't work too well and you've been sitting around waiting for some time in considerable pain, you have very likely ripped this card into small pieces by now.

The final section gives options of Agree, Disagree and Don't know.

> Do you agree with the following aspects of the centre's policy?
>
> - Children under 12 receive priority care for non-urgent conditions
> - Trained nurses manage minor conditions (no doctor involved)
> - Background music in the waiting room

Interestingly, it doesn't actually state what the centre's policies are with respect to these points. For example, if there is no background music playing, does that mean that this is their policy or does it mean that there should be music playing but something has gone wrong?

Summary

In this chapter, we have explored the importance of getting feedback from your customers as to how they believe you are performing. If you make assumptions about what your customers think about you and what their needs are, there will always be at least a 50 per cent chance that your assumptions are incorrect. Your customers are your life blood – you need to know how to keep them satisfied in order to retain their loyalty.

The following are key points to bear in mind when formulating a customer satisfaction survey:

● Determine exactly what you want to find out and include only those questions that will give you that result.

● You need to know what is important to your customers and how they feel you are performing in those areas.

● Avoid making your survey form too long – it becomes tedious and won't get completed.

● If you are posting forms out to your customers, you *must* include a pre-paid envelope for their return.

SUNDAY

MONDAY

TUESDAY

WEDNESDAY

THURSDAY

FRIDAY

SATURDAY

● Offering an incentive such as a prize draw or complimentary voucher will encourage your customers to complete a survey.

● If you have asked for suggestions, then you need to acknowledge them; otherwise, there will be an expectation that all suggestions will be implemented.

● When you've analysed results, find a way to publish them. This will make everyone who participated in the survey feel valued, as well as being a good public relations exercise for you.

Before reading any further, this is a good point at which to put together a draft version of a satisfaction survey. In addition to your own ideas, you could also ask for others' input and suggestions, ensuring that it retains a conciseness in its final form.

Fact-check (answers at the back)

Note: all questions require a single answer.

1. Which statement is true?
a) Your competitors define your service standards. ❏
b) Your service standards will always be the same as your customers' standards. ❏
c) Your customers define the standards you need to meet. ❏
d) As long as nobody is complaining, your standards are good enough. ❏

2. Which statement is true?
a) 17 per cent of dissatisfied customers don't complain. ❏
b) 83 per cent of dissatisfied customers complain loudly. ❏
c) The customers who don't complain each tell five others about your poor service. ❏
d) You can only resolve problems that your customers tell you about. ❏

3. Which statement is true?
a) You need to know what your customers expect from you. ❏
b) You probably know how well you are meeting their expectations. ❏
c) Your customers' future needs will be the same as they are now. ❏
d) Your customers must be happy if you don't hear anything negative from them. ❏

4. Which statement is true?
a) Feedback from customers is of little importance to your business. ❏
b) Feedback from customers contributes to planning the future of your business. ❏
c) Customers don't need to know whether their feedback will be taken seriously. ❏
d) As long as you smile at your customers, they will feel valued. ❏

5. Which statement is true?
a) It is important to know how far your customers travel to do business with you. ❏
b) People don't like being asked for their opinions. ❏
c) You need to know what is important to your customers about your product or service. ❏
d) There is no need to acknowledge suggestions put forward by your customers. ❏

6. Which statement is true?
a) As long as your prices are competitive, nothing else matters to your customers. ❏
b) If you think a particular aspect of your product/service should be important to your customers, then it will be. ❏
c) People need no incentives to encourage them to fill out lengthy satisfaction surveys. ❏
d) Responding positively to customer feedback can contribute to an organization's business success. ❏

7. Which statement is true?
a) Mixing different methods of scoring on a satisfaction survey is not good practice. ❏
b) People should expect to pay postage costs to return a completed survey form. ❏
c) The point of asking customers to give feedback is purely for your organization to look as if it cares. ❏
d) No customer would ever expect their suggestions to be implemented. ❏

8. Which statement is true?
a) Customers are just an inconvenience. ❏
b) Your customers are your life blood. ❏
c) Your customers shouldn't expect so much of you. ❏
d) Your customers are always wrong. ❏

9. Which statement is true?
a) If you make assumptions, they will always be correct. ❏
b) Product improvements based on assumptions may not represent the best investment of your time and money. ❏
c) There is a 70 per cent chance of an assumption being correct. ❏
d) The possible margin for error in an assumption is 20 per cent. ❏

10. Which statement is true?
a) Customers are not interested in seeing the results of a survey in which they have participated. ❏
b) Customers have no expectations related to service. ❏
c) It is okay to take customer loyalty for granted. ❏
d) People are more likely to complete a survey form if there is a chance of winning a prize as a result. ❏

SUNDAY

MONDAY

TUESDAY

WEDNESDAY

THURSDAY

FRIDAY

SATURDAY

WEDNESDAY

Deliver more than your customers expect

In the previous chapter, we explored how your customers define your service standards by their expectations, and it is their expectations that you need to fulfil in order to achieve a good standard of customer care. In this chapter, we will 'boldly go' beyond your customers' expectations and discover how to delight them by achieving customer excellence.

It is by consistently exceeding others' expectations that you not only retain your customers, but turn them into your 'raving fans'. The real bonus of this is that they will then do your marketing for you, by telling their friends, family and anyone else who is remotely interested that you are the best thing since sliced bread. Because people like to buy from people they know, like and trust, such 'referral marketing' is particularly effective. It also helps to build and sustain your reputation as an organization that really cares about its customers.

One of the key principles at work in achieving customer excellence is to under-promise and over-deliver. Even though your mission statement might encapsulate your customer service standards, by maintaining an attitude of constantly over-delivering on those standards you will build a reputation of outstanding customer care.

Included in this chapter are examples of organizations that have achieved, and continue to achieve, customer excellence. There are, of course, many more and, as you are reading this, others may come to mind for you. If so, notice exactly what it is that is generating this level of excellence, and whether there are any ideas that you could replicate for yourself and your organization.

Excellence doesn't need to cost a lot of money

Many years ago, I was recommended a stationery supplier that guaranteed next day delivery free of charge for all orders over £30 in value. They would also offer free gifts such as a box of envelopes, a pack of A4-sized writing pads, a personal CD player and so on. I started buying my stationery from them on a regular basis and found them to be very reliable and good value for money.

One January, during an outbreak of influenza, I rang in a stationery order and was told that I would also receive a free ream of photocopy paper. Sure enough, the next day, when my order was delivered and I unpacked all the items I had ordered, I was pleased to find the promised free ream of paper. However, the box wasn't empty. Down in one corner was a pack of three tubes of medicated throat sweets – not ordered, not expected as a free gift, just included as a complimentary extra. This impressed me more than the free ream of paper did, because I had been expecting that. I hadn't expected the throat sweets and, even though I was fortunate enough not to have the flu, there must have been many other customers who were delighted to receive them and probably put them to good use straight away!

This is a brilliant example of customer excellence. The stationery supplier had probably negotiated a good price for buying in these throat sweets in bulk, and then instructed their 'pick and pack' staff to drop a pack into every order that was being dispatched to their customers that month. All it needed was a good idea. The additional cost per order was just pennies but the value added must have been immense. I'm sure that I wasn't the only recipient who told others about it and it certainly assured my loyalty as their customer.

I should add that I never opened my pack of throat sweets. Instead, I have used them many, many times as a prop when I have been running customer care courses as an illustration of customer excellence in action. I still have them, and I notice that the expiry date is 1998 – so for this particular stationery supplier the return on their investment has been truly immeasurable. That's the value of just one good idea.

Exercise

Have you ever been the recipient of customer excellence – where, as a customer, your expectations were significantly exceeded? If so, jot down the key points below.

....

....

....

379

Customer excellence is showing that you care

The following is another example of customer excellence, as described by the manager of a casino based on the south coast of England:

Excellent customer service is paramount in everything we do and we are always looking at ways of improving what we do. This is done through customer feedback forms, which are given out at the casino, and the customer then goes online to answer some questions about their casino experience.

A couple of ways we have exceeded customer expectations are as follows.

A couple, who were regular customers of the casino, moved away but still visited the area regularly. When they were due to come back about six months ago, they couldn't find a hotel room for the three weeks they were here. As they visit us regularly, we decided to arrange and pay for their stay in a local hotel ourselves. The couple in question were overjoyed and couldn't thank us enough.

Another example of us going that extra mile is that if one of our regular customers is ill or in hospital, we always send them flowers as a way of saying that we are thinking of them. Also, anyone who visits us on their birthday is given a free drink and a small gift as our way of saying happy birthday.

I would add that this particular casino has a large bar/restaurant area in which regular events, such as business networking lunches, are hosted. When I attended a lunch there recently, it transpired that over the past 11 months the casino had been holding fundraising events for a local cancer relief charity and in that time had raised a total of £280,000. This clearly demonstrates a caring culture and, in addition to the examples already mentioned, shows that they really value their customers.

Also notice that they actively use customer feedback as a tool for thinking up new initiatives and responding positively to customers' wants, needs and ideas for improvements.

Think about the customer experience

The following is the story of how Waterstones bookshops originated, based on a desire to enhance the customer experience of browsing and buying books.

Following redundancy, Tim Waterstone opened his first bookshop in 1982 on Old Brompton Road, London. At the time, he had only £6,000 of his own money, but managed to raise the rest of the £100,000 he needed to get started. His intention was to build a chain of bookshops with a wide specialist range, a friendly atmosphere in which to browse and with knowledgeable staff on hand for advice. At that time, this was not how high street bookshops and newsagents operated, so his concept was quite different to the 'norm'. However, his ideas proved to be popular and, before long, Waterstones developed into a chain of bookshops throughout the UK.

What is particularly interesting is that at that time publishers were protected by the net book agreement, which meant that retailers of books were prevented from offering discounts on them. So Waterstones was selling the same products at exactly the same price as its competitors. In order to succeed, Tim Waterstone chose to step into his customers' shoes and focus on the whole experience of browsing and buying books in his stores. What would make the experience more enjoyable? What would make the customer want to come back and do it again? And what would encourage the customer to recommend the Waterstones experience to others?

The following are some of the features that contributed to the success of Waterstones. Although they probably sound quite commonplace now, back in the 1980s these things were different enough to make the difference:

- **Books put out on display on tables**. Generally, bookshops displayed their wares only on shelves, with their window displays featuring new publications. However, if a potential customer is browsing rather than looking for a specific book, their attention will be drawn to the books lying on a table. Rather like visiting someone in their home, if there are books or magazines lying on a coffee table, very soon your eyes will be drawn to them, probably out of curiosity.
- **Comfortable seating for customers**. Browsing while standing gets uncomfortable after a while, and if that element of discomfort kicks in before a desirable book has been discovered then the potential customer will probably leave without making a purchase. Where space allowed, squashy armchairs and other forms of seating were installed in Waterstones shops so that browsers could relax and take their time to review any books that interested them.

- **Knowledgeable staff**. I was fortunate enough to be seated next to Tim Waterstone at a business networking event several years ago. We had a fascinating discussion, during which he told me that many of his staff were themselves aspiring authors. This meant that, for them, working in an environment of books and literature was like living the dream. Staff were encouraged to select and review books themselves and to write a personal recommendation on a small piece of card and attach it to the shelf where the book was stocked. Anyone curious to know more about the book could then speak to the member of staff who had written the recommendation. Many of Waterstones' staff have indeed gone on to become successful authors, including the following:
  - David Mitchell (*Cloud Atlas*)
  - Anna Dale (*Dawn Undercover* and *Whispering to Witches*)
  - Stuart Hill (*The Cry of the Icemark* and *Blade of Fire*)
  - Alan Bissett (*The Incredible Adam Spark*)
  - Jeff Noon (*Vurt*)
  - Sonia Overall (*A Likeness*)
  - Oliver Jeffers (*Lost and Found*)
- **Coffee shops**. Again, space permitting, coffee shops with seating are included in the Waterstones' experience. This has the added advantage of also attracting passers-by, who pop in for a coffee and are then tempted to browse among the books while they are there.

- **Events**. Starting in a small way in the early days with storytelling sessions for children, in 2007 Waterstones shops held more than 5,000 events and activities. When a Harry Potter book was published in July of that year, some 250,000 people attended their midnight openings around the UK, Ireland and Europe. Branches throughout the UK regularly host book signings and stand-up shows featuring a wide range of celebrities. And Waterstones is also associated with 15 literary festivals, including the Cheltenham Literary Festival and the Bath Children's Literary Festival.
- **Spotting new market trends**. Tim Waterstone, who is himself a published author, anticipated a demand for books by writers who were just emerging in the 1980s, such as Salman Rushdie, Ian McEwan, John Banville and Martin Amis. By embracing this new, developing market, Waterstones shops were positioned as being a little different to other mainstream high street booksellers.

In more recent years, Waterstones has embraced online book sales, issued loyalty cards to its customers and gained a reputation for occupying buildings of architectural or historical interest while retaining their original character and features. Examples include the Piccadilly (London) branch, which used to be Simpsons of Piccadilly, a department store that originally opened in 1936. During the early 1950s, scriptwriter Jeremy Lloyd was employed as a junior assistant at Simpsons; he drew on his experiences to come up with the idea for the highly popular 1970s/80s television sitcom *Are You Being Served?*.

In the basement of Waterstones in Canterbury, and on display, are the remains of a Roman bath-house floor – a scheduled ancient monument.

Bradford's branch of Waterstones is housed in the city's former Wool Exchange and features a stunning gothic hammerbeam roof.

So, having set up Waterstones for £100,000 in 1982, Tim Waterstone sold it to WH Smith in 1993 for £47 million. Since then, it has been bought and sold a couple more times and, even though the book retailing industry has been impacted by the rise in popularity of e-books and e-book readers such as the Kindle, Waterstones remains a popular, respected high street presence. In 2006, in a BrandIndex survey, Waterstone's came top of the high street retailers for service, quality, satisfaction and corporate reputation.

In an earlier chapter, we looked at mission statements. Tim Waterstone has been quoted as saying that mission statements are no good if customers can't understand them and staff can't buy into them. The following is Waterstones' mission:

> *To be the leading bookseller on the high street and online, providing customers with the widest choice, great value and expert advice from a team passionate about bookselling. Waterstones aims to interest and excite its customers and continually inspire people to read and engage in books.*

Ideas for achieving customer excellence

Remember that the key concept of customer excellence is to consistently exceed your customers' expectations. This need not require a large financial investment, but it does require an investment of your thoughts and ideas.

Let's recap on the initiatives used by the organizations featured in this chapter:

- **Topical or seasonal add-ons**. The stationery supplier that was sending out free medicated throat sweets during a bout of influenza. When a customer receives something that is immediately helpful to them, and which they weren't expecting, they will attach great value to it. I know of accountants who email their clients the day after a budget has been announced, explaining exactly what all the changes mean in 'real language' instead of political speak.

What could you give to your clients that would be valued?

....

....

....

● **Showing that you care**. The casino that sends flowers to customers who are ill or in hospital, and gives them a free drink and small gift to celebrate their birthday. I have met independent financial advisors who make a point of sending out birthday cards to all their clients. This activity doesn't cost a huge amount of money but is very much appreciated by the recipients and is more personal than just sending out Christmas cards.

How can you demonstrate to your customers that you care?

....

....

....

● **Enhancing the customer experience**. When you can't compete on product quality and price because they are fixed variables, as in the early days of Waterstones, then you need to make the overall experience of buying from you more enticing. Step into the shoes of your typical customer and 'walk through' the buying process, at every stage being aware of their expectations and asking yourself how you can exceed them.

How can you enhance the customer's experience of dealing with you?

....

....

....

IT WAS EASY— I JUST GAVE THE ORDER, SOMEONE GOT THE STONE, AND HEY PRESTO!

● **Product display**. However you showcase your products or services, it must be visually appealing. Think about refreshing any physical displays to make them more eye-catching. If customers visit your premises, ensure that cleanliness is a high priority. If you sell through a website, cast a critical eye over the ease of navigation and visual appeal of the relevant pages.

How can you make your products more appealing to your customers?

....
....
....

● **Physical comfort**. Depending on the nature of your business, your customers may visit you and may need to be provided with seating, perhaps in a reception area. A stained, uncomfortable, 'seen better days' sofa or chair sends out a message to your customers that you really don't care about them. Well-thumbed, months-out-of-date magazines lying in an untidy heap on a coffee table don't help. Neither does the sight of used coffee cups that haven't been cleared away.

If you have a reception area, how can you improve the experience of spending time there?

....
....
....

● **Knowledgeable staff**. When dealing with customer-facing staff, there is only one thing worse than hearing the words 'I don't know' in response to a question – being told the wrong information. You need to ensure not only that everyone in your organization receives the training that they need to do their jobs, but also that they are kept informed of any new products or services introduced, new procedures or changes to existing ones. Communication starts at the top and it is essential that it cascades throughout all levels of staff. Anything less than that and you are doing your customers a great disservice.

How can training and knowledge sharing be improved in your business?

....

....

....

● **Refreshments**. In recent years, vending machines for customers' use have become more of a regular feature in businesses. Even department stores now have water coolers on the shop floor – retail therapy is thirsty work, after all! If you have a reception area, then at the very least you need to have a water cooler, if not a hot drinks vending machine as well. (Ensure that you also include a bin for the disposal of used plastic cups.) If your organization is an office environment with a staffed reception, then ensure that your reception staff offer a cup of tea or coffee to anyone who is likely to be kept waiting for ten minutes or more.

Do your customers have easy access to drinking water or hot drinks?

....

If not, what changes could you make to incorporate this facility?

....

....

....

● **Events**. This is an area where customer care and public relations can become very closely aligned. The casino mentioned earlier in this chapter was supporting a nominated charity for cancer relief. In holding fundraising events, they were not only helping the charity, but also promoting the casino as a venue to potential new customers who had never visited before. The activity also sent out a message that this was a caring business that chose to invest time and money to help people with serious illnesses.

Does your organization hold events? If not, how could this become a regular feature?

....

....

....

● **Spotting new market trends**. What are other businesses doing to look after their customers? It's always a good idea to be constantly vigilant, and not just by keeping an eye on other businesses in your industry. Novel and effective customer care initiatives that work in other industries may well work in yours too. Think about loyalty cards, newsletters and vouchers.

What customer care initiatives could you introduce that would differentiate you from your competitors?

....

....

....

Summary

In this chapter, we have explored the concept of achieving customer excellence by consistently exceeding the customer's expectations. The main benefits to be gained by doing this are:

- customer loyalty
- your customers become 'raving fans' and tell others about you, and your sales increase accordingly
- you build a reputation for yourself of being an organization that excels.

To illustrate this 'above and beyond' approach, examples included in this chapter spanned a variety of businesses, from a stationery supplier to a casino, with the main case study being Waterstones bookshops.

Also reiterated in this chapter is the close relationship between customer care, marketing and public relations functions. The more effective you become at customer care, and particularly customer excellence, the more your customers will fulfil your marketing and public relations activities for you!

SUNDAY

MONDAY

TUESDAY

WEDNESDAY

THURSDAY

FRIDAY

SATURDAY

And, perhaps the best part – achieving customer excellence needs only a good idea; for example, the stationery supplier who decided to send out medicated throat sweets during an influenza epidemic. Someone in that organization came up with a good idea that would cost only a minimal amount, it was taken seriously, implemented and raving fans were created overnight!

In your organization, who is responsible for coming up with ideas for customer care initiatives? The answer is – everyone. Do you have a suggestion scheme in place? If not, think seriously about creating one. *Anyone* in your business might be sitting on the best idea that you've never had. Encourage them to put it forward, and be prepared to reward them for doing so.

Fact-check (answers at the back)

Note: all questions require a single answer.

1. In order to achieve customer excellence:
   a) Over-promise and under-deliver ❏
   b) Meet customer expectations and nothing more ❏
   c) Under-promise and under-deliver ❏
   d) Consistently exceed customer expectations. ❏

2. Which statement is true?
   a) Achieving customer excellence is expensive. ❏
   b) Just one good idea can generate customer excellence. ❏
   c) Customer excellence is a one-off activity. ❏
   d) Customer excellence is impossible to achieve. ❏

3. Which statement is true?
   a) Small, thoughtful actions can make a big impression. ❏
   b) A customer will notice only major initiatives. ❏
   c) There is little point in sending birthday cards to customers. ❏
   d) Customer feedback should not be used for generating new ideas. ❏

4. Waterstones bookshops were founded by:
   a) Tom Waterstone ❏
   b) Jim Waterstone ❏
   c) Tim Waterstone ❏
   d) WH Smith. ❏

5. Which statement is true?
   a) Books for sale should be displayed only on shelves. ❏
   b) A table display attracts visual attention. ❏
   c) People should always stand up to browse books. ❏
   d) Seating customers is a waste of space. ❏

6. Which statement is true?
   a) As long as staff know how to work a cash register, they are knowledgeable enough. ❏
   b) Customers shouldn't expect staff to have product knowledge. ❏
   c) A little knowledge is a dangerous thing; better to have none at all. ❏
   d) It is important for staff to be knowledgeable about the products and services offered by their organization. ❏

7. Which statement is true?
   a) Loyalty cards and vouchers are valued by customers. ❏
   b) Customers do not need to feel valued. ❏
   c) There is no such thing as a customer who is a 'raving fan'. ❏
   d) Marketing and public relations have nothing to do with customer care. ❏

8. Which statement is true?

a) Events are for staff only, not customers. ❏

b) Hosting events for the benefit of customers builds loyalty and a good reputation. ❏

c) Events are a costly overhead, and therefore are not feasible. ❏

d) An event will be supported only if a top celebrity attends. ❏

9. Which statement is true?

a) Customers don't notice whether products are displayed well or not. ❏

b) As long as your business premises are cleared once a week, they are clean enough. ❏

c) Your website is also your shop window and needs to be visually appealing. ❏

d) There is no need to provide water coolers or vending machines for use by customers. ❏

10. Which statement is true?

a) The 'customer experience' has nothing to do with you; it's all in their mind. ❏

b) Customers will always buy the cheapest product or service available. ❏

c) Your reception area is a great place to dump very old magazines. ❏

d) Customer care initiatives being used in other industries may well work in your business too. ❏

SUNDAY

MONDAY

TUESDAY

WEDNESDAY

THURSDAY

FRIDAY

SATURDAY

THURSDAY

Excellence in communication

You cannot not communicate. Even if you are not speaking out loud, your body language is 'speaking' for you. The clothes you are wearing convey a message that will either enhance your degree of professionalism or detract from it. If you are wearing an overpowering perfume or cologne or, even worse, have a strong, unpleasant body odour, you have communicated a negative message to your customers and they may well decide that they don't want to interact with you and take their business elsewhere.

In this chapter, we will explore all aspects of communication, whether face to face, over the telephone or in writing. Using proven, effective NLP (Neuro-linguistic Programming) techniques, you will learn how to build rapport easily, effortlessly and rapidly. You will understand what makes everyone different and unique, and therefore why it is essential to have flexibility in your communication style.

You will also learn how to calm down an angry customer, easily and assertively, without getting sucked into their emotional state. You will discover the language to use and the actions to take to generate the best possible outcomes, which could even result in your most challenging customer becoming your biggest fan.

And, if you are an aspiring author, then there is a real gem in this chapter for you. I will share with you a technique that JK Rowling uses in every Harry Potter book to build rapport with her readers through the written word. So, if you're sitting comfortably, let's begin . . .

What makes everyone different and unique?

Each one of us is as individual as a fingerprint. We might be similar to others; however, there will always be differences that set us apart. The way that we process information, think, feel and behave creates our uniqueness, which influences the way that we communicate with others and how we like others to communicate with us.

The following diagram illustrates how we take in information (external events), pass it through our own individual set of 'filters', make sense of it, react to it emotionally and physically and, finally, behave in a way that feels appropriate to us.

Let's explore this in more detail.

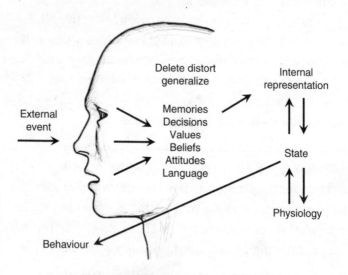

The only way that we can take in the world that is going on around us is through our five senses. However, if we tried to absorb *everything* that is going on around us all the time, it would be more than our conscious minds could handle.

Your conscious mind can process only seven plus or minus two things at a time; in other words, a maximum of nine things. Any more than that, and it will get overloaded and forget or overlook things. However, your unconscious mind makes two million neural connections a second; this is your 'power house'. When you hear it said that we use only 5 per cent of our brains, it is a reference to the very limited conscious mind. The remaining 95 per cent is our unconscious mind.

To protect the conscious mind from overload, everyone has a set of 'filters', made up of such things as memories, decisions, values, beliefs, attitudes, language and much more. These filters are created by our experiences as we progress through life, and because everyone's experience of life is different, everyone's filters are unique.

The role of the filters is to delete, distort or generalize information coming in, in order to make sense of it. The information then becomes an 'internal representation' – in other words, it is re-presented internally as a thought. Attached to the thought is a state of mind, so it may be a happy thought, a sad thought, an angry thought and so on. And allied to the state of mind is the physiology, or body language.

The connection between thought, state and physiology is a powerful one and we can test it out here.

Exercise

Sit up straight in your chair, look up at the ceiling, hold a big smile on your face and try to feel really miserable. Really try hard now.

You may have found that difficult, so now try the opposite. Slump down in your chair, look down at the ground, hold a miserable expression on your face and try to feel really happy.

What you may have discovered for yourself is that the mind and body are very much linked. All that occurred during that exercise was that you adopted two quite different types of body language, yet you may have found that it was difficult, perhaps even impossible, to experience a state of mind that was incongruent with your physiology.

Back to the diagram. The output from the information
processing that goes on in your mind is your behaviour. This
is your reaction to the 'external event' that you have just
experienced, according to how your filters interpreted it. In
your mind, you carry your own unique 'map of the world'
and you use it to make sense of the 'territory' out there. This
process determines how you conduct yourself at all times and
it will always feel right for you. Somebody else in identical
circumstances might behave differently in accordance with
their unique set of filters, and that will be right for him or her,
although it might appear to be completely wrong to you.

So how does this fit into customer care? Let's suppose your
customer has at some time in the past had a bad experience
with a product or service similar to the one they have
purchased from you. Perhaps they tried to complain in order
to get the fault corrected and were met with an extremely
negative, unhelpful response. Maybe this caused them to lose
money – it certainly made them very angry.

Now they have become your customer and a slight problem
has arisen with the product or service you have supplied.
Because they stored some very negative memories as a result
of the past bad experience, these may now come to the surface
and influence the way they behave towards you. To you, the
customer seems to be over-reacting to a minor problem. You
feel their behaviour is inappropriate and, being on the receiving
end, you are now becoming defensive and perhaps even angry.
If you continue in this vein, not only will you probably lose this

customer, and possibly your temper, but you will reinforce their now very negative perception of your organization and your industry.

There is a saying, often attributed to Eleanor Roosevelt: 'No-one upsets me unless I allow it.' No matter how someone is behaving towards you, they cannot make you feel anything that you haven't chosen to feel. It may have been an unconscious choice on your part, but, nevertheless, it *was* your choice.

Learning point 3

You are in control of your mind and your emotions, and you always have choice.

So, given that everyone is different and unique, we need to find a way to 'build a bridge' across to their personal model of the world. We do this through building rapport.

Rapport

What is rapport? It is a term used to describe how two or more people feel *in sync* or *on the same wavelength* because they feel alike. It stems from an old French verb, *'rapporter'*, which means, literally, to carry something back. In the sense of how people relate to each other, it means that what one person sends out, the other sends back. For example, they may realize that they share similar values, beliefs, knowledge or behaviours around common interests.

Rapport embodies empathy; it is a two-way connection and is, in effect, the bridge across from my model of the world to yours. Having rapport with someone nurtures a better understanding, leading to a greater spirit of mutual co-operation. Resistance or negativity in a customer may indicate that rapport is missing.

Rapport builds naturally and can often be witnessed when the body language of two people interacting with each other ends up matched or mirrored. Be clear on the difference between these two: matching means identical, i.e. both people have their right leg crossed over their left and are leaning to their left, whereas mirroring means that one person is the mirror image of the other. So, if one has his right leg crossed over his left and is leaning to his left, the other person will have her left leg crossed over her right and be leaning to her right. You are more likely to end up *matched* with someone you are sitting or standing next to and *mirrored* with someone opposite you. Both are external indicators that rapport has been built.

It is of course possible to hasten along the process of rapport building by deliberately matching or mirroring the other person. If you choose to do this, subtlety is essential! If what you are doing is too obvious, it can cause offence.

The following diagram is a pie chart showing the three elements of communication – physiology (body language),

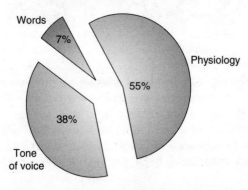

Segments of communication

Words 7%

Physiology 55%

38%

Tone of voice

tone of voice and words – and their relative proportions. Much research has been conducted on these figures, principally by Professor Emeritus of Psychology, Albert Mehrabian.

As you can see, the largest element in communication is physiology. Remember that you can't not communicate; your body language speaks for you, even before you've opened your mouth and uttered a single word. However, on the telephone, you have lost this largest piece of the pie; your body language cannot be seen, although a smile can be heard. When you speak with a smile, your voice sounds happier and more positive, so it's always a good idea to answer the phone with a smile on your face.

Let's look at each of these components in turn, to explore how you can utilize them to build rapport.

Physiology (55 per cent)

Matching or mirroring the other person's posture, gestures and movements, *with subtlety*, is the first place to start. Be very careful to avoid mimicry if, for example, they use very expansive arm gestures when they speak. If you suddenly start doing the same when this is not your normal behaviour, you may cause offence. Instead, use similar gestures on a smaller scale, i.e. hand movements rather than arm movements.

Match the breathing rate. When two people laugh together, their breathing is matched and if you're laughing with someone, you probably have a good rapport with them. Watch for the rise and fall of the shoulders and upper chest area, and match your breathing to theirs. If you are a man matching with a woman, be very careful that your eyes do not stray lower than shoulder level. It's no good excusing yourself by saying 'but I was just watching your breathing rate'; you won't get away with it and you may well get a slap round the face!

Let's imagine for a moment that you have an angry customer in front of you. What has happened to their breathing rate? It has probably speeded up because, as we know, emotional state has an effect on physiology. Perhaps you've been in this situation; you chose to stay really calm and your customer, instead of calming down, got even angrier. The reason for this is that rapport was lacking. Your customer's unconscious mind was telling him or her that because you were so different to them, clearly you just didn't understand the gravity of the situation and so they would have to ramp up their own behaviour in order to make their point more clearly.

In this scenario, you can use a technique called *pacing and leading*. If, while you are listening to your angry customer, you match their rapid breathing rate, you are expressing empathy and building a bridge across to their model of the world. This is called *pacing*. After a minute or so of doing this, start to slow down your breathing rate. If sufficient rapport has been built, they will now start to follow you and slow down their breathing, which in turn will move them towards a calmer state. You are now *leading*. This is a very effective strategy and because the other person is responding at an unconscious level, it will feel completely natural to them and not manipulative at all. Remember that matched breathing is something that occurs naturally; you are just hastening that process along to help your customer feel that you really do understand their grievance.

The final thing that you can match on body language is the blink rate. Be very careful if the other person has a squint, so as not to cause offence; however, this is another very effective way of creating a similarity and building rapport.

Tone of voice (38 per cent)

Have you ever been speaking with someone who has a very strong accent or dialect, and you unwittingly picked it up and started reflecting it back to them? This is a guaranteed way of offending through mimicry, caused by your unconscious mind's desire to create a similarity and build rapport. This is more likely to happen during a telephone conversation, when physiology plays very little part and tone of voice becomes approximately 80 per cent of the communication.

Instead, you can match the following elements of the other person's voice:

● volume
● speed
● tone
● energy
● intonation
● phrasing.

Pacing and leading can also play a part in calming down an angry customer over the telephone, without taking on board their angry emotional state. By sounding like them, even temporarily, they feel understood and it then becomes much easier for you to deal with their problem.

Exercise

In a very calm, quiet voice, read the following out loud:

'I cannot believe you've had this trouble, Mr Jones. This isn't like us at all. Now what I'm going to do is to make a note of everything you've told me, investigate it all personally and come back to you with an answer by the end of today. Is that acceptable to you?'

If you were saying this to a receptive, albeit angry, customer, they might let you get to the end of it without interrupting. However, there is a 50 per cent chance that they would jump in after the second sentence and start ranting again because there is a mismatch between your tone of voice and theirs.

So now read out the section in quotes again and this time, for the first two sentences, speak a little more loudly and faster. Then continue by gradually slowing down your speed and turning down the volume until you speak the final sentence in a calm voice.

This time, you have matched your angry customer's tone of voice. They feel understood and so are now prepared to enter into a calmer conversation with you. All you did was increase your energy levels for the first two sentences – and you didn't have to get angry to do that. The words you used were exactly the same both times – only the sound of your voice was different.

Words (7 per cent)

This is the smallest component of communication, but over the telephone it increases in value to about 20 per cent. In terms of matching, listen for the following:

● *Key words* – these are either individual words or short phrases that we like and use a lot. They vary from person to person and may include words such as:
   – basically
   – actually
   – cool
   – you know
   – okay
   – at the end of the day.

If you hear someone using any word or short phrase repeatedly, then you are hearing their key words. When you respond to them, incorporate those same words into your reply, and you are then 'speaking their language'.

● *VHF words* – when we speak, we tend to use words that fit into our preferred 'channel' of communication. These can be:
  - *visual* – examples are 'I see what you mean', 'Looks good to me', 'Show me more', etc.
  - *hearing* – examples are 'I hear what you're saying', 'That rings a bell', 'Sounds familiar', etc.
  - *feeling* – examples are 'I want to get a grip on this idea', 'I'm going with my gut feeling', 'That really touched me', etc.

If you can hear someone using vocabulary that falls predominantly into one of these three channels, then adjust your language so that you are using the same type of words. When you do this, you have 'tuned into their wavelength'.

Rapport in writing

If you are writing to someone and you don't know their preferred VHF channel, or if you are writing promotional material that will be read by many people, then balance the number of VHF words that you use. This will ensure that at least one-third of your text will be tuning into your reader's wavelength.

For example, 'We *see* from our records that it is some time since we have *spoken* and *felt* this was a good time to write to you.'

And JK Rowling? Open any Harry Potter book at any page and you will see that she uses a good balance of VHF words on every page. No wonder her books are so hard to put down . . .

Summary

In this chapter, we have explored the concept of everyone being different and unique, determined by our unique sets of internal 'filters', which in turn influence how we make sense of things and react to them. Perhaps you have watched a film with a friend; you thought it was brilliant and he or she thought it was rubbish. Neither of you is right or wrong – you are both evaluating the film using your own sets of filters, which are different.

We all create our own private 'model of the world' that enables us to make sense of what is going on around us and drives our behaviour. Past experiences play a huge part in the creation of our model and can mean that someone else's behaviour seems inappropriate to us, whereas it feels 'right' to them.

Rapport is the key to effective communication and enables us to build a bridge across into someone else's model of the world. By using the principles of matching and mirroring body language, tone of voice and words, we can replicate natural rapport building in a fraction of the 'normal' time.

Remember that it is impossible to not communicate. This means that everything covered in this chapter can be put into practice any time, anywhere, with anybody. Communication is the most essential skill you have in your 'toolbox' – use it well and it will reward you amply.

SUNDAY
MONDAY
TUESDAY
WEDNESDAY
THURSDAY
FRIDAY
SATURDAY

Fact-check (answers at the back)

Note: all questions require a single answer.

1. Which statement is true?
a) The conscious mind can process a minimum of 15 things at a time. ❑
b) The unconscious mind makes two million neural connections a second. ❑
c) The conscious mind is the 95 per cent of the brain that we use most. ❑
d) Your 'power house' is your conscious mind. ❑

2. Filters . . .
a) Are identical for everyone ❑
b) Remain exactly the same throughout life ❑
c) Can cause the conscious mind to become overloaded ❑
d) Make sense of incoming information. ❑

3. Which statement is true?
a) The fastest way to change how you feel is to eat chocolate. ❑
b) Body language has nothing to do with feelings. ❑
c) Changing your physiology instantly changes your state of mind. ❑
d) Thoughts and emotions are completely disconnected. ❑

4. In your mind, you carry your unique:
a) Model of the world ❑
b) Telephone directory ❑
c) Map of the London underground ❑
d) European road atlas. ❑

5. Which statement is true?
a) Matching and mirroring are not natural processes. ❑
b) 'Rapport' comes from an old Italian verb. ❑
c) When deliberately matching someone else, movements should be exaggerated. ❑
d) Rapport enables a bridge to be built across to someone else's model of the world. ❑

6. The three elements of communication are:
a) Physiology, tone of voice, words ❑
b) Eye contact, handshake, written word ❑
c) Dress code, smiling, gestures ❑
d) Telephone, face to face, email. ❑

7. Which statement is true?
a) Physiology is 58 per cent of communication. ❑
b) Words make up the smallest element of communication. ❑
c) Tone of voice is worth 70 per cent over the telephone. ❑
d) Spacing and leading is a rapport-building technique. ❑

8. Which statement is true?
a) Mimicking an accent builds rapport rapidly. ❏
b) Breathing is mismatched when people laugh together. ❏
c) Pacing and leading can help to calm down an angry customer. ❏
d) Matching somebody's blink rate serves no purpose. ❏

9. Which statement is true?
a) To 'speak somebody's language', match their key words. ❏
b) Until you speak, you are not communicating. ❏
c) If someone is quietly spoken, it's good to speak louder. ❏
d) It is impossible to build rapport over the telephone. ❏

10. Which statement is true?
a) 'I get the picture' indicates the hearing channel of communication. ❏
b) VHF stands for virtual, hearing, feeling. ❏
c) 'Feeling' people use words such as 'Tell me more'. ❏
d) To establish rapport in writing, use a balanced selection of VHF words. ❏

FRIDAY

Attitude is everything

In the last chapter, the point was made that it is impossible not to communicate. Even if you are not speaking, your body language speaks for you, and, in so doing, it conveys your state of mind. If a member of your customer-facing staff is feeling demotivated, not enjoying his or her job or even just having a 'bad hair day', his or her body language and general behaviour will reflect this. This means that there is a very strong chance that your customers will pick up on your staff member's negative attitude and this will damage their experience of doing business with you.

The definition of 'living the dream' in terms of a career is when your vocation is also your vacation. In other words, you love doing the work that you are employed to do and even if you weren't being paid to do it, you would still choose to do it anyway. Employees who are like this are totally self-motivated. They are natural peak performers and if every member of your staff is this type of person, then your organization is truly living the dream.

Probably, this is not quite the reality for you. So, in this chapter, we will explore attitude, motivation and how to positively enjoy being of service to customers.

SUNDAY

MONDAY

TUESDAY

WEDNESDAY

THURSDAY

FRIDAY

SATURDAY

When the customer is an inconvenience

Can you remember a time when, as a customer, you found yourself on the receiving end of somebody else's indifference, negativity even. Perhaps you dared to complain about a product or service and you were met with a hostile response, which was completely inappropriate. That may well have been the last time you dealt with that organization and, possibly, you warned others to avoid it too.

And yet, what you actually had was a bad experience with one individual, not with the whole organization. If you had been served by another member of staff, who was helpful, polite and genuinely interested in resolving your problem to the very best of their ability, your perception would have been completely different. You might even have ended up recommending that organization to your friends and family.

What this means is that every individual within an organization is, at any time, representative of that organization. If one of your customer-facing staff has a big argument with their partner before coming into work one morning, and carries that anger around with them all day, there is a strong chance that they will end up snapping at your customers. Anyone on the receiving end of this unjustified treatment may well form a negative impression of your entire organization. After all, if one of your staff behaves like that, perhaps they all do.

HAVE YOU TRIED STICKING PLASTER?

So how do you know how your staff behave towards customers? You may have personally witnessed their standard of service by being present when they were dealing with a customer, either face to face or over the telephone. However, their behaviour when there is nobody present to observe or supervise them may be quite different.

Mystery shopper

One very effective way of finding out exactly how your staff treat your customers is to carry out a mystery shopper exercise. This means that you, or someone appointed by you, adopts the role of a customer to ascertain how your staff behave in the following areas:

- dealing with telephone enquiries
- dealing with face-to-face enquiries
- selling goods or services
- ordering goods to be collected or delivered
- arranging delivery of goods to a customer's premises
- ensuring that delivery of the correct goods is carried out on schedule
- dealing with the return of faulty or unwanted goods
- dealing with complaints (face to face and over the telephone)
- dealing with a 'difficult' person and
- any other areas relative to your business.

By now, you will have created service standards and procedures, and communicated these to your staff, so carrying out a mystery shopper exercise is the ideal opportunity to check how well they have been understood and implemented. The results may also highlight situations that your staff need to deal with which you had not anticipated, so this provides an opportunity to revise and improve your standards and procedures.

Before carrying out a mystery shopper exercise, create a checklist of all the aspects you would like to review. For a face-to-face exercise, these could include:

- time taken to acknowledge and greet you
- if there was a queue, how many people were in it?
- friendliness of the greeting

- attentiveness of listening
- accurate understanding of your needs
- appropriateness of response
- accuracy of information provided
- speed of service
- standard of personal appearance
- general demeanour of the staff member(s)
- cleanliness and tidiness of the premises.

For a telephone exercise, the following could also be included:

- time taken to answer the phone
- friendliness and clarity of the greeting
- ease of being connected to the appropriate person
- if put on hold, for how long?
- if a request for a call back was made, did it happen and how long did it take?

If you are conducting a mystery shopper exercise by telephone, it is a good idea to record the call. There are many ways to do this, one of which is to use Skype, a free, downloadable software package that enables calls to be made via the internet. You can either use a headset connected to a desktop computer or laptop or use the computer's speakers and plug in a microphone. There are recording options that work in conjunction with Skype and these will generate a sound file at the end of the call. These recordings can then be used in staff training sessions as both good and not so good examples of how to handle incoming calls from customers.

I once worked with an estate agency that used a selection of recorded mystery shopper calls as part of their induction training for new staff. I remember one in particular in which the phone could be heard persistently ringing before the receiver was eventually picked up and put straight back down again to disconnect the call. This happened three times before the mystery shopper gave up. It transpired that these calls had been made just after 9.00 a.m. on a Monday morning and when the particular member of staff was 'confronted' with the evidence and asked for an explanation, he replied, 'I'm not a morning person!'

SUNDAY

MONDAY

TUESDAY

WEDNESDAY

THURSDAY

FRIDAY

SATURDAY

Learning point 1

If you have any members of staff with an attitude like this, you need to know about it before your customers let you know by taking their business elsewhere.

The motivated individual

In an earlier chapter, Waterstones featured as a case study in enhancing the 'customer experience'. Tim Waterstone personally recruited his first 500–600 staff and has been quoted as saying: 'A good attitude, good spirit and optimism in somebody is a precious thing. Without this, no matter how good somebody is technically, they'll bring you down.'

So motivation starts at the recruitment stage. Once employed, there needs to be a working environment that nurtures ongoing motivation for *all* staff. Research has shown that money (in terms of salary) is not the top motivator in the workplace. People need to feel acknowledged and valued for the job that they do and this can be achieved by verbal, genuine praise and awards, which may or may not be financial. In the world of cinema, an actor can be paid millions for appearing in a film and may receive great media reviews by critics, but what means the most to them is the ultimate accolade of being awarded an Oscar for their performance.

Motivation through employee involvement

A good example of an organization that fully involves its staff in its day-to-day operations and recognizes their contributions by awarding a performance-related bonus for everyone is the John Lewis Partnership.

Founded in 1864 by John Spedan Lewis, the company has a written constitution that sets out the principles, governance system and rules of the partnership. It states that the happiness of its members is the partnership's ultimate purpose, recognizing that such happiness depends on having a satisfying job in a successful business. It establishes a system of rights and responsibilities, which places on all partners the requirement to work for the improvement of the business in the knowledge that everyone shares the rewards of success.

This system works so well that in March 2014, the 91,000 staff, or 'partners', who co-own the retail group received a bonus of

15 per cent of their annual salary in that month's wages. It is considered that the motivation generated by employee ownership gives the company a competitive advantage. The John Lewis Partnership also won 'Multichannel Retailer of the Year' at the Oracle Retail Week Awards in 2014.

One of the methods used by the company to focus on the happiness of its members is the annual partner survey, which was first introduced in 2003. The survey is distributed to all partners and is anonymous, with each store receiving separate results so that concerns can be easily identified and acted upon without compromising that anonymity. Included in the survey are questions related to job satisfaction, pay, career development, management, their branch, the democratic bodies and the partnership as a business. Replies are processed by an external company so that no individual responses are seen by anyone in the partnership. In 2011, some 90 per cent of the partners took part in the survey, with the real value coming from the questions, discussions and actions prompted by the results.

As a democratic business, all major business decisions are shared with partners and active communication is nurtured through councils, forums and committees at local, divisional and partnership levels. There are also online communication channels and publications to keep partners fully informed of business developments. The company's weekly publication, *The Gazette*, was originally created by John Spedan Lewis to communicate news to partners and provide them with a forum for airing their views. It still serves the same purpose today, and partners can write in to *The Gazette* anonymously, if they wish, on any matter.

Considering that the John Lewis Partnership is a retail business that has flourished during an economic downturn that has hit many retail businesses hard, then staff attitude and motivation must be playing a major role in its success.

Employee engagement

Research has shown that the majority of employees would like to take on challenges and are prepared to put in the extra effort needed to excel in their work. However, the reality is that only a small minority actually do so. What this means is that most staff are performing well below their potential, which is known as the 'engagement gap'. Staff may physically be at work but they are not 'there' in any other sense. This is known as 'presenteeism', as opposed to 'absenteeism', when they don't even turn up at all.

Exercise

The following questions are designed to explore how well you know, develop, motivate, involve and reward your staff. The results will identify for you areas within your organization where improvements could be made.

● What does your organization do to build the kind of working relationships between managers and staff, such that staff feel they are 'known' and understood?

....
....
....

How does your organization measure staff morale and what actions are taken to address any morale issues?

....
....
....

How does your organization encourage staff to develop their skills and capabilities?

....
....
....

Does your organization have training programmes readily available (either in house or outsourced) and a budget to fund staff training and development?

....
....
....

Are staff recognized and rewarded for initiating their own development?

....
....
....

How well does your organization communicate its vision, mission and long-term goals?

....
....
....

Do staff fully understand how they fit into this 'big picture' and that everyone's job role plays an important part?

....
....
....

Are your directors seen to be ambassadors for fulfilling the organization's vision and mission, and how much do staff feel inspired by them?

....
....
....

What are the communication channels within your organization and how well is important information cascaded down from director level throughout the organization?

....
....
....

How well do different departments or functions interact with each other and are there any processes to encourage open communication/good working relationships between them?

....
....
....

How are people recognized and rewarded within your organization, such that they feel valued for their efforts?

....
....
....

Do your managers actively pursue a policy of 'catching them doing something right', praising in public and, if necessary, criticizing in private?

....
....
....

If you found yourself guessing at some of the answers related to how your staff feel, then you might like to consider carrying out an employee satisfaction survey. As with your customers, don't assume that no news is good news. Find out what's going on for your staff.

Is the glass half full or half empty?

Would you like the good news or the bad news? Here is the good news – optimism is contagious, and it can generate a fantastic, energized, friendly working environment where it is a joy to come into work.

Here is the bad news – pessimism is also contagious, and it can dampen anyone's enthusiasm, drain staff of their energy and even contribute to absenteeism. After all, who would look forward to spending their working day in an environment like that?

Your staff will also be positively or negatively influenced by the environment in which they work. This means that if they deal with customers, either face to face or over the telephone, their demeanour and attitude will determine their behaviour. The following is an example of a workplace where I cannot imagine any employee being able to feel miserable.

Fruit Towers

Innocent Drinks is a UK-based company founded in 1998 by three Cambridge graduates – Richard Reed, Adam Balon and Jon Wright. At the time, they were working in consulting and advertising; however, after spending six months working on recipes and £500 on fruit, they took a stall at a London music festival and sold their smoothies to the public. People were asked to deposit their empty bottles in a 'yes' or 'no' bin depending on whether they thought the three friends should quit their jobs to make smoothies full time. At the end of the festival, the 'yes' bin was full, with only three empty bottles in the 'no' bin. They went into work the next day and resigned, and Innocent Drinks was born. It now has a 75 per cent share of the £169 million UK smoothie market and the company sells two million smoothies a week.

The company's headquarters, Fruit Towers, has been relocated to another part of London in order to accommodate the growing staff head count. However, as with the original location, it has been furnished to promote the 'happy-go-lucky' image:

- Floors covered in artificial turf rather than carpets.
- Every office area has its own break-out space with soft seating, sofas and a small kitchen area.
- Picnic tables replace a cafeteria.
- An original red British phone box (in the office area).
- Banana-shaped telephones.
- A large lever with the instruction, 'Last leaver, pull the lever', which shuts down the power for the office at night.
- A green lamp that flashes when the outside temperature reaches a suitable level, prompting staff to open the windows as the air conditioning cuts out.
- Delivery vans, lined up outside the offices, are either covered in artificial turf or have been 'decorated' to look like cows.

Office tours take place regularly and members of the public are invited at random to attend the annual general meeting, which has been renamed 'A Grown-up Meeting'.

Add to this working environment the product, which is sugar free, healthy, tasty, consisting of whole fruit and vegetable products in minimal packaging, using 100 per cent recycled bottles, plus the fact that Innocent Drinks donates 10 per cent of its profits to charities every year, and it's not difficult to find happy, motivated staff on board.

Summary

Some people are naturally cheerful and helpful, with a genuine desire to be of service to others. If you are able to recruit people like this into your customer service function, then you will have a force to be reckoned with!

Others need to have these attributes nurtured. They need to feel valued, and they need to be openly recognized for doing a good job. They need to know that their voice will be heard if they have a point to make. They need to feel fully involved in the day-to-day running of their organization and to know that their job role makes a worthwhile contribution.

The quality of the communication within your organization will have a powerful effect on the morale and motivation of staff at all levels. When staff feel they are being 'kept in the dark', they start to shut down. They will find it hard to 'go the extra mile' for an unappreciative employer and a negative attitude will soon be conveyed to your customers.

SUNDAY

MONDAY

TUESDAY

WEDNESDAY

THURSDAY

FRIDAY

SATURDAY

However, just as customer excellence can be achieved with a good idea, so can employee excellence. It really takes very little effort to put in place the kind of initiatives that can generate consistently positive attitudes from your staff. You don't have to rip up the carpet and replace it with artificial turf; all you have to do is communicate with your staff. Ask them what they think, how they feel and what ideas they have to improve the business. And then listen . . .

Fact-check (answers at the back)

Note: all questions require a single answer.

1. An ideal career is when:
a) Your day-to-day work is a chore ❑
b) Your vocation is your vacation ❑
c) Somebody else has chosen your career for you ❑
d) Your work is just something that pays the bills. ❑

2. Which statement is true?
a) Natural peak performers are self-motivated. ❑
b) Peak performer means 'mountaineer'. ❑
c) Peak performers hate their jobs. ❑
d) There is an age limit to being a peak performer. ❑

3. Which statement is true?
a) It's acceptable to be indifferent to a complaining customer. ❑
b) Only directors are representative of their organization. ❑
c) Sales staff should not be expected to be representative of their organization. ❑
d) Every individual within an organization is representative of that organization. ❑

4. Which statement is true?
a) The only way to find out how your staff are performing is to install hidden cameras and microphones. ❑
b) If your staff insist that they're doing a fantastic job, then clearly there is no room for improvement. ❑
c) Using a mystery shopper is an effective way of stepping into your customers' shoes. ❑
d) There is no need to have a checklist prepared before making a mystery shopper call. ❑

5. Which statement is true?
a) Recorded mystery shopper calls can be used in staff training sessions. ❑
b) Staff shouldn't be expected to be polite in the mornings if that is not their preferred time of day. ❑
c) As long as there is music playing, it's acceptable to leave a caller on hold for any length of time. ❑
d) A 'difficult' customer deserves a hostile response. ❑

6. Which statement is true?
a) A positive attitude will not be apparent in a candidate at a recruitment interview. ❏
b) Motivation starts at the recruitment stage. ❏
c) A self-motivated person will never 'go the extra mile' without being asked. ❏
d) An optimistic attitude is unrealistic and irritating. ❏

7. Which statement is true?
a) Salary is the top motivator in the workplace. ❏
b) Nobody needs to be acknowledged for doing a good job. ❏
c) Criticizing in public is a good idea. ❏
d) Verbal, genuine praise contributes to motivation. ❏

8. Which statement is true?
a) The John Lewis Partnership was founded in 1864. ❏
b) Only the directors are 'partners'. ❏
c) It is considered to be an autocratic business. ❏
d) 50 per cent of the partners took part in the 2011 survey. ❏

9. Which statement is true?
a) Information is power; therefore communication should be severely restricted. ❏
b) People appreciate being 'kept in the dark' as ignorance is bliss. ❏
c) Good communication at all levels in an organization helps staff to feel valued. ❏
d) Communication has nothing to do with staff motivation. ❏

10. Which statement is true?
a) Innocent Drinks sells 100,000 smoothies a week. ❏
b) Fruit Towers has artificial turf instead of carpets in the office areas. ❏
c) It's easy to feel miserable in a 'happy-go-lucky' work environment. ❏
d) Innocent's delivery vans are covered in cotton wool to look like sheep. ❏

SUNDAY
MONDAY
TUESDAY
WEDNESDAY
THURSDAY
FRIDAY
SATURDAY

SATURDAY

Plan to excel

This chapter will focus on helping you to become a recognized market leader in customer care by creating and maintaining a reputation that will speak for you. In the previous chapters, much of the groundwork has been done in giving you an awareness of all the different aspects that contribute to customer excellence. In this chapter, we will aim to consolidate all those aspects into defining a 'way forward' that will generate an ongoing momentum throughout your organization.

For some businesses, this 'way forward' might just be a matter of reinforcing existing processes and practices. For others, the introduction of new customer care techniques may generate a culture change – for the better, of course! The common denominator is one of communicating service standards, amended processes, new initiatives and so on to staff at all levels, using the most appropriate methods.

The key concept, which *must* be embraced for customer excellence to be achieved, is that leadership in customer care comes from the top. It is not just the responsibility of customer-facing staff; it is the responsibility of *everyone* within an organization. This means that training programmes and workshops are as relevant for company directors as they are for staff manning a help desk.

Also, your customers are not just external to your organization. You also have internal customers who need to be accorded an appropriate level of service without being constantly compromised in favour of fee-paying customers. Let's look at this area first.

Internal customers

Every function within an organization exists to play a part in the overall process of the organization's business transactions. The relationships between these different functions are co-dependent. Some of these relationships run smoothly, like a well-oiled machine. However, others sometimes break down, often resulting in fingers of blame being pointed in multiple directions.

It is at times like these that departments can end up behaving as if they are in competition with each other and, consequently, working relationships deteriorate. Any spirit of co-operation that was in place ceases and somewhere, at the far end of all this turmoil going on, is an external customer being let down.

Again, direction and leadership needs to come from the top. Even though every department is focused on achieving goals and targets within allocated budgets, everyone is working for the same organization. It can be very easy to lose sight of this bigger picture, and this is where leadership by example plays a key role.

It is important that staff at all levels in an organization have visibility of their directors 'walking the walk', that is living the vision and the mission and demonstrating that they are in touch with, and care about, everyone within the organization. If any new key clients or major orders have been won, then it's good to communicate this to all staff and congratulate them on the parts that they have played in this achievement.

It is also a good plan to encourage cross-functional communication, in order to engender a better understanding of how other functions operate, timescales they are subject to, challenges they regularly encounter, and the role they play in the whole scheme of things. This can be done, for example, by inviting someone from another department to come along and give a presentation at your next department meeting.

This is the type of information that needs to be included in induction training for new staff, and perhaps also documented in an employee manual. In a large organization, it is easy for individuals to feel that they are just a cog in a large wheel; however, wheels cannot turn without those cogs. Everyone needs to know how they fit into the organization, how important their working relationships with others are and how their individual job role contributes to the overall success of the organization.

In short, the organization that has staff who feel informed and valued will be perceived by customers as an organization with which they would like to do business. The organization that cares about its staff also cares about its customers, and this is a great culture to nurture.

Training

Induction training for new staff is essential, and your customer service standards and procedures can be included in this. However, training in customer care should not be seen as a one-off. Even staff who have been on the head count for a few years will benefit from 'refresher' training; after all, customer expectations are constantly changing, particularly with developing technology. Also, if the attendees on a course are a mixture of some who have been with the company for only a short time and others who have been employed for many years, the exchange of experiences and knowledge between them will be invaluable.

Similarly, if the course is deliberately positioned to be cross-functional, with attendees drawn from a variety of different departments, then they will not only learn about customer care, but they will also learn and understand more about each other.

Beware of having too many attendees on a training session. There is nothing worse than being faced with a group of people with their arms folded defiantly, sighing heavily, telling you in an angry tone of voice that they are only there because their managers sent them. It is better to opt for smaller groups and to make the training a 'workshop' in which ideas, opinions and other contributions are welcomed.

It is also important that people know why they are attending the workshop. Uninformed people will be completely disconnected from the training; they will not be remotely interested in learning anything at all and they will resent the time they are having to spend away from their jobs.

Be aware that everyone's favourite radio station is WIIFM, or 'What's In It For Me?'. Think about how you can make the idea of attending a customer care workshop sound interesting and intriguing, exciting even. The following are some ideas that you could use.

- You are creating new customer service standards for the company and you are keen to get input from staff on their techniques for dealing with customers and their problems in order to get the best results. Everyone invited to attend will have the opportunity to review and comment on the new standards you are creating, as well as put forward their own ideas for 'best practice'.

  The best idea put forward at each workshop will win a prize (make this worth having, for example a £25 voucher for a retailer of their choice).

- The company is thinking of introducing incentives for outstanding customer service and everyone within the organization will be eligible, even those who do not deal directly with external customers.

  The workshop will be a vehicle for communicating the scheme to staff, gaining their input and agreement to criteria being set for achieving an award (which could be financial or something else they would prefer) and generally help them on their way to winning an award for themselves.

- Create a 'branded' customer service programme, to be rolled out throughout your organization. Make it fun and funky, without losing the underlying purpose, and start promoting it well before the training workshops start to generate curiosity and anticipation. For example, I once created a customer service programme for a client in the insurance industry and called it 'In Step'. The theme was all about being 'in step' with their customers, so it embraced rapport building on the telephone, listening skills, problem-solving and so on.

A logo for the programme was created, incorporating a couple of footprints, and posters were put up around the building along the lines of 'In Step – coming your way' and 'Are you In Step yet?' and so on. As part of the course content, I included a short session on line dancing! Part-way through the training day, we stopped and pushed all the tables and chairs back, I taught everyone a very simple line dancing routine and then everyone did it together to music. The whole point of line dancing is that everyone is 'in step' with each other, otherwise it doesn't work, so this made it relevant to the programme. Needless to say, everyone loved it: it was a great energizer and it made the programme memorable.

Note that if you choose to create a branded customer care programme and roll it out to your entire organization, this also generates a public relations opportunity. You can publicly announce that your organization cares so much about its customers that everyone, without exception, receives innovative training in being customer focused. However, be aware that this is a double-edged sword. Once you have gone public on this, customer expectations of service from your organization will increase, so staff must consistently put into practice what they have been taught.

Workshop content

In creating the content for a customer care workshop, think about including the following:

● **Objectives and outcomes for attendees** – people need to know why they are there and what they are going to get from it (WIIFM).
● **Definitions of all the elements that constitute customer care** – invite ideas from delegates as a brainstorming activity, ensuring that everything that needs to be identified does get identified. See Sunday's chapter for inspiration.

- **Examples of good and bad customer service** – this works well as an exercise. Divide into small groups and ask each group to come up with one example of outstandingly good customer service that they have received, and one example of extremely bad customer service. This often brings out some real horror stories, and also starts to get them into the idea of stepping into the shoes of the customer.
- **The expectations of your company's customers** – ask for their ideas, and then follow with the next question.
- **How well are you meeting their expectations?** Generally, delegates will believe that they are doing a good job of serving customers, so if you have any results from a customer satisfaction survey or from a mystery shopper exercise, this is a good time to present them.
- **Customer service standards** – these should encapsulate the principle of meeting customer expectations. In discussion with the group, check that the standards are seen as being realistic, to ensure that they are fully embraced by delegates.
- **Customer excellence** – leading on from just meeting service standards, this topic introduces the idea of going 'above and beyond' what the customer expects in order to achieve excellence. Relate it back to the earlier examples identified by the group of outstandingly good customer service.
- **How can we exceed customer expectations**? This encourages delegates to start identifying 'excellence initiatives'. The real bonus here is that because they are formulating these ideas themselves, any feasible ideas will automatically be fully supported by their 'authors'. Divide into small groups and ask each group to present three different ideas for achieving customer excellence. Among their answers there are bound to be some real 'gems', which could be implemented in your organization.
- **Rapport building** – this is an essential skill in customer service. You could include some of the tips and techniques explored in Thursday's chapter, 'Excellence in communication'.
- **Problem solving** – there are three golden rules that should always be observed when dealing with customers' problems, which are:

1 **Always say what you can do rather than what you can't do** when resolving a customer problem. This will make you sound more positive and helpful, even if you are unable to provide the exact solution that the customer wants.

2 **Always do what you say you will do**. It is essential to follow through on actions that you have promised a customer you will carry out. For example, if you have promised to ring them back by a certain time with an update, but at that time you have nothing new to tell them, ring them back anyway to tell them that. Don't leave them in the dark – they will assume that you don't care and you have abandoned them.

3 **Take ownership of a customer's problem** if it is reported to you first. Even if it does require the involvement of another department to resolve it, monitor progress to ensure that it does get sorted out to the customer's satisfaction and within an acceptable timeframe.

● **Mystery shop other organizations in your industry**. This is an optional exercise that I have included in workshops in the past and which has worked particularly well. Here's what you do:

1 Ask delegates to brainstorm all those elements that play a part in handling an incoming enquiry by telephone effectively, e.g. time taken to answer, friendliness of greeting, helpful attitude.

2 List all of these on a flip chart and then ask delegates to prioritize them in order of importance to a potential customer.

3 Divide into pairs and give each pair a pre-prepared list of four other organizations in your industry, with telephone numbers, and either provide them with a phone to make the calls or check that they are happy to use their own mobile phones. If necessary, lend them your mobile phone for the exercise.

4 Using the prioritized list of elements to listen out for, each pair makes telephone enquiries to the organizations on their list and allocates marks out of ten against each of the elements.

5 Reconvene the whole group and take feedback. Check for any calls that were handled particularly well or particularly badly.

6 Bring out the learning point that they were speaking to just one individual within that organization. They could ring that same company again and speak to somebody else and have a completely different experience. Every individual is representative of their organization, and you never get a second chance to make a first impression.

Post training

It is important to keep the momentum of training going after the course is over. If you have incorporated this training into an induction programme, then providing your new starters with mentors for their first few months in the company is always a good idea.

If you have been encouraging staff to propose customer excellence initiatives during training, then it is to everyone's benefit to keep this ball rolling. Your organization may already have a 'suggestion scheme' in place, under which anyone can submit ideas for improvement and cost savings in any area of the organization. Think about expanding this to include customer excellence initiatives, with a prize for the best one submitted each month of, say, £100 in value.

The real bonus of this course of action is that it keeps everyone thinking about customer care all the time. It also means that your organization has developed into one that is serious about continuous improvement in your levels of customer service. And that is a very good reputation to have.

One good idea

The teabag was originally invented in 1908 when Thomas Sullivan, a New York tea and coffee merchant, started packaging loose tea in small hand-sewn silk bags as a convenient way to send tea samples to his customers. Recipients of these silk bags thought that the tea was intended to be brewed in the bags and so put these directly into their cups instead of removing the contents. As a result, the teabag was born.

Tetley Tea launched its teabag in Britain in 1953, which, like other tea companies' teabags, was the conventional square shape. However, someone came up with the idea of introducing round teabags and, in 1989, Tetley embarked on an advertising campaign promoting the benefits of the new shape. In a television advert, an animation demonstrated how tea leaves got caught up in the corners of a square tea bag, whereas in a round bag they could circulate freely and give the tea drinker an improved 'all-round flavour'.

Tetley's sales of the new round teabag went through the roof. Before long, its inventory turnover had increased by 30 per cent, and within 18 months it had gained brand leadership in the UK – all as a result of one good idea.

Internet customers

So far, we have focused on dealing with customers face to face or over the telephone; however, people are increasingly purchasing goods and services over the internet. The principles of customer care remain the same, in particular that if people are buying through your website, then they need to be able to contact customer support just as easily through your website.

The main challenge is that of managing customer expectations. If people are 'surfing the net' and making purchases in the early hours of the morning, they may expect that a complaint they have emailed to you will be answered more promptly than is realistic. This particularly applies to international customers, where there may be a time difference of several hours. The best way to handle this is for an automatic response to be sent out in reply to a customer's email, acknowledging receipt and providing a timescale within which the customer can expect to receive a personal reply. It is then essential that a customer support person responds to the individual within this time frame.

One of the major benefits of achieving customer excellence via the internet is that a delighted customer may give you a 'viral referral'; in other words, they sing your praises to friends and followers through a variety of social media sites.

There is, of course, a downside to this. A dissatisfied customer can also spread the word very quickly and very widely, which could seriously damage the reputation of your organization. Remember the iceberg model from Tuesday's chapter.

Your customer service standards should include a time frame within which complaints will be investigated and resolved. If a problem cannot be resolved within that time, then there needs to be regular communication with the customer to keep them up to date with progress. Although this applies to all your customers, it is imperative that this happens with your internet customers because these people are more likely to be users of Facebook, Twitter, LinkedIn and other social media sites.

SUNDAY
MONDAY
TUESDAY
WEDNESDAY
THURSDAY
FRIDAY
SATURDAY

Summary

In this final chapter, we have explored those things that need to happen to move your organization forward to becoming a recognized market leader in customer care. Training is a key element of this, and for *everyone* in an organization, not just those who deal directly with external customers. It is also important that a training programme addresses the 'What's in it for me?' question in order to gain the support of staff.

Once a training programme has kickstarted the customer excellence mentality, it is important to keep that momentum going with incentives and awards. A suggestion box might sound very basic, yet it is a practical way of encouraging people to put forward their ideas, with the assurance that they will be taken seriously and reviewed in a confidential environment. And a suggestion box doesn't need to be a physical box; it can be a virtual box with a dedicated email address.

SUNDAY

MONDAY

TUESDAY

WEDNESDAY

THURSDAY

FRIDAY

SATURDAY

We have also looked at the concept of internal customers and the benefits to the entire organization of improving cross-functional communication and understanding.

Leadership from the top and leadership by example are the real drivers for creating and sustaining customer excellence. However, the following two 'rules' also work very well:

The golden rule of customer care is to treat others as you would like to be treated.

The platinum rule of customer care is to treat others as they would like to be treated, and then some.

Fact-check (answers at the back)

Note: all questions require a single answer.

1. Which statement is true?
   a) Customer care is purely the responsibility of customer-facing staff. ❑
   b) Leadership in customer care comes from the top. ❑
   c) Customer care is driven by your competitors. ❑
   d) Directors do not need training in customer care. ❑

2. Which statement is true?
   a) All customers are external to your organization. ❑
   b) Internal customers are other companies in your industry. ❑
   c) Internal customers are other departments in your organization. ❑
   d) Only external customers matter. ❑

3. Which statement is true?
   a) Directors need to be seen to 'walk the walk'. ❑
   b) Directors should be made to walk the plank. ❑
   c) Directors need to remain remote from their staff. ❑
   d) Only the sales force need to know about a major new order. ❑

4. Which statement is true?
   a) New starters should attend reduction training. ❑
   b) An induction course should not include any references to customer care. ❑
   c) Induction training is only necessary in large organizations. ❑
   d) Induction training is for new staff. ❑

5. Which statement is true?
   a) Customer care training needs to be recurring rather than a 'one-off'. ❑
   b) Customer expectations always remain the same. ❑
   c) If someone has been employed by the organization for five years, then there is nothing new they can learn about customer care. ❑
   d) Directors are exempt from customer care training. ❑

6. Which statement is true?
   a) 'Cross-functional' means that different functions get cross with each other. ❑
   b) Cross-functional training helps different departments understand each other. ❑
   c) There can never be too many attendees on a training course. ❑
   d) Delegates on a training course should all be from the same department. ❑

SUNDAY
MONDAY
TUESDAY
WEDNESDAY
THURSDAY
FRIDAY
SATURDAY

7. Which statement is true?
a) People don't need to know the reason they are attending a workshop. ❏
b) Everyone is comfortable to speak up in front of a large group of people. ❏
c) When attending a workshop, you must bring along a hammer and nails. ❏
d) Everyone's favourite radio station is WIIFM. ❏

8. Which statement is true?
a) A branded customer service programme can be rolled out throughout the organization. ❏
b) A good customer service programme is weird and meaningless. ❏
c) Incentives for delivering customer excellence are pointless. ❏
d) It is unlikely that any good ideas will come from staff on a workshop. ❏

9. Which statement is true?
a) Customers do not hold any expectations of service levels at all. ❏
b) Always tell a customer what you can't do for them. ❏
c) Always follow through and do what you say you will do. ❏
d) Never take ownership of a problem that isn't directly your fault. ❏

10. Which statement is true?
a) You should mystery shop only your own organization, not others. ❏
b) A suggestion scheme can help to maintain the momentum of training. ❏
c) Teabags have always been round in shape. ❏
d) Internet customers never shop outside of your working hours. ❏

Surviving in tough times

No one likes tough times. They bring fear to the marketplace. Employers don't know if their customers will survive, or even if their suppliers will survive. The great news, however, is that there is never more demand for good salespeople than in tough economic times.

The abilities of a key account manager will be tested even more than usual; the skills and experience of good key account managers will set them apart from those less capable, in allowing them to continue to negotiate successfully. When budgets are being squeezed, negotiation will be absolutely critical in securing the deal with which both parties are content.

When people are being careful about what they spend their money on, and indeed whether to spend it at all, the organizations that place great importance on the quality of their customer care are the ones that stand out from the rest.

Here are 40 crucial tips to help you to achieve your selling goals.

Christine Harvey: Tips 1–10; Grant Stewart: Tips 11–20; Peter Fleming: Tips 21–30; Di McLanachan: Tips 31–40.

1 Talk about targets

Whether you are looking for a better job, seeking a promotion or aiming for a pay rise, remember that *everyone* responds well to the concept of targets. When selling to a customer, talk to them about *their* targets. This shows them that you care and that you understand the challenges they face. Then, let them know how your product or service can help them reach *their* targets.

Let prospective employers hear you talk targets, targets, targets. This will tell them that you have systems that guarantee you will reach *their* targets. By talking about targets, you'll be talking their language! And don't forget to dwell on your own targets daily to maximize your success.

2 Visit current and past customers

Some salespeople avoid speaking with current and past clients, fearing that they might get complaints. Actually, the opposite is true. By interviewing past and current clients about the benefits they've derived from your product or service, you're likely to reinvigorate their interest and commitment. You're likely to pique their interest in other products and services you offer, leading to new sales. And in the process, you're likely to gain three valuable benefits for yourself: product knowledge, testimonials and referrals.

3 Understand buying motives

As many as 80 per cent of unsuccessful salespeople try to sell their product or service before they know the buying motives of the customer. They assume they know the motive but, as with anything in life, assumptions are often wrong. If you want to maximize your closings, you need to ask your prospect about the benefits and features they require. By doing this, you'll be able to zero in on their exact needs with your presentation. You'll save countless hours, which you'll be able to use to close more sales. You'll have time left over for more prospecting and you'll join the top 20 per cent of sales professionals.

4 Assume flexibility

An intriguing aspect of human nature is its flexibility. Customers often start out thinking that they must have features A, B and C in a product or service. However, when presented with X, Y and Z, they often become fascinated and shift their priorities. The lesson of this is simple: to maximize sales, don't be discouraged when you don't have all the features the customer first asks for. Other aspects of your product or service may satisfy or override those being initially sought. They may have more faith in you and your company than in your competitor. By exploring these concepts rather than settling for defeat, you will prosper.

5 Turn objections to your advantage

Objections never stop the top 2 per cent of sales professionals. In fact, they treasure objections. To join their ranks and learn to value objections, you need to understand that prospective customers are showing interest when they bring up objections. If a person has no interest, they won't waste time bringing up objections. The top 2 per cent choose to see the objection as a question, as an encouragement. Then they proceed with the three-part process shown in Wednesday's chapter. By adopting this attitude and skill yourself, you will join the top 2 per cent, and you'll not only survive in tough times, you'll also gain enormously.

6 Master the component parts

Successful selling is not a fly-by-the-seat-of-the-pants process. A successful sales process has a precise structure. Learn that structure and you'll succeed. Just as in the manufacturing process, there are component parts in the sales process, which include discovering the corporate and personal buying motive, gaining product expertise, knowing your competitors' strengths and weaknesses, linking needs to benefits, overcoming objections, reviewing their needs and the benefits we offer and – last, but not least – the successful close. By mastering these, you'll turn tough times into good times, possibly the best ever.

7 Strike while the iron is hot

Fewer than 20 per cent of salespeople maximize the closing of sales, because they miss the right time to ask for the business. After putting tremendous effort into prospecting, setting up appointments and making presentations, ineffective salespeople walk away from the business by not asking timely closing questions. They fool themselves into thinking that they don't need to ask for the business, or they wait too long. Don't let this happen to you. Study the 'customer interest cycle' in Friday's chapter and master 'striking while the iron is hot'.

8 Create your own action-provoking system

In order to survive in tough times, we need to make each minute count – be it in closing a sale or gaining more prospects. The best way to do this is to create a foolproof, easy-to-use system that will tell you which prospect needs to be closed each day, as well as how many new prospects need to be acquired. Friday's chapter gives you tried and true methods for creating a system perfect for you, that will allow you to know instantly where to put your efforts each day to maximize your sales.

9 Dare to be different

To succeed at the highest levels in sales, think of yourself as running your own business. If you owned a retail or a manufacturing business, you would undoubtedly run it according to your own judgement. You wouldn't follow the practices of other business owners, especially if they were unsuccessful or mediocre in their results. However, when salespeople have good ideas about how to run their sales practice but see no one else doing it, they often hold themselves back. Don't let this happen to you. To turn tough times into prosperous times, follow your inspiration and dare to be different.

10 Take the most challenging path

When you come to a crossroads in life, you have two choices. You can take the easy road, the familiar one that you've travelled before. Alternatively, you can take the more challenging road, the one you've not tried before. The choice is yours.

Research shows that the most successful people choose the challenging path. They do this because it offers personal growth, variety and a chance to use and improve their skills and knowledge. This leads to higher responsibility, higher income and high satisfaction. The next time you're faced with a decision, think about taking the most challenging path in order to survive and prosper in tough times.

11 Work harder at knowing your customer

Understanding your customer through your possession of knowledge of them and their sales is vitally important when profits are being squeezed. In more solvent times, when it is not necessary to watch every last pound, charm and a little knowledge may be all that are required to win a profitable deal with a customer. This is no longer the case; ensure you have fulfilled all your information requirements for a strong negotiating position.

12 Ensure your information management is up to date

To maximize your position in negotiations with the customer, not only must your knowledge and understanding of them be up to date, but so must your management of this information. In addition to knowing your customer, this information allows you to analyse your growth opportunities; it is no longer reasonable to assume that all accounts will grow, or at similar rates. Reassess the information you have gathered and continually update it to keep you as informed as possible.

13 Understand that your customer is also under pressure

This pressure will mean they are likely to enter negotiations with an ambitious price reduction in mind, which may well make the atmosphere more aggressive. You will need to work hard to ensure the tone of discussions is neither defensive nor offensive but one that allows constructive trading of ideas to achieve a positive result. Remember the best negotiations are a win-win situation: both parties should feel that they have gained something through the interaction.

14 Promote value-added services

One way to persuade your customer that a price reduction is not the best deal for either of you is to promote the value-added services that you can offer. During a time of lower sales, your own staff may well be in a position to take on functions that will assist the customer – for instance with weekly or monthly reports, on products and quantities, as appropriate – and will facilitate information management for both parties and keep your staff busier at a time when senior management may be querying whether your staff is fully occupied.

15 Develop working relationships

The value-added services you can offer your customer have a two-fold benefit. Not only can they assist with information management, but they can also facilitate the development of a rapport between your own staff and that of your customer. A rewarding and valuable relationship requires that every single member of your staff works within the guidelines established following the information-gathering stages. If an employee offends or pleases, be it a delivery driver or finance assistant, this will reflect on the key account manager.

16 Manage your staff

While it is always important that staff should be well managed, it is of benefit to not only maintain but perhaps increase the focus during straitened times. If the momentum of high sales and profitability is wavering, so might staff commitment and attention to detail. In your quest for sales, don't neglect appraisals, goal setting and performance reviews, all of which will remind your staff that best practice is still required. Hold regular meetings to keep your team involved.

17 Continually revisit your comparisons of account profitability

Comparisons that previously may have been made only annually, may now be relevant on a more frequent basis. Your strong information management and possession of customer knowledge will make the reviews simple. If your league tables of profitability are reviewed monthly for instance, if appropriate, you are more likely to maximize your potential to profit from peaks, even if they are short-lived. Your most profitable customer may not be consistent, or may revolve in profitability position with others, even if this would not be the case in more stable times.

18 Reassess costs

It may have become standard to host negotiations with customers in a hotel meeting room or to have outside caterers provide lunch. When profits are high, these costs are easily justified. Nowadays these may be considered luxuries that are ill-afforded. Inevitably the price of this hospitality will be included as a cost incurred in maintaining the contract and therefore ultimately the customer pays: perhaps they would rather not. It weakens your negotiating position if your customer considers you extravagant as they will feel you are making too much profit and will seek to reduce this.

19 Keep staff morale high

When sales and profits are growing, work is fulfilling, exciting and, to an extent, easy. When sales and profits are diminishing, the sales have to be chased, worked much harder for and often have lower financial returns. This can be demoralizing, particularly as bonuses for efforts come when the sales are easier and the rewards must come to an end when the boom time does. It need not be expensive, however, to make your staff feel valued and their efforts appreciated. Praise for a job well done is free and a bag of doughnuts offered round at a staff meeting costs little, but is a great mood improver.

20 Keep sight of the future

It is unlikely that tough times will continue forever. When sales and profits improve you will be quick to capitalize on this, with your monthly profitability comparisons and up-to-date information management revealing upward trends the moment they occur. Your negotiating position is already strong with the value-added services you have been supplying and may now be able to charge for; having come to rely on them, your customer may pay to continue receiving them. You have maintained a competent staff and can now reap the benefits of both this and their closer customer relations.

21 Build up your inner determination and confidence

Remember that the economic climate is challenging for everyone; and that external pressures should not cause us to break existing, healthy relationships (even though they may be under strain due to rising prices, costs and so on). So, a careful, dispassionate and continuing review of trading relationships – their relative importance to you, your organization and its customers – should be carried out as a fundamental part of your preparation *before* setting up a negotiation. This may help avoid premature or unwise decisions, such as to change suppliers, or simply to allow client relations to unwind gradually over time, through giving the impression that they are now a lower priority for you and your colleagues.

In your negotiating plan, make sure that your preparation is completely up to date, especially where this reflects budgets, market values and services offered by your competitors.

22 Give up shortcuts!

Invest quality time in your preparation – and avoid the temptation to make 'back-of-an-envelope' plans for meetings that could turn out to be more important than you expect. If you fail to prepare thoroughly, you risk preparing to fail! You should test all your assumptions and ensure that your research is really up to date. (If this means a tactical delay for an appointment, or the cost of an international call to check out current costings – so be it!) Use your critical thinking skills to stay ahead of the game.

23 Put meetings first – and make them productive

Build and reinforce confidence in you as a representative of your organization. While others may be relying on impersonal contacts, ensure that your positive influence is readily available to build confidence for your business. This might involve re-visiting your personal impact – for example, dressing for success, minimizing negative talk but also avoiding trite formulae. Ensure that you are seen by your contacts as a good and trusted person to do business with.

24 Resist the temptation to use win/lose tactics

Be goal centred. This is not an excuse to use questionable tactics! Being greedy can result in deals that become unenforceable (for example from having a contract with an organization that is about to go out of business). Consider the impact of 'sharp' tactics on longer-term relationships. (However, this does not mean you should become passive or non-assertive in your communication style.)

25 Be inventive and creative

Take advantage of technology. LinkedIn has links with groups of professionals in a vast array of subjects. Join these groups and make a contribution; get your name known. Use social networking sites to enrich your network rather than just catch up with friends' gossip. Review your profile on Facebook and Twitter – ensure you give a professional impression. Maintaining your personal brand is essential.

Take a new look at the method you use. For example, spreading a supply contract over a longer period – with phased deliveries – could result in retaining a contract which may otherwise have been under threat. There is evidence that this type of supply approach can ease cash flow stresses and give a win/win outcome. Pricing can be flexible, and so can timing (for example, dating invoices carefully, making/taking deliveries before/after stock-taking).

26 Prepare to make concessions

Concessions do not need to cost you money! They might involve support in kind (for example, soft skills such as advice, training, promotions support and so on) Even doing a favour or two may be effective – especially when you are able to ensure that these are short term and exceptional. However, be sure that concessions are *not* unilateral – they should always be conditional (something for something). Offering to run a training session for your client, aimed at increasing sales of your product could bring impressive results!

27 Be positive!

Resist the temptation to 'trade' negative stories – this can lead to a depressing atmosphere in the meeting. Rather, try to trade positive stories, such as other clients or suppliers who have tried a new approach that is working well. Spread the word because good news sells! However, do not invent stories that may breach trust/confidence in you. Try to be positive but be vigilant for symptoms of impending doom (such as a close-down).

28 Listen!

Seek and listen to the advice of peers and mentors. Advice is free and, although it may not always be correct, it helps to hear multiple perspectives and to consider all angles.

Concentrate on finding further opportunities to do business with this person – maybe in a different territory (even if it is not 'yours'). People can sometimes be economical with the truth, but also rather less controlled with their speech than they should be. Ask yourself: 'Is this half-suggestion I have heard one that could require a new source of help/supply/finance?'

29 Follow up

Be careful with, and limit, 'loose talk', which can dilute the persuasion value of your negotiation. Rather, reinforce the customer service issues contained in your proposals, which are designed to cement relationships. This might also include apocryphal stories of how other organizations have benefited from this type of support. Such approaches can be particularly helpful for 'opponents' who are depressed or feel that they have lost control.

30 Work hard – but also take all your holidays

Re-double your efforts! Resist the temptation to take that extra hour at lunchtime – and keep looking for more opportunities for new clients/alternative suppliers/

economies of scale/new negotiation targets. Listen to your contacts and feed back helpful suggestions/proposals to your organization. Work with professional standards in mind at all times. Take all your relaxation and holiday time – and use it to rebuild your energy levels and determination to succeed.

Remain confident in your abilities and take confidence from your experience. Understand that not every job is right for you. Rejection is a learning experience and can be used to your advantage. Reflect on and learn from every new opportunity.

31 Reward customer loyalty

When people are trying to be thrifty with their money, they love to receive vouchers and special offers. These could be in the form of, for example, money-off vouchers, buy one get one free vouchers or loyalty cards. Think about offers you could make to your customers that will save them money. If they have bought from you through your website, could you email them a unique code that will give them a personal discount off their next order? What about a free extended warranty or insurance? For inspiration, check out what other organizations in your industry are offering their customers and then explore what you could do that would be even better.

32 Run a testimonial-gathering exercise

Contact past and present customers and offer them the chance to win a prize for completing the phrase 'I love dealing with [your company] because . . .'. There could be different categories, for example the most original testimonial, the wittiest, the most appealing and so on. Award prizes for each category and publish a selection of the testimonials on your website. This activity will also make a good press release.

33 Put mirrors in front of your telephone staff

Invest in free-standing mirrors, but not with a magnifying lens, and position them so that your customer support staff can see their own reflections when they are talking to customers on the telephone. This will encourage them to smile, which will make them sound friendlier on the phone. There are also several other benefits of smiling – see Sunday's chapter to remind yourself of what they are.

34 Put on an event

Invite your customers to an event, such as a treasure hunt on a Sunday afternoon. This could be on foot or it could take the form of a car rally in which clues have to be solved. Tell them that they are welcome to bring along family and friends, and that there will be prizes for the winners. This type of event has a wide appeal, is relatively inexpensive to run and provides an opportunity to build good relationships with your customers in a relaxed atmosphere.

35 Give your customers an unexpected gift

This is one of the key routes to achieving customer excellence and need not be a costly option – see the example of the stationery supplier in Wednesday's chapter. The gift could accompany their next purchase or be sent to them as a thank you for referring a new customer to you.

36 Send birthday cards to your customers

Many organizations send out Christmas cards to their customers but very few send out birthday cards.

These are unexpected and far more personal, and they demonstrate that you care. Recipients will be pleasantly surprised and feel that yours is a genuinely caring, 'thoughtful' organization. The cost is minimal, but the value is huge.

37 Conduct a customer satisfaction survey

It is essential that you are in touch with your customers' views about your organization and that you willingly and positively respond to any complaints or suggestions that they make. Also, people like to be asked for their opinions – it makes them feel valued and keeps you uppermost in their minds. See Tuesday's chapter for ideas on what to include in a survey. There are online survey tools that you could utilize to conduct a survey by email.

38 Spring clean your business

Step into your customer's shoes and 'visit' your business, as if for the first time. Does it feel bright, warm and inviting? Does it feel like an organization you would enjoy doing business with? If not, why not? Experiment with making small changes – moving furniture around, updating displays or including an 'offer of the week' on your website. What would appeal to your customers and how can you supply it?

39 Go public with your customer care standards

People buy people first and if you are able to build a reputation as a customer-friendly organization, then customers will stay loyal to you. Monday's chapter focused on creating customer care standards while Saturday's chapter presented the idea of creating and rolling out a branded customer service programme. Going public on these initiatives will enhance your reputation significantly. Think of John Lewis's slogan, 'Never knowingly undersold', or Marks & Spencer's policy for exchanging unwanted goods.

40 Give awards to your outstanding staff

Recognize those members of your staff who, on their own initiative, 'go the extra mile' for customers. Some organizations nominate an employee of the month. Others give personal awards such as a dinner for two at a local, good-quality restaurant or a gift voucher that would be really appreciated by that particular individual. Whatever you choose to do, publicize it through your internal communications channels, e.g. your newsletter or intranet. Ideally, also include testimonials from customers relevant to the award winners.

Further reading

Advanced skills

Negotiating the Better Deal; Peter Fleming, International Thomson Press, 1997

Commercial/Sales

Bargaining for Results; John Winkler, Heinemann, 1989

Getting to Yes; Roger Fisher et al, Arrow, 1997

Managing Retail Sales; Peter Fleming, Management Books 2000 Ltd, 1997

Negotiate to Close: How to make more successful deals; Gary Karrass, Fontana, 1987

Retail Selling; Peter Fleming, Management Books 2000 Ltd, 2007

Successful Selling In A Week; Christine Harvey, Hodder Education, 2012

Industrial relations

Effective Negotiation; Alan Fowler, Chartered Institute of Personnel Development, 1986

Personal skills

Assertiveness at Work: a practical guide to handling awkward situations; Ken and Kate Back, McGraw Hill, 1999

Successful People Skills In A Week; Christine Harvey, Hodder Education, 2012

General

Managing Negotiation: how to get a better deal; Kennedy et al, Random House Business Books, 1987

The Skills of Negotiation; Bill Scott, Gower Publishing, 1981

Answers to Week 1

Sunday: 1d; 2d; 3b; 4c; 5b; 6d; 7a; 8c; 9d; 10b.

Monday: 1c; 2a; 3c; 4d; 5d; 6a; 7d; 8b; 9d; 10d.

Tuesday: 1d; 2a; 3b; 4a; 5c; 6d; 7d; 8d; 9b; 10b.

Wednesday: 1d; 2c; 3a; 4d; 5d; 6d; 7a; 8b; 9b; 10d.

Thursday: 1d; 2a; 3d; 4a; 5b; 6d; 7d; 8b; 9b; 10c.

Friday: 1b; 2b; 3d; 4d; 5d; 6d; 7a; 8d; 9d; 10d.

Saturday: 1d; 2a; 3d; 4b; 5c; 6d; 7c; 8c; 9d; 10d.

Answers to Week 2

Sunday: 1b; 2a,c,d; 3c; 4a,b,c; 5c; 6b,c,d; 7b; 8a,b,c; 9a; 10a,b,d.

Monday: 1d; 2c; 3a; 4b; 5d; 6b,c; 7a,b,c; 8a,b,c; 9b,c,d; 10a,c,d.

Tuesday: 1a,d; 2b; 3b; 4b,c,d; 5b,d; 6c; 7a,c,d; 8a,c; 9a,b; 10a,b.

Wednesday: 1a,b,c; 2a,c; 3c; 4b,c,d; 5a,b,c; 6b,c,d; 7a,c; 8b,c; 9b,c,d; 10,b,c,d.

Thursday: 1b,c,d; 2a,c; 3b,c; 4b; 5a,d; 6b,c; 7d; 8b,d; 9b,c; 10a,b,c.

Friday: 1a,c; 2a,b,d; 3d; 4b,d; 5c,d; 6c; 7c; 8;a,b,c; 9a,c,d; 10a,b,c.

Saturday: 1b; 2a,c; 3b; 4a,c; 5b,d; 6a,c,d; 7c; 8a,b,c; 9d; 10a,d.

Answers to Week 3

Sunday:
1. a) 0 b) 1 c) 2 d) 0
2. a) 1 b) 0 c) 0 d) 2
3. a) 1 b) 0 c) 2 d) 0
4. a) 1 b) 2 c) 0 d) 0
5. a) 2 b) 0 c) 0 d) 1
6. a) 0 b) 0 c) 2 d) 1
7. a) 0 b) 0 c) 1 d) 2
8. a) 2 b) 0 c) 1 d) 0
9. a) 1 b) 2 c) 0 d) 0
10. a) 0 b) 2 c) 1 d) 1

Monday:
1. a) 1 b) 1 c) 1 d) 2
2. a) 0 b) 1 c) 2 d) 1
3. a) 0 b) 2 c) 1 d) 0
4. a) 1 b) 1 c) 1 d) 2
5. a) 1 b) 1 c) 1 d) 2
6. a) 1 b) 2 c) 0 d) 0
7. a) 0 b) 1 c) 2 d) 0
8. a) 2 b) 0 c) 1 d) 0
9. a) 0 b) 0 c) 2 d) 0
10. a) 1 b) 0 c) 2 d) 1

Tuesday:
1. a) 1 b) 1 c) 2 d) 3
2. a) 0 b) 0 c) 2 d) 1
3. a) 2 b) 0 c) 0 d) 0
4. a) 2 b) 0 c) 0 d) 1
5. a) 1 b) 2 c) 3 d) 1
6. a) 3 b) 1 c) 0 d) 0
7. a) 0 b) 2 c) 3 d) 0
8. a) 0 b) 0 c) 0 d) 2
9. a) 0 b) 2 c) 1 d) 3
10. a) 1 b) 0 c) 1 d) 2

Wednesday:
1. a) 2 b) 2 c) 0 d) 0
2. a) 0 b) 1 c) 0 d) 2
3. a) 1 b) 2 c) 0 d) 1
4. a) 2 b) 0 c) 1 d) 1
5. a) 0 b) 1 c) 2 d) 0
6. a) 1 b) 1 c) 2 d) 0
7. a) 0 b) 2 c) 1 d) 0
8. a) 1 b) 2 c) 0 d) 0
9. a) 2 b) 0 c) 1 d) 0
10. a) 1 b) 0 c) 2 d) 1

Thursday:
1. a) 0 b) 0 c) 2 d) 1
2. a) 0 b) 0 c) 1 d) 2
3. a) 0 b) 1 c) 1 d) 2
4. a) 2 b) 2 c) 0 d) 2
5. a) 1 b) 0 c) 2 d) 1
6. a) 2 b) 1 c) 1 d) 0
7. a) 2 b) 0 c) 0 d) 1
8. a) 0 b) 1 c) 2 d) 0
9. a) 1 b) 2 c) 0 d) 0
10. a) 1 b) 0 c) 0 d) 2

Friday:
1. a) 0 b) 0 c) 2 d) 1
2. a) 1 b) 2 c) 0 d) 0
3. a) 0 b) 0 c) 1 d) 2
4. a) 1 b) 0 c) 2 d) 0
5. a) 1 b) 2 c) 1 d) 0
6. a) 2 b) 3 c) 1 d) 1
7. a) 0 b) 2 c) 0 d) 1
8. a) 0 b) 0 c) 1 d) 2
9. a) 2 b) 0 c) 1 d) 0
10. a) 0 b) 2 c) 0 d) 1

Total score out of a possible 126:

Answers to Week 4

Sunday: 1c; 2b; 3d; 4a; 5b.
Monday: 1c; 2b; 3d; 4b; 5b;
6a; 7d; 8b; 9a; 10c.
Tuesday: 1c; 2d; 3a; 4b; 5c;
6d; 7a; 8b; 9b; 10d.
Wednesday: 1d; 2b; 3a; 4c;
5b; 6d; 7a; 8b; 9c; 10d.

Thursday: 1b; 2d; 3c; 4a; 5d;
6a; 7b; 8c; 9a; 10d.
Friday: 1b; 2a; 3d; 4c; 5a; 6b;
7d; 8a; 9c; 10b.
Saturday: 1b; 2c; 3a; 4d; 5a;
6b; 7d; 8a; 9c; 10b.

Notes